KNIGHTS
OF
MADNESS

Also edited by Peter Haining

**THE WIZARDS OF ODD
THE FLYING SORCERERS**

KNIGHTS
OF
MADNESS

Further Comic Tales of Fantasy

Edited by
Peter Haining

ORBIT

An *Orbit* Book

First published in Great Britain by Souvenir Press Ltd 1998
This edition published by Orbit 2000

A CIP catalogue record for this book
is available from the British Library.

ISBN 1 85723 958 X

Typeset by Hewer Text Ltd, Edinburgh
Printed in Great Britain by
Mackays of Chatham PLC, Chatham, Kent

Orbit
A Division of
Little, Brown and Company (UK)
Brettenham House
Lancaster Place
London WC2E 7EN

When fishes flew and forests walked,
  And figs grew upon the thorn,
Some moment when the Moon was blood,
  Then surely I was born.

G.K. Chesterton, *The Song of Quoodle*

```
✓ +3        + = +1
C +2        Ø → UNREAD!
O + 1
X − 3
```

CONTENTS

Introduction   ix

1   FLIGHTS OF FANTASY: Stories of the Absurd   1
✓   Hollywood Chickens *by Terry Pratchett*   3
O   The New Utopia *by Jerome K. Jerome*   13
✓   The Angry Street *by G.K. Chesterton*   33
C   The Party at Lady Cusp-Canine's *by Mervyn Peake*   41
✗   The Little Man Who Wasn't All There *by Robert Bloch*   52
O   The Year the Glop-Monster Won
      the Golden Lion at Cannes *by Ray Bradbury*   78
C   Lila the Werewolf *by Peter S. Beagle*   95
O   The War With the Fnools *by Philip K. Dick*   125

2   THE MUDDLE AGES: Tales of Heroic Times   145
✓+ The Creation According to Spike Milligan
      by Spike Milligan   147
O   Mediaeval Romance *by Mark Twain*   155
✗   Ethelred the Unready *by Ben Travers*   166
C   Dream Damsel *by Evan Hunter*   173
O   Three Months in a Balloon *by John Kendrick Bangs*   187
O   How I Lost the Second World War *by Gene Wolfe*   196
C   Fifi and the Chilean Truffle *by Orson Welles*   220
    The Wastrel *by Peter Sellers*   228

3   MALICE IN BLUNDERLAND: Cases of Crime   237
C   Stirring the Pot *by Tom Sharpe*   239
O   The Suicide of Kiaros *by L. Frank Baum*   247

C The Rape of the Sherlock *by A.A. Milne*   264

✗ The White Rabbit Caper *by James Thurber*   268

C Wot the Eye Don't See *by Stan McMurtry*   279

∅ The Condemned *by Woody Allen*   292

O The Mulligan Stew *by Donald E. Westlake*   301

✓ The Dulwich Assassins *by David L. Stone*   308

Acknowledgements   323

INTRODUCTION

I once had a dream in which all my hair fell out. On waking up and finding, thankfully, that what little I possess was still there, I consulted a dictionary of dreams. It told me that my nocturnal experience was an omen: I would never be rich (which is true), but there was one sure way of ensuring that I did not go bald. You will not be surprised to learn that I turned up my nose at the suggestion, apparently based on an old tradition, that I could remedy any thinning areas by applying liberal portions of *goose dung*!

The imagination is a funny thing – which is just as well because it is in just such nightmares and daydreams as mine that humorous fantasy stories often originate. Some, though, don't even need a flash of inspiration, for facts can prove stranger than fiction. Take, for example, a story that appeared in the pages of that far-famed London newspaper *The Times* on 8 January 1998, headlined 'WHEN CHICKENS RULED THE EARTH'. Underneath it the paper reported: 'Chinese scientists are examining the remains of two chicken-sized dinosaurs which probably developed their feathers to keep warm rather than fly.'

According to *The Times*, the bones of two *Sinosaur-opteryx*, which lived more than 140 million years ago, had been found in north-eastern China. They were described as two-legged, with a pointed head, long tail and a three-fingered hand, one finger being large and clawlike, probably used to kill prey. The scientists concluded that vertical fibres from the head to the tail were intended to prevent the loss of body heat. The story had an even more curious footnote: a group of American scientists (obviously anxious not to be left behind in the search for even more curious lifeforms) claimed to have found a 370-million-year-old fin in Pennsylvania, which indicated to them that the fish from which it came had fingers. 'Until now,' the account added, 'most scientists believed that fingerlike digits evolved as animals colonised the land from the sea.'

So what has all this to do with the present book? Only that a not dissimilar idea about chickens – today rather than in the past – hatched in the mind of writer Terry Pratchett a few years ago, to become 'Hollywood Chickens', a fantasy of the absurd which sets the tone of this book. I just loved the coincidence when reading *The Times* story, and the thought was never far from my mind as I put together this anthology, the third in the series.

Unlike its predecessors, *The Wizards of Odd* and *The Flying Sorcerers*, this selection draws on material from an even wider field of humorous writing. In the first two books I chose predominantly fantasy and science fiction stories, but here the contributions come from three more genres. I have devoted the first section to tales of the absurd, while the second is given over to historical (even hysterical) tales in which the facts of the past are turned topsy-turvy. The third is a showcase for comic crime stories in which the crimes are more often than not bungled and the criminals inept. The mixture of these three themes will, I hope, prove enjoyable.

Among the contributors are many of the masters of comic fantasy – Terry Pratchett, Mervyn Peake, Philip K. Dick, Ray Bradbury and their ilk – but also several surprises in the persons of G.K. Chesterton, Evan Hunter, Orson Welles, James Thurber and Woody Allen. You will find the king of farce, Ben Travers; Tom Sharpe, that master of ancestral vices; and even a couple of Goons, Spike Milligan and Peter Sellers. Together they underline not only *why* comic fantasy is so popular today, but that it has attracted some formidable writing talents.

Poll after poll among readers in recent years has shown that J.R.R. Tolkien's epic fantasy, *The Lord of the Rings*, is by far the most popular book of this century. Works of fantasy by other great writers in the genre, such as C.S. Lewis and Mervyn Peake, have also scored highly. But those who put the emphasis on humour, like Terry Pratchett and Roald Dahl, are rising meteorically in the popularity stakes. Comic fantasy has an excellent future also, I believe, in the hands of the new generation of writers like young David L. Stone, who makes his debut in this collection with a sparkling tale of unionised criminality, 'The Dulwich Assassins'.

It has been a pleasure to return once again to the wellsprings (and offsprings) of comic fantasy to compile this collection. I hope it will provoke as much laughter and enjoyment as the previous two.

Perhaps, after all, that dream of going bald could hold something quite different for me. But *goose droppings*?

PETER HAINING,
Boxford, Suffolk.

1

FLIGHTS OF FANTASY

Stories of the Absurd

HOLLYWOOD CHICKENS

Terry Pratchett

It has been said of Terry Pratchett's fantasy worlds that all his heroes have feet of clay and magic has all the efficacy of a Tommy Cooper trick. Nonetheless, this amazingly successful combination has made his books into today's most popular fantasy works and their author one of the world's bestselling writers. Indeed, there is hardly a country on the face of the planet where his Discworld is unknown and readers have not heard of the city state of Ankh-Morpork with its Unseen University, or the motley band of characters including the skeletal DEATH on his white horse, 'Binkie'; Rincewind the hopeless wizard; Granny Weatherwax the witch; and Luggage, the psychopathic wooden chest on legs who has now acquired a wife, with the pair referring to themselves cosily as 'the Luggages'. But Terry's mastery of humorous fantasy has extended beyond Discworld as this first story, 'Hollywood Chickens', written in 1990, bears witness. If I say it is his own particular variation on that very old joke about why the chicken crossed the road, I shall not be giving away too much.

Terry Pratchett (1948–) was born in Beaconsfield, Buckinghamshire, where his father was a garage mechanic and the family lived in a cottage with no electricity and one cold tap. 'We were poor,' he has said, 'but, my God, we were miserable.' Reading Kenneth Grahame's The Wind in the Willows *when he was ten introduced Terry to the world of fantasy and, trying his own hand at it, he had his first story, 'The Hades Business', a little fable about the Devil's attempts to commercialise Hell, published in* Science Fantasy *magazine when he was just 15. After finishing his schooling at High Wycombe Technical High, he worked for a time on the local* Bucks Free Press *and was then a press officer for the Central Electricity Generating Board, writing fiction at night. The* Colour of Magic, *his first Discworld novel, published in 1983, put him on the road to financial independence. He was inspired to write the book, he says, 'because there was so much bad Tolkien imitation around' and the later volumes in the ongoing series have caused him to be compared to Lewis Carroll and P.G. Wodehouse, although he himself believes he is more in the tradition of Jerome K. Jerome (see the next story).*

Today, despite all his success, Terry Pratchett remains a friendly and amiable man who is always interested in the opinions of his fans and spends endless hours at signing sessions for his admirers. Despite the arcane nature of Discworld, Pratchett is fascinated by modern technology and is an inveterate Web-watcher, taking especial interest in the discussions and messages about his work which appear on sites like alt.fan.pratchett. Even before this collection appeared, the word was already out on the Web that Terry's Rhode Island Reds were about to hatch again. So meet them now . . .

The facts are these:

In 1973 a lorry overturned at a freeway interchange in Hollywood. It was one of the busiest in the United States and, therefore, the world.

It shed some of its load. It had been carrying chickens. A few crates broke.

Alongside the interchange, bordered on three sides by thundering traffic and on the fourth by a wall, was a quarter-mile of heavily-shrubbed verge.

No one bothered too much about a few chickens.

. . .

Peck peck.

Scratch. Scratch.

Cluck?

. . .

It is a matter of record that, after a while, those who regularly drove this route noticed that the chickens had survived. There were, and indeed still are, sprinklers on the verge to keep the greenery alive and presumably the meagre population of bugs was supplemented by edible fallout from the constant stream of traffic.

The chickens seemed to be settling in. They were breeding.

. . .

Peck peck. Scratch. Peck . . .

Peck?

Scratch peck?

Peck?

Peck + peck = squawk

Cluck?

. . .

A rough census indicated that the population stabilised at around fifty birds. For the first few years young chickens would frequently be found laminated to the backtop, but some sort of natural selection appeared to be operating, or, if we may put it another way, flat hens don't lay eggs.

Passing motorists did occasionally notice a few birds standing at the kerb, staring intently at the far verge.

They looked like birds with a problem, they said.

. . .

SQUAWK PECK PECK CROW!

I   Peck squawk peck
II   Squawk crow peck
III Squawk *squawk* crow
IV   Scratch crow peck waark
V   (Neck stretch) peck crow
VI   Peck peck peck (preen feathers)
VII (Peck foot) scratch crow
VIII Crow scratch
IX   Peck (weird gurgling noise) peck
X   Scratch peck *crow* waark (to keep it holy).

. . .

In fact, apart from the occasional chick or young bird, no chicken was found dead on the freeway itself apart from the incident in 1976, when ten chickens were seen to set out from the kerb together during the rush hour peak. This must have represented a sizeable proportion of the chicken population at that time.

The driver of a gas tanker said that at the head of the little group was an elderly cockerel, who stared at him with supreme self-confidence, apparently waiting for something to happen.

Examination of the tanker's front offside wing suggests that the bird was a Rhode Island Red.

. . .

Cogito ergo cluck.

. . .

Periodically an itinerant, or the just plain desperate, would dodge the traffic to the verge and liberate a sleeping chicken for supper.

This originally caused some concern to the Department of Health, who reasoned that the feral chickens, living as they did so close to the traffic, would have built up dangerously high levels of lead in their bodies, not to mention other noxious substances.

In 1978 a couple of research officers were sent into the thickets to bring back a few birds for a sacrifice to Science.

The birds' bodies were found to be totally lead-free.

We do not know whether they checked any eggs.

This is important (see Document C).

They did remark incidentally, however, that the birds appeared to have been fighting amongst themselves. (See Document F: *Patterns of Aggression in Enclosed Environments*, Helorksson and Frim, 1981.) We must assume, in view of later developments, that this phase passed.

. . .

Four peck-(neck stretch) *and seven* cluck-scratch *ago, our* crow-(peck left foot)-squawk *brought forth upon this* cluck-cluck-squawk . . .

. . .

In the early hours of 10 March 1981, Police Officer James Stooker Stasheff, in pursuit of a suspect following a chase which resulted in a seven-car collision, a little way from the verge, saw a construction apparently made of long twigs, held together with cassette tape, extending several feet into the carriageway. Two chickens were on the end of it, with twigs in their beaks. 'They looked as if they was nest building,' he now recalls. 'I went past again about 10 am, it was all smashed up in the gutter.'

Officer Stasheff went on to say, 'You always get tapes along the freeway. Any freeway. See, when they get snarled up in the Blaupunkt or whatever, people just rip 'em out and pitch them through the window.'

According to Ruse and Sixbury (*Bulletin of the Arkham*

Ornithological Society, vol. 17, pp. 124–132, 1968) birds may, under conditions of chronic stress, build nests of unusual size and complexity (Document D).

This is not necessarily advanced as an explanation.

. . .

Peck . . . peck . . . scratch.

Scratch scratch scratch scratch scratch scratch scratch scratch scratch scratch scratch.

. . .

The collapse of a small section of carriageway near the verge in the summer of 1983 is not considered germane to this study. The tunnel underneath it was put down to gophers. Or foxes. Or some other burrowing animal. What were irresponsibly described as shoring timbers must simply have been, for example, bits of timber that accidentally got carried into the tunnel by floodwater, as it were, and wedged. Undoubtedly the same thing happened with the feathers.

. . .

If Cluck *were meant to fly, they'd have bigger* (flap).

. . .

Testimony of Officer Stasheff again:

'This must have been around late August, 1984. This trucker told me, he was driving past, it would have been around mid-afternoon, when this thing comes flapping, he said *flapping*, out of the bushes and right across the freeway and he's watching it, and it doesn't lose height, and next thing he knows it bounces off his windshield and breaks up. He said he thought it was kids or something, so I went and had a look at the bushes, but no kids. Just a few of the chickens scratching about, and a load of junk, you know, you wouldn't believe the kind of junk that ends up by the side of roads. I found what was left of the thing that'd hit him. It was like a sort of cage with these kind of big wings on, and all full of pulleys and more bits of cassette tapes and levers and stuff. What? Oh, yeah. And these chickens. All smashed up. I mean, who'd do something like that? One minute flying chickens, next minute McNuggets. I recall there were three of them. All cockerels, and brown.'

. . . It's a (small scratch) for a *cluck*, a (giant flap) for *Cluck*.

. . .

Testimony of Officer Stasheff again (19 July 1986):

'Kids playing with fire. That's my opinion. They get over the wall and make hideouts in the bushes. Like I said, they just grab one of the chickens. I don't see why everyone's so excited. So some kids fill an old trashcan with junk and fireworks and stuff and push a damn *chicken* in it and blow it up in the air . . . It'd have caused a hell of a lot of damage if it hadn't hit one of the bridge supports on the far side. Bird inside got all smashed up. It'd got this cloth in there with strings all over. Maybe the kids thought the thing could use a parachute. Okay, so there's a crater, what the hell, plant a bush in it. What? Sure it'd be hot, it's where they were playing spacemen. Not that kind of hot? What kind of hot?'

. . .

Peck (Neck Twist)-crow = gurgle/C^2
Cluck?

. . .

We do know that at about 2 am on the morning of 3 May 1989, a purple glow was noticed by several drivers in the bushes around the middle of the verge. Some say it was a blue glow. From a cross-checking of the statements, it appeared to last for at least ten minutes.

There was also a noise. We have a number of descriptions of this noise. It was 'sort of weird', 'kind of a whooping sound', and 'rather like radio oscillation'. The only one we have been able to check is the description from Curtis V.J. McDonald, who said, 'You know in that *Star Trek* episode when they meet the fish men from an alternate Earth? Well, the fish men's matter transmitter made just the same noise.'

We have viewed the episode in question. It is the one where Captain Kirk falls in love with the girl (tape A).

. . .

Cluck?

(Foot twist) $\sqrt{2t\beta}$ . . . [Σ/peck]/Scratch^{2*} $*^{oon}$ (Gurgle) (Left-shoulder-preen) = (Right-shoulder-preen) . . .

HmmMMmmMMmmMMmmMMmmMMmm.

Cluck.

. . .

We also know that the person calling himself Elrond X, an itinerant, entered the area around 2 am. When located subsequently, he said: 'Yeah, well, maybe sometimes I used to take a chicken but there's no law against it. Anyway, I stopped because it was getting very heavy, I mean, it was the way they were acting. The way they looked at you. Their beady eyes. But times are tough and I thought, okay, why not . . .

'There's no chickens there, man. Someone's been through it, there's no chickens!'

When asked about the Assemblage, he said: 'There was only this pile of junk in the middle of the bushes. It was just twigs and wire and junk. And eggs, only you never touch the eggs, we know that, some of those eggs give you a shock, like electricity. 'Cos you never asked me before, that's why. Yeah, I kicked it over. Because there was this chicken inside it, okay, but when I went up close there was this flash and, like, a clap of thunder and it went all wavy and disappeared. I ain't taking that from no chicken.'

Thus far we have been unable to reassemble the Assemblage (photos A thru G). There is considerable doubt as to its function, and we have dismissed Mr X's view that it was 'a real *funky* microwave oven'. It appeared simply to have been a collection of roadside debris and twigs, held together with cassette tape.* It may have had some religious significance. From drawings furnished by Mr X, there appeared to have been space inside for one chicken at a time.

Document C contains an analysis of the three eggs found in the debris. As you will see, one of them seems normal but infertile, the second has been powering a flashlight bulb for two days, and a report on the third is contingent on our finding either it or Dr Paperbuck, who was last seen trying to cut into it with a saw.

For the sake of completeness, please note document B, which is an offprint of Paperbuck and Macklin's *Western Science Journal* paper: 'Exaggerated Evolutionary Pressures on Small Isolated Groups Under Stress'.

All that we can be certain of is that there are no chickens in the area where chickens have been for the last seventeen years.

However, there are now forty-seven chickens on the *opposite* verge.

Why they crossed is of course one of the fundamental riddles of popular philosophy.

That is not, however, the problem.

* 'The Best of Queen'.

We don't know *how*.

But it's not such a great verge over there, and they're all clustered together and some of the hens are laying.

We're just going to have to wait and see how they get back.

. . .

Cluck?

Author's note: In 1973 a lorry overturned at a freeway interchange in Hollywood. It was one of the busiest in the United States and, therefore, the world. Some chickens escaped and bred. They survived – are surviving – very well, even in the hazardous atmosphere of the roadside. But this story is about another Hollywood. And other chickens.

THE NEW UTOPIA

Jerome K. Jerome

*At the beginning of the twentieth century, Jerome K. Jerome
was styled as the 'New Humorist'. So popular were his books
that his publisher, J.W. Arrowsmith, once remarked with
evident delight, 'I can't imagine what becomes of all the
copies of his books I issue – I often think the public must
eat them!' In their time Jerome's comic novels, especially*
Three Men in a Boat *(1889), were as hugely successful as
Terry Pratchett's are today, and it is interesting to hear
Pratchett admit that 'my humour is in an incredibly British
tradition which can be traced back to Jerome K. Jerome.' Both
men enjoyed creating their own fantasy worlds, giving their
characters extraordinary names, and making the most of their
public notoriety. Like Pratchett, who once signed an anthology
for me with the exclamation 'Boo!', Jerome referred to himself
as ' 'Arry K. 'Arry' and often used this in preference to his own
signature in books.*

*Jerome Klapka Jerome (1859–1927) was born in Walsall in
Staffordshire, but his family moved to the East End of London
when he was still very young. His childhood was one of almost
unremitting misery, due largely to the tendency of his lay
minister father, Jerome Clap Jerome, to sink his own and then
his wife's money into a string of disastrous enterprises. 'Having a father with a name like that I felt I had no choice but to*

make my living from humour,' he said later. The boy left school at 14 and, after a number of dead-end jobs, managed to become a jobbing actor and later a penny-a-line journalist. In 1889 he became successful almost overnight with The Idle Thoughts of an Idle Fellow *which, with its slang and nonsense and spectacle of people making fools of themselves, had a profound effect on modern popular journalism. At a stroke, Jerome found it far easier to sell stories and essays to magazine editors.* Three Men in a Boat, *in the same year, made him a literary lion and, like Terry Pratchett today, he took to wearing stylish black clothing and a splendid hat (a boater) at a rakish angle. The book was soon translated into a dozen languages, filmed several times for both the cinema and TV, and has remained in print to this day, accepted as one of the classic humorous novels of all time.*

The critic Alfred Moss has said of Jerome K. Jerome that he could 'always find the comic element in the most trivial incidents', and because there was a shortage of humour he tried to remedy it – the self-same objectives that Terry Pratchett has also pursued. 'The New Utopia', written for Punch *in 1891, is Jerome K. Jerome's wry view of a new world of the future – and in it will be found the same threads of invention and characterisation which, a century later, so enliven the Discworld novels.*

I had spent an extremely interesting evening. I had dined with some very 'advanced' friends of mine at the 'National Socialist Club'. We had had an excellent dinner: the pheasant, stuffed with truffles, was a poem; and when I say that the '49 Chateau Lafite was worth the price we had to pay for it, I do not see what more I can add in its favour.

After dinner, and over the cigars (I must say they do

know how to stock good cigars at the National Socialist Club), we had a very instructive discussion about the coming equality of man and the nationalisation of capital.

I was not able to take much part in the argument myself, because, having been left when a boy in a position which rendered it necessary for me to earn my own living, I have never enjoyed the time and opportunity to study these questions.

But I listened very attentively while my friends explained how, for the thousands of centuries during which it had existed before they came, the world had been going on all wrong, and how, in the course of the next few years or so, they meant to put it right.

Equality of all mankind was their watchword – perfect equality in all things – equality in possessions, and equality in position and influence, and equality in duties, resulting in equality in happiness and contentment.

The world belonged to all alike, and must be equally divided. Each man's labour was the property, not of himself, but of the State which fed and clothed him, and must be applied, not to his own aggrandisement, but to the enrichment of the race.

Individual wealth – the social chain with which the few had bound the many, the bandit's pistol by which a small gang of robbers had thieved from the whole community the fruits of its labours – must be taken from the hands that too long had held it.

Social distinctions – the barriers by which the rising tide of humanity had hitherto been fretted and restrained – must be for ever swept aside. The human race must press onward to its destiny (whatever that might be), not as at present, a scattered horde, scrambling, each man for himself, over the broken ground of unequal birth and fortune – the soft sward reserved for the feet of the pampered, the cruel stones left for the feet of the cursed – but an ordered army, marching side by side over the level plain of equity and equality.

The great bosom of our Mother Earth should nourish all her children, like and like; none should be hungry, none should have too much. The strong man should not grasp more than the weak; the clever should not scheme to seize more than the simple. The earth was man's, and the fulness thereof; and among all mankind it should be portioned out in even shares. All men were equal by the laws of Nature, and must be made equal by the laws of man.

With inequality comes misery, crime, sin, selfishness, arrogance, hypocrisy. In a world in which all men were equal, there would exist no temptation to evil, and our natural nobility would assert itself.

When all men were equal, the world would be Heaven – freed from the degrading despotism of God.

We raised our glasses and drank to EQUALITY, sacred EQUALITY; and then ordered the waiter to bring us green Chartreuse and more cigars.

I went home very thoughtful. I did not go to sleep for a long while; I lay awake; thinking over this vision of a new world that had been presented to me.

How delightful life would be, if only the scheme of my socialistic friends could be carried out. There would be no more of this struggling and striving against each other, no more jealousy, no more disappointment, no more fear of poverty! The State would take charge of us from the hour we were born until we died, and provide for all our wants from the cradle to the coffin, both inclusive, and we should need to give no thought even to the matter. There would be no more hard work (three hours' labour a day would be the limit, according to our calculations, that the State would require from each adult citizen, and nobody would be allowed to do more – *I* should not be allowed to do more) – no poor to pity, no rich to envy – no one to look down upon us, no one for us to look down upon (not quite so pleasant this latter reflection) – all our life ordered and arranged for us – nothing to think about except the glorious destiny (whatever that might be) of Humanity!

Then thought crept away to sport in chaos, and I slept.

When I awoke, I found myself lying under a glass case, in a high, cheerless room. There was a label over my head; I turned and read it. It ran as follows:

MAN – ASLEEP

PERIOD – 19th CENTURY

This man was found asleep in a house in London, after the great social revolution of 1899. From the account given by the landlady of the house, it would appear that he had already, when discovered, been asleep for over ten years (she having forgotten to call him). It was decided, for scientific purposes, not to awake him, but to just see how long he would sleep on, and he was accordingly brought and deposited in the 'Museum of Curiosities,' on February 11th, 1900.

Visitors are requested not to squirt water through the air-holes.

An intelligent-looking old gentleman, who had been arranging some stuffed lizards in an adjoining case, came over and took the cover off me.

'What's the matter?' he asked. 'Anything disturbed you?'

'No,' I said. 'I always wake up like this, when I feel I've had enough sleep. What century is this?'

'This,' he said, 'is the twenty-ninth century. You have been asleep just one thousand years.'

'Ah! Well, I feel all the better for it,' I replied, getting down off the table. 'There's nothing like having one's sleep out.'

'I take it you are going to do the usual thing,' said the old gentleman to me, as I proceeded to put on my clothes, which had been lying beside me in the case. 'You'll want me to walk round the city with you, and explain all the changes to you, while you ask questions and make silly remarks?'

'Yes,' I replied, 'I suppose that's what I ought to do.'

'I suppose so,' he muttered. 'Come on, and let's get it over,' and he led the way from the room.

As we went downstairs, I said:

'Well, is it all right, now?'

'Is what all right?' he replied.

'Why, the world,' I answered. 'A few friends of mine were arranging, just before I went to bed, to take it to pieces and fix it up again properly. Have they got it all right by this time? Is everybody equal now, and sin and sorrow and all that sort of thing done away with?'

'Oh, yes,' replied my guide, 'you'll find everything all right now. We've been working away pretty hard at things while you've been asleep. We've just got this earth about perfect now, I should say. Nobody is allowed to do anything wrong or silly; and as for equality, tadpoles ain't in it with us.'

(He talked in rather a vulgar manner, I thought; but I did not like to reprove him.)

We walked out into the city. It was very clean and very quiet. The streets, which were designated by numbers, ran out from each other at right-angles, and all presented exactly the same appearance. There were no horses or carriages about; all the traffic was conducted by electric cars. All the people that we met wore a quiet, grave expression, and were so much like each other as to give one the idea that they were all members of the same family. Everyone was dressed, as was also my guide, in a pair of grey trousers, and a grey tunic, buttoning tight round the neck and fastened round the waist by a belt. Each man was clean shaven, and each man had black hair.

I said:

'Are all these men twins?'

'Twins! Good gracious, no!' answered my guide. 'Whatever made you fancy that?'

'Why, they all look so much alike,' I replied, 'and they've all got black hair!'

'Oh; that's the regulation colour for hair,' explained my companion: 'we've all got black hair. If a man's hair is not black naturally, he has to have it dyed black.'

'Why?' I asked.

'Why!' retorted the old gentleman, somewhat irritably. 'Why, I thought you understood that all men were now equal. What would become of our equality if one man or woman were allowed to swagger about in golden hair, while another had to put up with carrots? Men have not only got to be equal in these happy days, but to look it, as far as can be. By causing all men to be clean shaven, and all men and women to have black hair cut the same length, we obviate, to a certain extent, the errors of Nature.'

I said:

'Why black?'

He said he did not know, but that was the colour which had been decided upon.

'Who by?' I asked.

'By THE MAJORITY,' he replied, raising his hat and lowering his eyes, as if in prayer.

We walked further, and passed more men. I said:

'Are there no women in this city?'

'Women!' exclaimed my guide. 'Of course there are. We've passed hundreds of them!'

'I thought I knew a woman when I saw one,' I observed, 'but I can't remember noticing any.'

'Why, there go two, now,' he said, drawing my attention to a couple of persons near to us, both dressed in the regulation grey trousers and tunics.

'How do you know they are women?' I asked.

'Why, you see the metal numbers that everybody wears on their collar?'

'Yes: I was just thinking what a number of policemen you had, and wondering where the other people were!'

'Well, the even numbers are women; the odd numbers are men.'

'How very simple,' I remarked. 'I suppose after a little practice you can tell one sex from the other almost at a glance?'

'Oh yes,' he replied, 'if you want to.'

We walked on in silence for a while. And then I said:

'Why does everybody have a number?'

'To distinguish him by,' answered my companion.

'Don't people have names, then?'

'No.'

'Why?'

'Oh! there was so much inequality in names. Some people were called Montmorency, and they looked down on the Smiths; and the Smythes did not like mixing with the Joneses: so, to save further bother, it was decided to abolish names altogether, and to give everybody a number.'

'Did not the Montmorencys and the Smythes object?'

'Yes; but the Smiths and Joneses were in THE MAJORITY.'

'And did not the Ones and Twos look down upon the Threes and Fours, and so on?'

'At first, yes. But, with the abolition of wealth, numbers lost their value, except for industrial purposes and for double acrostics, and now No. 100 does not consider himself in any way superior to No. 1,000,000.'

I had not washed when I got up, there being no conveniences for doing so in the Museum, and I was beginning to feel somewhat hot and dirty. I said:

'Can I wash myself anywhere?'

He said:

'No; we are not allowed to wash ourselves. You must wait until half-past four, and then you will be washed for tea.'

'*Be* washed!' I cried. 'Who by?'

'The State.'

He said that they had found they could not maintain their equality when people were allowed to wash themselves. Some people washed three or four times a day, while others never touched soap and water from one year's end to the other, and in consequence there got to be two distinct classes, the Clean and the Dirty. All the old class prejudices began to be revived. The clean despised the dirty, and the dirty hated the clean. So, to end dissension, the State decided to do the washing itself, and each citizen was now washed twice a day by government-appointed officials; and private washing was prohibited.

I noticed that we passed no houses as we went along, only block after block of huge, barrack-like buildings, all of the same size and shape. Occasionally, at a corner, we came across a smaller building, labelled 'Museum', 'Hospital', 'Debating Hall', 'Bath', 'Gymnasium', 'Academy of Sciences', 'Exhibition of Industries', 'School of Talk', etc., etc.; but never a house.

I said:

'Doesn't anybody live in this town?'

He said:

'You do ask silly questions; upon my word, you do. Where do you think they live?'

I said:

'That's just what I've been trying to think. I don't see any houses anywhere!'

He said:

'We don't need houses – not houses such as you are thinking of. We are socialistic now; we live together in fraternity and equality. We live in these blocks that you see. Each block accommodates one thousand citizens. It contains one thousand beds – one hundred in each room – and bathrooms and dressing-rooms in proportion, a dining-hall and kitchens. At seven o'clock every morning a bell is rung, and everyone rises and tidies up his bed. At seven-thirty they go into the dressing-rooms, and are washed and shaved and have their hair done. At eight

o'clock breakfast is served in the dining-hall. It comprises
a pint of oatmeal porridge and half-a-pint of warm milk
for each adult citizen. We are all strict vegetarians now.
The vegetarian vote increased enormously during the last
century, and their organisation being very perfect, they
have been able to dictate every election for the past fifty
years. At one o'clock another bell is rung, and the people
return to dinner, which consists of beans and stewed
fruits, with roly-poly pudding twice a week, and plum
duff on Saturdays. At five o'clock there is tea, and at ten
the lights are put out and everybody goes to bed. We are
all equal, and we all live alike – clerk and scavenger,
tinker and apothecary – all together in fraternity and
liberty. The men live in blocks on this side of the town,
and the women are at the other end of the city.'

'Where are the married people kept?' I asked.

'Oh, there are no married couples,' he replied; 'we
abolished marriage two hundred years ago. You see,
married life did not work at all well with our system.
Domestic life, we found, was thoroughly anti-socialistic
in its tendencies. Men thought more of their wives and
families than they did of the State. They wished to labour
for the benefit of their little circle of beloved ones rather
than for the good of the community. They cared more for
the future of their children than for the Destiny of
Humanity. The ties of love and blood bound men together fast in little groups instead of in one great whole.
Before considering the advancement of the human race,
men considered the advancement of their kith and kin.
Before striving for the greatest happiness of the greatest
number, men strove for the happiness of the few who
were near and dear to them. In secret, men and women
hoarded up and laboured and denied themselves, so as,

in secret, to give some little extra gift of joy to their beloved. Love stirred the vice of ambition in men's hearts. To win the smiles of the women they loved, to leave a name behind them that their children might be proud to bear, men sought to raise themselves above the general level, to do some deed that should make the world look up to them and honour them above their fellow-men, to press a deeper footprint than another's upon the dusty highway of the age. The fundamental principles of Socialism were being daily thwarted and contemned. Each house was a revolutionary centre for the propagation of individualism and personality. From the warmth of each domestic hearth grew up the vipers, Comradeship and Independence, to sting the State and poison the minds of men.

'The doctrines of equality were openly disputed. Men, when they loved a woman thought her superior to every other woman, and hardly took any pains to disguise their opinion. Loving wives believed their husbands to be wiser and braver and better than all other men. Mothers laughed at the idea of their children being in no way superior to other children. Children imbibed the hideous heresy that their father and mother were the best father and mother in the world.

'From whatever point you looked at it, the Family stood forth as our foe. One man had a charming wife and two sweet-tempered children; his neighbour was married to a shrew, and was the father of eleven noisy, ill-dispositioned brats – where was the equality?

'Again, wherever the Family existed, there hovered, ever contending, the angels of Joy and Sorrow; and in a world where joy and sorrow are known, Equality cannot live. One man and woman, in the night, stand weeping beside a little cot. On the other side of the lath-and-plaster, a fair young couple, hand in hand, are laughing at the silly antics of a grave-faced, gurgling baby. What is poor Equality doing?

'Such things could not be allowed. Love, we saw, was our enemy at every turn. He made equality impossible. He brought joy and pain, and peace and suffering in his train. He disturbed men's beliefs, and imperilled the Destiny of Humanity; so we abolished him and all his works.

'Now there are no marriages, and, therefore, no domestic troubles; no wooing, therefore, no heartaching; no loving, therefore no sorrowing; no kisses and no tears.

'We all live together in equality, free from the troubling of joy or pain.'

I said:

'It must be very peaceful; but, tell me – I ask the question merely from a scientific standpoint – how do you keep up the supply of men and women?'

He said:

'Oh, that's simple enough. How did you, in your day, keep up the supply of horses and cows? In the spring, so many children, according as the State requires, are arranged for, and carefully bred, under medical supervision. When they are born, they are taken away from their mothers (who, else, might grow to love them), and brought up in the public nurseries and schools until they are fourteen. They are then examined by State-appointed inspectors, who decide what calling they shall be brought up to, and to such calling they are thereupon apprenticed. At twenty they take their rank as citizens, and are entitled to a vote. No difference whatever is made between men and women. Both sexes enjoy equal privileges.'

I said:

'What are the privileges?'

He said:

'Why, all that I've been telling you.'

We wandered on for a few more miles, but passed nothing but street after street of these huge blocks. I said:

'Are there no shops or stores in this town?'

'No,' he replied. 'What do we want with shops and stores? The State feeds us, clothes us, houses us, doctors us, washes and dresses us, cuts our corns, and buries us. What could we do with shops?'

I began to feel tired with our walk. I said:

'Can we go in anywhere and have a drink?'

He said:

'A "drink!" What's a "drink"? We have half-a-pint of cocoa with our dinner. Do you mean that?'

I did not feel equal to explaining the matter to him, and he evidently would not have understood me if I had; so I said:

'Yes; I meant that.'

We passed a very fine-looking man a little farther on, and I noticed that he only had one arm. I had noticed two or three rather big-looking men with only one arm in the course of the morning, and it struck me as curious. I remarked about it to my guide.

He said:

'Yes; when a man is much above the average size and strength, we cut one of his legs or arms off, so as to make things more equal; we lop him down a bit, as it were. Nature, you see, is somewhat behind the times; but we do what we can to put her straight.'

I said:

'I suppose you can't abolish her?'

'Well, not altogether,' he replied. 'We only wish we could. But,' he added afterwards, with pardonable pride, 'we've done a good deal.'

I said:

'How about an exceptionally clever man. What do you do with him?'

'Well, we are not much troubled in that way now,' he answered. 'We have not come across anything dangerous in the shape of brainpower for some very considerable time now. When we do, we perform a surgical operation upon the head, which softens the brain down to the average level.

'I have sometimes thought,' mused the old gentleman, 'that it was a pity we could not level *up* sometimes, instead of always levelling down; but, of course, that is impossible.'

I said:

'Do you think it right of you to cut these people up, and tone them down, in this manner?'

He said:

'Of course, it is right.'

'You seem very cocksure about the matter,' I retorted. 'Why is it "of course" right?'

'Because it is done by THE MAJORITY.'

'How does that make it right?' I asked.

'A MAJORITY can do no wrong,' he answered.

'Oh! is that what the people who are lopped think?'

'They!' he replied, evidently astonished at the question. 'Oh, they are in the minority, you know.'

'Yes; but even the minority has a right to its arms and legs and heads, hasn't it?'

'A minority has NO rights,' he answered.

I said:

'It's just as well to belong to the Majority, if you're thinking of living here, isn't it?'

He said:

'Yes; most of our people do. They seem to think it more convenient.'

I was finding the town somewhat uninteresting, and I asked if we could not go out into the country for a change.

My guide said:

'Oh, yes, certainly,' but did not think I should care much for it.

'Oh! but it used to be so beautiful in the country,' I urged, 'before I went to bed. There were great green trees, and grassy, wind-waved meadows, and little rose-decked cottages and—'

'Oh, we've changed all that,' interrupted the old gentleman; 'it is all one huge market-garden now, divided by roads and canals cut at right-angles to each other. There is no beauty in the country now whatever. We have abolished beauty; it interefered with our equality. It was not fair that some people should live among lovely scenery, and others upon barren moors. So we have made it all pretty much alike everywhere now, and no place can lord it over another.'

'Can a man emigrate into any other country?' I asked. 'It doesn't matter what country – *any* other country would do.'

'Oh, yes, if he likes,' replied my companion; 'but why should he? All lands are exactly the same. The whole world is all one people now – one language, one law, one life.'

'Is there no variety, no change anywhere?' I asked.

'What do you do for pleasure, for recreation? Are there any theatres?'

'No,' responded my guide. 'We had to abolish theatres. The histrionic temperament seemed utterly unable to accept the principles of equality. Each actor thought himself the best actor in the world, and superior, in fact, to most other people altogether. I don't know whether it was the same in your day?'

'Exactly the same,' I answered, 'but we did not take any notice of it.'

'Ah! we did,' he replied, 'and, in consequence, shut the theatres up. Besides, our White Ribbon Vigilance Society said that all places of amusement were vicious and degrading; and being an energetic and stout-winded band, they soon won THE MAJORITY over to their views; and so all amusements are prohibited now.'

I said: 'Are you allowed to read books?'

'Well,' he answered, 'there are not many written. You see, owing to our all living such perfect lives, and there being no wrong, or sorrow, or joy, or hope, or love, or grief in the world, and everything being so regular and so proper, there is really nothing much to write about – except, of course, the Destiny of Humanity.'

'True!' I said, 'I see that. But what of the old works, the classics? You had Shakespeare, and Scott, and Thackeray, and there were one or two little things of my own that were not half-bad. What have you done with all those?'

'Oh, we have burned all those old works,' he said. 'They were full of the old, wrong notions of the old, wrong, wicked times, when men were merely slaves and beasts of burden.'

He said all the old paintings and sculptures had been likewise destroyed, partly for that same reason, and partly because they were considered improper by the White Ribbon Vigilance Society, which was a great power now; while all new art and literature were forbidden, as such things tended to undermine the principles of equality. They made men think, and the men that thought grew cleverer than those that did not want to think; and those that did not want to think naturally objected to this, and being in THE MAJORITY, objected to some purpose.

He said that, from like considerations, there were no sports or games permitted. Sports and games caused competition, and competition led to inequality.

I said:

'How long do your citizens work each day?'

'Three hours,' he answered; 'after that, all the remainder of the day belongs to ourselves.'

'Ah! that is just what I was coming to,' I remarked. 'Now, what do you do with yourselves during those other twenty-one hours?'

'Oh, we rest.'

'What! for the whole twenty-one hours?'

'Well, rest and think and talk.'

'What do you think and talk about?'

'Oh! Oh, about how wretched life must have been in the old times, and about how happy we are now, and – and – oh, and the Destiny of Humanity!'

'Don't you ever get sick of the Destiny of Humanity?'

'No, not much.'

'And what do you understand by it? What *is* the Destiny of Humanity, do you think?'

'Oh! – why to – to go on being like we are now, only more so – everybody more equal, and more things done by electricity, and everybody to have two votes instead of one, and—'

'Thank you. That will do. Is there anything else that you think of? Have you got a religion?'

'Oh, yes.'

'And you worship a God?'

'Oh, yes.'

'What do you call him?'

'THE MAJORITY.'

'One question more – You don't mind my asking you all these questions, by-the-by, do you?'

'Oh no. This is all part of my three hours' labour for the State.'

'Oh, I'm glad of that. I should not like to feel that I was encroaching on your time for rest; but what I wanted to ask was, do many of the people here commit suicide?'

'No; such a thing never occurs to them.'

I looked at the faces of the men and women that were passing. There was a patient, almost pathetic, expression upon them all. I wondered where I had seen that look before; it seemed familiar to me.

All at once I remembered. It was just the quiet, troubled, wondering expression that I had always noticed upon the faces of the horses and oxen that we used to breed and keep in the old world.

No. These people would not think of suicide.

Strange! how very dim and indistinct all the faces are growing around me! And where is my guide? and why am I sitting on the pavement? and – hark! Surely that is the voice of Mrs Biggles, my old landlady. Has *she* been asleep a thousand years, too? She says it is twelve o'clock – only twelve? and I'm not to be washed till half-past four; and I do feel so stuffy and hot, and my head is aching. Hulloa!

why, I'm in bed! Has it all been a dream? And am I back in the nineteenth century?

Through the open window I hear the rush and roar of old life's battle. Men are fighting, striving, working, carving out each man his own life with the sword of strength and will. Men are laughing, grieving, loving, doing wrong deeds, doing great deeds – falling, struggling, helping one another – living!

And I have a good deal more than three hours' work to do today, and I meant to be up at seven; and, oh dear! I do wish I had not smoked so many strong cigars last night!

THE ANGRY STREET

G.K. Chesterton

The concept of Utopia has been a favourite theme with writers ever since the term was invented by Thomas More in 1516. Nor is Jerome K. Jerome the only author to have parodied the idea: there have notably also been Samuel Butler in Erewhon *(1872), Aldous Huxley with his* Brave New World *(1932) and G.K. Chesterton, the next contributor, who started a series of short stories in 1925 to be known as* Utopias Unlimited, *but sadly he got no further than two episodes, 'The Paradise of Human Fishes' and 'Concerning Grocers as Gods'. Although Chesterton is perhaps best known today for his detective stories about the little priest, Father Brown, he also made a substantial contribution to the fantasy genre with his novels* The Napoleon of Notting Hill *(1904) and* The Man Who Was Thursday *(1908), and his short stories include comic gems like 'The Taming of the Nightmare', 'The Curious Englishman' and 'The Angry Street', written for the* Daily News *in January 1908. Chesterton's influence can be seen in a number of the stories by R.A. Lafferty and Gene Wolfe, as well as in the whole new genre known as 'Steampunk'.*

Gilbert Keith Chesterton (1874–1936) studied art at the Slade School in London, but as soon as he began working in journalism, his inventive mind and natural wit marked him out as a very distinctive writer. Father Brown has been

*described as a detective unique in crime fiction, but Chesterton
also produced several humorous fantasy novels, including* The
Flying Inn *(1914) about a Turkish conspiracy to impose
Prohibition in England,* The Return of Don Quixote *(1927)
and* The Paradoxes of Mr Pond *(1937) which was greatly
admired by the Argentine writer Jorge Luis Borges. His love of
paradox, his whimsicality and his sense of the absurd were
particularly evident in the short stories collected as* The Club
of Queer Trades, *about a group whose members have only to
fulfil one requirement – the creation of an entirely new
profession, no matter how bizarre. Since it was first published
in 1905, the book has been constantly reprinted. Like so many
of Chesterton's stories, beneath its humour of the absurd 'The
Angry Street' has a point to make which is, if anything, even
more relevant now than when it was written at the start of the
century.*

I cannot remember whether this tale is true or not. If I
read it through very carefully I have a suspicion that I
should come to the conclusion that it is not. But, unfortunately, I cannot read it through very carefully,
because, you see, it is not written yet. The image and
idea of it clung to me through a great part of my boyhood; I may have dreamt it before I could talk; or told it
to myself before I could read; or read it before I could
remember. On the whole, however, I am certain that I
did not read it. For children have very clear memories
about things like that; and of the books of which I was
really fond I can still remember not only the shape and
bulk and binding, but even the position of the printed
words on many of the pages. On the whole, I incline to
the opinion that it happened to me before I was born.

* * *

At any rate, let us tell the story now with all the advantages of the atmosphere that has clung to it. You may suppose me, for the sake of argument, sitting at lunch in one of those quick-lunch restaurants in the City where men take their food so fast that it has none of the quality of food, and take their half-hour's vacation so fast that it has none of the qualities of leisure. To hurry through one's leisure is the most unbusinesslike of actions. They all wore tall shiny hats as if they could not lose an instant even to hang them on a peg, and they all had one eye a little off, hypnotised by the huge eye of the clock. In short they were the slaves of the modern bondage, you could hear their fetters clanking. Each was, in fact, bound by a chain; the heaviest chain ever tied to a man – it is called a watch-chain.

Now, among these there entered and sat down opposite to me a man who almost immediately opened an uninterrupted monologue. He was like all the other men in dress, yet he was startlingly opposite to them all in manner. He wore a high shiny hat and a long frock coat, but he wore them as such solemn things were meant to be worn; he wore the silk hat as if it were a mitre, and the frock coat as if it were the ephod of a high priest. He not only hung his hat up on the peg, but he seemed (such was his stateliness) almost to ask permission of the hat for doing so, and to apologise to the peg for making use of it. When he had sat down on a wooden chair with the air of one considering its feelings and given a sort of slight stoop or bow to the wooden table itself, as if it were an altar, I could not help some comment springing to my lips. For the man was a big, sanguine-faced, prosperous-looking man, and yet he treated everything with a care that almost amounted to nervousness.

For the sake of saying something to express my interest I said, 'This furniture is fairly solid; but, of course, people do treat it much too carelessly.'

As I looked up doubtfully my eye caught his, and was fixed as his was fixed, in an apocalyptic stare. I had thought him ordinary as he entered, save for his strange, cautious manner; but if the other people had seen him then they would have screamed and emptied the room. They did not see him, and they went on making a clatter with their forks, and a murmur with their conversation. But the man's face was the face of a maniac.

'Did you mean anything particular by that remark?' he asked at last, and the blood crawled back slowly into his face.

'Nothing whatever,' I answered. 'One does not mean anything here; it spoils people's digestions.'

He leaned back and wiped his broad forehead with a high handkerchief; and yet there seemed to be a sort of regret in his relief.

'I thought perhaps,' he said in a low voice, 'that another of them had gone wrong.'

'If you mean another digestion gone wrong,' I said, 'I never heard of one here that went right. This is the heart of the Empire, and the other organs are in an equally bad way.'

'No, I mean another street gone wrong,' he said heavily and quietly, 'but as I suppose that doesn't explain much to you, I think I shall have to tell you the story. I do so with all the less responsibility; because I know you won't believe it. For forty years of my life I invariably left my office, which is in Leadenhall Street, at half-past five in the afternoon, taking with me an umbrella in the right hand and a bag in the left hand. For forty years two months and four days I passed out of the side office door, walked down the street on the left-hand side, took the first turning to the left and the third to the right, from where I bought an evening paper, followed the road on the right-hand side round two obtuse angles, and came out just outside a Metropolitan station, where I took a train home. For forty years two months and four days I fulfilled this course by accumulated habit: it was not a long street that I traversed, and it took me about four and a half minutes to do it. After forty years two months and four days, on the fifth day I went out in the same manner, with my umbrella in the right hand and my bag in the left, and I began to notice that walking along the familiar street tired me somewhat more than usual. At first I thought I must be breathless and out of condition; though this, again, seemed unnatural, as my habits had always been like clockwork. But after a little while I became convinced that the road was distinctly on a more steep incline that I had known previously; I was positively panting uphill. Owing to this no doubt the corner of the street seemed farther off than usual; and when I turned it I was convinced that I had turned down the wrong one. For now the street shot up quite a steep slant, such as one only sees in the hilly parts of London, and in this part there were no hills at all. Yet it was not the wrong street. The name written on it was the same; the shuttered shops were the same; the lamp-posts and the whole look of the perspective was the same; only it was tilted upwards like a lid. Forgetting any trouble about breathlessness or fatigue I ran furiously forward, and reached the second of my accustomed turnings, which ought to bring me almost within sight of the station. And as I turned that corner I nearly fell on the pavement. For now the street went up straight in front of my face like a steep staircase or the side of a pyramid. There was not for miles round that place so much as a slope like that of Ludgate Hill. And this was a slope like that of the Matterhorn. The whole street had lifted itself like a single wave, and yet every speck and detail of it was the same, and I saw in the high distance, as at the top of an Alpine pass, picked out in pink letters the name over my paper shop.

'I ran on and on blindly now, passing all the shops, and coming to a part of the road where there was a long grey row of private houses. I had, I know not why, an irrational feeling that I was on a long iron bridge in empty space. An impulse seized me, and I pulled up the iron trap of a coal hole. Looking down through it I saw empty space and the stars.

'When I looked up again a man was standing in his front garden, having apparently come out of his house; he was leaning over the railings and gazing at me. We were all alone on that nightmare road; his face was in shadow; his dress was dark and ordinary; but when I saw him standing so perfectly still I knew somehow that he was not of this world. And the stars behind his head were larger and fiercer than ought to be endured by the eyes of men.

' "If you are a kind angel," I said, "or a wise devil, or have anything in common with mankind, tell me what is this street possessed of devils."

'After a long silence he said, "What do you say that is?"

' "It is Bumpton Street, of course," I snapped. "It goes to Oldgate Station."

' "Yes," he admitted gravely; "it goes there sometimes. Just now, however, it is going to heaven."

' "To heaven?" I said. "Why?"

' "It is going to heaven for justice," he replied. "You must have treated it badly. Remember always that there is one thing that cannot be endured by anybody or anything. That one unendurable thing is to be over-worked and also neglected. For instance, you can overwork women – everybody does. But you can't neglect women – I defy you to. At the same time, you can neglect tramps and gipsies and all the apparent refuse of the State, so long as you do not overwork them. But no beast of the field, no horse, no dog can endure long to be asked to do more than his work and yet have less than his honour. It is the same with streets. You have worked this street to death, and yet you have never remembered its existence. If you had owned a healthy democracy, even of pagans, they would have hung this street with garlands and given it the name of a god. Then it would have gone quietly. But at last the street has grown tired of your tireless insolence; and it is bucking and rearing its head to heaven. Have you never sat on a bucking horse?"

'I looked at the long grey street, and for a moment it seemed to me to be exactly like the long grey neck of a horse flung up to heaven. But in a moment my sanity returned, and I said, "But this is all nonsense. Streets go to the place they have to go to. A street must always go to its end."

' "Why do you think so of a street?" he asked, standing very still.

' "Because I have always seen it do the same thing," I replied, in reasonable anger. "Day after day, year after year, it has always gone to Oldgate Station; day after . . ."

'I stopped, for he had flung up his head with the fury of the road in revolt.

' "And you?" he cried terribly. "What do you think the

road thinks of you? Does the road think you are alive? Are you alive! Day after day, year after year, *you* have gone to Oldgate Station . . ." Since then I have respected the things called inanimate.'

And bowing slightly to the mustard-pot, the man in the restaurant withdrew.

THE PARTY AT LADY CUSP-CANINE'S

Mervyn Peake

The Gormenghast Trilogy by Mervyn Peake (published in an omnibus edition in 1983) is, like Tolkien's The Lord of the Rings, *one of the great fantasy works of the twentieth century. But apart from this sprawling epic concerning the fortunes of Titus, heir to the Earldom of Groan, Peake was also a master of the comic short story and poem, as 'The Dwarf of Battersea', 'An Angry Cactus Does No Good' and 'The Men in Bowler Hats are Sweet' bear hilarious witness. Like G.K. Chesterton, he was a wonderfully skilled artist and illustrated many of his works with his own highly individual sketches. But for his tragic early death his stature as a major fantasy writer might well have been further enhanced with more stories like 'Danse Macabre' (which I included in my previous collection,* The Flying Sorcerers) *and books such as* Captain Slaughterboard Drops Anchor *(1939), for children, and* Mr Pye *(1953), about a man who is so good he grows angel's wings. This novel was recently adapted for television and it is hoped that its success will encourage Walt Disney studios, which owns the films rights to the Gormenghast Trilogy, to bring this unique saga to the screen.*

Mervyn Laurence Peake (1911–68) was born in China where his father was a missionary, and some of his early drawings and writings were clearly influenced by his impressions of that vast and mysterious country. It was while he was serving in the Royal Engineers during the Second World War that he began to work on the adventures of Titus Groan, and it is said that some of the darker episodes of the books were directly influenced by the trauma he suffered when sent to Belsen concentration camp as a war artist. Scarcely had the success of the Gormenghast books been acknowledged, however, than Peake was diagnosed as suffering from Parkinson's disease. Among his papers were found a number of episodes obviously intended for the final book in the trilogy, Titus Alone, which the author had either deleted or simply left out. 'The Party at Lady Cusp-Canine's' is one such and was intended for the beginning of the story when Titus finds himself in a glittering city over which aircraft glide menacingly. Trying to avoid them, he suddenly finds himself looking through a skylight at an incredible party going on below. Originally published in New Worlds *in September/ October 1969, it is a superlative piece of comic writing in which Peake ingeniously puts the reader in the position of a guest at the party, overhearing the most extraordinary snatches of conversation.*

And so, by a whim of chance, yet another group of guests stood there beneath him. Some had limped and some had slid away. Some had been boisterous: some had been aloof.

This particular group were neither and both, as the offshoots of their brain-play merited. Tall guests they were, and witless that through the accident of their height and slenderness they were creating between them a grove – a human grove. They turned, this group, this grove of guests, turned as a newcomer, moving sideways an inch at a time, joined them. He was short, thick and sapless, and was most inappropriate in that lofty copse, where he gave the appearance of being pollarded.

One of this group, a slender creature, thin as a switch, swathed in black, her hair as black as her dress and her eyes as black as her hair, turned to the newcomer.

'Do join us,' she said. 'Do talk to us. We need your steady brain. We are so pitifully emotional. *Such* babies.'

'Well I would hardly—'

'Be quiet, Leonard. You have been talking quite enough,' said the slender, doe-eyed Mrs Grass to her fourth husband. 'It is Mr Acreblade or nothing. Come along dear Mr Acreblade. There . . . we are . . . there . . . we are.'

The sapless Mr Acreblade thrust his jaw forward, a sight to be wondered at, for even when relaxed his chin gave the impression of a battering ram; something to prod with; in fact, a *weapon*.

'Dear Mrs Grass,' he said, 'you are always so unaccountably kind.'

The attenuate Mr Spill had been beckoning a waiter, but now he suddenly crouched down so that his ear was level with Acreblade's mouth. He did not face Mr Acreblade as he crouched there, but swivelling his eyes to their eastern extremes, he obtained a very good view of Acreblade's profile.

'I'm a bit deaf,' he said. 'Will you repeat yourself? Did you say – "unaccountably kind"? How droll.'

'Don't be a bore,' said Mrs Grass.

Mr Spill rose to his full working height, which might have been even more impressive were his shoulders not so bent.

'Dear lady,' he said. 'If I am a bore, who made me so?'

'Well who *did*, darling?'

'It's a long story—'

'Then we'll skip it, shall we?'

She turned herself slowly, swivelling on her pelvis until her small conical breasts, directed at a Mr Kestrel, were for all the world like some kind of delicious *threat*. Her husband, Mr Grass, who had seen this manoeuvre at least a hundred times, yawned horribly.

'Tell me,' said Mrs Grass, as she let loose upon Mr Kestrel a fresh broadside of naked eroticism, 'tell me, dear Mr Acreblade, all about *yourself*.'

Mr Acreblade, not really enjoying being addressed in this off-hand manner by Mrs Grass, turned to her husband.

'Your wife is very special. Very rare. Conducive to speculation. She talks to me through the back of her head; staring at Kestrel the while.'

'But that is as it should be!' cried Kestrel, his eyes swimming over with excitement, 'for life must be various, incongruous, vile and electric. Life must be ruthless and as full of love as may be found in a jaguar's fang.'

'I like the way you talk, young man,' said Grass, 'but I don't know *what* you're saying.'

'What are you mumbling about?' said the lofty Spill, bending one of his arms like the branch of a tree and cupping his ear with a bunch of twigs.

'You are somewhat divine,' whispered Kestrel, addressing Mrs Grass.

'I think I spoke to you, dear,' said Mrs Grass over her shoulder to Mr Acreblade.

'Your wife is talking to me again,' said Acreblade to Mr Grass. 'Let's hear what she has to say.'

'You talk about my wife in a very peculiar way,' said Grass. 'Does she annoy you?'

'She would if I lived with her,' said Acreblade. 'What about you?'

'O, but my dear chap, how naive you are! Being *married* to her I seldom *see* her. What is the point of getting married if one is always bumping into one's wife? One might as well not be married. Oh no, dear fellow, she does what she wants. It is quite a coincidence that we found each other here tonight. You see? And we enjoy it – it's like the first love all over again without the heartache – without the *heart* in fact. Cold love's the loveliest love of all. So clear, so crisp, so empty. In short, so civilised.'

'You are out of a legend,' said Kestrel, in a voice that was so muffled with passion that Mrs Grass was quite unaware that she had been addressed.

'I'm as hot as a boiled turnip,' said Mr Spill.

'But tell me, you horrid man, how do I feel?' cried Mrs Grass, lacerating her beauty with the edge of her voice. 'I'm looking so well these days, even my husband said so, and you know what husbands are.'

'I have no idea what they *are*,' said the fox-like man newly arrived at her elbow. 'But you must tell me. What are they? I only know what they become . . . and perhaps . . . what drove them to it.'

'Oh, but you are *clever*. Wickedly clever. But you must tell me all. How *am* I, darling?'

The fox-like man (a narrow-chested creature with reddish hair above his ears, a very sharp nose and a brain far too large for him to manage with comfort) replied:

'You are feeling, my dear Mrs Grass, in need of something sweet. Sugar, bad music, or something of that kind might do for a start.'

The black-eyed creature, her lips half open, her teeth

shining like pearls, her eyes fixed with excited animation on the foxy face before her, clasped her delicate hands together at her conical breasts.

'You're quite right! O, but *quite*!' she said breathlessly. 'So absolutely and miraculously *right*, you brilliant, *brilliant* little man; something sweet is what I *need*!'

Meanwhile Mr Acreblade was making room for a long-faced character dressed in a lion's pelt. Over his head and shoulders was a black mane.

'Isn't it a bit hot in there?' said young Kestrel.

'I am in agony,' said the man in the tawny skin.

'Then why?' said Mr Grass.

'I thought it was Fancy Dress,' said the skin, 'but I mustn't complain. Everyone has been most kind.'

'That doesn't help the heat you're generating in there,' said Mr Acreblade. 'Why don't you just whip it off?'

'It is all I have on,' said the lion's pelt.

'How delicious,' cried Mrs Grass, 'you thrill me utterly. Who are you?'

'But my *dear*,' said the lion, looking at Mrs Grass, 'surely you . . .'

'What is it, O King of Beasts?'

'Can't you remember me?'

'Your nose seems to ring a bell,' said Mrs Grass.

Mr Spill lowered his head out of the clouds of smoke. Then he swivelled it until it lay alongside Mr Kestrel. 'What did she say?' he asked.

'She's worth a million,' said Kestrel. 'Lively, luscious, what a plaything!'

'Plaything?' said Mr Spill. 'How do you mean?'

'You wouldn't understand,' said Kestrel.

The lion scratched himself with a certain charm. Then he addressed Mrs Grass.

'So my nose rings a bell – is that all? Have you forgotten me? *Me!* Your one-time Harry?'

'Harry? What . . . my . . . ?'

'Yes, your Second. Way back in time. We were married, you remember, in Tyson Street.'

'Lovebird!' cried Mrs Grass. 'So we *were*. But take that foul mane off and let me see you. Where have you been all these years?'

'In the wilderness,' said the lion, tossing back his mane and twitching it over his shoulder.

'What sort of wilderness, darling? Moral? Spiritual? O but tell us about it!' Mrs Grass reached forward with her breasts and clenched her little fists at her sides, which attitude she imagined would have appeal. She was not far wrong, and young Kestrel took a step to the left which put him close beside her.

'I believe you said, "wilderness" ', said Kestrel. 'Tell me, how wild *is* it? Or isn't it? One is so at the mercy of words. And would you say, sir, that what is wilderness for one might be a field of corn to another with little streams and bushes?'

'What sort of bushes?' said the elongated Mr Spill.

'What does that matter?' said Kestrel.

'*Everything* matters,' said Mr Spill. '*Everything*. That is part of the pattern. The world is bedevilled by people thinking that some things matter and some things don't. Everything is of equal importance. The wheel must be complete. And the stars. They *look* small. But are they? No. They are large. Some are very large. Why, I remember—'

'Mr Kestrel,' said Mrs Grass.

'Yes, my dear lady?'

'You have a vile habit, dear.'

'What is it, for heaven's sake? Tell me about it that I may crush it.'

'You are too *close*, my pet. But *too* close. We have our little areas you know. Like the home waters, dear, or fishing rights. Don't trespass, dear. Withdraw a little. You know what I mean, don't you? Privacy is *so* important.'

Young Kestrel turned the colour of a boiled lobster and retreated from Mrs Grass who, turning her head to him, by way of forgiveness switched on a light in her face, or so it seemed to Kestrel, a light that inflamed the air about them with a smile like an eruption. This had the effect of drawing the dazzled Kestrel back to her side, where he stayed, bathing himself in her beauty.

'Cosy again,' she whispered.

Kestrel nodded his head and trembled with excitement until Mr Grass, forcing his way through a wall of guests, brought his foot down sharply upon Kestrel's instep. With a gasp of pain, young Kestrel turned for sympathy to the peerless lady at his side, only to find her radiant smile was now directed at her own husband where it remained for a few moments before she turned her back upon them both and, switching off the current, she gazed across the room with an aspect quite drained of animation.

'On the other hand,' said the tall Spill, addressing the man in the lion's pelt, 'there is something in the young man's question. This wilderness of yours. Will you tell us more about it?'

'But oh! But do!' rang out the voice of Mrs Grass, as she gripped the lion's pelt cruelly.

'When I say "wilderness",' said the lion, 'I only speak of the heart. It is Mr Acreblade that you should ask. His wasteland is the very earth itself.'

'Ah me, that Wasteland,' said Acreblade, jutting out his

chin, 'knuckled with ferrous mountains. Peopled with termites, jackals, and to the north-west – hermits.'

'And what were *you* doing out there?' said Mr Spill.

'I shadowed a suspect. A youth not known in these parts. He stumbled ahead of me in the sandstorm, a vague shape. Sometimes I lost him altogether. Sometimes I all but found myself beside him, and was forced to retreat a little way. Sometimes I heard him singing, mad, wild, inconsequential songs. Sometimes he shouted out as though delirious – words that sounded like "Fuchsia", "Flay", and other names. Sometimes he cried out "Mother!" and once he fell to his knees and cried, "Gormenghast, Gormenghast, come back to me again!'

'It was not for me to arrest him – but to follow him for my superiors informed me his papers were not in order, or even in *existence*.

'But on the second evening the dust rose up more terribly than ever, and as it rose it blinded me so that I lost him in a red and gritty cloud. I could not find him, and I never found him again.'

'Darling.'

'What is it?'

'Look at Gumshaw.'

'Why?'

'His polished pate reflects a brace of candles.'

'Not from where I am.'

'No?'

'No. But look – to the left of centre I see a tiny image, one might almost say of a boy's face, were it not that faces are unlikely things to grow on ceilings.'

'Dreams. One always comes back to dreams.'

'But the silver whip RK 2053722220 – the moon circles, first of the new—'

'Yes, I know all about that.'

'But love was nowhere near.'

'The sky was smothered with planes. Some of them, though pilotless, were bleeding.'

'Ah, Mr Flax, how is your son?'

'He died last Wednesday.'

'Forgive me, I am so sorry.'

'Are you? I'm not. I never liked him. But mark you – an excellent swimmer. He was captain of his school.'

'This heat is horrible.'

'Ah, Lady Crowgather, let me present the Duke of Crowgather; but perhaps you have met already?'

'Many times. Where are the cucumber sandwiches?'

'Allow me—'

'Oh I beg your pardon. I mistook your foot for a tortoise. What is happening?'

'No, indeed, I do not like it.'

'Art should be artless, not heartless.'

'I am a great one for beauty.'

'Beauty, that obsolete word.'

'You beg the question, Professor Salvage.'

'I beg nothing. Not even your pardon. I do not even beg to differ. I differ without begging, and would rather beg from an ancient, rib-staring, sightless groveller at the foot of a column, than beg from you, sir. The truth is not in you, and your feet smell.'

'Take that . . . and that,' muttered the insultee, tearing off one button after another from his opponent's jacket.

'What fun we do have,' said the button-loser, standing on tip-toe and kissing his friend's chin: 'Parties would be unbearable without abuse, so don't go away, Harold. You sicken me. What is that?'

'It is only Marblecrust making his bird noises.'

'Yes, but . . .'

'Always, somehow . . .'

'Oh no . . . no . . . and yet I like it.'

'And so the young man escaped me without knowing,' said Acreblade, 'and judging by the hardship he must have undergone he must surely be somewhere in the City . . . where else could he be?'

THE LITTLE MAN
WHO WASN'T ALL THERE

Robert Bloch

Robert Bloch's stories of Lefty Feep have been described as a mixture of Damon Runyon and Groucho Marx, and as a legend in the annals of comic fantasy. The fast-talking racetrack-tout who is constantly getting involved in supernatural tall tales was, like Mervyn Peake's Titus, a creation of the Second World War and his language is full of the coloquialisms of America in the Forties. Lefty has an eye for curvaceous blondes 'poured into low-cut dresses with ruby-red lips', while his circle of acquaintances includes such unforgettable characters as Gorilla Gabface, Out-of-Business Oscar, Black Art the rug-seeker, Klondike Ike the prospector, Boogie Mann the jive musician and Magistrate Donglepootzer. The titles of some of the funniest of Lefty Feep's adventures speak for themselves: 'Jerk the Giant Killer', 'The Weird Doom of Floyd Scrich' and 'The Pied Piper Fights the Gestapo'. In 1987 a collection of the best of these exploits was published as Lost in Time and Space with Lefty Feep, *introducing the character to a whole new generation of fantasy fans.*

Robert Bloch (1917–94) is best-known as the author of Psycho *(1959) which Alfred Hitchcock made into one of the most famous horror films of all time. However, from the*

1930s, when he made his debut with short stories in the pages of the American pulp magazine, Weird Tales, he also showed a rare talent for tales of black comedy which were notable for the author's use of the most excruciating puns in both text and titles. For the background to the Feep stories Bloch drew on the Chicago in which he grew up, as well as on items of news that caught his eye. The story of 'The Little Man Who Wasn't All There', published in Fantastic Adventures in August 1942, although partly influenced by H.G. Wells' classic, The Invisible Man, has an even stranger association about which the author knew nothing when he wrote it. There is a reference in the story to Dunninger, a popular stage magician who specialised in hypnotism and mind reading, and helped the US Navy's war efforts with tests for invisibility. In 1943, a year after the story was published, the Navy actually conducted invisibility experiments with the USS Eldridge, a warship based at Norfolk, Virginia, which allegedly vanished and reappeared a short while later in Philadelphia. The events have since been thoroughly documented, and in 1987 Robert Bloch was asked if 'The Little Man Who Wasn't All There' was a case of 'psychic foresight'. He denied it emphatically. 'As far as my story is concerned, I made it up,' he said. 'Nothing more. Those things happen once in a while.' Coincidence or not, prepare for one of the most side-splitting of all Lefty Feep's adventures.

I walked into Jack's Shack accompanied by a terrific appetite. It tugged me towards a table with a haste not to be denied. I didn't notice the thin and melancholy figure in the booth until a thin and melancholy arm grabbed my coat-tails.

'Hey!' said a voice, plaintively.

'Why, Lefty Feep! I didn't see you when I came in.'

A grimace of positive horror crossed Mr Feep's face, together with half of the sandwich he was eating.

'Don't say that,' he pleaded.

'But I really didn't notice you.'

Feep trembled violently.

'Please put a collar on that kind of holler,' he begged. 'It makes me queasy but uneasy when you say you do not see me.'

'Oh, I see you now, all right.'

'That's better.' Feep pushed a relieved smile through the sandwich lettuce and waved me to a seat opposite him. 'Now you're cooking with sterno.'

I gave my order and sank back in my chair.

'Well, Lefty, what's new? Haven't seen hide nor hair of you for a few days.'

'Don't say it that way!' Feep grated.

'What's biting you?'

'The finance company,' Lefty Feep replied. 'But that is neither here nor there. It is this stuff about not seeing me that disturbs and perturbs.'

I began to feel a question coming on. I struggled to resist, but it was no use.

'What's the reason you're so upset when I mention not seeing you?'

Feep wiggled his ears impressively.

'Do you really want to know?' he asked.

'No. But you're going to tell me, anyway.'

'Seeing you are so inquisitive,' said Lefty Feep, 'I suppose there is nothing else I can do but spill it. The whole thing starts out when I get tangled up with this Gorgonzola.'

'The cheese?' I inquired.

'No – the magician,' Feep replied.

Waving a stalk of celery in mysterious rhythm, Lefty Feep hunched forward and began his story.

I know this great Gorgonzola for many a year. In fact, I know him when he is just plain Eddie Klotz, doing a vaudeville act. Then he gets a magic show of his own, and pretty soon he calls himself the Great Gorgonzola and becomes tops in the sleight-of-hand racket.

I see his latest show just recently, and it is only a couple of days later that I run into him in front of a brass rail I happen to be standing on.

I give him the old once-over, because he is dressed very stylish, like a corpse, and he has a dance-floor moustache – full of wax. Then I recognise him.

'Well, if it isn't the Great Gorgonzola,' I yap. 'How are tricks in the magic game?'

'Fair,' he tells me. 'The legerdemain is all right, but the prestidigitation is lousy.'

'I am sorry to hear that,' I reply. 'But by the way, as one magician to another – who is that lady I saw you in half with last night?'

'That is no lady, that is my wife,' he comes back, with a straight puss. 'She is my assistant in the show we are doing. How do you like it?'

'Very nice,' I tell him. 'Strictly uptown. I figure I will go again this week.'

He shakes his head.

'The show closes last night,' he informs me. 'I have a little business to attend to the rest of this week, so I close up and get ready to leave town. But I hate to do it.'

'Why?'

'Do you ever hear of my rival?'

'Rival?'

'Yes,' he sneers. 'Gallstone the Magician.'

'What's with him?'

'My wife, mostly,' says Gorgonzola, looking very sad. 'Gallstone is nothing but a bushy-haired wolf. He is making passes at my wife, and not just to practise his hypnotism, either.'

'That is a tough break,' I agree. 'But why do you not give him a tough break too – say, his neck, for instance?'

'An excellent idea,' Gorgonzola tells me. 'But I simply must leave on this business trip. Meanwhile, this Gallstone will be hanging around my wife, trying to insinuate himself with her.'

'That is a lousy thing to do,' I pronounce. 'There is nothing I hate worse than an insinuator. Isn't there a law?'

'You do not seem to understand me,' says Gorgonzola. 'He wants to worm something out of her.'

'That is even worse.'

'I mean, Gallstone is trying to get my wife to give away the secrets of my new magical effects for the next season's show. He wants her to tell him my new tricks.'

'Aha! Then why don't you take your wife with you?'

'That's out. Private business, very important and just a little dangerous. I'm leaving her out at the house. Futzi will have to take care of her.'

'Futzi?'

'My houseboy,' Gorgonzola explains. 'He's a Filipino.' Then he slaps his hand on the bar. 'Say, there's an idea. Listen, Feep – why can't you come out to the house and stay there these next three days? It would solve everything if you'd keep your eyes open.'

'I am sorry,' I tell him. 'But it is necessary for me to stay downtown and look after my interests.'

'You mean those lousy two-dollar horse bets?'

'Well, if you choose to put it that way.'

'But you can come down every day anyway. Just so you are on hand if this Gallstone shows up. It means a lot to me, Lefty – more than I can tell you now.'

'All right,' I agree. 'When do I go, and where?'

'Today,' Gorgonzola tells me. 'Here's what I'll do – I'll go home, pack, and leave. Then I'll have Futzi come around and call for you with the car. You can carry your things easier that way.'

'What things?' I reply, very bitterly. 'One toothbrush and a pair of socks is not exactly a load.'

'Nevertheless, Futzi will call for you. He'll bring the keys and everything. Expect him at your place around two. And thanks a million.'

With that, Gorgonzola breezes out and I go home and dry out that pair of socks. I am shredding the bristles on my toothbrush when the doorbell rings.

I yank it open, careful, and look out into the hall. I do not see anybody. Then I glance down. Somewhere about a few feet from the floor is a little guy with a face like yellow jaundice.

This face is all plastered up in a big grin with the teeth sticking out like they want to use my toothbrush.

The little yellow guy bows up and down.

'Honourable Feep?' he asks.

I give him the nod.

'Honourable Feep, honourable Gorgonzola say for me to carry you to honourable house. Myself, humble Futzi, am yours truly to command.'

This is Filipino double-talk meaning I am going to Gorgonzola's dump with him.

So I grab my handclasp – it is so small, you can hardly call it a grip – and close the door.

'OK,' I tell this Futzi. 'Lead the way, my Japanese sandman.'

He turns and gives me an unlaundered look.

'Me Filipino boy, not Japanese,' he hisses. 'I do not enjoy it when you stick amusement at me.'

'You mean poke fun at you?' I ask.

'Correctly. If I one of those Japanzees I go out commit hootchie-kootchie.'

'Hotsy-totsy?'

'No, hocus-pocus.'

Then I get it. 'You mean hari-kari.'

'No. Hocus-pocus. I kill myself with magician's knife.'

This kind of talk is hard to follow, and so is this guy's driving. We skid through traffic in Gorgonzola's car, and a dozen times I think we are morgue-meat, but little Futzi just sings away at the wheel. Then I decide to take advantage of the chance to find out a few things about the setup I am heading into.

'Does Mrs Gorgonzola expect me?'

'Of coarsely. She expectorate you right away. Mr Gorgonzola he tell her you coming down on weekend and then he take it on the sheep.'

'On the lam, you mean.'

'Honourable correction noted. And here we arrive.'

We pull into the driveway of a two-storey bungalow.

'What kind of woman is Mrs Gorgonzola?' I ask, just to be on the safe side.

'She very female person,' Futzi answers. 'But so sorry. Too skinny for suiting me. Not too skinny for honourable Gallstone though. He all the time dangle around like ants in the pants.'

'You mean snake in the grass.'

'Surely. Shrubbery serpent, that honourable skunk. Mr

Gorgonzola say if you catch Gallstone hanging around you cut his throat from ear to there.'

We get out and head for the door. Futzi rings, grinning at me.

'Mrs Gorgonzola arrive now,' he says.

Sure enough, the door opens.

'Slide in,' Futzi suggests.

'Not me!' I yelp. I do not like what is standing in the doorway. I dislike it so much my knees begin to knock.

'Listen, my fine Filipino friend,' I whisper. 'You tell me Mrs Gorgonzola is thin, but you do not tell me she is *that* thin.'

Because the thing that opens the door is nothing else than a white, grinning skeleton!

'Squeeze yourself together,' Futzi giggles. 'This is not Mrs Gorgonzola. Is just a trick. Gorgonzola he very tricky honourable baby, you betcha! This just harmless bones.'

Sure enough, I see the skeleton is attached to the doorpost. We edge inside.

'Now here are keys to honourable house,' Futzi tells me in the hall. 'Especially keys to Mr Gorgonzola's bedroom. He does tricks up there so nobody steals. He say you take nice care of these, so Gallstone cannot stick honourable schnozzola into secret business.'

I pocket the keys and then I hear somebody coming.

'So there you are,' snaps a voice. Futzi turns around.

'Honourable Mrs, allow me to gift to you honourable Feep, Lefty, Esq. He is here to sit down on week end.'

Mrs Gorgonzola gives me the old eye, and a very pretty eye it is too, under all that mascara and pencil work. She is a tall, thin damsel, the drugstore-blonde hair. I hold out my hand, but she must think I have a bad case of tattle-tale grey, because she does not take it. Instead, she hands me a stuffed-fish look.

'My husband tells me you're going to be here until he gets back,' she freezes.

'I hope it does not put you out,' I tell her.

'Oh, it's perfectly all right, I suppose. Futzi, show Mr Feep to his room. Dinner's at seven. Now, if you'll pardon me, I must go lock myself in a trunk.'

'What kind of talk is that?' I ask Futzi, when we walk upstairs.

'Straight from elbow talk,' he says. 'Mrs Gorgonzola always lock herself in trunk or safe or something. She makes practice for magic act. What you call, escape artist?'

'I see.'

When I get into Gorgonzola's room upstairs, I see a lot more. The place is filled with trunks and boxes and cases, and when I hang my coat in the closet I find still more. There are packs of cards under the bed, and artificial flowers and flags and wands. I head for the bath to wash my hands and Futzi leaps for the door ahead of me.

'Wait!' he hollers. 'You wish to release rabbits?'

'Rabbits?'

'Honourable Gorgonzola keeps rabbits in bath. Bathtub full of lettuce, you notice.'

Sure enough, the place is full of bunnies. I start to wash, and the lop-ears flop around and jump up on me, while Futzi tries to shoo them off.

'Oww!' I mention, with my eyes full of soap, because a rabbit jumps onto the washbowl and starts tickling my stomach. But it is too late for me to do anything, and I get my coat splashed up plenty.

'Do you spend any attention to that,' Futzi grins. 'I send honourable coat to honourable cleaners.'

'Fie upon that noise,' I bark. 'If I do not get back downtown this afternoon I am going to the cleaners myself. I have to place a bet on a pet, and I cannot run down there in my shirtsleeves. The snappy dressers at the pool hall will laugh at me.'

'Why not wear coat of Mr Gorgonzola?' Futzi suggests. 'He got plenty clothes in closet. Enough for whole nudist colony, I gamble you.'

This seems to be an idea. After Futzi takes my wet coat away and tells me I can use the car to drive down, I go to the big bedroom closet and start looking around.

The place is full of magic paraphernalia like I say, but there do not seem to be any clothes hanging there at all, except costumes. I do not wish to wear a turban or a Chinese kimono, and I am about ready to give up when I see this trunk.

It is a great big iron chest locked away at the bottom of the closet, and I pull it out and see that it is closed very tight indeed. For a minute I give up, because I do not carry any nitroglycerine on my person for many years. Then I remember the keys Futzi gives me.

Sure enough, the first key I try unlocks the trunk. It is filled with mirrors and folding stuff and glass balls – and I realise this must be the trunk full of new tricks that Gorgonzola is so anxious for me to watch over.

But there at one side is just what I am looking for – a nice tuxedo. There is a coat, a vest, a pair of pants, and a top hat to match.

I merely remove the coat and slip it on for size. It fits pretty well and I am just going to yank on the trousers when I look at the clock and see I must beat it downtown in a hurry if I wish to catch the fifth race.

So I keep my old trousers and wear Gorgonzola's coat. I

run down the hall and out into the yard, climb into the car, and make like crazy.

Ten minutes later I am entering Gorilla Gabface's pool palace. It is here that I make my modest investments on the races from time to time.

There are quite a bunch of bananas standing around phoning in their wagers, and big fat Gorilla Gabface is making book. When I rush in, they turn around and stare.

Now I admit it is unusual for me to wear a tuxedo coat and check trousers. Such a spectacle is worth a stare any day of the week. But the kind of look I get from the personalities around the phone is quite queer indeed. And there is a very quaint silence along with it.

I rush up to Gorilla Gabface and hold up my hand. He is standing there with his mouth open and his tongue hanging out a mile, and when I come close he sort of shudders and puts his hands over his eyes.

'No!' he gasps. 'No – no!'

'What's the matter, you big ape?' I ask, kindly. 'You look like you never see me before in your life.'

'I don't!' he gasps. 'And if I never see you again I am very satisfied.'

'But you know me. I'm Lefty Feep!'

Gorilla moans a little.

'The face is familiar,' he groans. 'And so are the trousers. But what happens to the rest of you?'

'Nothing at all,' I tell him. 'I merely borrow this tuxedo coat to wear here.'

'What tuxedo coat?' Gabface asks. 'I don't see any.'

'Then what do you think I'm wearing?'

'I don't know.' Gorilla is sweating. He backs farther

away. 'From the looks of you, you should be wearing a shroud. I don't know what holds your neck up.'

'Are you giving me the rib?' I ask.

'No–you're giving me the shivers,' he says. 'Coming in here like that; just a face and a pair of pants underneath. What happens to the rest of you?'

He pulls me along the wall by the seat of my trousers, very careful, until I am facing a mirror.

'Tell me what you see,' he whispers.

I look, and then it is my turn to gasp.

Because in the mirror I see a pair of pants, a neck, and a head. There is nothing in between. I am cut off at the hips, and my head and neck are floating around about three feet above in the empty air!

'You must do a lot of betting in the first races today,' Gorilla whispers. 'I hear of guys losing their shirts on the horses before, but you go ahead and lose your whole torso!'

I just stand there. Looking down, I can see my tuxedo coat very plain. But it does not show in the mirror and it is not visible to anybody else.

'You say you borrow that coat?' one of the specimens at the phone inquires.

'Yes, I find it in a closet.'

'Maybe the thing is full of moths,' he suggests.

'Very hungry moths,' Gorilla chimes in. 'So hungry they not only eat up the coat but your chest and arms, too.'

I just stare at the mirror. Because now I find I know what happens. I look around for clothes in a trunk where Gorgonzola keeps his magic tricks and I get a trick coat. One that makes me invisible.

Just to prove it, I take the coat off. And sure enough, I

am all right again. I stand there in my shirtsleeves looking foolish, but not so foolish as the rest of these mugs.

'How do you do it?' Gabface asks me.

'It is a magician's coat,' I admit.

'Well, do not put it back on,' he begs. 'You give us all
quite a shock with that trick. For a minute I think you
must be suffering from an overdose of vanishing cream.'

'Never mind that,' I snap. 'I want to place a wager in
the fifth race at Santa Anita. On Bing Crosby's horse.'

'You are too late,' Gorilla tells me. 'It just finishes.'

I let out an unkind remark. 'Curse this coat business,' I
suggest. 'It spoils a sure 15-to-1 shot for me.'

'Cheer up,' says Gabface. 'You are lucky you do not
make the bet, because you lose anyway.'

'How come?'

'Well, Bing Crosby's horse is disqualified at the post, so
Crosby runs the race himself instead. And loses.'

This cheers me up a little, and so I take my leave and go
back to Gorgonzola's house for supper. I am very careful
not to wear this coat in the car, because if I do it will look
like the jalopy has no driver in it.

Besides, I cannot get used to the idea of what I see
when I look in the mirror. Being invisible is a very funny
feeling, and every time I remember it I have to close my
eyes and shudder.

The last time I do so I am just ready to park. And I run
smack into the back of a big Packard.

'Aha!' yells a voice from inside. 'Watch where you're
going, you hoodlum!'

I look around to see what kind of uncouth person he is
talking to, and then I realise the remark is made to me.
More and over, the owner of the voice jumps out of the
Packard and climbs up to the running board. He is

waving one hand in front of my face and he does not have any flag in it, either. Just a big fist.

'I am sorry,' I say. 'I must be driving with my eyes closed.'

'That is the way you will drive for a long time, you oaf,' he says. 'Because I am going to black both eyes for you.'

I notice he is a big, beefy fellow with a red face and a shock of bushy hair that stands out from his head like a dust mop.

'Can't we talk this over?' I suggest.

One big arm reaches in and grabs me. He lifts me out of the car and holds me up by the neck.

'The only thing I will talk over is your dead body,' he snarls. 'You smash both my rear bumpers and that is what I am going to do to you.'

Just then the front door opens and Mrs Gorgonzola runs out. She smiles at the big bushy-haired specimen.

'Why, Mr Gallstone, you've arrived for dinner,' she simpers. 'I see you and Mr Feep already know each other.'

'Yes,' I gasp. 'I bump into him just now coming in.'

'Mr Feep is a house-guest,' says Mrs Gorgonzola.

'So?' Gallstone drops me down to my feet and takes his paw off my collar. 'I am pleased to meet you,' he snarls, and holds out his hand. I take it, and he nearly breaks my fingers off at the joints.

'So you are Gallstone the Magician,' I manage to get out. 'Gorgonzola tells me a lot about you.'

'He does, huh? Well – he can't prove it.' Gallstone sneers. Then he turns to Mrs Gorgonzola and gives her a look at his big teeth.

'I hear your husband is away,' he says.

'That's right.'

'Too bad. Ha-ha!'

'Yes, isn't it, tee-hee!' cracks Mrs Gorgonzola.

So right away I figure it is one of *those* things. I get out of the way to avoid being hit by any flying mush they are slinging at each other.

Then Futzi sticks his head around the door.

'Dinner is swerved!' he yells. 'Rush to put on honourable food-sack.'

Mrs Gorgonzola turns to me. 'When you leave, I think you're not coming back for dinner,' she says. 'So—'

I catch on to this, also.

'I eat downtown,' I lie. 'I will just go up to my room, if you don't mind. You two go right ahead and entertain each other. If you don't mind, of course.'

Gallstone smiles and now I know what he reminds me of with his bushy hair. A wolf. It is like Gorgonzola says. And now he is sneaking around Gorgonzola's wife.

I just go upstairs but already I have an idea in the old noggin. When I get into the room I make for the trunk and pull out the rest of the tuxedo, also the top hat. I put these on, and then go for the mirror.

For a minute I am afraid to look. I stare down at my coat and pants. They are very ordinary-looking to me, and I can see them very plainly. So naturally I know I must be able to see them in the mirror.

But when I do look in the mirror, there is nothing. Nothing at all. The coatsleeves come down over my hands and the pants cuffs cover my shoes, and the top hat pulls down over my face – all this I know, but I do not see it in the mirror. The mirror is blank. Absolutely blank.

Maybe there is some new chemical in the cloth, or some fibre that does not reflect light. Whatever it is, Gorgonzola has an invisible suit, and I am wearing it. This is enough for me.

Because I have this plan. I do not like Gallstone the Magician and I promise to watch Gorgonzola's wife. So I decide to go ahead.

I wait a while and then I sneak downstairs wearing the invisible suit. Sure enough, Gallstone and Mrs Gorgonzola are at the supper table, flirting with each other.

When I slide in, he is showing off by juggling three water glasses in the air at once. She giggles and watches him and he smirks all over the place. Pretty soon he puts down the glasses and pulls out his napkin. A big rubber plant grows from underneath it.

'Oh, Mr Gallstone, you are so clever,' she says.

'Just call me Oscar,' he says. And pulls a live snake out from the potatoes. 'I'll bet your husband can't do this,' he remarks.

'Oh – him,' sniffs Mrs Gorgonzola. 'He doesn't do anything. Before we marry he is so cute – always grabbing rabbits out of my neck and surprising me by turning coffee into champagne. Now he doesn't even juggle the dinner plates any more.

'Such neglect! Shameful!' says Gallstone. He reaches over and tweaks her ear. A gopher jumps out.

'You're wonderful, Oscar,' she tells him.

'That's nothing at all to what I can do,' boasts Gallstone. 'Come into the living-room.'

'Why?'

'I want to show you some of my parlour tricks.'

They go into the living room. Mrs Gorgonzola grabs his arm. I follow right behind, but of course they cannot see me at all.

'You ought to leave that clumsy oaf of a husband,' Gallstone suggests. 'A woman like you deserves only the best kind of <u>thaumatugry</u>, to say nothing of a little goety now and then.'

'Oh – I couldn't,' she says.

'Why not? What has your husband got that I haven't got? What if he does saw you in half? I've got a trick where I can saw you into four parts. Six, even. And if you'll join my act instead, I'll promise not to stop until I can cut you into sixteen pieces.'

'That would be thrilling,' she blushes.

'Why, your husband doesn't even know how to stick knives into you in the basket trick,' Gallstone sneers. 'Me, I can use axes on you.'

'You make it all sound so fascinating,' she simpers, snuggling up against him.

'Tricks? Why, I've got tricks Gorgonzola never even dreams of,' whispers Gallstone, grabbing her in a half nelson and giving her the kind of look a rat gets when he grabs a piece of cheese.

'I know what kind of tricks you have,' I burst out. 'And you can stick them back up your sleeve, Gallstone.'

'What's that?' Mrs Gorgonzola shrieks, jumping up.

'Huh?' Gallstone looks around. 'That voice – it spoke to me out of empty air.'

They stare but they do not see me, of course, even though I am standing right in front of them.

'You must be imagining things,' says Gallstone, with a puzzled look.

'*Ouch!* I didn't imagine *that*,' snaps Mrs Gorgonzola.

Because I decide to pinch her in a likely spot at this moment, and do so, hard.

'What?' asks Gallstone.

'*That!*' shrieks the lady. 'There – you did it again. You naughty boy. You pinched me.'

'Where?'

'On the davenport there.'

'How can I pinch you when you're holding both my hands?'

'Well, somebody pinched me.'

I stick my face down close.

'You'll get pinched again if you don't stop holding hands with that bushy-haired baboon,' I mutter.

'Eeek – that voice again!' Mrs Gorgonzola wails. 'Don't tell me you don't hear it this time, Oscar.'

Gallstone is on the spot now. All at once he smiles.

'Oh, *that* voice,' he says. 'Just another little trick of mine your husband can't duplicate. That's a spirit. A ghost. I'm psychic, you know. I can call ghosts out of the empty air.'

She gives him a sick-calf look.

'Oh, how wonderful you are!' she says. They go into another clinch. I break this up by stepping on Gallstone's toes, hard. Then I let out a long groan. They jump apart fast.

'Cut out that romantic stuff, Goldilocks,' I grate. 'Or you'll be a ghost yourself in a couple of minutes.'

'I don't think I'd like to live with such spirits,' Mrs Gorgonzola wails. 'Oscar, make that voice go away.'

Gallstone is plenty confused. But he stands up, and tries to smile.

'Listen, darling – once and for all, let's forget all these things. I want you to go away with me and join my act. That's what I've come to tell you. You and I can take your husband's new tricks with us and—'

Aha, that was it! He was after those tricks, just the way Gorgonzola warns me. I watch the two of them close.

'I'm not sure,' Mrs Gorgonzola flutters. 'You must let me decide.'

'No time for that. I'll prove to you that I'm a better magician than Gorgonzola any day. And then you must come with me.'

'Well—'

'Come on. Name a trick your husband can't do and I'll do it for you right now.'

'Let me see. Oh yes, that safe trick. You know that big iron safe he has. He tries to get out of it after it's locked and he just can't seem to master the combination.'

'Let me at it,' Gallstone boasts. 'Lead me to it. I'll show you.'

'It's in the cellar,' she says.

'Show me.'

They go downstairs and I follow. I try to trip Gallstone on the stairs, but miss. And there we are in the cellar; the two standing in front of a big iron safe and me invisible next to them.

The safe is really a terrific box, big and heavy, with a large lock on it. Gallstone looks at it and laughs.

'Why, breaking that is like breaking a baby bank,' he sneers. 'I'll climb in and let you lock me up. In three minutes I'll be out again and we'll be off together. Is it a deal?'

Mrs Gorgonzola blushes.

'Very well, Oscar,' she says. 'You have my consent. If you can break out of this safe I'll run away with you.'

'Kiss me, darling,' moos Gallstone. They clinch, but I stick my face in between and Gallstone kisses my neck. He blinks a little but breaks away. Then he wraps his coat around himself and opens the safe.

'Here I go,' he says, crawling inside and bending himself double to squeeze in. 'Lock the door, darling. I'll be out in no time.'

I stoop down and notice, when he pulls his feet in, that there is a little steel pick attached to the sole of one shoe. But Mrs Gorgonzola does not see this. She closes the door and blows him a kiss and then steps back to wait.

In about a minute I can hear this Gallstone fumbling around inside with his pick, working on the combination. I just wait. The tumblers start to click.

Another minute goes by and another. Still no Gallstone. Mrs Gorgonzola stoops down.

'Are you all right, Oscar?' she calls.

'Sure – be with you in a jiffy,' he gasps.

But a jiffy passes and so do five minutes. And no Gallstone.

Mrs Gorgonzola is getting impatient.

'Can I help you?' she asks.

'No – I'm – getting on fine – just a second,' he groans.

Fifteen more minutes go by. Gallstone is thumping around and rattling the combination and panting for breath.

Mrs Gorgonzola is getting redder and redder. All at once she looks at her wristwatch.

'You got in there twenty-five minutes ago,' she calls. 'I'll give you five minutes more.'

There is a grunt from inside and a lot of rattling. But five minutes pass, and Gallstone is still in the safe. The noise stops. Gallstone gives up trying to get out. Mrs Gorgonzola gives a sigh and looks stern.

'Very well, Oscar, you show your true colours. You are nothing but an impostor. You are not a good magician. You cannot find your way out of a telephone booth, let alone a safe. I will never run away with you. Good night!'

She turns around and marches upstairs. I follow her, because there is nothing more I have to do. I do my job when I keep turning the dial of the safe after Gallstone lines up the tumblers.

So I go to bed very happy. Gallstone will sneak away like the pup he is. Now I know Mrs Gorgonzola is all through with him, and there is nothing to worry about. Gorgonzola will be back in a day or so and his tricks are safe after all.

I take off my coat and hat and am just going to remove the tuxedo trousers, when the door opens. Futzi walks in.

'Honourable Feep, I expect you are – oh mercy, what in name is honourable that?' he yells.

He is staring at my trousers, or rather at the place where my trousers should be. But because of the pants I wear, he does not see anything below my waist at all.

'Oh what unhappy accident!' he wails. 'You can cut in twice by auto car?'

'No, of course not,' I say.

'Then perhaps you lose on races?'

'There are some things,' I answer with dignity, 'which I will never bet. No, I do not lose anything.'

'But you have no limbs downstairs,' Futzi wails. 'Just head and torso.'

'I have more so than torso,' I assure him, stepping out of the trousers. 'There, you see? All that happens, Futzi, is I wear this suit of Gorgonzola's. It is some kind of trick suit, because when I wear it I am invisible.'

'So? whispers Futzi. 'That is remarkable, also strange.'

'Sure,' I say. 'This must be one of the new tricks that Gorgonzola wishes me to protect. I prefer you do not mention this around. Now I lock the suit up again and that is that.'

So I haul out the trunk and lock up the tuxedo and hat. Futzi hangs around staring at me.

'Where is honourable Gallstone?' he asks.

'Downstairs on ice,' I tell him. 'He locks himself up in a safe like a war bond.'

'Then he does not rush away with Mrs Gorgonzola?' Futzi asks. 'I expect they lope off together.' His face falls.

'No elopement,' I tell him. 'You better go down and unlock the safe now and let Gallstone go home.'

Futzi still hangs around.

'Maybe you like me to press honourable suit?' he asks. 'Make it nice and fresh for Mr Gorgonzola to be invisible in? Gorgonzola always proud to look his best even if invisible, I gamble you.'

'No, get out of here,' I snap.

'I press and iron plenty fast,' he begs. 'Please, let me press nice invisible coat and trousers.'

'I'll press your trousers for you with my foot if you don't scram,' I suggest.

So Futzi scrams.

I go to bed. I tuck the keys right under my pillow, too, because I do not wish to lose them. An invisible suit is plenty valuable and I am taking no chances. I figure on keeping awake.

But I am not awake a couple of hours later. In fact, I am very much asleep, and dreaming about rabbits with big teeth and bushy hair that are locking me into a safe. The dream is so real I can even hear the tumblers clicking.

The clicking gets louder and I wake up. Then I know what is making the sound. The keys under my pillow.

They are sliding out, in a hand.

It is a yellow hand. Futzi's hand.

He is standing over my bed in the dark, grabbing for those keys.

'Hey!' I yell, jumping up.

'Hey!' I yell, going down again.

Because Futzi's hand drops the keys and grabs my wrist. He jerks it and I go back on my head. Then his other hand gets hold of my waist. I turn over on my stomach. Then he uses both hands in a very busy fashion and we have quite a scramble.

In a minute I am sitting on the bed looking straight into a pair of legs wrapped around my neck.

Something about them looks quite familiar to me. And I suddenly realise that these are my legs. Around my neck. I am tied up like a Christmas package.

Futzi stands in front of me, grinning.

'Very sorry to disturb,' he says.

'What is this?' I gasp, trying to get loose.

'Jiu-jitsu,' he tells me.

'Jiu-jitsu? But that's a Japanese trick, isn't it? Then you're not a Filipino, you're a—'

Futzi bows.

'That is most correct,' he tells me. 'I am not a Filipino, Mr Feep. Nor do I need to continue the disguise with that ridiculous accent, either. All I require now are those keys of yours. I shall take the suit and leave.'

'But I don't understand –' I say.

'Of course not.' Futzi laughs, very low. 'Why should I disguise myself as a Filipino house boy, get a job in a magician's house, and act as a servant?

'The answer is obvious. Gorgonzola is a clever man, but I know his secret. He does not leave town – he's here now, down at local headquarters of Army Ordnance. He'll tell them he has a new chemical treatment which renders clothing invisible and offer it to the army as a military weapon. Like Dunninger's work in camouflage that makes battleships invisible. The invisible suit is just a sample of the material. Quite a valuable secret.

'Now I have that suit. I shall wear it, slip downtown and put Gorgonzola out of the way once and for all. Information comes to me that his conference with ordnance officials is scheduled for late tonight.

'Naturally I would not be admitted to such a gathering under normal circumstances.' Here Futzi gives a little smirk and bow. 'But with this suit on as a passport I think I can slip in quite freely. With your curiosity thus satisfied, I leave you.'

I still sit there with my legs tied into Boy Scout knots while Futzi goes over to the closet, hauls out the trunk, and opens it. He gets the dress suit and hat and slips them on very fast. He is so small the clothes hang over him and in a few seconds he is gone. Disappears into thin air. I see the door open. His voice chuckles.

'Goodnight, honourable Feep,' he says, sarcastic. 'We must discuss hari-kari again some time. Perhaps you will prefer committing it yourself when you think of what's going to happen to your friend Gorgonzola.'

Then the door closes and I am left tied to be fit. I grunt and groan and wrestle with myself, but I cannot get my legs loose. Finally I roll off the bed onto the floor. That does it. It cracks my skull, but it loosens my legs.

I stagger downstairs to the phone and look up the ordnance headquarters number. I ring and there is no answer. Then I decide to call the cops – until I remember this invisible suit stuff is a military secret. Also, it will not sound so good to ask the cops to chase an invisible man at midnight.

So there is only one thing to do. I spot Gallstone's Packard still standing outside. Futzi has the other car, of course.

I have some trouble sitting down inside, with my sore

legs, but no trouble at all in getting that car up to ninety. When I think of that invisible little Jap sneaking around and trying to knock off Gorgonzola and steal his plans, I know there is no time to lose.

In exactly seven minutes I pull up in front of the old destination. The joint is dark, but open, and I make the stairs very fast to the second floor. There is a light burning in an office room and the door is open. They are inside – and I am sure from the open door that Futzi is with them. Invisible.

I tiptoe in and look through the inside door. There are four characters sitting around a desk, and sure enough, Gorgonzola is with them. He has a briefcase open in front of him and he is talking very fast.

I am the only one who sees what is behind him, though. It hangs in the air very still, but it is ready for action. A big black revolver, in the hands of that invisible Jap.

I throw myself through the doorway and grab the revolver. There is a lot of yelling, but I get it in my hands. Then there is a real yell.

Naturally, all these birds can see is me, waving a gun. They do not see any invisible Futzi, and I cannot yell out to them to look for him, either. He can be hiding anywhere in the room and nobody can spot him.

So I just turn my gun around, point it at a perfect bull's-eye, and shoot Futzi.

And that is how I save a military secret.

Lefty Feep stopped waving the celery and put it in his mouth.

'I can understand now why it upset you when I spoke of not seeing you,' I said. 'You must have had quite an experience.'

'Sure. But it is OK now. Gorgonzola gives the ordnance department his new chemical invisibility formula, his wife gives Gallstone the air, and I give that little Jap spy some lead poisoning where it does him the least good.'

I coughed.

'About that business of shooting the Jap,' I said. 'There's just one question that bothers me.'

'Yes?'

'Well, you say he was wearing this invisible suit and nobody could see him. Yet you managed to shoot him at once. Just what were you aiming at?'

Feep blushed.

'I do not like to say, exactly,' he confessed. 'But I will mention that I get suspicious that night when Futzi hangs around wanting to get his hands on the suit. I decide to figure out a way to make the suit a little less invisible, in case it is worn by anybody else. So I do, and as a result when Futzi wears it he gives me a target he does not notice himself in his hurry putting it on.'

'What target?' I persisted.

'I refuse to say,' Feep grinned. 'All I can tell you is that before I lock honourable suit up for the night, I take a scissors and cut a big hole in seat of honourable pants.'

THE YEAR THE GLOP-MONSTER WON THE GOLDEN LION AT CANNES

Ray Bradbury

Few modern short-story writers have employed whimsical and sombre fantasy so well or in so rich a vein as Ray Bradbury. His novels The Martian Chronicles *(1950) and* Fahrenheit 451 *(1951), and his collection of stories* The Illustrated Man *(1952), are recognised as classics and all have been filmed, though with varying degrees of success. Indeed, Bradbury has a love-hate relationship with the film business: he has written a number of screenplays – including two Fifties B films,* It Came from Outer Space *(1953) and* The Beast from Twenty Thousand Fathoms *(1953), both of which are now cult favourites – as well as being hired to work on several proposed productions of his work which have never reached the screen. He has lived close to Hollywood for much of his life, and his sense of irony about the way film-makers operate is obvious not only in some of his stories, but also in the occasional outspoken magazine article – for example, 'The Fahrenheit Chronicles' (1964), 'Films that are Frightful' (1979) and 'The Future According to Disney' (1980).*

Raymond Douglas Bradbury (1920–) was born in Wau-kegan, Illinois, where his father was a power linesman. When the family fell on hard times during the 1930s Depression, they moved to Los Angeles where young Ray became a film fan

*and spent endless hours after school hanging around the
studios, trying to meet the stars like W.C. Fields, Bing Crosby
and Marlene Dietrich and to get their autographs. 'I also
collected scripts out of studio dustbins so I could learn to write
better,' he admits today. Writing, even then, was his main
preoccupation, and after getting a few stories published in
amateur fanzines, his particular brand of fantasy and sf
caught the eye of the editor of* Weird Tales *and he found
himself being published alongside Robert Bloch who later
became a close friend.*

*In fictional terms, Bradbury has perhaps most clearly
demonstrated his attitude towards Hollywood in his novel*
A Graveyard for Lunatics *(1990), about a wildly eccentric
bunch of characters who operate around the show business
circles of the city with varying degrees of success, and in the
following short story, 'The Year the Glop-Monster Won the
Golden Lion at Cannes', which he wrote for* Cavalier *magazine in July 1967. I am especially delighted now to be giving
the tale its first appearance in book form.*

Remember the Aaron Stolittz jokes? How they called him
the Vampire Bat because he was a fly-by-night producer?
Remember his two studios? One a piano box, the other a
cracker bin? I worked in the cracker bin near the Santa
Monica graveyard. Great! Dead, you just moved 90 feet
south to a good address.

Me? I plagiarised scripts, borrowed music and edited
film on *Slime Monster, The Creature from across the Hall*
(my mother liked it, it resembled *her* mother), *The Mobile
Mammoth* and all the other Giant Yeast, Elephantine
Aphid and Berserk Bacillus films we shot between sunset
and sunrise the next day.

But all that changed. I lived through that great and

awful night when Aaron Stolittz became world-famous, rich, and nothing was the same after that.

The phone rang early one hot September evening. Aaron was up front of his studio. That is, he was hiding in one two-by-four office, beating vinegar-gnat sheriffs off the screen door. I was in the back splicing our latest epic film, using stolen equipment, when the phone buzzed. We jumped, afraid of bill-collector wives shrieking long-distance from forgotten years.

Finally, I lifted the receiver.

'Hey,' a voice cried, 'this is Joe Samasuku at the Samasuku Samurai Theatre. Tonight at 8.30 we scheduled a genuine Japanese surprise studio feature preview. But the film has been waylaid at a film festival in Pacoima or San Luis Obispo—who knows? Look. You got ninety minutes of film any way resembles a Samurai widescreen or even a Chinese fairy tale? There's a fast fifty bucks in it. Give me the titles of your latest somebody-stepped-on-Junior-and-now-he-looks-better-than-ever pictures.'

'*The Island of Mad Apes*?' I suggested.

Uneasy silence.

'*Two Tons of Terror*?' I went on.

The manager of the Samasuku Theatre stirred to disconnect.

'*The Dragon Dances at Midnight*!' I cried, impulsively.

'Yeah.' The voice smoked a cigarette. 'That *Dragon*. Can you finish shooting, cutting, and scoring it in . . . eh . . . one hour and thirty minutes?'

'Monster Apple Pie!' I hung up.

The Dragon Dances at Midnight?' Aaron loomed behind me. 'We got no such film!'

'Watch!' I snapped some title letters under our camera,

'as *The Island of Mad Apes* becomes *The Dragon Dances* et cetera!'

So I retitled the film, finished the music (old Leonard Bernstein out-takes run backwards) and jockeyed 24 film reels into our Volkswagen. Usually films run nine reels, but, editing, you keep film on dozens of short spools so it's easier to handle. There wasn't time to rewind our epic. The Samasuku would have to make do with a couple dozen cans.

We dented bumpers roaring to the theatre and ran the reels up to the projection booth. A man with a dire pirate's eye, and a breath like King Kong's, exhaled sherry wine, grabbed our reels, slammed and locked the metal door.

'Hey!' cried Aaron.

'Quick,' I said. 'After the show may be too late, let's go grab that fifty bucks and . . .'

'I'm ruined, ruined!' said a voice, as we went down the stairs.

There was Joe Samasuku, the manager, staring at the mob as it jostled into the theatre.

'Joe!' we both said, alarmed.

'Look,' he groaned. 'I sent telegrams warning them off. There's been a foulup. And here comes *Variety, Saturday Review, Sight and Sound, Manchester Guardian, Avant-Garde Cinema Review*. Give me poisoned American food, go on!'

'Calmness, Joe,' said Aaron. 'Our film ain't all that bad.'

'It's *not*?' I asked. 'Aaron, those supersnobs! It's Hari-Kari Productions after tonight!'

'Calmness,' said Aaron quietly, 'is a drink we can buy in the bar next door. Come.'

The film started with a great explosion of Dimitri Tiomkin themes upside down, backward and super-reversed.

We ran for the bar. We were halfway through a double glass of serenity when the ocean crashed on the shore. That is to say, the audience in the theatre gasped and sighed.

Aaron and I raced out, opened the theatre door to gaze in at whatever dragon happened to be dancing that midnight.

I let out a small bleat, whirled, and leaped upstairs to beat on the projection-room door with my tiny fists. 'Nincompoop! Louse! The reels are reversed. You got No. 4 reel in where it should be reel 2!'

Aaron joined me, gasping, to lean against the locked door.

'Listen!'

Behind the door a tinkling sound like ice and something that wasn't water.

'He's drinking.'

'He's *drunk*!'

'Look,' I said, sweating, 'he's five minutes into the reel now. Maybe no one noticed. You, in there!' I kicked the door. 'You're warned! Line 'em up! Get 'em right. Aaron,' I said, leading him shakily downstairs, 'let's buy you some more calmness.'

We were finishing our second Martini when another tidal wave hit the coastline.

I ran into the theatre. I ran upstairs. I scrabbled at the projection-room peek-hole. 'Maniac! Destroyer! Not reel six. Reel three! Open up, so I can strangle you with my bare hands!'

He opened up . . . another bottle behind the metal door. I heard him stumble over tin cans of film strewn on the concrete floor.

Clawing my hair, like a scene in *Medea*, I wandered back down to find Aaron gazing deep into his glass.

'Do all movie projectionists drink?'

'Do whales swim underwater,' I replied, eyes shut. 'Does leviathan plumb the ocean seas?'

'Poet,' said Aaron reverently. 'Speak on.'

'My brother-in-law,' I spoke, 'has been projectionist at TriLux Studios for fifteen years, which means fifteen years in which he has not drawn a sober breath.'

'Think of that.'

'I *am* thinking. Fifteen years seeing day after day the rushes for *Saddle of Sin*, the rerun of *Sierra Love Nest*, the recut of *Pitfall of Passion*. The concussion alone would give a man bends. Worse in long-run theatres. Imagine, the ninetieth time you see Carroll Baker in *Harlow*. Think, Aaron, think! Madness, huh? Up-the-wall panics! Sleepless midnights. Impotency. Brown tastes. So? So you start drinking. All across night America at this very hour, conjure up the little settlements, the brave small forts, the big neon cities, and in every one, this second, Aaron, all the film projectionists, no exceptions, are drunker than hoot owl skunks. Drunk, drunk, drunk to a man.'

We brooded over this and sipped our drinks. My eyes watered, imagining ten thousand projectionists alone with their films and bottles far across the prairie continent.

The theatre audience stirred.

'Go see what the madman is doing now,' said Aaron.

'I'm afraid.'

The theatre shook with a tremor of emotion.

We went out and stared up at the projection-room window above.

'He's got twenty-four reels of film there. Aaron, how

many combinations can you put together out of that?
Reel nine for reel five. Reel eleven for reel sixteen. Reel
eight for reel twenty. Reel—'

'Stop!' Aaron groaned, and shuddered.

Aaron and I did not so much walk as run round the
block.

We made it round six times. Each time we came back
the shouts, squeals and improbable roars of the crowd in
the theatre got louder.

'My God, they're ripping up the seats!'

'They wouldn't do that.'

'They're killing their mothers!'

'Movie critics? You ever *see* their mothers, Aaron?
Epaulettes down to here. Battle ribbons across to there.
Work out at the gym five days a week. Build and launch
battleships in their off-hours. Naw, Aaron, break each
other's wrists, sure, but kill their *mothers* . . . ?'

There was a gasp, a hiss, a long-drawn sigh from the
midnight dark within the California architecture. The big
mission dome of the theatre sifted dust.

I went in to stare at the screen until the reels changed. I
came out.

'Reel nineteen in for reel ten,' I said.

At which moment the theatre manager staggered out,
tears in his eyes, face all pale cheese, reeling from wall to
wall with despair and shock.

'What have you done to me? What kind of film is
that?' he shouted, wildly. 'Ingrates, the Joe Samasuku
Samurai Theatre is ruined forever!'

He lunged at us, and I held him off. 'Joe, Joe,' I pleaded,
'don't talk like that!'

The music swelled. It was as if film and audience were
inflating themselves towards a vast ripped-forth explo-

sion which might tear mind from matter as flesh from bone.

Joe Samasuku fell back, pressed a key in my hand and said, 'Call the cops, telephone the janitor service to clean up after the riot, lock the doors if the doors are left, and don't call me; I'll call *you*!'

Then he fled.

We would have dogged him out of his old California patio and down the mean streets had not at that instant a huge stolen chunk of Berlioz and a cymbal smash straight out of Beethoven ended the film.

There was a stunned silence.

Aaron and I turned to stare madly at the shut-tight theatre doors.

They banged wide open. The mob, in full cry, burst into view. It was a beast of many eyes, many arms, many legs, many shoes, and one immense and ever-changing body.

'I'm too young to die,' Aaron remarked.

'You should've thought of that before you messed with things better left to God,' said I.

The mob, the great beast, stopped short, quivering. We eyed it. It eyed us.

'There they are!' someone shouted at last. 'The producer, the director!'

'So long, Aaron,' I said.

'It's been great,' said Aaron.

And the beast, rushing forward with an inarticulate cry, threw itself upon us . . . hoisted us to its shoulders and carried us, yelling happily, singing, slapping us on the back, three times around the patio, out into the street, then back onto the patio again.

'Aaron!'

I stared down aghast into a swarming sea of beatific smiles. Here loped the reviewer of the *Manchester Guardian*. There bounded the mean and dyspeptic critic from the *Greenwich Village Avanti*. Beyond gambolled ecstasies of second-string film reviewers from the *Saturday Review*, *The Nation*, and the *New Republic*. And far out on the shore of this tumultuous sea, in all directions, there was a frolic and jump, a laughing and waving of columnists from the *Partisan Review, Sight and Sound, Cinema*, multitudinous beyond belief.

'Incredible!' they cried. 'Marvellous! Superior to *Hiroshima Mon Amour*! Ten times better than *Last Year at Marienbad*! One hundred times greater than *Greed*! Classic! Genius! Makes *Giant* look like a Munchkin! My God, the New American wave is *in*! How did you *do* it?!'

'Do *what*?' I yelled, looking over at Aaron being carried for the fourth time around the lobby.

'Shut up and ride high in the saddle!' Aaron sailed over the ocean of humanity on a sea of smiles.

I blinked up, wild strange tears in my eyes. And there in the projection room window above a shadow loomed with wide-sprung eyes. The projectionist, bottle in numbed hand, gaped down upon our revelry, ran his free fingers over his face in self-discovery, stared at the bottle and fell away in shadow before I could shout.

When at last, the hopping dancing dwarfs and gazelles were exhausted and laughing out their final compliments, Aaron and I were set back down on our feet with:

'The most tremendous avant-garde film in history!'

'We had high hopes,' said I.

'The most daring use of camera, editing, the jump cut, and the multiple reverse story line I can remember!' everyone said at once.

'Planning pays off,' said Aaron, modestly.

'You're competing it in the Edinburgh Film Festival of course?'

'No,' said Aaron, bewildered, 'we—'

'– planned on it after we show at the Cannes Film competition,' I cut in.

A battalion of flash cameras went off and, like the tornado that dropped Dorothy in Oz, the crowd whirled on itself and went away, leaving behind a litter of cocktail parties promised, interviews set, and articles that must be written tomorrow, next week, next month – remember, remember!

The patio stood silent. Water dripped from the half-dry mouth of a satyr cut in an old fountain against the theatre wall. Aaron, after a long moment of staring at nothing, walked over and bathed his face with water.

'The projectionist!' he cried, suddenly remembering.

We pounded upstairs and paused. This time we scratched at the tin door like two, small, hungry, white mice.

After a long silence a faint voice mourned, 'Go away. I'm sorry. I didn't mean to do it.'

'Didn't *mean*? Hell, open up! All is forgiven!' said Aaron.

'You're nuts,' the voice replied faintly. 'Go away.'

'Not without you, honey. We love you. Don't we, Sam?'

I nodded. 'We love you.'

'You're out of your mother-minds.'

Feet scraped tin lids and rattling film.

The door sprang open.

The projectionist, a man in his mid-forties, eyes blood-shot, face a furious tint of boiled-crab red, stood swaying before us, palms out and open to receive the driven nails.

'Beat me,' he whispered. 'Kill me.'

'Kill you? You're the greatest thing ever happened to dog meat in the can!'

Aaron darted in and planted a kiss on the man's cheek. He fell back, beating the air as if attacked by wasps, spluttering.

'I'll fix it all back just the way it was,' he cried, bending to scrabble the strewn film snakes on the floor. 'I'll find the right pieces and . . .'

'Don't!' said Aaron. The man froze. 'Don't change a thing.' Aaron went on, more calmly. 'Sam, take this down. You got a pencil? Now, you, what's your name?'

'Willis Hornbeck.'

'Willis, Willie, give us the order. Which reels first, second, third, which reversed, upside down, backwards, the whole deal.'

'You mean . . . ?' the man blinked, stupid with relief.

'I mean we got to have your blueprint, the way you ran the greatest avant-garde film in history tonight.'

'Oh, for God's sake.' Willis let out a hoarse, choking laugh, crouched among the tumbled reels, the insanely littered floor where his 'art' lay waiting.

'Willis, honey,' said Aaron. 'You know what your title is going to be as of this hour of this fantastic night of creation?'

'Mud?' inquired Hornbeck, one eye shut.

'Associate producer of Hasurai Productions! Editor, cutter, director even, maybe! A ten-year contract! Escalations. Privileges, Stock buy-ins. Percentages. Okay now. Ready, Sam, with the pencil? Willis. What did you *do*?'

'I—' said Willis Hornbeck, 'don't remember.'

Aaron laughed lightly. '*Sure* you remember.'

'I was drunk. Then I got scared sober. I'm sober now. I don't remember.'

Aaron and I gave each other a look of pure animal panic. Then I saw something else on the floor and picked it up.

'Hold on. Wait,' I said.

We all looked at the half-empty sherry bottle.

'Willis,' said Aaron.

'Yes, sir?'

'Willis, old friend . . .'

'Yes, sir?'

'Willis,' said Aaron. 'I will now start this projection machine.'

'Yes.'

'And you, Willis, will finish drinking whatever is in that bottle.'

'Yes, sir.'

'And you, Sam?'

'Sir?' said I, saluting.

'You, Sam,' said Aaron, flicking the machine so a bright beam of light struck out into the quiet night theatre and touched an emptiness that lay waiting for genius to paint incredible pictures on a white screen. 'Sam, please shut and lock that heavy tin door.'

I shut and locked the heavy tin door.

Well, the dragon danced at midnight film festivals all round the world.

We tamed the Lion of Venice at the Venice Film Festival, we took first honours at the New York Film Fete and the Brasilia Special Prize at the World Film Competition. And not just with one film, no, with six! After the

Dragon Danced there was the big smash international success of our *The Dreadful Ones*. There was *Mr Massacre* and *Onslaught*, followed by *The Name Is Horror* and *Wattle*.

With these, the names of Aaron Stolittz and Willis Hornbeck were honey on the lips of reviewers under every flag.

How did we make five more smash hits in a row?

The same way we made the first one.

As we finished each film we grabbed Willis, rented the Samasuku Theatre at twelve midnight, poured a bottle of the finest sherry down Willis' throat, handed him the film, started the projector, and locked the door.

By dawn our epic was slashed to ribbons, tossed like monster salad, gathered, respliced, glued fast with the epoxy of Willis Hornbeck's subliminal genius, and ready for release to the waiting avant-garde theatres in Calcutta and Far Rockaway. To the end of my insignificant life I shall never forget those nights with Willis shambling among his whirring, shadow-flickering machines, floundering about from midnight until dawn filled the patio of the Samasuku Theatre with a gold the pure colour of money.

So it went, film after film, beast after beast, while the pesos and roubles poured in, and one night Aaron and Willis grabbed their Academy Oscar for Experimental Film, and we all drove XKE-Jags and lived happy ever after, yes?

No.

It was three, glorious, fine, loving years high on the avant-garde hog. But . . .

One afternoon when Aaron was chortling over his bank account, in walks Willis Hornbeck to stand facing the big picture window overlooking Hasurai Productions' huge back lot. Willis shuts his eyes and laments in a quiet voice, beating his breast gently and tearing ever so tenderly at his own lapels.

'I am an alcoholic. I drink. I am a terrible lush. I booze. Just name it. Rubbing alcohol? Sure. Methylated spirits? Why not? Turpentine? Spar varnish? Hand it over. Nail-polish remover? Pure gargle. Rumdummy, mad fool, long-time-no-see-the-light-of-day Willis Hornbeck, but that's all over. The Pledge! Give me the Pledge!'

Aaron and I ran over and circled Willis, trying to get him to open his eyes.

'Willis! What's wrong?'

'Nothing's wrong. All's right.' He opened his eyes. Tears dripped down his cheeks. He took our hands. 'I hate to do this to you nice guys. But, last night . . .'

'Last night?' bleated Aaron.

'I joined Alcoholics Anonymous.'

'You *what*?' screamed Aaron.

'Alcoholics Anonymous. I joined.'

'You can't do that to me!' Aaron jumped up and down. 'Don't you know you're the heart, soul, lungs and lights of Hasurai Productions?'

'Don't think I haven't put it that way to myself,' said Willis, simply.

'Aren't you happy being a genius, Willie?' shrieked Aaron. 'Feted wherever you go? Internationally famed? That ain't enough, you got to be *sober*, too?'

'We're all so famous now,' said Willis, 'and loved and accepted, it has filled me up. I'm so full of fame there's no room for drink.'

'*Make* room!' yelled Aaron. '*Make* room!'

'Ironic, huh?' said Willis. 'Once I drank because I felt I

was nobody. Now if I quit, the whole studio falls down.
I'm sorry.'

'You can't break your contract!' I said.

Willis looked as if I had stabbed him.

'I wouldn't dream of breaking my word. But where
does it say in plain English in the contract I got to be a
drunk to work for you?'

My tiny shoulders sagged. Aaron's tiny shoulders sagged.
Willis finished, gently.

'I'll go on working for you, always. But you know, and I
know, sober it won't be the same.'

'Willis,' Aaron sank into a chair and, after a long and
private agony, went on. 'Just *one* night a year?'

'The Pledge, Mr Stolittz. Not a drop, not once a year,
even for dear and beloved friends.'

'Holy Moses,' said Aaron.

'Yeah,' I said. 'We're halfway across the Red Sea. And
here come the waves.'

When we glanced up again, Willis Hornbeck was gone.

It was indeed the twilight of the gods. We had been
turned back into mice. We sat a while, squeaking gently.
Then Aaron got up and circled the liquor cabinet. He put
out his hand to touch it.

'Aaron,' I said, 'You're not going to . . . ?'

'What?' said Aaron. 'Cut and edit our next avant-garde
epic, *Sweet Beds of Revenge*?' He seized and opened a
bottle. He swigged. 'All by myself? *Yes!*'

No.

The dead rocket fell out of the sky. The gods knew not
only twilight but that awful sleepless three o'clock in the
morn when death improves on circumstance.

Aaron tried drinking. I tried drinking. Aaron's brother-
in-law tried drinking.

But, look, none of us had the euphoric muse which once walked with Willis Hornbeck. In none of us did the small worm of intuition stir when alcohol hit our blood. Bums sober, we were bums drunk. But Willis Hornbeck drunk was almost everything the critics claimed, a wildman who blind-wrestled creativity in a snake pit, who fought an inspired alligator in a crystal tank for all to see, and sublimely won.

Oh, sure, Aaron and I bulled our way through a few more film festivals. We sank all our profits in three more epics, but you smelled the change when the titles hit the screen. Hasurai Films folded. We sold our whole package to Educational TV.

Willis Hornbeck? He lives in a Monterey Park tract house, goes to Sunday School with his kids, and only occasionally is reminded of the maggot of genius buried in him when a critic from Glasgow or Paris strays by to chat for an hour, finds Willis a kindly but sober bore, and departs in haste.

Aaron and me? We got this little shoe-box studio thirty feet closer to that graveyard wall. We make little pictures and profits to match and still edit them in 24 reels and hit previews around greater California and Mexico, smash and grab. There are 300 theatres within striking distance. That's 300 projectionists. So far, we have previewed our monsters in 120 of them. And still, on warm nights like tonight, we sweat and wait and pray for things like this to happen:

The phone rings. Aaron answers and yells: 'Quick! The Arcadia Barcelona Theatre needs a preview! Jump!'

And down the stairs and past the graveyard we trot, our little arms full of film, always laughing, always running towards that future where somewhere another projectionist waits behind some locked projection-room door, bottle in hand, a look of unravelled genius in his red eye, a great blind worm in his soul waiting to be kissed awake.

'Wait!' I cry, as our car rockets down the freeway. 'I left Reel 7 behind.'

'It'll never be missed!' Aaron bangs the throttle. Over the roar he shouts, 'Willis Hornbeck, Jr! Oh, Willis Hornbeck, the Second, wherever you are! Watch out! Sing it, Sam, to the tune of *Someday I'll Find You!*'

LILA THE WEREWOLF

Peter S. Beagle

Stories of mythical animals and magical spells that are both credible and have an impact on the reader are not easy to achieve, though a great many authors have tried. Peter S. Beagle is one of the few to have succeeded, thanks partly to his gorgeous sense of fun which has made his work so highly regarded in the field of comic fantasy. He has understandably been compared to Lewis Carroll and J.R.R. Tolkien for what has been described as his unmistakable brand of 'magical nonsense'. Beagle utilised a cemetery in the Bronx close to where he grew up as the background for his first fantasy, A Fine and Private Place, *published in 1960. Eight years later he secured his reputation with* The Last Unicorn, *a sophisticated and often hilarious story about the quest of a lonely unicorn to find others of her kind.*

Peter Soyer Beagle (1939–) was born in a run-down area of New York, but escaped from the bleakness all around him by reading the work of the great fantasists. When he himself began writing, he added a new dimension to the genre he so admired by uniting mythology with the contemporary world. As he has explained, 'It is no less absurd and presumptuous to try on the skin of a bank teller than that of a Bigfoot or dragon.' Not a prolific writer, he has at the time of writing published only five novels throughout his career, the most recent being The Innkeeper's Song *(1993), a masterly and complex fantasy using traditional motifs in a highly individual way; and* <u>The Unicorn Sonata</u> *(1996), in which he returns to the mythological animal that made him famous. His recent collection of linked novellas,* Giant Bones *(1997), is set in the world of* The Innkeeper's Song. *In 1965 he crossed America on a motorbike, which resulted in an amusing travelogue,* I See By My Outfit. *Since settling in California, he has produced a number of screenplays and the script for the Ralph Bakshi film of* The Lord of the Rings. *'Lila the Werewolf', written in 1969, is Beagle at his most ingenious, recounting the story of a girl from New York's Upper West Side who is to all appearances the same as any other in the Big Apple. She lives with her boyfriend, Joe Farrell, visits her analyst three times a week, and plays the guitar for relaxation. What's different is that Lila is a werewolf – and Joe's discovery of the fact after they have been together for three weeks threatens the bizarre balance of their relationship in ways that neither expects.*

Lila Braun had been living with Farrell for three weeks before he found out she was a werewolf. They had met at a party when the moon was a few nights past the full, and by the time it had withered to the shape of a lemon Lila had moved her suitcase, her guitar, and her Ewan Mac-Coll records two blocks north and four blocks west to Farrell's apartment on Ninety-Eighth Street. Girls sometimes happened to Farrell like that.

One evening Lila wasn't in when Farrell came home from work at the bookstore. She had left a note on the table, under a can of tunafish. The note said that she had gone up to the Bronx to have dinner with her mother, and would probably be spending the night there. The

coleslaw in the refrigerator should be finished up before
it went bad.

Farrell ate the tunafish and gave the coleslaw to Grunewald. Grunewald was a half-grown Russian wolf-
hound, the colour of sour milk. He looked like a goat,
and had no outside interests except shoes. Farrell was
taking care of him for a girl who was away in Europe for
the summer. She sent Grunewald a tape-recording of her
voice every week.

Farrell went to a movie with a friend, and to the West
End afterwards for beer. Then he walked home alone
under the full moon, which was red and yellow. He
reheated the morning coffee, played a record, read
through a week-old 'News of the Week in Review' section
of the Sunday *Times*, and finally took Grunewald up to
the roof for the night, as he always did. The dog had been
accustomed to sleep in the same bed with his mistress,
and the point was not negotiable. Grunewald mooed and
scrabbled and butted all the way, but Farrell pushed him
out among the looming chimneys and ventilators and
slammed the door. Then he came back downstairs and
went to bed.

He slept very badly. Grunewald's baying woke him
twice; and there was something else that brought him
half out of bed, thirsty and lonely, with his sinuses full
and the night swaying like a curtain as the figures of his
dream scurried offstage. Grunewald seemed to have gone
off the air – perhaps it was the silence that had awakened
him. Whatever the reason, he never really got back to
sleep.

He was lying on his back, watching a chair with his
clothes on it becoming a chair again, when the wolf came
in through the open window. It landed lightly in the

middle of the room and stood there for a moment, breathing quickly, with its ears back. There was blood on the wolf's teeth and tongue, and blood on its chest.

Farrell, whose true gift was for acceptance, especially in the morning, accepted the idea that there was a wolf in his bedroom and lay quite still, closing his eyes as the grim, black-lipped head swung towards him. Having once worked at a zoo, he was able to recognise the beast as a Central European subspecies: smaller and lighter-boned than the northern timber wolf variety, lacking the thick, ruffy mane at the shoulders and having a more pointed nose and ears. His own pedantry always delighted him, even at the worst moments.

Blunt claws clicking on the linoleum, then silent on the throw rug by the bed. Something warm and slow splashed down on his shoulder, but he never moved. The wild smell of the wolf was over him, and that did frighten him at last – to be in the same room with that smell and the Miró prints on the walls. Then he felt the sunlight on his eyelids, and at the same moment he heard the wolf moan softly and deeply. The sound was not repeated, but the breath on his face was suddenly sweet and smoky, dizzyingly familiar after the other. He opened his eyes and saw Lila. She was sitting naked on the edge of the bed, smiling, with her hair down.

'Hello, baby,' she said. 'Move over, baby. I came home.'

Farrell's gift was for acceptance. He was perfectly willing to believe that he had dreamed the wolf; to believe Lila's story of boiled chicken and bitter arguments and sleeplessness on Tremont Avenue; and to forget that her first caress had been to bite him on the shoulder, hard enough so that the blood crusting there as he got up and made breakfast might very well be his own. But then he left the coffee perking and went up to the roof to get Grunewald. He found the dog sprawled in a grove of TV antennas, looking more like a goat than ever, with his throat torn out. Farrell had never actually seen an animal with its throat torn out.

The coffeepot was still chuckling when he came back into the apartment, which struck him as very odd. You could have either werewolves or Pyrex nine-cup perco-lators in the world, but not both, surely. He told Lila, watching her face. She was a small girl, not really pretty, but with good eyes and a lovely mouth, and with a curious sullen gracefulness that had been the first thing to speak to Farrell at the party. When he told her how Grunewald had looked, she shivered all over, once.

'Ugh!' she said, wrinkling her lips back from her neat white teeth. 'Oh baby, how awful. Poor Grunewald. Oh, poor Barbara.' Barbara was Grunewald's owner.

'Yeah,' Farrell said. 'Poor Barbara, making her little tapes in Saint-Tropez.' He could not look away from Lila's face.

She said, 'Wild dogs. Not really wild, I mean, but with owners. You hear about it sometimes, how a pack of them get together and attack children and things, run-ning through the streets. Then they go home and eat their Dog Yummies. The scary thing is that they probably live right around here. Everybody on the block seems to have a dog. God, that's scary. Poor Grunewald.'

'They didn't tear him up much,' Farrell said. 'It must have been just for the fun of it. And the blood. I didn't know dogs killed for the blood. He didn't have any blood left.'

The tip of Lila's tongue appeared between her lips, in the unknowing reflex of a fondled cat. As evidence, it wouldn't have stood up even in old Salem; but Farrell knew the truth then, beyond laziness or rationalisation, and went on buttering toast for Lila. Farrell had nothing against werewolves, and he had never liked Grunewald.

He told his friend Ben Kassoy about Lila when they met in the Automat for lunch. He had to shout it over the clicking and rattling all around them, but the people sitting six inches away on either hand never looked up. New Yorkers never eavesdrop. They hear only what they simply cannot help hearing.

Ben said, 'I told you about Bronx girls. You better come stay at my place for a few days.'

Farrell shook his head. 'No, that's silly. I mean, it's only Lila. If she were going to hurt me, she could have done it last night. Besides, it won't happen again for a month. There has to be a full moon.'

His friend stared at him. 'So what? What's that got to do with anything? You going to go on home as though nothing had happened?'

'Not as though nothing had happened,' Farrell said lamely. 'The thing is, it's still only Lila, not Lon Chaney or somebody. Look, she goes to her psychiatrist three afternoons a week, and she's got her guitar lesson one night a week, and her pottery class one night, and she cooks eggplant maybe twice a week. She calls her mother every Friday night, and one night a month she turns into a wolf. You see what I'm getting at? It's still Lila, whatever she does, and I just can't get terribly shook about it. A little bit, sure, because what the hell. But I don't know. Anyway, there's no mad rush about it. I'll talk to her when the thing comes up in the conversation, just naturally. It's okay.'

Ben said, 'God damn. You see why nobody has any

respect for liberals anymore? Farrell, I know you. You're just scared of hurting her feelings.'

'Well, it's that too,' Farrell agreed, a little embarrassed. 'I hate confrontations. If I break up with her now, she'll think I'm doing it because she's a werewolf. It's awkward, it feels nasty and middleclass. I should have broken up with her the first time I met her mother, or the second time she served the eggplant. Her mother, boy, there's the real werewolf, there's somebody I'd wear wolfbane against, that woman. Damn, I wish I hadn't found out. I don't think I've ever found out anything about people that I was the better for knowing.'

Ben walked all the way back to the bookstore with him, arguing. It touched Farrell, because Ben hated to walk. Before they parted, Ben suggested, 'At least you could try some of that stuff you were talking about, the wolfbane. There's garlic, too – you put some in a little bag and wear it around your neck. Don't laugh, man. If there's such a thing as werewolves, the other stuff must be real too. Cold iron, silver, oak, running water—'

'I'm not laughing at you,' Farrell said, but he was still grinning. 'Lila's shrink says she has a rejection thing, very deep-seated, take us years to break through all that scar tissue. Now if I start walking around wearing amulets and mumbling in Latin every time she looks at me, who knows how far it'll set her back? Listen, I've done some things I'm not proud of, but I don't want to mess up anyone's analysis. That's the sin against God.' He sighed and slapped Ben lightly on the arm. 'Don't worry about it. We'll work it out, I'll talk to her.'

But between that night and the next full moon, he found no good, casual way of bringing the subject up. Admittedly, he did not try as hard as he might have: it was true that he feared confrontations more than he feared werewolves, and he would have found it almost as difficult to talk to Lila about her guitar playing, or her pots, or the political arguments she got into at parties. 'The thing is,' he said to Ben, 'it's sort of one more little weakness not to take advantage of. In a way.'

They made love often that month. The smell of Lila flowered in the bedroom, where the smell of the wolf still lingered almost visibly, and both of them were wild, heavy zoo smells, warm and raw and fearful, the sweeter for being savage. Farrell held Lila in his arms and knew what she was, and he was always frightened; but he would not have let her go if she had turned into a wolf again as he held her. It was a relief to peer at her while she slept and see how stubby and childish her fingernails were, or that the skin around her mouth was rashy because she had been snacking on chocolate. She loved secret sweets, but they always betrayed her.

It's only Lila after all, he would think as he drowsed off. Her mother used to hide the candy, but Lila always found it. Now she's a big girl, neither married nor in a graduate school, but living in sin with an Irish musician, and she can have all the candy she wants. What kind of a werewolf is that. Poor Lila, practising *Who killed Davey Moore? Why did he die?* . . .

The note said that she would be working late at the magazine, on layout, and might have to be there all night. Farrell put on about four feet of Telemann laced with Django Reinhardt, took down *The Golden Bough*, and settled into a chair by the window. The moon shone in at him, bright and thin and sharp as the lid of a tin can, and it did not seem to move at all as he dozed and woke.

Lila's mother called several times during the night, which was interesting. Lila still picked up her mail and most messages at her old apartment, and her two room-mates covered for her when necessary, but Farrell was absolutely certain that her mother knew she was living with him. Farrell was an expert on mothers. Mrs Braun called him Joe each time she called and that made him wonder, for he knew she hated him. Does she suspect that we share a secret? Ah, poor Lila.

The last time the telephone woke him, it was still dark in the room, but the traffic lights no longer glittered through rings of mist, and the cars made a different sound on the warming pavement. A man was saying clearly in the street, 'Well, *I*'d shoot'm. *I*'d shoot'm.' Farrell let the telephone ring ten times before he picked it up.

'Let me talk to Lila,' Mrs Braun said.

'She isn't here.' What if the sun catches her, what if she turns back to herself in front of a cop, or a bus driver, or a couple of nuns going to early Mass? 'Lila isn't here, Mrs Braun.'

'I have reason to believe that's not true.' The fretful, muscular voice had dropped all pretence of warmth. 'I want to talk to Lila.'

Farrell was suddenly dry-mouthed and shivering with fury. It was her choice of words that did it. 'Well, I have reason to believe you're a suffocating old bitch and a bourgeois Stalinist. How do you like them apples, Mrs B?' As though his anger had summoned her, the wolf was standing two feet away from him. Her coat was dark and lank with sweat, and yellow saliva was mixed with the blood that strung from her jaws. She looked at Farrell and growled far away in her throat.

'Just a minute,' he said. He covered the receiver with his palm. 'It's for you,' he said to the wolf. 'It's your mother.'

The wolf made a pitiful sound, almost inaudible, and scuffed at the floor. She was plainly exhausted. Mrs Braun pinged in Farrell's ear like a bug against a lighted window. 'What, what? Hello, what is this? Listen, you put Lila on the phone right now. Hello? I want to talk to Lila. I know she's there.'

Farrell hung up just as the sun touched a corner of the window. The wolf became Lila. As before, she only made one sound. The phone rang again, and she picked it up without a glance at Farrell. 'Bernice?' Lila always called her mother by her first name. 'Yes – no, no – yeah, I'm fine. I'm all right, I just forgot to call. No, I'm all right, will you listen? Bernice, there's no law that says you have to get hysterical. Yes, you are.' She dropped down on the bed, groping under her pillow for cigarettes. Farrell got up and began to make coffee.

'Well, there was a little trouble,' Lila was saying. 'See, I went to the Zoo, because I couldn't find – Bernice, I know, I *know*, but that was, what, three months ago. The thing is, I didn't think they'd have their horns so soon. Bernice, I had to, that's all. There'd only been a couple of cats and a – well, sure they chased me, but I – well, Momma, Bernice, what did you want me to do? Just what did you want me to do? You're always so dramatic – why do I shout? I shout because I can't get you to listen to me any other way. You remember what Dr Schechtman said – what? No, I told you, I just forgot to call. No, that is the reason, that's the real and only reason. Well, whose fault is that? What? Oh, Bernice. Jesus Christ, Bernice. All right, *how* is it Dad's fault?'

She didn't want the coffee, or any breakfast, but she sat at the table in his bathrobe and drank milk greedily. It was the first time he had ever seen her drink milk. Her face was sandy-pale, and her eyes were red. Talking to her mother left her looking as though she had actually gone ten rounds with the woman. Farrell asked, 'How long has it been happening?'

'Nine years,' Lila said. 'Since I hit puberty. First day, cramps; the second day, this. My introduction to womanhood.' She snickered and spilled her milk. 'I want some more,' she said. 'Got to get rid of that taste.'

'Who knows about it?' he asked. 'Pat and Janet?' They were the two girls she had been rooming with.

'God, no. I'd never tell them. I've never told a girl. Bernice knows, of course, and Dr Schechtman – he's my head doctor. And you now. That's all.' Farrell waited. She was a bad liar, and only did it to heighten the effect of the truth. 'Well, there was Mickey,' she said. 'The guy I told you about the first night, you remember? It doesn't matter. He's an acidhead in Vancouver, of all the places. He'll never tell anybody.'

He thought: I wonder if any girl has ever talked about me in that sort of voice. I doubt it, offhand. Lila said, 'It wasn't too hard to keep it secret. I missed a lot of things. Like I never could go to the riding camp, and I still want to. And the senior play, when I was in high school. They picked me to play the girl in *Liliom*, but then they changed the evening, and I had to say I was sick. And the winter's bad, because the sun sets so early. But actually, it's been a lot less trouble than my goddamn allergies.' She made a laugh, but Farrell did not respond.

'Dr Schechtman says it's a sex thing,' she offered. 'He says it'll take years and years to cure it. Bernice thinks I should go to someone else, but I don't want to be one of those women who runs around changing shrinks like hair colours. Pat went through five of them in a month one time. Joe, I wish you'd say something. Or just go away.'

'Is it only dogs?' he asked. Lila's face did not change, but her chair rattled, and the milk went over again. Farrell said, 'Answer me. Do you only kill dogs, and cats, and zoo animals?'

The tears began to come, heavy and slow, bright as knives in the morning sunlight. She could not look at him; and when she tried to speak she could only make creaking, cartilaginous sounds in her throat. '*You* don't know,' she whispered at last. 'You don't have any idea what it's like.'

'That's true,' he answered. He always was very fair about that particular point.

He took her hand, and then she really began to cry. Her sobs were horrible to hear, much more frightening to Farrell than any wolf noises. When he held her, she rolled in his arms like a stranded ship with the waves slamming into her. I always get the criers, he thought sadly. My girls always cry, sooner or later. But never for me.

'Don't leave me!' she wept. 'I don't know why I came to live with you – I knew it wouldn't work – but don't leave me! There's just Bernice and Dr Schechtman, and it's so lonely. I want somebody else, I get so lonely. Don't leave me, Joe. I love you, Joe. I love you.'

She was patting his face as though she were blind. Farrell stroked her hair and kneaded the back of her neck, wishing that her mother would call again. He felt skilled and weary, and without desire. I'm doing it again, he thought.

'I love you,' Lila said. And he answered her, thinking, I'm doing it again. That's the great advantage of making the same mistake a lot of times. You come to know it, and you can study it and get inside it, really make it yours. It's the same good old mistake, except this time the girl's hangup is different. But it's the same thing. I'm doing it again.

The building superintendent was thirty or fifty: dark, thin, quick and shivering. A Lithuanian or a Latvian, he spoke very little English. He smelled of black friction tape and stale water, and he was strong in the twisting way that a small, lean animal is strong. His eyes were almost purple, and they bulged a little, straining out – the terrible eyes of a herald angel stricken dumb. He roamed in the basement all day, banging on pipes and taking the elevator apart.

The superintendent met Lila only a few hours after Farrell did; on that first night, when she came home with him. At the sight of her the little man jumped back, dropping the two-legged chair he was carrying. He promptly fell over it, and did not try to get up, but cowered there, clucking and gulping, trying to cross himself and make the sign of the horns at the same time. Farrell started to help him up, but he screamed. They could hardly hear the sound.

It would have been merely funny and embarrassing, except for the fact that Lila was equally as frightened of the superintendent, from that moment. She would not go down to the basement for any reason, nor would she enter or leave the house until she was satisfied that he was nowhere near. Farrell had thought then that she took the superintendent for a lunatic.

'I don't know how he knows,' he said to Ben. 'I guess if you believe in werewolves and vampires, you probably recognise them right away. I don't believe in them at all, and I live with one.'

He lived with Lila all through the autumn and the winter. They went out together and came home, and her cooking improved slightly, and she gave up the guitar and got a kitten named Theodora. Sometimes she wept, but not often. She turned out not to be a real crier.

She told Dr Schechtman about Farrell, and he said that it would probably be a very beneficial relationship for her. It wasn't but it wasn't a particularly bad one either. Their love-making was usually good, though it bothered Farrell to suspect that it was the sense and smell of the Other that excited him. For the rest, they came near being friends. Farrell had known that he did not love Lila before he found out that she was a werewolf, and this made him feel a great deal easier about being bored with her.

'It'll break up by itself in the spring,' he said, 'like ice.'

Ben asked, 'What if it doesn't? They were having lunch in the Automat again. 'What'll you do if it just goes on?'

'It's not that easy.' Farrell looked away from his friend and began to explore the mysterious, swampy innards of his beef pie. He said, 'The trouble is that I know her. That was the real mistake. You shouldn't get to know people if you know you're not going to stay with them, one way or another. It's all right if you come and go in ignorance, but you shouldn't know them.'

A week or so before the full moon, she would start to become nervous and strident, and this would continue until the day preceding her transformation. On that day, she was invariably loving, in the tender, desperate

Searching for
a book?

www.waterstones.co.uk

Visit us 24 hours
a day at

www.waterstones.co.uk

Any book at the
touch of a button

www.waterstones.co.uk

Visit us 24 hours
a day at

www.waterstones.co.uk

Free delivery to
any branch

www.waterstones.co.uk

Visit us 24 hours
a day at

WATERSTONE'S BOOKSELLERS
174 - 176 Argyle Street
GLASGOW
G2 8BT
Tel.No: 0141 248 4814
Fax No: 0141 248 4622
VAT No: 710 6311 84

112 CASH-1   4367 0099 005

STROLLER'S GUIDE T	QTY 1	8.99
FLYING SORCERERS,	QTY 1	5.99
KNIGHTS OF MADNESS	QTY 1	5.99
WIZARDS OF ODD, TH	QTY 1	5.99
	TOTAL	26.96

Travellers Cheque	50.00
CHANGE	23.04

www.waterstones.co.uk

9.10.00 13:38

manner of someone who is going away; but the next day would see her silent, speaking only when she had to. She always had a cold on the last day, and looked grey and patchy and sick, but she usually went to work anyway.

Farrell was sure, though she never talked about it, that the change into wolf shape was actually peaceful for her, though the returning hurt. Just before moonrise she would take off her clothes and take the pins out of her hair, and stand waiting. Farrell never managed not to close his eyes when she dropped heavily down on all fours; but there was a moment before that when her face would grow a look that he never saw at any other time, except when they were making love. Each time he saw it, it struck him as a look of wondrous joy at not being Lila any more.

'See, I know her,' he tried to explain to Ben. 'She only likes to go to colour movies, because wolves can't see colour. She can't stand the Modern Jazz Quartet, but that's all she plays the first couple of days afterwards. Stupid things like that. Never gets high at parties, because she's afraid she'll start talking. It's hard to walk away, that's all. Taking what I know with me.'

Ben asked, 'Is she still scared of the super?'

'Oh, God,' Farrell said. 'She got his dog last time. It was a Dalmatian – good-looking animal. She didn't know it was his. He doesn't hide when he sees her now, he just gives her a look like a stake through the heart. That man is a really classy hater, a natural. I'm scared of him myself.' He stood up and began to pull on his overcoat. 'I wish he'd get turned onto her mother. Get some practical use out of him. Did I tell you she wants me to call her Bernice?'

Ben said, 'Farrell, if I were you, I'd leave the country. I would.'

They went out into the February drizzle that sniffed back and forth between snow and rain. Farrell did not speak until they reached the corner where he turned towards the bookstore. Then he said very softly, 'Damn, you have to be so careful. Who wants to know what people turn into?'

May came, and a night when Lila once again stood naked at the window, waiting for the moon. Farrell fussed with dishes and garbage bags, and fed the cat. These moments were always awkward. He had just asked her, 'You want to save what's left of the rice?' when the telephone rang.

It was Lila's mother. She called two and three times a week now. 'This is Bernice. How's my Irisher this evening?'

'I'm fine, Bernice,' Farrell said. Lila suddenly threw back her head and drew a heavy, whining breath. The cat hissed silently and ran into the bathroom.

'I called to inveigle you two uptown this Friday,' Mrs Braun said. 'A couple of old friends are coming over, and I know if I don't get some young people in we'll just sit around and talk about what went wrong with the Progressive party. The Old Left. So if you could sort of sweet-talk our girl into spending an evening in Squaresville—'

'I'll have to check with Lila.' She's *doing* it, he thought, that terrible woman. Every time I talk to her, I sound married. I see what she's doing, but she goes right ahead anyway. He said, 'I'll talk to her in the morning.' Lila struggled in the moonlight, between dancing and drowning.

'Oh,' Mrs Braun said. 'Yes, of course. Have her call me

back.' She sighed. 'It's such a comfort to me to know you're there. Ask her if I should fix a fondue.'

Lila made a handsome wolf: tall and broad-chested for a female, moving as easily as water sliding over stone. Her coat was dark brown, showing red in the proper light, and there were white places on her breast. She had pale green eyes, the colour of the sky when a hurricane is coming.

Usually she was gone as soon as the changing was over, for she never cared for him to see her in her wolf form. But tonight she came slowly towards him, walking in a strange way, with her hindquarters almost dragging. She was making a high, soft sound, and her eyes were not focusing on him.

'What is it?' he asked foolishly. The wolf whined and skulked under the table, rubbing against the leg. Then she lay on her belly and rolled and as she did so the sound grew in her throat until it became an odd, sad, thin cry; not a hunting howl, but a shiver of longing turned into breath.

'Jesus, don't do that!' Farrell gasped. But she sat up and howled again, and a dog answered her from somewhere near the river. She wagged her tail and whimpered.

Farrell said, 'The super'll be up here in two minutes flat. What's the matter with you?' He heard footsteps and low frightened voices in the apartment above them. Another dog howled, this one nearby, and the wolf wriggled a little way towards the window on her haunches, like a baby, scooting. She looked at him over her shoulder, shuddering violently. On an impulse, he picked up the phone and called her mother.

Watching the wolf as she rocked and slithered and moaned, he described her actions to Mrs Braun. 'I've never seen her like this,' he said. 'I don't know what's the matter with her.'

'Oh, my God,' Mrs Braun whispered. She told him.

When he was silent, she began to speak very rapidly. 'It hasn't happened for such a long time. Schechtman gives her pills, but she must have run out and forgotten – she's always been like that, since she was little. All the thermos bottles she used to leave on the school bus, and every week her piano music—'

'I wish you'd told me before,' he said. He was edging very cautiously towards the open window. The pupils of the wolf's eyes were pulsing with her quick breaths.

'It isn't a thing you tell people!' Lila's mother wailed in his ears. 'How do you think it was for me when she brought her first little boyfriend—' Farrell dropped the phone and sprang for the window. He had the inside track, and he might have made it, but she turned her head and snarled so wildly that he fell back. When he reached the window, she was already two fire-escape landings below, and there was eager yelping waiting for her in the street.

Dangling and turning just above the floor, Mrs Braun heard Farrell's distant yell, followed immediately by a heavy thumping on the door. A strange, tattered voice was shouting unintelligibly beyond the knocking. Footsteps crashed by the receiver and the door opened.

'My dog, my dog!' the strange voice mourned. 'My dog, my dog, my dog!'

'I'm sorry about your dog,' Farrell said. 'Look, please go away. I've got work to do.'

'I got work,' the voice said. 'I know my work.' It climbed and spilled into another language, out of which English words jutted like broken bones. 'Where is she? Where is she? She kill my dog.'

'She's not here.' Farrell's own voice changed on the last word. It seemed a long time before he said, 'You'd better put that away.'

Mrs Braun heard the howl as clearly as though the wolf were running beneath her own window: lonely and insatiable, with a kind of gasping laughter in it. The other voice began to scream. Mrs Braun caught the phrase *silver bullet* several times. The door slammed; then opened and slammed again.

Farrell was the only man of his own acquaintance who was able to play back his dreams while he was having them: to stop them in mid-flight, no matter how fearful they might be – or how lovely – and run them over and over studying them in his sleep, until the most terrifying reel became at once utterly harmless and unbearably familiar. This night that he spent running after Lila was like that.

He would find them congregated under the marquee of an apartment house, or romping around the moonscape of a construction site: ten of fifteen males of all races, creeds, colours and previous conditions of servitude; whining and yapping, pissing against tyres, inhaling indiscriminately each other and the lean, grinning bitch they surrounded. She frightened them, for she growled more wickedly than coyness demanded, and where she snapped, even in play, bone showed. Still they tumbled on her and over her, biting her neck and ears in their turn; and she snarled but she did not run away.

Never, at least, until Farrell came charging upon them, shrieking like any cuckold, kicking at the snuffling lovers. Then she would turn and race off into the spring dark, with her thin, dreamy howl floating behind her like the train of a smoky gown. The dogs followed, and so did

Farrell, calling and cursing. They always lost him quickly, that jubilant marriage procession, leaving him stumbling down rusty iron ladders into places where he fell over garbage cans. Yet he would come upon them as inevitably in time, loping along Broadway or trotting across Columbus Avenue towards the Park; he would hear them in the tennis courts near the river, breaking down the nets over Lila and her moment's Ares. There were dozens of them now, coming from all directions. They stank of their joy, and he threw stones at them and shouted, and they ran.

And the wolf ran at their head, on sidewalks and on wet grass; her tail waving contentedly, but her eyes still hungry, and her howl growing ever more warning than wistful. Farrell knew that she must have blood before sunrise, and that it was both useless and dangerous to follow her. But the night wound and unwound itself, and he knew the same things over and over, and ran down the same streets, and saw the same couples walk wide of him, thinking he was drunk.

Mrs Braun kept leaping out of a taxi that pulled up next to him; usually at corners where the dogs had just piled by, knocking over the crates stacked in market doorways and spilling the newspapers at the subway kiosks. Standing in broccoli, in black taffeta, with a front like a ferryboat – yet as lean in the hips as her wolf-daughter – with her plum-coloured hair all loose, one arm lifted, and her orange mouth pursed in a bellow, she was no longer Bernice but a wronged fertility goddess getting set to blast the harvest. 'We've got to split up!' she would roar at Farrell, and each time it sounded like a sound idea. Yet he looked for her whenever he lost Lila's trail, because she never did.

The superintendent kept turning up too, darting after Farrell out of alleys or cellar entrances, or popping from the freight elevators that load through the sidewalk. Farrell would hear his numberless passkeys clicking on the flat piece of wood tucked into his belt.

'You see her? You see her, the wolf, kill my dog?' Under the fat, ugly moon, the Army .45 glittered and trembled like his own mad eyes.

'Mark with a cross.' He would pat the barrel of the gun and shake it under Farrell's nose like maracas. 'Mark with a cross, bless by a priest. Three silver bullets. She kill my dog.'

Lila's voice would come sailing to them then, from up in Harlem or away near Lincoln Center, and the little man would whirl and dash down into the earth, disappearing into the crack between two slabs of sidewalk. Farrell understood quite clearly that the superintendent was hunting Lila underground, using the keys that only superintendents have to take elevators down to the black sub-sub-basements, far below the bicycle rooms and the wet, shaking laundry rooms, and below the furnace rooms, below the passages walled with electricity meters and roofed with burly steam pipes; down to the realms where the great dim water mains roll like whales, and the gas lines hump and preen, down where the roots of the apartment houses fade together; and so along under the city, scrabbling through secret ways with silver bullets, and his keys rapping against the piece of wood. He never saw Lila, but he was never very far behind her.

Cutting across parking lots, pole-vaulting between locked bumpers, edging and dancing his way through fluorescent gaggles of haughty children; leaping uptown like a salmon against the current of the theatre crowds;

walking quickly past the random killing faces that floated down the night tide like unexploded mines, and especially avoiding the crazy faces that wanted to tell him what it was like to be crazy – so Farrell pursued Lila Braun, of Tremont Avenue and CCNY, in the city all night long. Nobody offered to help him, or tried to head off the dangerous-looking bitch bounding along with the delirious raggle of admirers streaming after her; but then, the dogs had to fight through the same clinched legs and vengeful bodies that Farrell did. The crowds slowed Lila down, but he felt relieved whenever she turned towards the emptier streets. *She must have blood soon, somewhere.*

Farrell's dreams eventually lost their clear edge after he played them back a certain number of times, and so it was with the night. The full moon skidded down the sky, thinning like a tatter of butter in a skillet, and remembered scenes began to fold sloppily into each other. The sound of Lila and the dogs grew fainter whichever way he followed. Mrs Braun blinked on and off at longer intervals; and in dark doorways and under subway gratings, the superintendent burned like a corposant, making the barrel of his pistol run rainbow. At last he lost Lila for good, and with that it seemed that he woke.

It was still night, but not dark, and he was walking slowly home on Riverside Drive through a cool, grainy fog. The moon had set, but the river was strangely bright: glittering grey as far up as the Bridge, where headlights left shiny, wet paths like snails. There was no one else on the street.

'Dumb broad,' he said aloud. 'The hell with it. She wants to mess around, let her mess around.' He wondered whether werewolves could have cubs, and what

sort of cubs they might be. Lila must have turned on the
dogs by now, for the blood. Poor dogs, he thought. They
were all so dirty and innocent and happy with her.

'A moral lesson for all of us,' he announced senten-
tiously. 'Don't fool with strange, eager ladies, they'll kill
you.' He was a little hysterical. Then, two blocks ahead of
him, he saw the gaunt shape in the grey light of the river;
alone now, and hurrying. Farrell did not call to her, but as
soon as he began to run, the wolf wheeled and faced him.
Even at that distance, her eyes were stained and streaked
and wild. She showed all the teeth on one side of her
mouth, and she growled like fire.

Farrell trotted steadily towards her, crying, 'Go home,
go home! Lila, you dummy, get on home, it's morning!'
She growled terribly, but when Farrell was less than a
block away she turned again and dashed across the street,
heading for West End Avenue. Farrell said, 'Good girl,
that's it,' and limped after her.

In the hours before sunrise on West End Avenue, many
people came out to walk their dogs. Farrell had done it
often enough with poor Grunewald to know many of the
dawn walkers by sight, and some to talk to. A fair number
of them were whores and homosexuals, both of whom
always seem to have dogs in New York. Quietly, almost
always alone, they drifted up and down the Nineties,
piloted by their small, fussy beasts, but moving in a kind
of fugitive truce with the city and the night that was
ending. Farrell sometimes fancied that they were all
asleep, and that this hour was the only true rest they
ever got.

He recognised Robie by his two dogs, Scone and
Crumpet. Robie lived in the apartment directly below
Farrell's, usually unhappily. The dogs were horrifying

little homebrews of Chihuahua and Yorkshire terror, but Robie loved them.

Crumpet, the male, saw Lila first. He gave a delighted yap of welcome and proposition (according to Robie, Scone bored him, and he liked big girls anyway) and sprang to meet her, yanking his leash through Robie's slack hand. The wolf was almost upon him before he realised his fatal misunderstanding and scuttled desperately in retreat, meowing with utter terror.

Robie wailed, and Farrell ran as fast as he could, but Lila knocked Crumpet off his feet and slashed his throat while he was still in the air. Then she crouched on the body, nuzzling it in a dreadful way.

Robie actually came within a step of leaping upon Lila and trying to drag her away from his dead dog. Instead, he turned on Farrell as he came panting up, and began hitting him with a good deal of strength and accuracy. 'Damn you, damn you!' he sobbed. Little Scone ran away around the corner, screaming like a mandrake.

Farrell put up his arms and went with the punches, all the while yelling at Lila until his voice ripped. But the blood frenzy had her, and Farrell had never imagined what she must be like at those times. Somehow she had spared the dogs who had loved her all night, but she was nothing but thirst now. She pushed and kneaded Crumpet's body as though she were nursing.

All along the avenue, the morning dogs were barking like trumpets. Farrell ducked away from Robie's soft fists and saw them coming; tripping over their trailing leashes, running too fast for their stubby legs. They were small, spoiled beasts, most of them, overweight and shortwinded, and many were not young. Their owners cried unmanly pet names after them, but they waddled gallantly towards their deaths, barking promises far bigger than themselves, and none of them looked back.

She looked up with her muzzle red to the eyes. The dogs did falter then, for they knew murder when they smelled it, and even their silly, nearsighted eyes understood vaguely what creature faced them. But they knew the smell of love too, and they were all gentlemen.

She killed the first two to reach her – a spitz and a cocker spaniel – with two snaps of her jaws. But before she could settle down to her meal, three Pekes were scrambling up to her, though they would have had to stand on each others' shoulders. Lila whirled without a sound, and they fell away, rolling and yelling but unhurt. As soon as she turned, the Pekes were at her again, joined now by a couple of valiant poodles. Lila got one of the poodles when she turned again.

Robie had stopped beating on Farrell, and was leaning against a traffic light, being sick. But other people were running up now: a middle-aged black man, crying; a plump youth in a plastic car coat and bedroom slippers, who kept whimpering, 'Oh God, she's eating them, look at her, she's really eating them!' two lean, ageless girls in slacks, both with foamy beige hair. They all called wildly to their unheeding dogs, and they all grabbed at Farrell and shouted in his face. Cars began to stop.

The sky was thin and cool, rising pale gold, but Lila paid no attention to it. She was ramping under the swarm of little dogs; rearing and spinning in circles, snarling blood. The dogs were terrified and bewildered, but they never swerved from their labour. The smell of love told them that they were welcome, however ungraciously she seemed to receive them. Lila shook herself, and a pair of squealing dachshunds, hobbled in a double harness, tumbled across the sidewalk to end at Farrell's feet. They scrambled up and immediately towed themselves back into the maelstrom. Lila bit one of them almost in half, but the other dachshund went on trying to climb her hindquarters, dragging his ripped comrade with him. Farrell began to laugh.

The black man said, 'You think it's funny?' and hit him. Farrell sat down, still laughing. The man stood over him, embarrassed, offering Farrell his handkerchief. 'I'm sorry, I shouldn't have done that,' he said. 'But your dog killed my dog.'

'She isn't my dog,' Farrell said. He moved to let a man pass between them, and then saw that it was the superintendent, holding his pistol with both hands. Nobody noticed him until he fired; but Farrell pushed one of the foamy-haired girls, and she stumbled against the superintendent as the gun went off. The silver bullet broke a window in a parked car.

The superintendent fired again while the echoes of the first shot were still clapping back and forth between the houses. A Pomeranian screamed that time, and a woman cried out, 'Oh, my God, he shot Borgy!' But the crowd was crumbling away, breaking into its individual components like pills on television. The watching cars had sped off at sight of the gun, and the faces that had been peering down from windows disappeared. Except for Farrell, the few people who remained were scattered halfway down the block. The sky was brightening swiftly now.

'For God's sake, don't let him!' the same woman called from the shelter of the doorway. But two men made shushing gestures at her, saying, 'It's all right, he knows how to use that thing. Go ahead, buddy.'

The shots had at last frightened the little dogs away from Lila. She crouched among the twitching splotches of fur, with her muzzle wrinkled back and her eyes more black than green. Farrell saw a plaid rag that had been a dog jacket protruding from under her body. The superintendent stooped and squinted over the gun barrel, aiming with grotesque care, while the men cried to him to shoot. He was too far from the werewolf for her to reach him before he fired the last silver bullet, though he would surely die before she died. His lips were moving as he took aim.

Two long steps would have brought Farrell up behind the superintendent. Later he told himself that he had been afraid of the pistol, because that was easier than remembering how he had felt when he looked at Lila. Her tongue never stopped lapping around her dark jaws; and even as she set herself to spring, she lifted a bloody paw to her mouth. Farrell thought of her padding in the bedroom, breathing on his face. The superintendent grunted and Farrell closed his eyes. Yet even then he expected to find himself doing something.

Then he heard Mrs Braun's unmistakable voice. *'Don't you dare!'* She was standing between Lila and the superintendent: one shoe gone, and the heel off the other one; her knit dress torn at the shoulder, and her face tired and smudgy. But she pointed a finger at the startled superintendent, and he stepped quickly back, as though she had a pistol too.

'Lady, that's a wolf,' he protested nervously. 'Lady, you please get, get out of the way. That's a wolf, I go shoot her now.'

'I want to see your licence for that gun.' Mrs Braun held out her hand. The superintendent blinked at her, muttering in despair. She said, 'Do you know that you can be sent to prison for twenty years for carrying a concealed weapon in this state? Do you know what the fine is for having a gun without a licence? The fine is Five. Thousand. Dollars.' The men down the street were shouting at her, but she swung around to face the creature snarling among the little dead dogs.

'Come on, Lila,' she said. 'Come on home with Bernice. I'll make tea and we'll talk. It's been a long time since we've really talked, you know? We used to have nice long talks when you were little, but we don't any more.' The wolf had stopped growling, but she was crouching even lower, and her ears were still flat against her head. Mrs Braun said, 'Come on, baby. Listen, I know what – you'll call in sick at the office and stay for a few days. You'll get a good rest, and maybe we'll even look around a little for a new doctor, what do you say? Schechtman hasn't done a thing for you, I never liked him. Come on home, honey. Momma's here, Bernice knows.' She took a step towards the silent wolf, holding out her hand.

The superintendent gave a desperate, wordless cry and pumped forward, clumsily shoving Mrs Braun to one side. He levelled the pistol point-blank, wailing, 'My dog, my dog!' Lila was in the air when the gun went off, and her shadow sprang after her, for the sun had risen. She crumpled down across a couple of dead Pekes. Their blood dabbed her breasts and her pale throat.

Mrs Braun screamed like a lunch whistle. She knocked the superintendent into the street and sprawled over Lila, hiding her completely from Farrell's sight. 'Lila, Lila,' she keened her daughter, 'poor baby, you never had a chance. He killed you because you were different, the way they kill everything different.' Farrell approached her and stooped down, but she pushed him against a wall without looking up. 'Lila, Lila, poor baby, poor darling, maybe it's better, maybe you're happy now. You never had a chance, poor Lila.'

The dog owners were edging slowly back, and the surviving dogs were running to them. The superintendent squatted on the curb with his head in his arms. A weary, muffled voice said, 'For God's sake, Bernice, would you get up off me? You don't have to stop yelling, just get off.'

When she stood up, the cars began to stop in the street again. It made it very difficult for the police to get through.

Nobody pressed charges, because there was no one to lodge them against. The killer dog – or wolf, as some insisted – was gone; and if she had an owner, he could not be found. As for the people who had actually seen the wolf turn into a young girl when the sunlight touched her, most of them managed not to have seen it, though they never really forgot. There were a few who knew quite well what they had seen, and never forgot it either, but they never said anything. They did, however, chip in to pay the superintendent's fine for possessing an un-licenced handgun. Farrell gave what he could.

Lila vanished out of Farrell's life before sunset. She did not go uptown with her mother, but packed her things and went to stay with friends in the Village. Later he heard that she was living on Christopher Street; and later still, that she had moved to Berkeley and gone back to school. He never saw her again.

'It had to be like that,' he told Ben once. 'We got to know too much about each other. See, there's another side to knowing. She couldn't look at me.'

'You mean because you saw her with all those dogs? Or because she knew you'd have let that little nut shoot her?' Farrell shook his head.

'It was that, I guess, but it was more something else, something I know. When she sprang, just as he shot at her that last time, she wasn't leaping at him. She was going straight for her mother. She'd have got her too, if it hadn't been sunrise.'

Ben whistled softly. 'I wonder if her old lady knows.'

'Bernice knows everything about Lila,' Farrell said.

Mrs Braun called him nearly two years later to tell him that Lila was getting married. It must have cost her a good deal of money and ingenuity to find him (where Farrell was living then, the telephone line was open for four hours a day), but he knew by the spitefulness in the static that she considered it money well spent.

'He's at Stanford,' she crackled. 'A research psychologist. They're going to Japan for their honeymoon.'

'That's fine,' Farrell said. 'I'm really happy for her, Bernice.' He hesitated before he asked, 'Does he know about Lila? I mean, about what happens—?'

'Does he know?' she cried. 'He's proud of it – he thinks it's wonderful! It's his field!'

'That's great. That's fine. Goodbye, Bernice. I really am glad.'

And he was glad, and a little wistful, thinking about it. The girl he was living with here had a really strange hangup.

THE WAR WITH THE FNOOLS

Philip K. Dick

Contact with aliens, with the possibility of the earth being invaded, is one of the most popular themes in both science fiction and fact at the present time. The idea has, of course, been well worked in mainstream sf for many years, but it is not so familiar in comic fantasy. An exception to this is the next story by Philip K. Dick. Labelled 'the funniest sf writer of his time' by The Encyclopedia of Science Fiction *(1993), in the years since his death a virtual cult has developed around his work. The adapting of some of his most powerful stories for the screen – especially,* Blade Runner *(1982) and* Total Recall *(1990) – has done much to enhance his reputation, and in the USA his keenest fans pay tribute to his literary talents and fondness for drug-taking by referring to themselves as 'Dickheads'.*

Philip Kindred Dick (1928–82) spent most of his life in California, where he was a record store manager and then a disc jockey at a radio station before beginning to publish the short stories and novels which made his name in the Fifties and Sixties. Books such as The Man whose Teeth were All Exactly Alike *(1960),* Humpty Dumpty in Oakland *(1960) and* Dr Bloodmoney, *or* How We Got Along After the Bomb *(1965), gave a clear indication of his humorous inclinations, while later works tended to reflect his interest in drugs, religion and paranoia. Despite his acclaim among fans, it was not until the 1970s that he began to win prizes, getting the John W. Campbell Memorial Award in 1974 for the brilliant, hallucinatory* Flow My Tears, the Policeman Said.

After Philip Dick's death his work was reassessed, and two of his best-known advocates, Terry Gilliam and Brian W. Aldiss, went to some lengths to dismiss a number of the sweeping religio-psychological statements made about his work – and to point out that he was actually a very funny *writer. Of him, Aldiss said, 'Like many a good man, Philip K. went around the bend. He was actually a very sane man who saw the bend coming.'*

Among the dozens of comic fantasies that he published, 'The War with the Fnools', written for Galactic Outpost *magazine in 1964, when talk of alien invasion was much in the air, remains especially topical. Commenting on the story later, Philip Dick said, 'My colleague Tim Powers once said that Martians could invade us simply by putting on funny hats and we'd never notice. Well, once again we are invaded – and, humiliatingly, by a life form which is absurd.' I think the story very neatly closes this opening section of* flights of fantasy.

Captain Edgar Lightfoot of CIA said, 'Darn it, the Fnools are back again, Major. They've taken over Provo, Utah.'

With a groan, Major Hauk signalled his secretary to bring him the Fnool dossier from the locked archives. 'What form are they assuming this time?' he asked briskly.

'Tiny real-estate salesmen,' Lightfoot said.

Last time, Major Hauk reflected, it had been filling station attendants. That was the thing about the Fnools.

When one took a particular shape they all took that shape. Of course, it made detection for CIA fieldmen much easier. But it did make the Fnools look absurd, and Hauk did not enjoy fighting an absurd enemy; it was a quality which tended to diffuse over both sides and even up to his own office.

'Do you think they'd come to terms?' Hauk said, half-rhetorically. 'We could afford to sacrifice Provo, Utah, if they'd be willing to circumscribe themselves there. We could even add those portions of Salt Lake City which are paved with hideous old red brick.'

Lightfoot said, 'Fnools never compromise, Major. Their goal is Sol System domination. For all time.'

Leaning over Major Hauk's shoulder, Miss Smith said, 'Here is the Fnool dossier, sir.' With her free hand she pressed the top of her blouse against herself in a gesture indicating either advanced tuberculosis or advanced modesty. There were certain indications that it was the latter.

'Miss Smith,' Major Hauk complained, 'here are the Fnools trying to take over the Sol System and I'm handed their dossier by a woman with a forty-two-inch bosom. Isn't that a trifle schizophrenic – for me, at least?' He carefully averted his eyes from her, remembering his wife and the two children. 'Wear something else from here on out,' he told her. 'Or swaddle yourself. I mean, my God, let's be reasonable: let's be realistic.'

'Yes, Major,' Miss Smith said. 'But remember, I was selected at random from the CIA employees pool. I didn't *ask* to be your secretary.'

With Captain Lightfoot beside him, Major Hauk laid out the documents that made up the Fnool dossier.

In the Smithsonian there was a huge Fnool, standing

three feet high, stuffed and preserved in a natural habitat-type cubicle. School-children for years had marvelled at this Fnool, which was shown with pistol aimed at Terran innocents. By pressing a button, the school-children caused the Terrans (not stuffed but imitation) to flee, whereupon the Fnool extinguished them with its advanced solarpowered weapon . . . and the exhibit reverted to its original stately scene, ready to begin all over again.

Major Hauk had seen the exhibit, and it made him uneasy. The Fnools, he had declared time and time again, were no joke. But there was something about a Fnool that – well, a Fnool was an idiotic life form. That was the basis of it. No matter what it imitated it retained its midget aspect; a Fnool looked like something given away free at supermarket openings, along with balloons and moist purple orchids. No doubt, Major Hauk had ruminated, it was a survival factor. It disarmed the Fnool's opponents. Even the name. It was just not possible to take them seriously, even at this very moment when they were infesting Provo, Utah, in the form of miniature real-estate salesmen.

Hauk instructed, 'Capture a Fnool in this current guise, Lightfoot, bring it to me and I'll parley. I feel like capitulating, this time. I've been fighting them for twenty years now. I'm worn out.'

'If you get one face to face with you,' Lightfoot cautioned, 'it may successfully imitate you and that would be the end. We would have to incinerate both of you, just to be on the safe side.'

Gloomily, Hauk said, 'I'll set up a key password situation with you right now, Captain. The word is *masticate*. I'll use it in a sentence . . . for instance, "I've got to thoroughly masticate these data." The Fnool won't know that – correct?'

'Yes, Major,' Captain Lightfoot sighed and left the CIA office at once, hurrying to the 'copter field across the street to begin his trip to Provo, Utah.

But he had a feeling of foreboding.

When his 'copter landed at the end of Provo Canyon on the outskirts of the town, he was at once approached by a two-foot-high man in a grey business suit carrying a briefcase.

'Good morning, sir,' the Fnool piped. 'Care to look at some choice lots, all with unobstructed views? Can be subdivided into—'

'Get in the 'copter,' Lightfoot said, aiming his Army-issue .45 at the Fnool.

'Listen, my friend,' the Fnool said, in a jolly tone of voice. 'I can see you've never really given any hard-headed thought to the meaning of our race having landed on your planet. Why don't we step into the office a moment and sit down?' The Fnool indicated a nearby small building in which Lightfoot saw a desk and chairs. Over the office there was a sign:

EARLY BIRD
LAND DEVELOPMENT
INCORPORATED

' "The early bird catches the worm," ' the Fnool declared. 'And the spoils go to the winner, Captain Lightfoot. By nature's laws, if we manage to infest your planet and pre-empt you, we've got all the forces of evolution and biology on our side.' The Fnool beamed cheerily.

Lightfoot said, 'There's a CIA major back in Washington, DC who's on to you.'

'Major Hauk has defeated us twice,' the Fnool admitted. 'We respect him. But he's a voice crying in the wilderness, in this country, at least. You know perfectly well, Captain, that the average American viewing that exhibit at the Smithsonian merely smiles in a tolerant fashion. There's just no awareness of the *menace*.'

By now two other Fnools, also in the form of tiny real-estate salesmen in grey business suits carrying briefcases, had approached. 'Look,' one said to the other. 'Charley's captured a Terran.'

'No,' its companion disagreed, 'the Terran captured him.'

'All three of you get in the CIA 'copter,' Lightfoot ordered, waving his .45 at them.

'You're making a mistake,' the first Fnool said, shaking its head. 'But you're a young man; you'll mature in time.' It walked to the 'copter. Then, all at once, it spun and cried, '*Death to the Terrans!*'

Its briefcase whipped up, a bolt of pure solar energy whined past Lightfoot's right ear. Lightfoot dropped to one knee and squeezed the trigger of the .45; the Fnool, in the doorway of the 'copter, pitched head-forward and lay with its briefcase beside it. The other two Fnools watched as Lightfoot cautiously kicked the briefcase away.

'Young,' one of the remaining Fnools said, 'but with quick reflexes. Did you see the way he dropped on one knee?'

'Terrans are no joke,' the other agreed. 'We've got an uphill battle ahead of us.'

'As long as you're here,' the first of the remaining

Fnools said to Lightfoot, 'why don't you put a small deposit down on some valuable unimproved land we've got a listing for? I'll be glad to run you out to have a look at it. Water and electricity available at a slight additional cost.'

'Get in the 'copter,' Lightfoot repeated, aiming his gun steadily at them.

In Berlin, an *Oberstleutnant* of the SHD, the *Sicherheits-dienst* – the West German Security Service – approaching his commanding officer, saluted in what is termed Roman style and said, '*General, die Fnoolen sind wieder zurück. Was sollen wir jetzt tun?*'

'The Fnools are *back*?' Hochflieger said, horrified. 'Already? But it was only three years ago that we uncovered their network and eradicated them.' Jumping to his feet General Hochflieger paced about his cramped temporary office in the basement of the *Bundesrat Gebaude*, his large hands clasped behind his back. 'And what guise this time? Assistant Ministers of Domestic Finance, as before?'

'No sir,' the *Oberstleutnant* said. 'They have come as gear inspectors of the VW works. Brown suit, clipboard, thick glasses, middle-aged. Fussy. And, as before, *nur* six-tenths of a metre high.'

'What I detest about the Fnools,' Hochflieger said, 'is their ruthless use of science in the service of destruction, especially their medical techniques. They almost defeated us with that virus infection suspended in the gum on the backs of multicolour commemorative stamps.'

'A desperate weapon,' his subordinate agreed, 'but rather too fantastic to be successful, ultimately. This time they'll probably rely on crushing force combined with an absolutely synchronised timetable.'

'*Selbsverstandlich*,' Hochflieger agreed. 'But we've none-theless got to react and defeat them. Inform Terpol.' That was the Terra-wide organisation of counterintelligence with headquarters on Luna. 'Where, specifically, have they been detected?'

'In Schweinfurt only, so far.'

'Perhaps we should obliterate the Schweinfurt area.'

'They'll only turn up elsewhere.'

'True.' Hochflieger brooded. 'What we must do is pursue Operation *Hundefutter* to successful culmination.' *Hundefutter* had developed for the West German Government a sub-species of Terrans six-tenths of a metre high and capable of assuming a variety of forms. They would be used to penetrate the network of Fnool activity and de-stroy it from within. *Hundefutter*, financed by the Krupp family, had been held in readiness for just this moment.

'I'll activate *Kommando Einsatzgruppe II*,' his subordi-nate said. 'As counter-Fnools they can begin to drop behind Fnool lines near the Schweinfurt area immedi-ately. By nightfall the situation should be in our hands.'

'*Gruss Gott*,' Hochflieger prayed, nodding. 'Well, get the *kommando* started, and we'll keep our ears open to see how it proceeds.'

If it failed, he realised, more desperate measures would have to be initiated.

The survival of our race is at stake, Hochflieger said to himself. The next four thousand years of history will be determined by the brave act of a member of the SHD at this hour. Perhaps myself.

He paced about, meditating on that.

* * *

In Warsaw the local chief of the People's Protective Agency for Preserving the Democratic Process – the NNBNDL – read the coded teletype dispatch several times as he sat at this desk drinking tea and eating a late breakfast of sweet rolls and Polish ham. This time disguised as chess players, Serge Nicov said to himself. And each Fnool making use of the queen's pawn opening, Qp to Q3 . . . a weak opening, he reflected, especially against Kp to K4, even if they draw white. But—

Still a potentially dangerous situation.

On a piece of official stationery he wrote *select out class of chess players employing queen's pawn opening*. For Invigorating Forest-renewal Team, he decided. Fnools are small, but they can plant saplings . . . we must get some use out of them. Seeds; they can plant sunflower seeds for our tundra-removal vegetable-oil venture.

A year of hard physical work, he decided, and they'll think twice before they invade Terra again.

On the other hand, we could make a deal with them, offer them an alternative to invigorating forest-renewal activity. They could enter the Army as a special brigade and be used in Chile, in the rugged mountains. Being only sixty-one centimetres high, many of them could be packed into a single nuclear sub for transport . . . but can Fnools be trusted?

The thing he hated most about Fnools – and he had learned to know them in their previous invasions of Terra – was their deceitfulness. Last time they had taken the physical form of a troupe of ethnic dancers . . . and what dancers they had turned out to be. They had massacred an audience in Leningrad before anyone could intervene, men, women and children all dead on the spot by weapons of ingenious design and sturdy although monotonous construction which had masqueraded as folk-instruments of a five-stringed variety.

It could never happen again; all Democratic lands were alert, now; special youth groups had been set up to keep vigil. But something new – such as this chess-player deception – could succeed as well, especially in small towns in the East republics, where chess players were enthusiastically welcomed.

From a hidden compartment in his desk Serge Nicov brought out the special non-dial phone, picked up the receiver and said into the mouthpiece, 'Fnools back, in North Caucasus area. Better get as many tanks as possible lined up to accept their advance as they attempt to spread out. Contain them and then cut directly through their centre, bisecting them repeatedly until they're splintered and can be dealt with in small bands.'

'Yes, Political Officer Nicov.'

Serge Nicov hung up and resumed eating his – now cold – late breakfast.

As Captain Lightfoot piloted the 'copter back to Washington, DC, one of the two captured Fnools said, 'How is it that no matter what guise we come in, you Terrans can always detect us? We've appeared on your planet as filling station attendants, Volkswagen gear inspectors, chess champions, folk singers complete with native instruments, minor government officials, and now real-estate salesmen—'

Lightfoot said, 'It's your size.'

'That concept conveys nothing to us.'

'You're only two feet tall!'

The two Fnools conferred, and then the other Fnool patiently explained, 'But size is relative. We have all the absolute qualities of Terrans embodied in our temporary forms, and according to obvious logic—'

'Look,' Lightfoot said, 'stand here next to me.' The Fnool, in its grey business suit, carrying its briefcase, came cautiously up to stand beside him. 'You just come up to my knee cap,' Lightfoot pointed out. 'I'm six feet high. You're only one-third as tall as I. In a group of Terrans you Fnools stand out like an egg in a barrel of kosher pickles.'

'Is that a folk saying?' the Fnool asked. 'I'd better write that down.' From its coat pocket it produced a tiny ball-point pen no longer than a match. 'Egg in a barrel of pickles. Quaint. I hope, when we've wiped out your civilisation, that some of your ethnic customs will be preserved by our museums.'

'I hope so, too,' Lightfoot said, lighting a cigarette.

The other Fnool, pondering, said, 'I wonder if there's any way we can grow taller. Is it a racial secret reserved by your people?' Noticing the burning cigarette dangling between Lightfoot's lips, the Fnool said, 'Is that how you achieve unnatural height? By burning that stick of compressed dried vegetable fibres and inhaling the smoke?'

'Yes,' Lightfoot said, handing the cigarette to the two-foot-high Fnool. 'That's our secret. Cigarette-smoking makes you grow. We have all our offspring, especially teenagers, smoke. Everyone that's young.'

'I'm going to try it,' the Fnool said to its companion. Placing the cigarette between its lips, it inhaled deeply.

Lightfoot blinked. Because the Fnool was now four feet high, and its companion instantly imitated it; both Fnools were twice as high as before. Smoking the cigarette had augmented the Fnools' height incredibly by two whole feet.

'Thank you,' the now four-foot-high real-estate sales-man said to Lightfoot, in a much deeper voice than before. 'We are certainly making bold strides, are we not?'

Nervously, Lightfoot said, 'Gimme back the cigarette.'

In his office at the CIA building, Major Julius Hauk pressed a button on his desk, and Miss Smith alertly opened the door and entered the room, dictation pad in hand.

'Miss Smith,' Major Hauk said, 'Captain Lightfoot's away. Now I can tell you. The Fnools are going to win this time. As senior officer in charge of defeating them, I'm about to give up and go down to the bomb-proof shelter constructed for hopeless situations such as this.'

'I'm sorry to hear that, sir,' Miss Smith said, her long eyelashes fluttering. 'I've enjoyed working for you.'

'But you, too,' Hauk explained. '*All* Terrans are wiped out; our defeat is planet-wide.' Opening a drawer of his desk he brought out an unopened fifth of Bullock & Lade Scotch which he had been given as a birthday present. 'I'm going to finish this B & L Scotch off first,' he informed Miss Smith. 'Will you join me?'

'No thank you, sir,' Miss Smith said. 'I'm afraid I don't drink, at least during the daylight hours.'

Major Hauk drank for a moment from a dixie cup, then tried a little more from the bottle just to be sure it was Scotch all the way to the bottom. At last he put it down and said, 'It's hard to believe that our backs could be put to the wall by creatures no larger than domestic orange-striped tomcats, but such is the case.' He nodded courteously to Miss Smith. 'I'm off for the concrete sub-surface bomb-proof shelter, where I hope to hold out after the general collapse of life as we know it.'

'Good for you, Major Hauk,' Miss Smith said, a little uneasily. 'But are you – just going to *leave* me here to become a captive of the Fnools? I mean –' Her sharply pointed breasts quivered in becoming unison beneath her blouse. 'It seems sort of mean.'

'You have nothing to fear from the Fnools, Miss Smith,' Major Hauk said. 'After all, two feet tall—' He gestured. 'Even a neurotic young woman could scarcely—' He laughed. 'Really.'

'But it's a terrible feeling,' Miss Smith said, 'to be abandoned in the face of what we know to be an unnatural enemy from another planet entirely.'

'I tell you what,' Major Hauk said thoughtfully. 'Perhaps I'll break a series of strict CIA rulings and allow you to go below to the shelter with me.'

Putting down her pad and pencil and hurrying over to him, Miss Smith breathed, 'Oh, Major, how can I thank you!'

'Just come along,' Major Hauk said, leaving the bottle of B & L Scotch behind in his haste, the situation being what it was.

Miss Smith clung to him as he made his way a trifle unsteadily down the corridor to the elevator.

'Drat that Scotch,' he murmured. 'Miss Smith, Vivian, you were wise not to touch it. Given the cortico-thalamic reaction we are all experiencing in the face of the Fnoolian peril, Scotch isn't the beneficial balm it generally is.'

'Here,' his secretary said, sliding under his arm to help prop him up as they waited for the elevator. 'Try to stand firm, Major. It won't be long now.'

'You have a point there,' Major Hauk agreed. 'Vivian, my dear.'

*   *   *

The elevator came at last. It was the self-service type.

'You're being really very kind to me,' Miss Smith said, as the Major pressed the proper button and the elevator began to descend.

'Well, it may prolong your life,' Major Hauk agreed. 'Of course, that far underground . . . the average temperature is much greater than at the Earth's surface. Like a deep mine shaft, it runs in the near-hundreds.'

'But at least we'll be alive,' Miss Smith pointed out.

Major Hauk removed his coat and tie. 'Be prepared for the humid warmth,' he told her. 'Here, perhaps you would like to remove your coat.'

'Yes,' Miss Smith said, allowing him in his gentlemanly way to remove her coat.

The elevator arrived at the shelter. No one was there ahead of them, fortunately; they had the shelter all to themselves.

'It *is* stuffy down here,' Miss Smith said as Major Hauk switched on one dim yellow light. 'Oh dear.' She stumbled over something in the gloom. 'It's so hard to see.' Again she stumbled over some object; this time she half-fell. 'Shouldn't we have more light, Major?'

'What, and attract the Fnools?' In the dark, Major Hauk felt about until he located her; Miss Smith had toppled onto one of the shelter's many bunks and was groping about for her shoe.

'I think I broke the heel off,' Miss Smith said.

'Well, at least you got away with your life,' Major Hauk said. 'If nothing else.' In the gloom, he began to assist her in removing her other shoe, it being worthless now.

'How long will we be down here?' Miss Smith asked.

'As long as the Fnools are in control,' Major Hauk informed her. 'You'd better change into radiation-proof garb in case the rotten little non-terrestrials try H-bombing the White House. Here, I'll take your blouse and skirt – there should be overalls somewhere around.'

'You're being really kind to me,' Miss Smith breathed, as she handed him her blouse and skirt. 'I can't get over it.'

'I think,' Major Hauk said, 'I'll change my mind and go back up for that Scotch; we'll be down here longer than I anticipated and we'll need something like that as the solitude frays our nerves. You stay here.' He felt his way back to the elevator.

'Don't be gone long,' Miss Smith called anxiously after him. 'I feel terribly exposed and unprotected down here alone, and what is more I can't seem to find that radiation-proof garb you spoke of.'

'Be right back,' Major Hauk promised.

At the field opposite the CIA Building, Captain Lightfoot landed the 'copter with the two captive Fnools aboard. 'Get moving,' he instructed them, digging the muzzle of his Service .45 into their small ribs.

'It's because he's bigger than us, Len,' one of the Fnools said to the other. 'If we were the same size he wouldn't dare treat us this way. But now we understand – finally – the nature of the Terrans' superiority.'

'Yes,' the other Fnool said. 'The mystery of twenty years has been cleared up.'

'Four feet tall is still suspicious-looking,' Captain Lightfoot said, but he was thinking, If they grow from two feet to four feet in one instant, just by smoking a cigarette, what's to stop them from growing two feet more? Then they'll be six feet and look exactly like us.

And it's all my fault, he said to himself miserably.

Major Hauk will destroy me, career-wise if not body-wise.

However, he continued on as best he could; the famous tradition of the CIA demanded it. 'I'm taking you directly to Major Hauk,' he told the two Fnools. 'He'll know what to do with you.'

When they reached Major Hauk's office, no one was there.

'This is strange,' Captain Lightfoot said.

'Maybe Major Hauk has beaten a hasty retreat,' one of the Fnools said. 'Does this tall amber bottle indicate anything?'

'That's a tall amber bottle of Scotch,' Lightfoot said, scrutinising it. 'And it indicates nothing. However –' he removed the cap – 'I'll try it. Just to be on the safe side.'

After he had tried it, he found the two Fnools staring at him intently.

'This is what Terrans deem drink,' Lightfoot explained. 'It would be bad for you.'

'Possibly,' one of the two Fnools said, 'but while you were drinking from that bottle I obtained your .45 Service revolver. Hands up.'

Lightfoot, reluctantly, raised his hands.

'Give us that bottle,' the Fnool said. 'And let us try it for ourselves; we will be denied nothing. For in point of fact, Terran culture lies open before us.'

'Drink will put an end to you,' Lightfoot said desperately.

'As that burning tube of aged vegetable matter did?' the nearer of the two Fnools said with contempt.

It and its companion drained the bottle as Lightfoot watched.

Sure enough, they now stood six feet high. And, he knew, everywhere in the world, all Fnools had assumed equal stature. Because of him, the invasion of the Fnools would this time be successful. He had destroyed Terra.

'Cheers,' the first Fnool said.

'Down the hatch,' the other said. 'Ring-a-ding.' They studied Lightfoot. 'You've shrunk to our size.'

'No, Len,' the other said. 'We have expanded to his.'

'Then at last we're all equal,' Len said. 'We're finally a success. The magic defence of the Terrans – their unnatural size – has been eradicated.'

At that point a voice said, 'Drop that .45 Service revolver.' And Major Hauk stepped into the room behind the two thoroughly drunken Fnools.

'Well I'll be goddamned,' the first Fnool mumbled. 'Look, Len, it's the man most responsible for previously defeating us.'

'And he's little,' Len said. 'Little, like us. We're all little, now. I mean, we're all huge; goddamn it, it's the same thing. Anyhow we're equal.' It lurched towards Major Hauk—

Major Hauk fired. And the Fnool named Len dropped. It was absolutely undeniably dead. Only one of the captured Fnools remained.

'Edgar, they've increased in size,' Major Hauk said, pale. 'Why?'

'It's due to me,' Lightfoot admitted. 'First because of the cigarette, then second because of the Scotch – your Scotch, Major, that your wife gave you on your last birthday. I admit their now being the same size as us makes them undistinguishable from us . . . but consider this, sir. *What if they grew once more?*'

'I see your idea clearly,' Major Hauk said, after a pause.

'If eight feet tall, the Fnools would be as conspicuous as they were when—'

The captured Fnool made a dash for freedom.

Major Hauk fired, low, but it was too late; the Fnool was out into the corridor and racing towards the elevator.

'Get it!' Major Hauk shouted.

The Fnool reached the elevator and without hesitation pressed the button; some extra-terrestrial Fnoolian knowledge guided its hand.

'It's getting away,' Lightfoot grated.

Now the elevator had come. 'It's going down to the bombproof shelter,' Major Hauk yelled in dismay.

'Good,' Lightfoot said grimly. 'We'll be able to capture it with no trouble.'

'Yes, but—' Major Hauk began, and then broke off. 'You're right, Lightfoot; we must capture it. Once out on the street – it would be like any other man in a grey business suit carrying a briefcase.'

'How can it be made to grow again?' Lightfoot said, as he and Major Hauk descended by means of the stairs. 'A cigarette started it, then the Scotch – both new to Fnools. What would complete their growth, make them a bizarre eight feet tall?' He racked his brain as they dashed down and down, until at last the concrete and steel entrance of the shelter lay before them.

The Fnool was already inside.

'That's, um, Miss Smith you hear,' Major Hauk admitted. 'She was, or rather actually, we were – well, we were taking refuge from the invasion down here.'

Putting his weight against the door, Lightfoot swung it aside.

Miss Smith at once hopped up, ran towards them and a moment later clung to the two men, safe now from the

Fnool. 'Thank God,' she gasped. 'I didn't realise what it was until—' She shuddered.

'Major,' Captain Lightfoot said. 'I think we've stumbled on it.'

Rapidly, Major Hauk said, 'Captain, you get Miss Smith's clothes, I'll take care of the Fnool. There's no problem now.'

The Fnool, eight feet high, came slowly towards them, its hands raised.

ᔕ

2

THE MUDDLE AGES

Tales of Heroic Times

THE CREATION
ACCORDING TO SPIKE MILLIGAN

Spike Milligan

*Spike Milligan has been called 'the grandfather of British
humour' and in recent years has made something of a speciality
of rewriting history and the classic works of literature from his
own zany viewpoint – for example* Adolf Hitler: My Part in
His Downfall *(1971),* Monty: His Part in My Victory *(1976)
and D.H. Lawrence's* 'John Thomas and Lady Jane' *(1995).
It is a concept that can be traced back to* The Goon Show, *the
riotously funny radio programme he was largely instrumental
in creating in 1951, from which, it is said, modern British
comedy sprang. In it, he, Michael Bentine, Harry Secombe and
Peter Sellers portrayed four archetypal figures of fun – Eccles,
Grytpype Thynne, Ned Seagoon and Bluebottle. Recently, while
talking again about the show, Milligan said, 'Peter Sellers and I
saw ourselves as comic Bolsheviks. We wanted to destroy all
that had come before and create something totally new.' It
therefore seems only right that as Spike Milligan opens this part
of the book, devoted to heroic fantasy, Peter Sellers should bring
it to a close. Spike, incidentally, has one typical memento of his
friend-in-comedy. 'Just before he died, Peter sent me a tape of a
trombone player growling low notes accompanied by his own
gibberish commentary – how could you forget anyone like
that!'*

Terence Alan Milligan (1918–) was born at Ahmadnagar in India and received his first lessons in a tent in the Hyderabad Sindh desert. A natural performer from his childhood, he made his first stage appearance at the age of eight in a nativity play at a convent school in Poona. Milligan completed his education in England at Lewisham Polytechnic and began his working life as a trumpet player. But comedy was his driving force, and after the success of The Goon Show, *his first television series,* A Show Called Fred, *won the 1956 Television Producers and Directors award. Milligan later extended his talent for comedy to films and the theatre as well as writing essays, short stories and an uproarious bestseller about Irish life,* Puckoon (1963). *The success of this book has resulted in him producing almost fifty more titles. 'The Creation According to Spike Milligan' was written for* Punch *in February 1989 and makes an ideal opening to Part 2 with its alternative views of history.*

CHAPTER 1

1 In the beginning, God created heaven and earth, Maggie Thatcher created hell on earth.

2 And darkness was upon the face of the deep, this was due to a malfunction at Lots Road Power Station.

3 And God said, 'Let there be light,' and there was light, but Eastern Electricity Board said He would have to wait until Thursday to be connected.

4 And God saw the light and it was good, He saw the quarterly bill and that was not good.

5 And God called the light Day, and the Darkness He called Night and so passed his GCSE.

6 And God said, 'Let there be a firmament,' and God called the firmament Heaven, Freephone 999.

7 And God said, 'Let the waters be gathered together unto one place and let the dry land appear,' and in London it went on the market at six hundred pounds a square foot.

8 And God said, 'Let the Earth bring forth grass,' and the Earth brought forth grass and the Rastafarians sat down on it and smoked it.

9 God said, 'And let there be lights in Heaven to give light to the Earth,' and it was so, except over England where there was a heavy cloud and snow on high ground.

10 God said, 'Let the seas bring forth that that hath life,' flooding the market with fish fingers, fishburgers and grade three salmon.

11 And God blessed them saying, 'Be fruitful, multiply and fill the sea, and let fowl multiply on earth,' where Prince Charles and Prince Philip would shoot them.

12 And God said, 'Let the earth bring forth cattle and creeping things,' and there came cows, the BBC Board of Governors and Derek Jameson.

13 And God said, 'Let us make man in our own image,' alas many came out like Spitting Image.

14 And He said, 'Let man have dominion over fish, fowl, cattle and every creepy thing that creepeth upon the earth,' especially the SDP.

15 So God created man in his own image, all except C of E homosexual vicars.

16 And God said, 'Behold, I have given you the first of a free yielding seed, to you this shall be meat,' but to the EEC it will be a Beef Mountain.

CHAPTER 2

1 On the seventh day God ended His work, but Datsun of Coventry car workers went on to time and a half, and

God rested from all His work with complete backing from Arthur Scargill and the miners.

2 God blessed the seventh day, as did all the Pakistani corner shops.

3 Every plant, every herb was in Earth for the Good Lord had not caused it to rain. Because of this Bob Geldof had to raise fifty million quid with Band Aid.

4 And the Lord formed man of the dust of the ground and breathed into his nostrils the breath of life. It was done privately and not on the National Health.

5 The Lord planted a garden in Eden and there He put the man He had formed, who sold the idea to BBC TV as *Gardeners' World*.

6 And out of the ground the Lord grew every tree that was pleasant to the sight, but He had not reckoned with the dodgy weather forecast from Michael Fish, and they were all blown down in the hurricane.

7 And the Lord took man and put him in the Garden of Eden to dress it and keep, subject to compulsory purchase by Brent Council.

8 The Lord God said of every tree of the garden, 'Thou mayest freely eat,' but He was apprehended at the checkout and forced to pay.

9 But of the Tree of Knowledge, thou shall not eatest or thou shall surely die,' due to crop spraying with DDT.

10 And the Lord said, 'It is not good that man should be alone,' and caused a deep sleep to fall on Adam. The shop steward penalised him for doing it during working hours, deducting a day's pay. The Lord took one of Adam's ribs and made her a woman and brought her unto man, which immediately qualified for common law wife allowance.

11 And they were both naked, the man and the wife, and

were not ashamed; however, at Bow Street they were both charged with indecency, and the judge was very jealous of Adam.

CHAPTER 3

1 Now the serpent was more subtle than beasts of the field, he said unto the woman, 'Come eat the fruit of this tree,' and woman said, 'Nay if we eat or touch it we die,' and the serpent said, 'Fear not, they are not from South Africa,' whereupon she ate and gave of it to her husband.
2 And the eyes of them were both opened and they knew they were naked, and Adam said to her, 'Stand back, I don't know how big this is going to get,' and they sewed fig leaves together, one for Eve and seventy-eight for Adam.
3 And unto Adam the Lord said, 'Cursed is the ground for thy sake; in sorrow thou shall eat of it all the days of your life,' but only during official tea breaks.
4 The Lord said unto the serpent, 'Thou art cursed, upon the belly thou shall go, and dust thou shall eat all the days of your life,' and appear in wildlife programmes with a commentary by David Attenborough.
5 Unto the woman He said, 'In sorrow thou shall bring forth children,' which will qualify you for child allowance; 'and your desire shall be your husband, and he shall rule over thee,' and he will go on to become Dirty Den.
6 Unto Adam and his wife the Lord God made coats of skin to clothe them, and lo there were demos by the anti-fur lobby.
7 The Lord God sent him forth from Eden to till the ground from whence he came and he went on Camden Council housing list. When he came upon the place, it

had already been planted with pine trees, a tax dodge by Terry Wogan and Cliff Richard.

CHAPTER 4

1 And Adam knew Eve, and she conceived and bore Cain, and said, 'I have gotten a man from the Lord,' and *The Sun* newspaper named the Lord in a paternity case.

2 And again she bore his brother Abel, upping the child benefit by one. Abel was a sheep keeper, Cain was a tiller of the ground, but Cain was jealous of Abel because he was copping compensation for radioactive sheep caused by Chernobyl, so Cain slew Abel, having first insured him with the Prudential.

3 The Lord said, 'What has thou done? The voice of thy brother's blood cryeth unto me, thou art cursed, whenest thou tillest the ground, it shall not yield unto thee her strength,' and woe it would cost Cain a fortune in fertilisers.

4 And Cain went and dwelt in the land of Nod, on the East of Eden, where he signed on.

CHAPTER 5

1 And it came to pass that man began to multiply on Earth, there being no condoms.

2 And God saw that wickedness was great on earth with many Page Threes and Cynthia Paynes and Swedish Relief Massage Parlours.

3 The Lord said, 'I will destroy man save one,' Noah, who found grace in the eyes of the Lord because he was a mason. He was also a shipwright and had a degree in Carpentry.

4 The Earth was corrupt before God and the Earth was filled with violence and *Rambo I, II* and *III*.

5 And God said unto Noah, 'Make thee an Ark, three hundred cubits long and fifty cubits wide,' and Noah then did go to the nearest DIY shop and put the house up for sale with Hamptons.

6 The Lord said, 'Of every living thing, two of every sort shall thou bring into thee,' and Noah did fill the Ark with animals, and Noah and his family did enter the Ark and were knee deep in it.

7 And lo the rain was upon the earth for forty days and forty nights, whereas the BBC weather man predicted sunshine.

8 And the waters prevailed exceedingly high, but in England no one noticed the difference and there was racing at Newmarket.

CHAPTER 6

1 And after the end of one hundred and fifty days the waters were abated and Noah opened the windows of the Ark and let it all out. He sent forth a dove and lo in her beak was an olive branch plucked off. Noah himself was pretty plucked off and he took in the dove and saw it had been ringed by the Slimbridge Wild-Fowl Trust.

2 On the seventeenth day the Ark rested on Mount Ararat, and God spake to Noah saying, 'Go forth from the Ark.' He did and fell three thousand feet.

CHAPTER 7

1 And God blessed Noah and his sons and said, 'Be fruitful and multiply,' so very little work was done.

2 And Noah became a husbandman and planted a vineyard.

3 And he drank of the wine and was drunken, and he was uncovered within his tent and when breathalysed had 100 millilitres of alcohol per litre of blood.

4 And Ham, the father of Canan, saw the nakedness of his father and being jealous told the neighbours.

5 And Shem and Japeth took a garment (they were in the trade) and went backwards and covered the nakedness of their father and their faces were backward, and were in sore need of an Osteopath.

6 And Noah woke from his wine and knew what his youngest son had done to him, he could see the marks, and Noah lived after the flood, three hundred and fifty years.

MEDIAEVAL ROMANCE

Mark Twain

The first American writer fully to exploit the possibilities of humour in science fiction was Mark Twain, a fact not as widely appreciated today as it deserves to be. His influence has been seen in the work of a number of leading writers in the genre, including Philip José Farmer and Kurt Vonnegut Jr. Certainly, books like his time travel adventure, A Connecticut Yankee in King Arthur's Court *(1889), are still in print today, and* Captain Stormfield's Visit to Heaven *(1909) came out in a new edition only a few years ago. But how many readers have heard of Twain's Utopian novel,* The Curious Republic of Gondour *(1875), in which people classed as intelligent are given more votes than the rest, or his short stories 'The Secret History of Eddypus, the World-Empire' (1901), 'Three Thousand Years Among the Microbes' (1905), and the wonderful hoax-tale, 'The Petrified Man'? Probably just as little known is 'Mediaeval Romance', a comic fantasy about the not-so-heroic past which he wrote in 1871 and sub-titled 'A story that will bring a smile upon the gruffest countenance'.*

Mark Twain was the pseudonym of Samuel Langhorne Clemens (1835–1910) and famous as the author of two enduring masterpieces, Tom Sawyer *(1876) and* Huckleberry Finn *(1884), both of which were drawn from his own boyhood experiences in Florida, Missouri. Clemens was a printer, Mississippi pilot and unsuccessful gold-miner before becoming a newspaperman in Virginia City where he wrote his first comic stories under the name of Mark Twain. The* Innocents Abroad, *published in 1869, established his reputation as a humorist, and throughout the rest of his life his interest in history prompted occasional excursions into comic fantasy. It is high time that these short stories were collected and published in a single volume.*

In many of his stories Mark Twain enjoyed poking fun at entrenched institutions and traditions, and 'Mediaeval Romance' is just such a tale in which the lord of an ancient feudal castle decides to preserve his line by disguising the sex of his child. But although he convinces everyone that his daughter is his son, the real *problems begin when an heir becomes necessary . . .*

1

THE SECRET REVEALED

It was night. Stillness reigned in the grand old feudal castle of Klugenstein. The year 1222 was drawing to a close. Far away up in the tallest of the castle's towers a single light glimmered. A secret council was being held there. The stern old lord of Klugenstein sat in a chair of state meditating. Presently he said, with a tender accent:

'My daughter!'

A young man of noble presence, clad from head to heel in knightly mail, answered:

'Speak, father!'

'My daughter, the time is come for the revealing of the mystery that hath puzzled all your young life. Know, then, that it had its birth in the matters which I shall now unfold. My brother Ulrich is the great Duke of Brandenburgh. Our father, on his death-bed, decreed that if no son were born to Ulrich the succession should pass to my house, provided a *son* were born to me. And further, in case no son were born to either, but only daughters, then the succession should pass to Ulrich's daughter if she proved stainless; if she did not, my daughter should succeed if she retained a blameless name. And so I and my old wife here prayed fervently for the good boon of a son, but the prayer was vain. You were born to us. I was in despair. I saw the mighty prize slipping from my grasp, and the splendid dream vanishing away. And I had been so hopeful! Five years had Ulrich lived in wedlock, and yet his wife had borne no heir of either sex.

' "But hold," I said: "all is not lost." A saving scheme had shot athwart my brain. You were born at midnight. Only the leech, the nurse, and six waiting-women knew your sex. I hanged them every one before an hour sped. Next morning all the barony went mad with rejoicing over the proclamation that a *son* was born to Klugenstein, an heir to mighty Brandenburgh! And well the secret has been kept. Your mother's own sister nursed your infancy, and from that time forward we feared nothing.

'When you were ten years old a daughter was born to Ulrich. We grieved, but hoped for good results from measles, or physicians, or other natural enemies of infancy, but were always disappointed. She lived, she throve – Heaven's malison upon her! But it is nothing. We are safe. For, ha ha! have we not a son? And is not our son the future Duke? Our well-beloved Conrad, is it not so? – for, woman of eight-and-twenty years as you are, my child, none other name than that hath ever fallen to *you*!

'Now it hath come to pass that age hath laid its hand upon my brother, and he waxes feeble. The cares of state do tax him sore. Therefore he wills that you shall come to him and be already Duke in act, though not yet in name. Your servitors are ready – you journey forth tonight.

'Now listen well. Remember every word I say. There is a law as old as Germany, that if any woman sit for a single instant in the great ducal chair before she hath been absolutely crowned in presence of the people *she shall die*! So heed my words. Pretend humility. Pronounce your judgements from the Premier's chair, which stands at the *foot* of the throne. Do this until you are crowned and safe. It is not likely that your sex will ever be discovered, but still it is the part of wisdom to make all things as safe as may be in this treacherous earthly life.'

'Oh, my father, is it for this my life hath been a lie? Was it that I might cheat my unoffending cousin of her rights? Spare me, father, spare your child!'

'What, hussy! Is this my reward for the august fortune my brain has wrought for thee? By the bones of my father, this puling sentiment of thine but ill accords with my humour. Betake thee to the Duke instantly! And beware how thou meddlest with my purpose!'

Let this suffice of the conversation. It is enough for us to know that the prayers, the entreaties, and the tears of the gentle-natured girl availed nothing. Neither they nor anything could move the stout old lord of Klugenstein. And so, at last, with a heavy heart, the daughter saw the castle gates close behind her, and found herself riding away in the darkness surrounded by a knightly array of armed vassals and a brave following of servants.

The old baron sat silent for many minutes after his daughter's departure, and then he turned to his sad wife and said:

'Dame, our matters seem speeding fairly. It is full three months since I sent the shrewd and handsome Count Detzin on his devilish mission to my brother's daughter Constance. If he fail we are not wholly safe, but if he do succeed no power can bar our girl from being Duchess e'en though ill fortune should decree she never should be Duke!'

'My heart is full of bodings, yet all may still be well.'

'Tush, woman! Leave the owls to croak. To bed with ye, and dream of Brandenburgh and grandeur!'

2
FESTIVITY AND TEARS

Six days after the occurrences related in the above chapter, the brilliant capital of the Duchy of Brandenburgh was resplendent with military pageantry, and noisy with the rejoicings of loyal multitudes, for Conrad, the young heir to the crown, was come. The old Duke's heart was full of happiness, for Conrad's handsome person and graceful bearing had won his love at once. The great halls of the palace were thronged with nobles, who welcomed Conrad bravely; and so bright and happy did all things seem that he felt his fears and sorrows passing away, and giving place to a comforting contentment.

But in a remote apartment of the palace a scene of a different nature was transpiring. By a window stood the Duke's only child, the lady Constance. Her eyes were red and swollen, and full of tears. She was alone. Presently she fell to weeping anew, and said aloud:

'The villain Detzin is gone – has fled the dukedom! I could not believe it at first, but, alas! it is too true. And I loved him so. I dared to love him though I knew the Duke my father would never let me wed him. I loved him – but now I hate him! With all my soul I hate him! Oh, what is to become of me? I am lost, lost, lost! I shall go mad!'

3
THE PLOT THICKENS

A few months drifted by. All men published the praises of the young Conrad's government, and extolled the wisdom of his judgements, the mercifulness of his sentences, and the modesty with which he bore himself in his great office. The old Duke soon gave everything into his hands, and sat apart and listened with proud satisfaction while his heir delivered the decrees of the crown from the seat of the premier. It seemed plain that one so loved and praised and honoured of all men as Conrad was could not be otherwise than happy. But, strangely enough, he was not. For he saw with dismay that the Princess Constance had begun to love him! The love of the rest of the world was happy fortune for him, but this was freighted with danger! And he saw, moreover, that the delighted Duke had discovered his daughter's passion likewise, and was already dreaming of a marriage. Every day somewhat of the deep sadness that had been in the princess's face faded away; every day hope and animation beamed brighter from her eye; and by and by even vagrant smiles visited the face that had been so troubled.

Conrad was appalled. He bitterly cursed himself for having yielded to the instinct that had made him seek the companionship of one of his own sex when he was new and a stranger in the palace – when he was sorrowful and yearned for sympathy such as only a woman can give or feel. He now began to avoid his cousin. But this only made matters worse, for, naturally enough, the more he avoided her the more she cast herself in his way. He marvelled at this at first, and next it startled him. The girl haunted him; she hunted him; she happened upon him at all times and in all places, in the night as well as in the day. She seemed singularly anxious. There was surely a mystery somewhere.

This could not go on for ever. All the world was talking about it. The Duke was beginning to look perplexed. Poor Conrad was becoming a very ghost through dread and dire distress. One day as he was emerging from a private ante-room attached to the picture gallery Constance confronted him, and, seizing both his hands in hers, exclaimed:

'Oh, why do you avoid me? What have I done – what have I said, to lose your kind opinion of me – for surely I had it once? Conrad, do not despise me, but pity a tortured heart? I cannot, cannot hold the words unspoken longer, lest they kill me – I LOVE YOU, CONRAD. There, despise me, if you must, but they *would* be uttered!'

Conrad was speechless. Constance hesitated a moment, and then, misinterpreting his silence, a wild gladness flamed in her eyes, and she flung her arms about his neck and said:

'You relent! you relent! You *can* love me – you *will* love me! Oh, say you will, my own, my worshipped Conrad!'

Conrad groaned aloud. A sickly pallor overspread his countenance, and he trembled like an aspen. Presently, in desperation, he thrust the poor girl from him, and cried:

'You know not what you ask! It is for ever and ever impossible!' And then he fled like a criminal, and left the princess stupefied with amazement. A minute afterwards she was crying and sobbing there, and Conrad was crying and sobbing in his chamber. Both were in despair. Both saw ruin staring them in the face.

By and by Constance rose slowly to her feet and moved away, saying:

'To think that he was despising my love at the very moment that I thought it was melting his cruel heart! I hate him! He spurned me – did this man – he spurned me from him like a dog!'

4

THE AWFUL REVELATION

Time passed on. A settled sadness rested once more upon the countenance of the good Duke's daughter. She and Conrad were seen together no more now. The Duke grieved at this. But as the weeks wore away Conrad's colour came back to his cheeks, and his old-time vivacity to his eye, and he administered the government with a clear and steadily ripening wisdom.

Presently a strange whisper began to be heard about the palace. It grew louder; it spread farther. The gossips of the city got hold of it. It swept the dukedom. And this is what the whisper said:

'The Lady Constance hath given birth to a child!'

When the lord of Klugenstein heard it he swung his plumed helmet thrice around his head and shouted:

'Long live Duke Conrad! – for lo, his crown is sure from

this day forward! Detzin has done his errand well, and the good scoundrel shall be rewarded!'

And he spread the tidings far and wide, and for eight-and-forty hours no soul in all the barony but did dance and sing, carouse and illuminate, to celebrate the great event, and all at proud and happy old Klugenstein's expense.

5
THE FRIGHTFUL CATASTROPHE

The trial was at hand. All the great lords and barons of Brandenburgh were assembled in the Hall of Justice in the ducal palace. No space was left unoccupied where there was room for a spectator to stand or sit. Conrad, clad in purple and ermine, sat in the premier's chair, and on either side sat the great judges of the realm. The old Duke had sternly commanded that the trial of his daughter should proceed without favour, and then had taken to his bed broken-hearted. His days were numbered. Poor Conrad had begged, as for his very life, that he might be spared the misery of sitting in judgment upon his cousin's crime, but it did not avail.

The saddest heart in all that great assemblage was in Conrad's breast.

The gladdest was in his father's, for, unknown to his daughter 'Conrad,' the old Baron Klugenstein was come, and was among the crowd of nobles, triumphant in the swelling fortunes of his house.

After the heralds had made due proclamation and the other preliminaries had followed the venerable Lord Chief Justice said, 'Prisoner, stand forth!'

The unhappy princess rose, and stood unveiled before the vast multitude. The Lord Chief Justice continued:

'Most noble lady, before the great judges of this realm it hath been charged and proven that out of holy wedlock your Grace hath given birth unto a child, and by our ancient law the penalty is death excepting in one sole contingency, whereof his Grace the acting Duke, our good Lord Conrad, will advertise you in his solemn sentence now; wherefore give heed.'

Conrad stretched forth the reluctant sceptre, and in the self-same moment the womanly heart beneath his robe yearned pityingly towards the doomed prisoner, and the tears came into his eyes. He opened his lips to speak, but the Lord Chief Justice said quickly:

'Not there, your Grace, not there! It is not lawful to pronounce judgment upon any of the ducal line *save from the ducal throne!*'

A shudder went to the heart of poor Conrad, and a tremor shook the iron frame of his old father likewise. *Conrad had not been crowned* – dared he profane the throne? He hesitated and turned pale with fear. But it must be done. Wondering eyes were already upon him. They would be suspicious eyes if he hesitated longer. He ascended the throne. Presently he stretched forth the sceptre again, and said:

'Prisoner, in the name of our sovereign lord Ulrich, Duke of Brandenburgh, I proceed to the solemn duty that hath devolved upon me. Give heed to my words. By the ancient law of the land, except you produce the partner of your guilt and deliver him up to the executioner who must surely die. Embrace this opportunity – save yourself while yet you may. Name the father of your child!'

A solemn hush fell upon the great court – a silence so

profound that men could hear their own hearts beat. Then the princess slowly turned, with eyes gleaming with hate, and pointing her finger straight at Conrad, said, 'Thou art the man!'

An appalling conviction of his helpless hopeless peril struck a chill to Conrad's heart like the chill of death itself. What power on earth could save him! To disprove the charge he must reveal that he was a woman, and for an uncrowned woman to sit in the ducal chair was death! At one and the same moment he and his grim old father swooned and fell to the ground.

The remainder of this thrilling and eventful story will *not* be found in this or any other publication, either now or at any future time.

The truth is, I have got my hero (or heroine) into such a particularly close place that I do not see how I am ever going to get him (or her) out of it again, and therefore I will wash my hands of the whole business, and leave that person to get out the best way that offers – or else stay there. I thought it was going to be easy enough to straighten out that little difficulty, but it looks different now.

ETHELRED THE UNREADY

Ben Travers

Rewriting history with comic effect appealed also to the English dramatist, Ben Travers, best remembered for his farces staged at the Aldwych Theatre in London. Apart from his hugely successful plays like A Cuckoo in the Nest *(1925),* Rookery Nook *(1926) and* Plunder *(1928), he wrote a number of hilarious short stories based on historical and mythological characters, under the general title 'Misguided Lives'. He produced these stories for* The Passing Show *magazine in the Twenties, maintaining that it was no longer possible to expect children to learn moral lessons from the lives of wicked people because 'the wrong 'uns in history were, after all, usually successful.' Instead he believed cautionary characters should be drawn from 'the ranks of the weak, the beetle-headed and the piffling'. All these stories, with the curious exception of 'Ethelred the Unready,' were later included in his book* The Collection Today *(1929).*

Ben Travers (1886–1980) is still regarded as one of the twentieth century's most important comic writers for the theatre. His last, and typically near-the-knuckle comedy, The Bed Before Yesterday, *opened in December 1975 to be greeted by one critic: 'Short of Rip Van Winkle making a comeback as an alternative comedian with a ring through his eyebrow, it is hard to find any comparison to the opening of*

Ben Travers' new comedy.' The author himself explained that he had come out of retirement to see the play produced because he had been nursing the idea for years, but until then had felt the story of a frigid potted-meat heiress who awakens in middle age to the joys of sex 'would have been like scrawling "bum" on the nursery wall and sure to be strangled by the Lord Chamberlain.' Thanks to the end of British stage censorship it proved to be one of the biggest successes of his career.

Travers, who was born in Hendon and started writing comedy while he was a publisher's reader in London, had the rights to his first novel, The Dipper *(1920), bought for the stage and thereafter his career was set. The wonderful farces he created for the Aldwych made him and the theatre famous all over the world. Later, these plays became very popular with repertory and amateur dramatic companies, allowing Travers to pursue his other interest of writing comic short stories which are unjustly neglected today. Although Ben Travers disliked being compared to his contemporary, P.G. Wodehouse – as he was on more than one occasion – the following story demonstrates that he had a style and wit every bit the equal of that other great farceur.*

If the word 'unready' as applied to this stiff, had meant 'unpunctual', I, for one, couldn't put anything over at him. But it doesn't. It is Old English, and meant 'not having a rede.'

Many words bore a different meaning in those days. Inchbald the Industrious was so called because he was always short of dust. Donald the Discordant meant that Donald literally 'lacked a cord'; in other words, that he was trying to get around without his braces.

It was lucky that Ethelred never had a read at what some of our schoolroom historians have to say of him.

Here are some samples 'Quarrelsome, jealous, suspicious, cowardly, idle, lazy, selfish, indolent and weak.' On these Ethelred scores one better than I do on my prize school report and goes without question into the mug-list.

Anyhow, here is the story of how Ethelred got stung by his Danish neighbours and failed to save his bacon. So you can judge for yourselves.

One morning Ethelred received a visit from his Archbishop of Canterbury, one Ælf-heah; a name which is honoured to this day, being frequently applied to restive horses by cabmen.

'O King,' says Ælf-heah, 'the great Dane ravageth thy country. He has become an absolute nuisance. He invadeth the coast with savage barques. He bones things right and left. What to do about it thy wretched subjects, their pillaged homes and desecrated borders, wot not.'

'Well, he ought not to be allowed in the house at all,' replies Ethelred the Unready. 'Can't he be kept tied up in the yard or something? They needn't think I'm going round replacing the boarders' desecrated whatnots for them. It's entirely their own look-out.'

(Was not this rather flippant in a king? Worse, it was positively sordid. But Ethelred was notoriously slow in the uptake, and perhaps he didn't quite get Ælf-heah.)

'Nay, but I prate me rather of the foreign invaders, the Danes,' says the Archbishop of Canterbury. 'There's a whole bunch of these shysters knocking around, you know.'

'Oh, *those* skates?' says Ethelred. 'Tell 'em to go to Helsingfors.'

'I have, and they won't,' says Ælf-heah. 'They're a regular pest, and one is as bad as another. What's the difference between any two of them? One waxes slack in somebody else's shack and makes tracks for the next-door inn and shirks his labour; and the other necks great whacks of somebody's else's sack from the back-door bin and lurks his neighbour. I tell you, it's high time we rid ourselves of these hoboes.'

'Well, offer them money to quit,' says Ethelred. 'Will they go then, do you think?'

Ælf-heah shakes his head thoughtful.

' 'Tis a difficult riddle,' he says. 'But I'll see whether I can find a solution. Something about – shaking the dough to buzz off these bally misters, and making them go and jazz off like the Dolly Sisters. We'll try it anyhow.'

Did this answer, do you suppose? Why the Danes that were here already simply toured the country getting paid to leave every town in turn; and the Danes that had stayed behind in Denmark rushed England like lunch-time on a German steam-boat. Only the very high-principled ones left these shores at all, and they all took return tickets. Even their king came along – Swaine by name, a noted photographer.

'What are we going to do now?' asks Ethelred after a bit.

'Well, it's obviously one of two choices,' says Ælf-heah. 'Either you must raise more money from your subjects or else go for these blinking Danes. There's not much to it that I can see. What's the difference? Either you noise a hasty vow of your needs and make them sell up their houses for a tax; or else you voice a nasty row with these Swedes and give them hell with an axe.'

'I'll try fighting 'em first,' says Ethelred. 'I'll organise a scrap and get Brithnoth the Old to lead our boys.'

(Was this a wise decision? No, dashed silly. Fancy choosing a leader whose very name indicated that he was well past his prime and suffering severely from adenoids. It was asking for it. And got it.)

'Well, what do you advise now?' asks Ethelred, as he and Ælf-heah were walking home together from the funeral of Brithnoth the Old.

Ælf-heah tilts his mitre and does some head-scratch.

'We're getting pretty near through,' he says. 'But there seem to me to be just a couple of hopes left. We might get the Normans to come and lend us a hand. Richard of Normandy has a sister named Emma. It would be worth about six army corps to him to get rid of her. She has a face exactly like Lon Chaney in *The Hunchback of Notre Dame*. You might marry her.'

'What's the other hope?' asks Ethelred quick.

'The other hope is to fall on these Danes when they're not looking and all pretty well primed with victory and syrup, and to massacre them till they look like first prize in the *Daily Mirror* Rat Week Competition,' says Ælf-heah.

'That sounds the best to me,' says Ethelred.

Ælf-heah shrugs. 'After all,' he says, 'what's the difference? One means that you will merely be fated to get mixed up in a dirty shame in order to get trusted by the rabble; and the other means that you will really be fated to get fixed up with a shirty dame in order to get mustard for your trouble.'

'By heck, I'll do both,' says Ethelred. 'I'll have the massacre Thursday, and marry Emma Friday.'

(Was this a prudent and statesmanlike move? Shut up. Anybody with any experience would have had the marriage Thursday and the massacre Friday.)

Unfortunately several hitches occurred. For one thing, there were, by this time, several million more Danes in the country than there were Britons to massacre them. In consequence the massacre was a flivver.

In fact, most of the Danes took advantage of it to send over quick for their wives' relations who had been left behind in Denmark, so that they could arrive while the massacre was still on. Meanwhile Richard of Normandy hauled Emma along all right, but took good care it was the last he saw of her; and he never sent so much as a Dental Flight Lieutenant to fight for England.

'What shall I do now?' says Ethelred after this.

'You've about shot your bolt, I reckon,' says Ælf-heah. 'You'd better flee to the Low Countries.'

'Are there any lower than this?' asks Ethelred.

'Oh, rather,' says Ælf-heah. 'You try some of those French seaport towns. Oh, boy!'

'I wish you'd told me about this before,' says Ethelred, as he packs his grip.

So Swaine, the royal photographer, was left to carry on unhampered. He took pretty nearly all the country and developed it. It was a sitter for him. Then one day he took more than he could manage on one plate and it fixed him.

On hearing this, Ethelred, who had seen all there was to be seen in the Low Countries, came sneaking back to see what was doing. But this availed him nothing, because reigning in Swaine's place was that prince of the lads, King Knut, or Canute, the celebrated discoverer of paddling. And when Knut heard he was back it wasn't long before Emma was going around in a black toque.

*   *   *

So that's him. We needn't go on roasting him, especially after what the historians have said. In fact, on one point, I'm rather for him against the historians.

Tout says 'The King was a boy'; and Warner backs this up by saying, 'He was a prey to bad favourites.' Well, dash it, I must admit, children, if I had a chance of falling a prey to some of the favourites one sees at the theatre, I shouldn't hesitate to be a bit of a boy myself: especially if the favourites were bad. The only favourite I ever got to know at all well turned out to be quite good – which was tough luck, was it not?

Still, on the whole, Ethelred was undoubtedly a perfect boob. And I hope we shall all realise from his story how grateful we should be to have nowadays so good and wise a Monarch, and such a capital Archbishop of Canterbury.

DREAM DAMSEL

Evan Hunter

The dragon is one of the most fabled creatures of ancient legend. First described in Chinese mythology, it has been the subject of tales by writers as diverse as Kenneth Grahame, L. Frank Baum, Lord Dunsany, Robert Bloch and, of course, J.R.R. Tolkien. Evan Hunter is perhaps the most unexpected name to find in this company, for he is generally associated with mainstream novels and the bestselling police procedurals about the 87th Precinct which he writes as Ed McBain. Yet as a young writer fantasy fiction was one of his main interests, and his first three published novels, Find the Feathered Serpent *(1952),* Rocket to Luna *(1953) and* Danger: Dinosaurs! *(1953), were all about time travel and space exploration. In the Fifties he also contributed short stories to a number of fantasy magazines, revealing his interest in history which was one of the subjects he taught as a teacher in New York. 'Dream Damsel' first appeared in* Fantastic Universe *in 1954 and features a love-struck knight who slays dragons for his lady, cleverly satirising a legendary era which has fascinated many writers.*

Evan Hunter is the adopted name of Salvatore Lombino (1926–) who attended Evander Childs High School and Hunter College in New York, although he has always denied that the names are connected. His experiences as a teacher

provided the background for <u>The Blackboard Jungle</u> *(1954),
a dramatic story of racial tension and violence in a secondary
school which became a bestseller and a benchmark movie
notorious for the riots it allegedly generated among teenagers
with its sound track of rock 'n' roll music. Hunter broadened
his appeal with the long-running series of 87th Precinct novels
which have also been adapted for television. Despite the tough
themes of many of his stories, a streak of humour can often be
found in his work, though rarely as strong as in this journey
into the past – a fact which many readers of 'Dream Damsel'
will doubtless regret.*

I went first to the Lady Eloise, since I was her champion,
and it was only fair and knightly that she should be the
first to know.

There was a fair sky overhead that day, with scudding
clouds beyond the bannered towers of Camelot, and
below their stately ramparts the rich green curve of
the earth bending to meet the egg-shell blue of the
sky. We sat in the stone courtyard while an attendant
played the lute, plucking gently at the strings, and I did
not bid him cease because music seemed somehow fitting for the sorrow of the occasion. The Lady Eloise sat
with her hands folded demurely in her lap, awaiting my
pleasure. I raised my visored helmet and said, 'Elly . . .'

She lifted incredibly long lashes, tilting her amber eyes
to mine. The bodice of her gown rose and fell with her
gentle breathing. 'Yes, my Lord Larimar,' she said.

'I've something on my mind,' I told her, 'and it behoves me to give tongue to it.'

'Give it tongue, then,' Eloise said. 'Trippingly, I pray you.'

I rose and began pacing the courtyard. I had recently
jousted with Sir Mordred, and a few of my armour joints

were loose, and I'm afraid I made a bit of noise as I paced. I lifted my voice above the noise and said, 'As you know, I've been your champion for, lo, these many months.'

'Yes, m'lord,' she said.

'Many a dragon have I slain for you,' I said. I gave heed to the lute music, and corrected it to, 'For thee,' waxing flowery to befit the occasion.

'That's true,' Eloise said. 'Most true, Larry.'

'Yes.' I nodded my head, and my helmet rattled. 'And many an ogre have I sent to a dishonourable death, Elly, many a vile demon have I decapitated in thy name, wearing thy favour, charging forth to do battle upon my courageous steed, rushing over hill and dale, down valley, across stream . . .'

'Yes, m'lord,' Eloise said.

'Yes. And all for thy love, Elly, all for thy undying love.'

'Yes, Larry?' she said, puzzled.

'Arthur himself has seen fit to honour me for my undaunting courage, my unwavering valour. I carry now, among others, the Medal of the Sainted Slayer, the *Croix de Tête de Dragon*, and even . . .'

'Yes?' Eloise asked excitedly.

'Even,' I said, modestly, 'the much coveted Clustered Blueberry Sprig.'

'You are very brave,' Eloise said, lowering her lashes, 'and a most true knight, m'lord.'

'Fie,' I shouted over the music of the lute, 'I come not to speak of bravery. For what is bravery?' I snapped my gauntleted fingers. 'Bravery is naught!'

'Naught, m'lord?'

'Naught. I come because I must speak my mind, else I cannot live with honour or keep my peace with mine own self.'

'Thine own self? Speak then, m'lord,' Eloise said, 'and trippingly, pray you.'

'I desire,' I said, 'to call it quits.'

'Sir?'

'Quits. Finis. *Pfttt*.'

'*Pfttt*, m'lord?'

'Pftt, Elly.'

'I see.'

'It is not that I do not love thee, Elly,' I said. 'Perish the thought.'

'Perish it,' she said.

'For you are lovely and fair and true and constant and a rarity among women. And I am truly nothing when compared to thee.'

'True,' Eloise said, nodding her head. 'That's true.'

'So it is not that I do not love thee. It is that . . .'

I paused because my visor fell over my face.

'Yes?'

I lifted the visor. 'It is that I love another better than thee.'

'Oh.'

'Yes.'

'Guinevere?' she asked. 'Has that wench . . .'

'Nay, not Guinevere, our beloved queen.'

'Elaine, then? Elaine the fair, Elaine the . . .'

'Nay, nor is it Elaine.'

'Pray who then, pray?'

'The Lady Agatha.'

'The Lady who?'

'Agatha.'

'I know of no maiden named Agatha. Are you jesting with me, my Lord Larimar? Do you pull my maidenly leg?'

'Nay. There is an Agatha, Elly, and I do love her, and she doth love me, and we do intend to join our plights in holy matrimony.'

'I see,' Eloise said.

'I have therefore petitioned Arthur to release me from my vows concerning thee, Eloise. I tell you this now because it would not be fair if I am to marry Agatha, which I fully intend doing, to maintain me as a champion when my heart would elsewhere be.'

'I see,' Eloise said again.

'Yes. I hope you understand, Elly. I hope we can still be friends.'

'Of course,' Eloise said, smiling weakly. 'And I suppose you'll want your Alpha Beta Tau pin back.'

'Keep it,' I said magnanimously. And then, to show how magnanimous I really was, I reached into my tunic and said, 'Ho, lute player! Here are a pair of dragon ears for thee, for thy fine music!'

The lute player dropped to the stones and kissed both my feet, and I smiled graciously.

I killed two small dragons that day, catching the second one with my mace before he'd even had a chance to breathe any fire upon me. I cut off their heads and slung them over my jewelled saddle and then rode back to the shining spires of Camelot. Lancelot and Guinevere were just leaving for their afternoon constitutional, so I waved at them and then took my gallant steed to the stables where I left him with my squire, a young boy named Gawain.

I wandered about a bit, watching Merlin playing pinochle with some unsuspecting knight trainees, and then stopping to pass the time of day with Galahad, a fellow I've never enjoyed talking to because his white armour and helmet are so blinding in the sun. Besides, he is a bit of a braggart, and I soon tired of his talk and went to eat a small lunch of roast pheasant, lamb, mutton, cheese, bread, wine, nuts, apples, and grapes, topping it off with one of Arthur's best cigars.

I went back to the stables after lunch to get my gallant steed, and then I rode in the jousting exercises, knocking Mordred for a row of beer barrels, and being in turn knocked head over teacups by Lancelot, whose ride with Guinevere seemed to have done him well.

I gathered myself together afterwards, and was leading my horse back to the stables when Arthur caught up with me.

'Larry!' he called, 'Ho there, Larry! Wait up!'

I stopped and waited for Arthur to come alongside, and I said, 'What's up, beloved king?'

'Just what I wanted to ask you, Larry,' he said, blowing out a tremendous cloud of cigar smoke. 'What *is* all this nonsense?'

'What nonsense, my liege?'

'About wanting to break your champion vows. Now, hell, Larry, that just isn't done, and you know it.'

'It's the only honourable thing to do, Art,' I said.

'Honour, shmonour,' Arthur answered. 'I'm thinking of the paper work involved. These dispensations are a pain in the neck, Larry. After all, you should have thought of this when you took the vows. Any knight . . .'

'I'm sorry, Art,' I said, 'but it's the only way. I've given it a lot of thought, believe me.'

'But I don't understand,' Arthur said, blowing some more smoke at me. 'What's wrong between you and Elly? Now, she's a damn fine kid, Larry, and I hope . . .'

'She is a damn fine kid,' I agreed, 'but it's all off between us.'

'Why?'

'I've found another damsel.'

'This Agatha? Now look, Larry, this is old Artie you're talking to, and not some kid still wet behind the ears. Now you know as well as I do that there's no Agatha in my court, so now . . .'

'I know that, Art. I never said she was in your court.'

'But you call her the Lady Agatha!' Arthur said.

'I know.'

'A foreign broad?' Arthur asked.

'No. A dream damsel.'

'A *what*?'

'A dream damsel. I dream her.'

'Now, what was that again, Larry?'

'I dream her. I dream the Lady Agatha.'

'That's what I thought you . . . say, Larry, did Lancelot hurt you today during the joust? He plays rough, that fellow, and I've been meaning to . . .'

'No, he didn't hurt me at all. Few ribs, but nothing serious. I really do dream my lady, Art.'

'You mean at night? When you're asleep.'

'Aye.'

'You mean you just think her up?'

'Aye.'

'Then she isn't real?' Arthur asked.

'Oh, she's real all right. Not during the day, of course, but when I dream her up at night, she's real as can be.'

'Foo,' Arthur said. 'This is all nonsense. Now you get back to Elly and tell her . . .'

'No, my liege,' I said. 'I intend to marry the Lady Agatha.'

'But she's only a dream!' Arthur protested.

'Not *only* a dream, noble king. Much more than a dream to me. A woman of flesh and blood. A woman who loves me truly, and whom I do truly love.'

'Fie,' Arthur said. 'You're being absurd. I'll send Merlin around to say a few incantations over you. You're probably bewitched.'

'Nay, my lord, I'm not bewitched. I dream the Lady Agatha of my own accord. There's no enchantment whatever attached to it.'

'No enchantment, eh? Perhaps you've been taking to the grape then, Larry? Perhaps the enchantment is all in a cup?'

'Nay, that neither. I tell you I dream her of my own accord.'

Arthur puffed on his cigar again.

'How on earth do you do that?'

'It's really quite simple,' I said. 'I set me down on my couch, and I close my eyes, and I visualise a damsel with blonde hair and blue eyes, and lips like the blushing rose, and skin like Oriental ivory. Carmine nails, like pointed drops of blood, and an hourglass waist. A voice like the brush of velvet, flanks like a good horse in joust, a wit as sharp as any pike, a magic as potent as Merlin's. That is my Lady Agatha, Art. I visualise her and then I fall asleep, and she materialises.'

'She . . . materialises,' Arthur said, stroking his beard.

'Aye. And she loves me.'

'You?' Arthur asked, examining me with scrutiny.

'Yes, me.' I paused. 'What's wrong with that?'

'Nothing, nothing,' Arthur said hastily. 'But tell me, Larry, how do you plan on marrying her? I mean, a dream, after all . . .'

'Look at it this way, Art,' I said. 'During the daytime, I go to work anyway. There's always another dragon to kill, or some giant to fell, and ogres by the dozen Lord knows, not to mention other assorted monsters of various sizes and shapes, and maidens in distress, and sea serpents, and . . . oh, you know. You've been in the business much longer than I.'

'So?'

'So what does a man need a wife for during the daytime? He'd never get to see her anyway. Do you follow me?'

'Yes,' Arthur said, 'but . . .'

'Therefore, I'll marry the Lady Agatha and see her at night, when most knights see their wives anyway. Why, I wouldn't be surprised if that's why they're called knights, Art.'

'But how do you propose to marry her? Who will . . .?'

'I shall dream a friar, and he shall marry us.'

'I do believe you've been slaying too many dragons, my Lord Larimar,' Arthur said. 'After all, your dream girl – in all fairness – doesn't sound any lovelier than the fair Eloise.'

I poked the king in the ribs and said, 'Art you're just getting old, that's all.'

'Maybe so, boy,' he reflected, 'but I think I'll send Merlin around, anyway. Few incantations never hurt anyone.'

'Art, please . . .'

'He's salaried,' Arthur said, and so I conceded . . .

Merlin and Eloise came to me together, he looking very wise and very magical in his pointed hat and flowing robes; she looking very sad and very lovely, though not as lovely as my Lady Agatha.

'Tell me,' Merlin said, 'all about your dream damsel.'

'What is there to tell?'

'Well, what does she look like?'

'She's blond . . .'

'Um-huh, then we shall need some condor livers,' Merlin said.

'And blue-eyed,' I went on.

'Then we'll need a few dragon eggs, pastel-hued.'

'And . . . oh, she's very lovely.'

'I see,' Merlin said wisely. 'And do you love her?'

'I do indeed.'

'And she you?' he asked, cocking an eyebrow.

'Verily.'

'She truthfully loves thee?'

'Of course.'

'She is lovely you say, and she loves – forgive me – *thee*?'

'Why, yes,' I said.

'She loves . . . *thee*?'

'Three times already has she loved me, and still you do not hear? Turn up your hearing aid, wizard,' I said.

'Forgive me,' Merlin said, shaking his head. 'I just . . .'

'She has told me upon many an occasion that I am just what she has been waiting for,' I said. 'Tall, manly, bold, courageous and very handsome!'

'She said these things about *you*?' Merlin asked.

'Yes, of course.'

'That you were the man she waited for? That you were . . . tall?'

'Yes.'

'And . . . and manly?'

'Yes.'

Merlin coughed, perhaps first realising how tall and

manly I really was. 'And . . . and . . .' he coughed again '. . . handsome?'

'All those,' I said.

Merlin continued coughing until I thought he would choke. 'And all those she waited for, and all those she found in . . .' He coughed again. '. . .*you*?'

'And why not, wizard?' I asked.

'You are truly bewitched, Lord Larimar,' he said, 'truly.'

He pulled back the sleeve of his robe, and spread his fingers wide, and then he said, '*Alla-bah-roo-muh-jig-bah-roo, zing, zatch, zootch*!'

I listened to the incantation and I yawned. But apparently Eloise was taking all this nonsense to heart because she stared at Merlin wide-eyed, looking lovely but not so lovely as my Lady Agatha, and then she looked at me, and her eyes got wider and wider and wider . . .

Oh, there was so much to do in preparation. My dispensation from Arthur came through the next week, and I went about busily making plans for my wedding to Agatha. I wanted to dream up something really special, something that would never be forgotten as long as England had a history. I wanted a big wedding, and so I had to plan beforehand so that I could dream it all up in one night, which was no easy task.

I wanted to dream up the entire court on white stallions, their shields blazing, their swords held high to catch the gleaming rays of the sun, the gallery packed with damsels in pink and white and the palest blue. I wanted to dream the banners of Camelot fluttering in green and yellow and orange over the towers, with a pale sky beyond, and a mild breeze blowing. I wanted to dream a friar who would be droll and yet serious, chucklingly fat, but piously religious.

And most of all, I wanted to dream the Lady Agatha in her wedding gown, a fine thing of lace and pearls, with a low bodice and a hip-hugging waist. All these things I wanted to dream, and they had to be planned beforehand. So what with slaying dragons and ogres and planning for the wedding, I was a fairly busy young knight, and I didn't get around to visiting Eloise again until the night before the wedding.

Her lady-in-waiting was most cordial.

'My mistress is asleep,' she said.

'Asleep?' I glanced at my hourglass. 'Why, it's only four minutes past six.'

'She has been retiring early of late,' the woman said.

'Poor child,' I said, wagging my head. 'Her heart is doubtless breaking. Ah well, *c'est la guerre.*'

'*C'est,*' the woman said.

'When she awakes on the morrow, tell her I am going to dream her a seat of honour at the wedding. Tell her. She will be pleased.'

'Sir?'

'Just tell her. She'll understand.'

'Yes, sir.'

'Matter of fact,' I said, 'I'd better get to bed myself. Want to practise up. I've a lot to dream tomorrow night.'

'Sir?'

'Never mind,' I said. I reached into my tunic and said, 'Here's a dragon's tooth for lending a kind ear.'

I ripped the tooth from my hourglass fob and deposited it in her excitedly overwhelmed, shaking, grateful palm.

Then I went home and to bed and to dream of my Lady Agatha.

I went first to the Lady Eloise on the morrow, since it was only fair and knightly that she should be the first to know. I did not raise my visor for I did not desire her to see my face.

'Elly,' I said, 'I've got something on my mind, and it behoves me to give tongue to it.'

'Give it tongue, then,' Eloise said. 'Trippingly, pray you.'

'It's all off,' I told her. 'The Lady Agatha and me. We're through. She called it quits.'

'Quits?' Eloise said. 'Finis? *Pftt?*'

'Even so,' I said.

'Really now,' Eloise said, smiling.

'There's someone else, Elly. My Lady Agatha has someone else. Someone taller, manlier, handsomer. I know it's hard to believe. But there is someone else, someone who just came along . . . suddenly.'

'How terrible for you,' Eloise said happily.

'Yes. I can't understand it. He just popped up, just like that, right there beside her. I . . . I saw him, Elly, a big handsome knight on a white horse. Right there in my dream, I saw him.'

'Did you really?' Eloise asked sadly, clapping her hands together.

'Yes,' I said. 'So she wants him, and not me. So I thought, if you'll still have me, Elly, if you'll still take me as your champion . . .'

'Well . . .'

'. . . and perhaps someday as your husband, then . . .'

Eloise stepped forward, and there was a twinkle in her eye when she lifted my visor.

'You're tall and manly and handsome enough for me, you goof,' she said. I looked at her and suddenly remembered that she'd been doing an awful lot of sleeping lately, and I started to say, 'Hey!'

But she wrapped her arms around my armour and kissed me soundly on the mouth, and all I could do was stare at her in wonder and murmur, 'Eloise! I never dreamed!'

Eloise smiled secretly and said, '*I* did.'

ç

THREE MONTHS IN A BALLOON

John Kendrick Bangs

More than two hundred years after it was written, The
Singular Travels, Campaigns, Voyages and Sporting Adventures of Baron Münchhausen *by Rudolf Erich Raspe
remains one of the most popular of all 'tall-tale' fantasies. The
story of the Baron's exploits – including shooting a horse down
from a steeple, performing equestrian feats on a tea-table,
vanquishing the Turkish army and climbing up to the Moon
and back – became so popular with eighteenth century readers
that the character is today as famous as those other great
fictional heroes, Don Quixote, Falstaff and Gulliver. Apart
from endless reprints, Raspe's book has been adapted many
times for the radio, television and films – most notably in
1989 with Terry Gilliam's spectacular version starring John
Neville. This picture, the biggest shot in Europe for over 25
years, was beset with problems for the cast and crew – huge
overspending, dogs with liver complaints, and actors having to
cope with all manner of special effects, from bizarre make-up
to riding in a balloon wearing inflatable silken underwear.*

*The events were almost as bizarre as the lifestyle of the
book's author, Raspe, who has been described as 'one of those
seedy figures who sidled in and out of the shadows of eighteenth century history.' A German scholar turned rogue, he fled
to England where he was taken up and dropped by various*

patrons. Although the success of the book, first published in 1785, briefly made him a rich man, he squandered his wealth and died a pathetic and impoverished figure in 1794. His work thereafter became the subject of a whole battery of sequels, parodies and imitations, all of which have helped to maintain the status of the legendary Baron.

John Kendrick Bangs (1862–1922) was one of the writers who was intrigued and inspired by Raspe's original novel. He was also one of America's leading writers of humorous fantasies during the early years of the twentieth century. Born in New York, he worked for several years as a staff member on the city's leading magazines, including Harper's *Magazine and* Puck, *where his ability to satirise well-known individuals soon earned him a large readership. He became famous with* A House-Boat on the Styx *(1895), in which a number of familiar historical figures like Noah, Shakespeare and Napoleon form a club from which women are banned, and then have to face a rebellion from a group of females led by Cleopatra. A sequel,* The Pursuit of the House-Boat *(1897), included Sherlock Holmes as a character, while in* Olympian Nights *(1902) he featured a quartet of Greek gods whose greatest pleasure is using the planet Mars as a giant golf course.*

Bangs' influence was to prove far-reaching and his ideas can be seen in the works of such writers of comic fantasy as Thorne Smith and Philip José Farmer. It was inevitable that he should be attracted to the Münchhausen legend, and in 1901 he published Mr Munchhausen *subtitled, 'Being a True Account of some of the Recent Adventures beyond the Styx of the late Baron Munchausen'. The Baron recounts these tales to his two nephews, referred to as the 'Imps' or 'Heavenly Twins', and they are recorded by Mr Ananias of the* Gehenna Gazette. *The story of 'Three Months in a Balloon' has*

Munchausen coming to the aid of a beleaguered Napoleon and echoes the attempts of modern balloonists to circumnavigate the globe. Perhaps they could learn something from the remarkable Baron?

Mr Munchausen was not handsome, but the Imps liked him very much; he was so full of wonderful reminiscences, and was always willing to tell anybody that would listen, all about himself. To the Heavenly Twins he was the greatest hero that had ever lived. Napoleon Bonaparte, on Mr Munchausen's own authority, was not half the warrior that he, the late Baron, had been, nor was Cæsar in his palmiest days one-quarter so wise or so brave. How old the Baron was no one ever knew, but he had certainly lived long enough to travel the world over, and stare every kind of death squarely in the face without flinching. He had fought Zulus, Indians, tigers, elephants – in fact, everything that fights, the Baron had encountered, and in every contest he had come out victorious. He was the only man the children had ever seen that had lost three legs in battle and then had recovered them after the fight was over; he was the only visitor to their house that had been lost in the African jungle and wandered about for three months without food or shelter, and best of all he was, on his own confession, the most truthful narrator of extraordinary tales living. The youngsters had to ask the Baron a question only, any one, it mattered not what it was – to start him off on a story of adventure, and as he called upon the Twins' father once a month regularly, the children were not long in getting together a collection of tales beside which the most exciting episodes in history paled into insignificant commonplaces.

'Uncle Munch,' said the Twins one day, as they climbed up into the visitor's lap and disarranged his necktie, 'was you ever up in a balloon?'

'Only once,' said the Baron calmly. 'But I had enough of it that time to last me for a lifetime.'

'Was you in it for long?' queried the Twins, taking the Baron's watch out of his pocket and flinging it at Cerberus, who was barking outside the window.

'Well, it seemed long enough,' the Baron answered, putting his pocket-book in the inside pocket of his vest where the Twins could not reach it. 'Three months off in the country sleeping all day long and playing tricks all night seems a very short time, but three months in a balloon and the constant centre of attack from every source is too long for comfort.'

'Were you up in the air for three whole months?' asked the Twins, their eyes wide open with astonishment.

'All but two days,' said the Baron. 'For two of those days we rested in the top of a tree in India. The way of it was this: I was always, as you know, a great favourite with the Emperor Napoleon, of France, and when he found himself involved in a war with all Europe, he replied to one of his courtiers who warned him that his army was not in condition: "Any army is prepared for war whose commander-in-chief numbers Baron Munchausen among his advisers. Let me have Munchausen at my right hand and I will fight the world." So they sent for me and as I was not very busy I concluded to go and assist the French, although the allies and I were also very good friends. I reasoned it out this way: In this fight the allies are the stronger. They do not need me. Napoleon does. Fight for the weak, Munchausen, I said to myself, and so I went. Of course, when I reached Paris I went at once to the Emperor's palace and remained at his side until he took the field, after which I remained behind for a few days to put things to rights for the Imperial family. Unfortunately for the French, the King of Prussia heard of my delay in going to the front, and he sent word to his forces to intercept me on my way to join Napoleon at all hazards, and this they tried to do. When I was within ten miles of the Emperor's headquarters, I was stopped by the Prussians, and had it not been that I had provided myself with a balloon for just such an emergency, I should have been captured and confined in the King's palace at Berlin, until the war was over.

'Foreseeing all this, I had brought with me a large balloon packed away in a secret section of my trunk, and while my bodyguard was fighting with the Prussian troops sent to capture me, I and my valet inflated the balloon, jumped into the car and were soon high up out of the enemy's reach. They fired several shots at us, and one of them would have pierced the balloon had I not, by a rare good shot, fired my own rifle at the bullet, and hitting it squarely in the middle, as is my custom, diverted it from its course, and so saved our lives.

'It had been my intention to sail directly over the heads of the attacking party and drop down into Napoleon's camp the next morning, but unfortunately for my calculations, a heavy wind came up in the night and the balloon was caught by a northerly blast, and blown into Africa where, poised in the air directly over the desert of Sahara, we encountered a dead calm, which kept us stalled up for two miserable weeks.'

'Why didn't you come down?' asked the Twins, 'wasn't the elevator running?'

'We didn't dare,' explained the Baron, ignoring the

latter part of the question. 'If we had we'd have wasted a great deal of our gas, and our condition would have been worse than ever. As I told you, we were directly over the centre of the desert. There was no way of getting out of it except by long and wearisome marches over the hot, burning sands with the chances largely in favour of our never getting out alive. The only thing to do was to stay just where we were and wait for a favouring breeze. This we did, having to wait four mortal weeks before the air was stirred.'

'You said two weeks a minute ago, Uncle Munch,' said the Twins critically.

'Two? Hem! Well, yes it was two, now that I think of it. It's a natural mistake,' said the Baron stroking his mustache a little nervously. 'You see two weeks in a balloon over a vast desert of sand, with nothing to do but whistle for a breeze, is equal to four weeks anywhere else. That is, it seems so. Anyhow, two weeks or four, whichever it was, the breeze came finally, and along about midnight left us stranded again directly over an Arab encampment near Wady Halfa. It was a more perilous position really, than the first, because the moment the Arabs caught sight of us they began to make frantic efforts to get us down. At first we simply laughed them to scorn and made faces at them, because as far as we could see, we were safely out of reach. This enraged them and they apparently made up their minds to kill us if they could. At first their idea was to get us down alive and sell us as slaves, but our jeers changed all that, and what should they do but whip out a lot of guns and begin to pepper us.

' "I'll settle them in a minute," I said to myself, and set about loading my own gun. Would you believe it, I found that my last bullet was the one with which I had saved the balloon from the Prussian shot?'

'Mercy, how careless of you Uncle Munch!' said one of the Twins. 'What did you do?'

'I threw out a bag of sand ballast so that the balloon would rise just out of range of their guns, and then, as their bullets got to their highest point and began to drop back, I reached out and caught them in a dipper. Rather neat idea, eh? With these I loaded my own rifle and shot every one of the hostile party with their own ammunition, and when the last of the attacking Arabs dropped I found there were enough bullets left to fill the empty sand bag again, so that the lost ballast was not missed. In fact, there were enough of them in weight to bring the balloon down so near to the earth that our anchor rope dangled directly over the encampment, so that my valet and I, without wasting any of our gas, could climb down and secure all the magnificent treasures in rugs and silks and rare jewels these robbers of the desert had managed to get together in the course of their depredations. When these were placed in the car another breeze came up, and for the rest of the time we drifted idly about in the heavens waiting for a convenient place to land. In this manner we were blown hither and yon for three months over land and sea, and finally we were wrecked upon a tall tree in India, whence we escaped by means of a convenient elephant that happened to come our way, upon which we rode triumphantly into Calcutta. The treasures we had secured from the Arabs, unfortunately, we had to leave behind us in the tree, where I suppose they still are. I hope some day to go back and find them.'

Here Mr Munchausen paused for a moment to catch his breath. Then he added with a sigh. 'Of course, I went back to France immediately, but by the time I reached Paris the war was over, and the Emperor was in exile. I was too late to save him – though I think if he had lived some sixty or seventy years longer I should have managed to restore his throne, and Imperial splendour to him.'

The Twins gazed into the fire in silence for a minute or two. Then one of them asked:

'But what did you live on all that time, Uncle Munch?'

'Eggs,' said the Baron. 'Eggs and occasionally fish. My servant had had the foresight when getting the balloon ready to include, among the things put into the car, a small coop in which were six pet chickens I owned, and without which I never went anywhere. These laid enough eggs every day to keep us alive. The fish we caught when our balloon stood over the sea, baiting our anchor with pieces of rubber gas pipe used to inflate the balloon, and which looked very much like worms.'

'But the chickens?' said the Twins. 'What did they live on?'

The Baron blushed.

'I am sorry you asked that question,' he said, his voice trembling somewhat. 'But I'll answer it if you promise never to tell anyone. It was the only time in my life that I ever practised an intentional deception upon any living thing, and I have always regretted it, although our very lives depended upon it.'

'What was it, Uncle Munch?' asked the Twins, awed to think that the old warrior had ever deceived anyone.

'I took the egg shells and ground them into powder, and fed them to the chickens. The poor creatures supposed it was corn-meal they were getting,' confessed the Baron. 'I know it was mean, but what could I do?'

'Nothing,' said the Twins softly. 'And we don't think it was so bad of you after all. Many another person would have kept them laying eggs until they starved, and then he'd have killed them and eaten them up. You let them live.'

'That may be so,' said the Baron, with a smile that showed how relieved his conscience was by the Twins' suggestion. 'But I couldn't do that, you know, because they were pets. I had been brought up from childhood with those chickens.'

Then the Twins, jamming the Baron's hat down over his eyes, climbed down from his lap and went to their play, strongly of the opinion that, though a bold warrior, the Baron was a singularly kind, soft-hearted man after all.

HOW I LOST THE SECOND WORLD WAR AND HELPED TURN BACK THE GERMAN INVASION

Gene Wolfe

'Alternate Worlds' – a term for stories in which an alteration to history has changed the course of people's lives – has attracted many writers of comic fantasy, including G.K. Chesterton, Philip K. Dick, Spike Milligan and the next contributor, Gene Wolfe. Usually defined as tales of 'if it had happened otherwise', the favourite characters have, perhaps inevitably, proved to be Napoleon and Hitler. It is not generally known that Winston Churchill wrote one such tale, 'If Lee had not Won the Battle of Gettysburg' (1932), which gives an added piquancy to Wolfe's story set in the year 1938, when the great statesman was not yet at the centre of the world stage. The theme of 'Alternate Worlds' has also been utilised in bestselling novels like Queen Victoria's Bomb *by Ronald W. Clark (1967), in which the atom bomb is developed ahead of its time;* Martin Cruz Smith's The Indians Won *(1970); Len Deighton's* SS-GB *(1978); and in Kevin Brownlow's intriguing film of a successful German invasion of Britain,* It Happened Here *(1966), starring Pauline Murray and Sebastian Shaw.*

Gene Wolfe (1931–) has been called 'un Proust de l'espace' by L'Express *in Paris, and is generally regarded* as one of the finest modern writers of sf. Born in New York but raised in Texas, he served in the Korean War which earned him a Combat Infantry badge but deeply influenced his thinking. After graduating in mechanical engineering, he worked for a time as the editor of a trade magazine before finding his real talent as a writer of fiction. A short story, 'The Doctor of Death Island', in 1978 signalled the arrival of a remarkable new talent, and his later group of 'Archipelago' stories and 'The Book of the New Sun' series confirmed his reputation as well as winning the first of many prizes, among them the World Fantasy Award and prestigious Nebula Award.

Wolfe has recently turned to historical themes in his books such as There Are Doors (1988), set in a parallel world like the United States during the Depression; Castleview (1990), in which King Arthur takes up a new cause in contemporary Illinois; and Soldier of Arete (1989) about Ancient Greece. The parody element in all these books has caused him to be compared by some critics to G.K. Chesterton, and there are similar strains in the short story here, written for Analog in May 1973. It makes the point in a quite irresistibly comic way that not all wars are fought with guns and bombs, and that the ultimate weapon, always, is the mind of man.

1 April, 1938

Dear Editor:

As a subscriber of some years standing – ever since taking up residence in Britain, in point of fact – I have often noted with pleasure that in addition to dealing with the details of the various *All New and Logical, Original Games* designed by your readers, you have some-times welcomed to your columns vignettes of city and rural life, and especially those having to do with games.

Thus I hope that an account of a gamesing adventure which lately befell me, and which enabled me to rub elbows (as it were) not only with Mr W.L.S. Churchill – the man who, as you will doubtless know, was dismissed from the position of First Lord of the Admiralty during the Great War for his sponsorship of the ill-fated Dardanelles Expedition, and is thus a person of particular interest to all those of us who (like myself) are concerned with Military Boardgames – but also with no less a celebrity than the present *Reichschancellor*, of Germany, Herr Adolf Hitler.

All this, as you will already have guessed, took place in connection with the great Bath Exposition; but before I begin my account of the extraordinary events there (events observed – or so I flatter myself – by few from as advantageous a position as was mine), I must explain, at least in generalities (for the details are exceedingly complex) the game of *World War*, as conceived by my friend Lansbury and myself. Like many others we employ a large world map as our board; we have found it convenient to mount this with wallpaper paste upon a sheet of deal four feet by six, and to shellac the surface; laid flat upon a commodious table in my study this serves us admirably. The nations siding with each combatant are determined by the casting of lots; and naval, land, and air units of all sorts are represented symbolically by tacks with heads of various colours; but in determining the *nature* of these units we have introduced a new principle – one not found, or so we believe, in any other game. It is that either contestant may at any time propose a new form of ship, firearm, or other weapon; if he shall urge its probability (not necessarily its utility, please note – if it prove not useful the loss is his only) with sufficient force to convince his opponent, he is allowed to convert such of his units as he desires to the new mode, and to have the exclusive use of it for three moves, after which his opponent may convert as well if he so chooses. Thus a player of *World War*, as we conceive it, must excel not only in the strategic faculty, but in inventive and argumentative facility as well.

Now as it happened Lansbury and I had spent most of the winter now past in setting up the game and settling the rules for the movement of units. Both of us have had considerable experience with games of this sort, and knowing the confusion and ill feeling often bred by a rulebook treating inadequately of (what may once have appeared to be) obscure contingencies, we wrote ours with great thoroughness. On February 17th (Lansbury and I caucus weekly) we held the drawing: it allotted Germany, Italy, Austria, Bulgaria, and Japan to me; Britain, France, China and the Low Countries to Lansbury. I confess that these alignments appear improbable – the literal-minded man might well object that Japan and Italy, having sided with Britain in the Great War, would be unlikely to change their coats in a second conflict. But a close scrutiny of history will reveal even less probable reversals (as when France, during the sixteenth century, sided with Turkey in what has been called the Unholy Alliance) and Lansbury and I decided to abide by the luck of the draw. On the 24th we were to make our first moves.

On the 20th, as it happened, I was pondering my strategy when paging casually through the *Guardian*, my eye was drawn to an announcement of the opening of the Exposition; and it at once occurred to me that among the representatives of the many nations exhibiting I might find someone whose ideas would be of value to me. In any event I had nothing better to do, and so – little knowing that I was to become a witness to history – I thrust a small memorandum book in my pocket and I was off to the fair!

I suppose I need not describe the spacious grounds to the readers of this magazine. Suffice it to say that they were, as everyone has heard, surrounded by an oval hippodrome nearly seven miles in length, and dominated by the Dirigible Tower that formed a most impressive part of the German exhibit, and by the vast silver bulk of the airship *Graf Spee*, which, having brought the chief functionary of the German *Reich* to Britain, now waited, a slave of the lamp of *Kultur* (save the Mark!) to bear him away again. This was, in fact, the very day that *Reichschancellor* Hitler – for whom the Exposition itself had opened early – was to unveil the 'People's Car' exhibit. Banners stretched from poles and even across the main entry carried such legends as:

WHICH PEOPLE SHOULD HAVE A
'PEOPLE'S CAR' ?????
THE ENGLISH PEOPLE!!

and

GERMAN CRAFTSMANSHIP
BRITISH LOVE OF FINE MACHINES

and even

IN SPIRIT THEY ARE AS BRITISH
AS THE ROYAL FAMILY

Recollecting that Germany was the most powerful of the nations that had fallen to my lot in our game, I made for the German exhibit.

There the crowd grew dense; there was a holiday atmosphere, but within it a note of sober calculation – one heard workingmen discussing the mechanical merits (real and supposed) of the German machines, and their extreme cheapness and the interest-free loans available from the *Reichshauptkasse*. Vendors sold pretzels, *Lebkuchen*, and Bavarian creams in paper cups, shouting their wares in raucous Cockney voices. Around the great showroom where, within the hour, the *Reichschancellor* himself was to begin the 'People's Car' invasion of Britain by demonstrating the vehicle to a chosen circle of celebrities, the crowd was now ten deep, though the building (as I learned subsequently) had long been full, and no more spectators were being admitted.

The Germans did not have the field entirely to themselves, however. Dodging through the crowd were driverless model cars only slightly smaller (or at least so it seemed) than the German 'People's Cars'. These 'toys', if I may so style something so elaborate and yet inherently frivolous, flew the rising sun banner of the Japanese Empire from their aerials, and recited through speakers, in ceremonious hisses, the virtues of that industrious nation's products, particularly the gramophones, wirelesses, and so on employing those recently invented wonders, transistors.

Like others I spent a few minutes sightseeing – or rather, as I should say, craning myself upon my toes in an attempt to sightsee. But my business was no more with the 'People's Car' and the German *Reichschancellor* than with the Japanese marionette motorcars, and I soon turned my attention to searching for someone who might aid me in the coming struggle with Lansbury. Here I was fortunate indeed, for I had no sooner looked around than I beheld a portly man in the uniform of an officer of the *Flugzeugmeisterei* buying a handful of Germanic confections from a hawker. I crossed to him at once, bowed, and after apologising for having ventured to address him without an introduction made bold to congratulate him upon the great airship floating above us.

'Ah!' he said. 'So you like that' (it was almost 'dot') 'fat sailor up there? Well, he is a fine ship, and no mistake.' He puffed himself up in the good-natured German way as he said this and popped a sweet into his mouth, and I could see that he was pleased. I was about to ask him if he had ever given any consideration to the military aspects of aviation when I noticed the decorations on his uniform jacket. Seeing the direction of my gaze he asked, 'You know what those are?'

'I certainly do,' I replied. 'I was never in combat myself, but I would have given anything to have been a flier. I was about to ask you, Herr—'

'Goering.'

'Herr Goering, how do you feel the employment of aircraft would differ if – I realise this may sound absurd – the Great War were to take place now?'

I saw from a certain light in his eyes that I had found a kindred soul. 'That is a good question,' he said, and for a moment he stood staring at me, looking for all the world like a Dutch schoolmaster about to give a favourite pupil's inquiry the deep consideration it deserved. 'And I will tell you this – what we had then was nothing. Kites, with guns. If war was to come again now . . .' He paused.

'It is unthinkable, of course.'

'*Ja*. Today the *Vaterland*, that could not conquer Europe with bayonets in that war, conquers all the world with money and our little cars. With those things our leader has brought down the enemies of the party, and all the industry of Poland, of Austria, is ours. The people say, "Our company, our bank," but now the shares are in Berlin.'

I knew all this, of course, as every well-informed person does; and I was about to steer the conversation back towards new military techniques, but it was unnecessary. 'But you,' Goering continued, his mood suddenly lightening, 'and I, my friend, what do we care? That is for the financial people, *nicht wahr*? Do you know what I' (he thumped his broad chest) 'would do when the war came? I would build *Stutzkampfbombers*.'

'*Stutzkampfbombers*?'

'Each to carry one bomb! Only one, but a big one. Fast planes—' he stooped and made a diving motion with his right hand, at the last moment 'pulling out' and releasing a Bavarian cream in such a way that it struck my shoe. 'Fast planes. I would put my tanks – you know tanks?'

I nodded and said, 'A little.'

'– in columns. The *Stutzkampfbombers* ahead of the tanks, the storm troops behind. Fast tanks too – not so much armour, but fast, with big guns.'

'Brilliant . . . a lightning war.'

'*Ja, blitzkrieg*; but listen, my friend. I must go now and wait upon our *Führer*, but there is someone here you should meet. You like tanks – this man is their father – he was in the navy here in the war, and when the army would not do it he did it from the navy, and they told the newspapers they were making water tanks. You use that silly name still, and when you stand on the outside talk about decks on it because of him. He is in there—' He jerked a finger at the huge pavilion where the *Reichschancellor* was shortly to demonstrate the 'People's Cars' to a delighted British public.

I told him I could not possibly get in there – the place was packed already, and the crowd twenty deep outside now.

'You watch. With Hermann you will get in. You come with me, and look like you might be from the newspaper.'

Docilely I followed the big, blond German as he bulled his way – as much by his bulk and loud voice as by his imposing uniform – through the crowd. At the door the guard (in *lederhosen*) saluted him and made no effort to prevent my entering at all.

In a moment I found myself in an immense hall, the work of the same Germanic engineering genius that had recently stunned the world with the *Autobahn*. A vaulted metallic ceiling as bright as a mirror reflected with lustrous distortion every detail below. In it one saw the tiled floor, and the tiles, each nearly a foot on a side, formed an enormous image of the small car that had made German industry pre-eminent over half the world. By an artistry hardly less impressive than the wealth and power which had caused this great building to be erected on the exposition grounds in a matter of weeks, the face of the driver of this car could be seen through the windshield – not plainly, but dimly, as one might actually see the features of a driver about to run down the observer; it was, of course, the face of Herr Hitler.

At one side of this building, on a dais, sat the 'customers', those carefully selected social and political notables whose good fortune it would be to have the 'People's Car' demonstrated personally to them by no less a person than the German nation's leader. To the right of this, upon a much lower dais, sat the representatives of the press, identifiable by their cameras and notepads, and their jaunty, sometimes lightly shabby, clothing. It was towards this group that Herr Goering boldly conducted me, and I soon identified (I believe I might truthfully say, 'before we were halfway there') the man he had mentioned when we were outside.

He sat in the last row, and somehow seemed to sit higher than the rest; his chin was upon his hands, which in turn were folded on the handle of his stick. His remarkable face, broad and rubicund, seemed to suggest both the infant and the bulldog. One sensed here an innocence, an unspoiled delight in life, coupled with that courage to which surrender is not, in the ordinary conversational sense, 'unthinkable', but is actually never thought. His clothes were expensive and worn, so that I would have imagined he might be a valet save that they fit him so perfectly, and that something about him forbade his ever having been anyone's servant save, perhaps, the King's.

'Herr Churchill,' said Goering, 'I have brought you a friend.'

His head lifted from his stick and he regarded me with keen blue eyes. 'Yours,' he asked, 'or mine?'

'He is big enough to share,' Goering answered easily. 'But for now I leave him with you.'

The man on Churchill's left moved to one side and I sat down.

'You are neither a journalist nor a panderer,' Churchill rumbled.

'Not a journalist because I know them all, and the

panderers all seem to know me – or say they do. But since
I have never known that man to like anyone who wasn't
one of the second or be civil to anyone except one of the
first, I am forced to ask how the devil you did it.'

I began to describe our game, but I was interrupted
after five minutes or so by the man sitting in front of me,
who without looking around nudged me with his elbow
and said, 'Here he comes.'

The *Reichschancellor* had entered the building, and,
between rows of *Sturmsachbearbeiters* (as the elite sales
force was known), was walking stiffly and briskly towards
the centre of the room; from a balcony fifty feet above
our heads a band launched into *Deutschland, Deutschland
über alles* with enough verve to bring the place down,
while an American announcer nearby me screamed to
our compatriots on the far side of the Atlantic that Herr
Hitler was *here*, that he was even now, with commend-
able German punctuality, nearing the place where he was
supposed to be.

Unexpectedly a thin, hooting sound cut through the
music – and as it did the music halted as abruptly as
though a bell jar had been dropped over the band. The
hooting sounded again, and the crowd of onlookers
began to part like tall grass through which an approaching animal, still unseen, was making its way. Another
hoot, and the last of the crowd, the lucky persons who
stood at the very edge of the cordoned-off area in which
the *Reichschancellor* would make his demonstrations,
parted, and we could see that the 'animal' was a small,
canary-yellow 'People's Car', as the *Reichschancellor* approached the appointed spot from one side, so did this
car approach him from the other, its slow, straight course
and bright colour combining to give the impression of a

personality at once docile and pert, a pleasing and fun-
damentally obedient insouciance.

Directly in front of the notables' dais they met and
halted. The 'People's Car' sounded its horn again, three
measured notes, and the *Reichschancellor* leaned forward, smiled (almost a charming smile because it was
so unexpected), and patted its hood; the door opened
and a blonde German girl in a pretty peasant costume
emerged; she was quite tall, yet she had – as everyone
had seen – been comfortably seated in the car a moment
before. She blew a kiss to the notables, curtsied to
Hitler, and withdrew; the show proper was about to
begin.

I will not bore the readers of this magazine by rehears-
ing yet again those details they have already read so
often, not only in the society pages of *The Times* and
other papers but in several national magazines as well.
That Lady Woolberry was cheered for her skill in backing
completely around the demonstration area is a fact already, perhaps, too well known. That it was discovered
that Sir Henry Braithewaite could not drive only after he
had taken the wheel is a fact hardly less famous. Suffice it
to say that things went well for Germany; the notables
were impressed, and the press and the crowd attentive.
Little did anyone present realise that only after the last of
the scheduled demonstrations was History herself to
wrest the pen from Tattle. It was then that Herr Hitler
made one of the unexpected and indeed utterly unfore-
seeable intuitive decisions for which he is famous. (The
order, issued from Berchtesgaden at a time when nothing
of the kind was in the least expected, and, indeed, when
every commentator believed that Germany would be
content, at least for a time, to exploit the economic

suzerainty she had already gained in Eastern Europe and elsewhere, by which every 'People's Car' sold during May, June, and July would be equipped with Nordic Sidewalls at no extra cost comes at once to mind.) Having exhausted the numbers, if not the interest, of the nobility, Herr Hitler turned towards the press dais and offered a demonstration to any journalist who would step forward.

The offer, as I have said, was made to the dais at large; but there was no doubt – there could be no doubt – for whom it was actually intended; those eyes, bright with fanatic energy and the pride natural to one who commands a mighty industrial organisation, were locked upon a single placid countenance. That man rose and slowly, without speaking a word until he was face to face with the most powerful man in Europe, went to accept the challenge; I shall always remember the way in which he exhaled the smoke of his cigar as he said: 'I believe this is an automobile?'

Herr Hitler nodded. 'And you,' he said, 'I think once were of the high command of this country. You are Herr Churchill?'

Churchill nodded. 'During the Great War,' he said softly, 'I had the honour – for a time – of filling a post in the Admiralty.'

'During that time,' said the German leader, 'I myself was a corporal in the Kaiser's army. I would not have expected to find you working now at a newspaper.'

'I was a journalist before I ever commenced being a politician,' Churchill informed him calmly. 'In fact, I covered the Boer War as a correspondent with a roving commission. Now I have returned to my old trade, as a politician out of office should.'

'But you do not like my car?'

'I fear,' Churchill said imperturbably, 'that I am hopelessly prejudiced in favour of democratically produced products – at least, for the people of the democracies. We British also manufacture a small car, you know – the Centurion.'

'I have heard of it. You put water in it.'

By this time the daises were empty. We were, to the last man and woman, and not only the journalists but the notables as well, clustered about the two (I say, intentionally, *two*, for greatness remains greatness even when stripped of power) giants. It was a nervous moment, and might have become more so had not the tension been broken by an unexpected interruption. Before Churchill could reply we heard the sibilant syllables of a Japanese voice, and one of the toy automobiles from Imperial Nippon came scooting across the floor, made as though to go under the yellow 'People's Car' (which it was much too large to do), then veered to the left and vanished in the crowd of onlookers again. Whether it was madness that seized me at the sight of the speeding little car, or inspiration, I do not know – but I shouted, 'Why not have a race?'

And Churchill, without an instant's delay, seconded me: 'Yes, what's this we hear about this German machine? Don't you call it the race master?'

Hitler nodded. '*Ja*, it is very fast, for so small and economical a one. Yes, we will race with you, if you wish.' It was said with what seemed to be perfect poise; but I noted, as I believe many others did, that he had nearly lapsed into German.

There was an excited murmur of comment at the *Reichschancellor*'s reply, but Churchill silenced it by raising his cigar. 'I have a thought,' he said. 'Our cars, after all, were not constructed for racing.'

'You withdraw?' Hitler asked. He smiled, and at that moment I hated him.

'I was about to say,' Churchill continued, 'that vehicles of this size are intended as practical urban and suburban transportation. By which I mean for parking and driving in traffic – the gallant, unheralded effort by which the average Englishman earns his bread. I propose that upon the circular track which surrounds these exposition grounds we erect a course which will duplicate the actual driving conditions the British citizen faces – and that in the race the competing drivers be required to park every hundred yards or so. Half the course might duplicate central London's normal traffic snarl, while the other half simulates a residential neighbourhood; I believe we might persuade the Japanese to supply us with the traffic using their driverless cars.'

'Agreed!' Hitler said immediately. 'But you have made all the rules. Now we Germans will make a rule. Driving is on the right.'

'Here in Britain,' Churchill said, 'we drive on the left. Surely you know that.'

'My Germans drive on the right and would be at a disadvantage driving on the left.'

'Actually,' Churchill said slowly, 'I had given that some consideration before I spoke. Here is what I propose. One side of the course must, for verisimilitude, be lined with shops and parked lorries and charabancs. Let the other remain unencumbered for spectators. Your Germans, driving on the right, will go clockwise around the track, while the British drivers, on the left—'

'Go the other direction,' Hitler exclaimed. 'And in the middle – *ZERSTOREND GEWALT!*'

'Traffic jam,' Churchill interpreted coolly. 'You are not afraid?'

The date was soon set – precisely a fortnight from the day upon which the challenge was given and accepted. The Japanese consented to supply traffic with their drone cars, and the exposition officials to cooperate in setting up an artificial street on the course surrounding the grounds. I need not say that excitement was intense; an American firm, Movietone News, sent not less than three crews to film the race, and there were several British newsreel companies as well. On the appointed day excitement was at a fever pitch, and it was estimated that more than three million pounds had been laid with the bookmakers, who were giving three to two on the Germans.

Since the regulations (written, largely, by Mr Churchill) governing the race and the operation of the unmanned Japanese cars were of importance, and will, in any event, be of interest to those concerned with logical games, allow me to give them in summary before proceeding further. It was explained to the Japanese operators that their task would be to simulate actual traffic. Ten radio-controlled cars were assigned (initially) to the 'suburban' half of the course (the start for the Germans, the home-stretch for the British team), while fifty were to operate in the 'urban' section. Eighty parking positions were distributed at random along the track, and the operators – who could see the entire course from a vantage point on one of the observation decks of the dirigible tower – were instructed to park their cars in these for fifteen seconds, then move onto the course once more and proceed to the next unoccupied position according to the following formula: if a parking space were in the urban sector it was to be assigned a 'distance value' equal to its actual distance from the operator's machine, as determined by counting the green 'distance lines' with which the course was striped at five-yard intervals – but if a parking position were in the suburban section of the track, its distance value was to be the counted distance plus two. Thus the 'traffic' was biased – if I may use the expression – towards the urban sector. The participating German and English drivers, unlike the Japanese, were required to park in every position along the route, but could leave each as soon as they had entered it. The spaces between positions were filled with immobile vehicles loaned for the occasion by dealers and the public, and a number of London concerns had erected mock buildings similar to stage flats along the *parking* side of the course.

I am afraid I must tell you that I did not scruple to make use of my slight acquaintance with Mr Churchill to gain admission to the paddock (as it were) on the day of the race. It was a brilliant day, one of those fine early spring days of which the west of England justly boasts, and I was feeling remarkably fit, and pleased with myself as well. The truth is that my game with Lansbury was going very satisfactorily indeed; putting into operation the suggestions I had received from Herr Goering I had overrun one of Lansbury's most powerful domains (France) in just four moves, and I felt that only stubbornness was preventing him from conceding the match. It will be understood then that when I beheld Mr Churchill hurrying in my direction, his cigar clamped between his teeth and his old Homburg pulled almost about his ears, I gave him my broadest smile.

He pulled up short, and said, 'You're Goering's friend, aren't you – I see you've heard about our drivers.'

I told him I had heard nothing.

'I brought five drivers with me – racing chaps who had volunteered. But the Huns have protested about them. They said their own drivers were going to have to be *Sturmsachbearbeiters*, and it wasn't sporting to run professionals against them; the exposition committee has sided with them, and now I'm going to have to get up a scratch team to drive for England. All amateurs – I can offer them nothing but blood, toil, tears and sweat, and those blasted SS are nearly professional calibre. I've got three men but I'm still one short even if I drive myself . . .'

For a moment we looked at one another; then I said: 'I have never raced, but my friends all tell me I drive too fast, and I have survived a number of accidents; I hope you don't think my acquaintance with Herr Goering would tempt me to abandon fair play if I were enlisted for Britain.'

'Of course not.' Churchill puffed out his cheeks. 'So you drive, do you? May I ask what marque?'

I told him I owned a Centurion, the model the British team would field; something in the way he looked at me and drew on his cigar told me that he knew I was lying – and that he approved.

I wish that my stumbling pen could do justice to the race itself, but it cannot. With four others – one of whom was Mr Churchill – I waited with throbbing engine at the British starting line. Behind us, their backs towards us, were the five German *Sturmsachbearbeiters* in their

'People's Cars'. Ahead of us stretched a weirdly accurate imitation of a London street, wherein the miniature Japanese cars already dodged back and forth in increasing disorder.

The starting gun sounded and every car shot forward; as I jockeyed my little vehicle into its first park I was acutely aware that the Germans, having entered at the suburban end of the course, would be making two or three positions to our one. Bumpers crumpled and tempers flared, and I – all of us – drove and parked, drove and parked, until it seemed that we had been doing it forever. Sweat had long since wilted my shirt collar, and I could feel the blisters growing on my hands; then I saw, about thirty yards in front of me, a tree in a tub – and a flat painted to resemble, not a city shop but a suburban villa. It dawned on me then – it was as though I had been handed a glass of cold champagne – that we *had not yet met the Germans*. We had not yet met them, and the demarcation was just ahead, the halfway point. I knew then that we had won.

Of the rest of the race, what is there to say? We were two hundred yards into the suburban sector before we saw the slanted muzzle of the first 'People's Car'. My own car finished dead last – among the British team – but fifth in the race when the field was taken as a whole, which is only to say that the British entries ran away with everything. We were lionised (even I); and when *Reichschancellor* Hitler himself ran out onto the course to berate one of his drivers and was knocked off his feet by a Japanese toy, there was simply no hope for the German 'People's Car' in the English-speaking world. Individuals who had already taken dealerships filed suits to have their money returned, and the first ships carrying 'People's Cars' to reach London (Hitler had ordered them to sail well in advance of the race, hoping to exploit the success he expected with such confidence) simply never unloaded. (I understand their cargo was later sold cheaply in Morocco.)

All this, I realise, is already well known to the public; but I believe I am in a position to add a postscript which will be of special interest to those whose hobby is games.

I had, as I have mentioned, explained the game Lansbury and I had developed to Mr Churchill while we were waiting for the demonstrations of the 'People's Car' to begin, and had even promised to show him how we played if he cared to come to my rooms; and come he did, though it was several weeks after the race. I showed him our board (the map shellacked over) and regretted that I could not also show him a game in progress, explaining that we had just completed our first, which (because we counted the great War as *one*) we called World War Two.

'I take it you were victorious,' he said.

'No, I lost – but since I was Germany that won't discomfort you, and anyway I would rather have won that race against the real Germans than all the games Lansbury and I may ever play.'

'Yes,' he said. 'Never have so many owed so much to you – at least, I suppose not.'

Something in his smile raised my suspicions; I remembered having seen a similar expression on Lansbury's face (which I really only noticed afterwards) when he persuaded me that he intended to make his invasion of Europe by way of Greece; and at last I blurted out: 'Was that race really fair? I mean to say – we did surprisingly well.'

'Even you,' Churchill remarked, 'beat the best of the German drivers.'

'I know,' I said. 'That's what bothers me.'

He seated himself in my most comfortable armchair and lit a fresh cigar. 'The idea struck me,' he said, 'when that devilish Japanese machine came scooting out while I was talking to Hitler. Do you remember that?'

'Certainly. You mean the idea of using the Japanese cars as traffic?'

'Not only that. A recent invention, the transistor, makes those things possible. Are you by any chance familiar with the operating principle of the transistor?'

I said that I had read that in its simplest form it was merely a tiny chip or flake of material which was conductive in one direction only.

'Precisely so,' Churchill puffed his cigar. 'Which is only to say that electrons can move through the stuff more readily in one direction than in another. Doesn't that seem remarkable? Do you know how it is done?'

I admitted that I did not.

'Well, neither did I before I read an article in *Nature* about it, a week or two before I met Herr Hitler. What the sharp lads who make these things do is to take a material called germanium – or silicon will do as well, though the transistor ends up acting somewhat differently – in a very pure state, and then add some impurities to it. They are very careful about what they put in, of course. For example, if they add a little bit of antimony the stuff they get has more electrons in it than there are places for them to go, so that some are wandering about loose all the time. Then there's other kinds of rubbish – boron is one of them – that makes the material have more spots for electrons than electrons to occupy them. The experts call the spots "holes", but I would call them "parking places", and the way you make your transistor is to put the two sorts of stuff up against each other.'

'Do you mean that our track was . . .'

Churchill nodded. 'Barring a little terminological inexactitude, yes I do. It was a large transistor – primitive if you like but big. Take a real transistor now. What happens at the junction point where the two sorts of material come together? Well, a lot of electrons from the side that has them move over into the side that doesn't – there's so much more space there for them, you see.'

'You mean that if a car – I mean an electron – tries to go the other way, from the side where there are a great many parking places—'

'It has a difficult time. Don't ask me why, I'm not an electrical engineer, but some aspects of the thing can't be missed by anyone, even a simple political journalist like myself. One is that the electron you just mentioned is swimming upstream, as it were.'

'And we were driving downstream,' I said. 'That is, if you don't mind my no longer talking about electrons.'

'Not at all. I pass with relief from the tossing sea of cause and theory to the firm ground of result and fact. Yes, we were driving with the current, so to speak; perhaps it has also occurred to you that our coming in at the urban end, where most of the Japanese cars were, set up a wave that went ahead of us; we were taking up the spaces, and so they were drawn towards the Germans when they tried to find some and of course a wave of that sort travels much faster than the individuals in it. I suppose a transistor expert would say that by having like charges we repelled them.'

'But eventually they would pile up between the teams –

I remember that the going did get awfully thick just about when we passed through the Germans.'

'Correct. And when that happened there was no further reason for them to keep running ahead of us – the Jerries were repelling them too by then, if you want to put it that way – and then the rules (my famous distance formula, if you recall) pulled them back into the urban area, where the poor Huns had to struggle with them some more while we breezed home.'

We sat silent for a time; then I said, 'I don't suppose it was particularly honest; but I'm glad you did it.'

'Dishonesty,' Churchill said easily, 'consists in violating rules to which one has – at least by implication – agreed. I simply proposed rules I felt would be advantageous, which is diplomacy. Don't you do that when you set up your game?' He looked down at the world map on the table. 'By the way, you've burnt your board.'

'Oh, there,' I said. 'Some coals fell from Lansbury's pipe towards the end of the game – they cost us a pair of cities in south Japan, I'm afraid.'

'You'd better be careful you don't burn up the whole board next time. But speaking of the Japanese, have you heard that they are bringing out an automobile of their own? They received so much attention in the press in connection with the race that they're giving it a name the public will associate with the toy motorcars they had here.'

I asked if he thought that that would mean Britain would have to beat off a Japanese invasion eventually, and he said that he supposed it did, but that we Americans would have to deal with them first – he had heard that the first Japanese-made cars were already being unloaded in Pearl Harbor. He left shortly after that, and I doubt that I will ever have the pleasure of his company again, much though I should like it.

But my story is not yet finished. Readers of this magazine will be glad to learn that Lansbury and I are about to begin another game, necessarily to be prosecuted by mail, since I will soon be leaving England. In our new struggle the United States, Britain, and China will oppose the Union of Soviet Socialist Republics, Poland, Romania, and a number of other Eastern European states. Since Germany should have a part in any proper war, and Lansbury would not agree to my having her again, we have divided her between us. I shall try to keep Mr Churchill's warning in mind, but my opponent and I are both heavy smokers.

Sincerely,
'Unknown Soldier'

Editor's Note. While we have no desire to tear aside the veil of the *nom de guerre* with which 'Unknown Soldier' concluded his agreeable communication, we feel we are yet keeping faith when we disclose that he is an American officer of Germanic descent, no longer young (quite) and yet too young to have seen action in the Great War, though we are told he came very near. At present 'Unknown Soldier' is attached to the American embassy in London, but we understand that, as he feels it unlikely his country will ever again have need of military force within his lifetime, he intends to give up his commission and return to his native Kansas, where he will operate an agency for Buick motorcars. Best of luck, Dwight.

FIFI AND THE CHILEAN TRUFFLE

Orson Welles

This is the story of a crisis that could have spiralled into a world war but for an unexpected intervention. The author was one of the most multitalented men of this century, who triumphed at everything he turned his hand to – broadcaster, actor, screenwriter, producer, the list is almost endless. Even as a child Orson Welles was apparently outstanding at poetry, painting, cartooning, playing the piano and performing magic. Small wonder that he should have succeeded as a short-story writer, too, as this historical episode, written with his own brand of irony and wit, clearly shows. The only sadness is that the author did not write more of the same.

Orson Welles (1915–85) was born in Kenosha, Wisconsin, the second son of a wealthy inventor and a beautiful concert pianist, and showed precocious gifts from infancy. Acting had a special attraction for him, and after graduating in 1931 he travelled to Ireland where he convinced the director of the famous Gate Theatre in Dublin that he was a star of the New York stage and landed a leading role in a major production of Jew Suss. Once launched on his career, he never looked back, although it was his first film, Citizen Kane *(1941), that established his enduring reputation. When, after several box office failures, he fell out with Hollywood and moved to Europe, he continued to appear in films – including the classic*

The Third Man *(1949)* – *as well as producing, and in 1955 he started work in Paris on a humorous adaptation of* Don Quixote *which was sadly never completed.*

In 1975, after almost three decades of voluntary exile, Welles returned to America where he was given the American Film Institute's Life Achievement Award. Thereafter he enjoyed the remaining years of his life as a widely admired prodigal son. 'Fifi and the Chilean Truffle' was written in 1956 and first published in Ellery Queen's Mystery Magazine *where, as one might expect of Orson Welles, it was hailed as the best comic story of the year.*

There was once a truffle that almost started a world war. Not a 'trifle' – truffle. *Tuber Melanosporum* – the black things they put into goose livers. Pigs dig for them, but they almost never get to eat them. Any pig you're likely to find rooting about under an oak tree in the French Province of Perigord is bound to be heavily chaperoned by a keen-eyed farmer with a pocketful of corn. The pig gets the corn, and what the farmer gets for the truffle is a pretty penny (or '*joli sou*').

That Shakespeare among chefs, Brillat-Savarin, referred to the truffle as 'the black diamond of the kitchen' – and the little roots are priced accordingly.

In the autumn months optimistic porkers in Northern Italy turn up an outstandingly succulent 'white' truffle – actually a lovely, clouded grey. These are grated into silky paper-thin flakes and heaped over the fluffy *risottos* of Milan. But luckily these superb rarities are seasonal, and travel poorly – and thereby hangs my tale.

It happened in Paris and the tragic hero was a Minister in the French Cabinet.

The villain was a truffle.

This truffle was neither black nor white.

'It pretends,' said Henri, the Minister's chef, 'to be grey. But in point of fact, it is the most abominable green.'

The truffle was, moreover, enormous. It was the size of a cantaloupe and it came from Chile, where the father of the Minister's wife had once been *en poste*.

This lady's childhood memories of Chilean truffles were so glamorous that she had pulled strings, and the striking example now under her chef's suspicious eye had been flown all the way from Santiago to Paris in the diplomatic pouch.

His Excellency the Minister had at first mistaken it for some exotic meteorological specimen, while the First Under-Secretary, with a nice flair for melodrama, took the precaution of immersing the truffle in a tub of water under the impression that it was a bomb.

Madame, the Minister's wife, lost no time in setting everybody straight. As they well knew, an official dinner of the highest importance was to be given that very evening.

'It is July,' she pointed out. 'The white truffles of Italy are not to be found, and people eat black truffles every day.'

This last, of course, was not strictly accurate, but her husband contented himself with hinting that perhaps his honoured guests, being dignitaries from Soviet Russia, would not, during their brief stay in Paris, have already become sated to the point of boredom with French truffles.

'The truffle of Chile,' said Madame with finality, 'is a pleasing novelty. Inform the chef to use it with the sole.' And with this she leaves our story, for the dinner was a stag affair.

'It would not be wise,' said the Minister with typical understatement, 'to disregard my wife's wishes. And besides, the Russians will not know the difference.'

But the chef, a man of vivid temperament, was not to be placated. 'Think of the responsibility!' he cried, holding the mossy truffle at arm's length. 'Sixteen high-ranking dignitaries of the Soviet Union! Suppose they die?'

'Now, now, Henri, don't make a drama of it.'

'Drama?' – first placing the truffle gingerly on the floor, Henri started waving his arms – 'Drama? Let me assure Your Excellency that to involve such vegetable growth in a fish sauce, and to feed it to a group of men schooled in the most direct methods of political action – that is not to make drama, but to encourage tragedy!'

'He is thinking,' said the First Under-Secretary in a discreet undertone, 'of reprisals.'

'Well, now, Henri, don't forget the Ministry is behind you.'

'Your Excellency forgets to what I owe my first loyalty.'

'Naturally, your professional pride—'

'Not at all. I refer to my position as a member of the Communist Party.'

It had slipped the Cabinet Minister's mind that his chef was a Communist. 'That does make it awkward, doesn't it?'

'I am already suspected of deviationism,' said Henri. 'Imagine my fate if so much as one minor gastric upset—'

'Henri, my wife stands behind those truffles.'

'She is a brave woman, Your Excellency.'

'Now if one of you,' said the Minister, 'would care to act as a guinea-pig—'

There followed an uneasy silence disturbed only by the asthmatic snufflings of Fifi, an aged Peke.

'It boils down to this,' the Minister resumed, staring bleakly out of the window, 'we have the choice of poisoning the entire Soviet delegation or defying the express wishes of my wife. Either contingency is un-thinkable. Fifi! Come back with that!'

The Pekingese had seized upon the truffle, and was worrying it drearily across the parquet floor. The First Under-Secretary jumped forward as Fifi dug her teeth into the vegetable's greenish flesh; but suddenly the First Under-Secretary stopped – the dog was chewing, with evident relish, a generous hunk of the Chilean delicacy. And a terrible look had come into the Minister's eye.

'Long ago,' he said, speaking in tones he generally reserved for funerals of the highest pomp, 'this elderly and ailing beast should have been put quietly away. Give it another piece of truffle. Should it survive until dinner we are safe to proceed with the menu as planned by my wife. But should Fifi perish – it will be in a good cause: the security of the Republic of France.'

By dinner time everyone was breathing easier. Fifi was perhaps the only exception. Not that the truffle hadn't agreed with her, it had; but in the evening hours Fifi's asthma was always a bit troublesome. The Minister let her out to graze in the garden and turned back with a light heart to receive his guests.

A bare hour later the Comrade Vice-Commissar of Soviet Fisheries was already on his feet proposing a toast to peace. Henri had turned the hated truffle into one of his most subtle triumphs, chopping it with shallots and mushrooms into a sauce of white wine thickened with butter and yolks of eggs.

To a man the Russians had mopped their plates with bread and asked for more, and now, over his second glass

of an excellent champagne, the Minister was congratu-
lating himself on a diplomatic success when the First
Under-Secretary slipped a pencilled note under his hand.
The message read simply:

'FIFI IS DEAD.'

The Minister mumbled his excuses and rushed into the
kitchen.

'Call an ambulance!' he cried. 'If the Russians die here
in the Ministry it will bring down the Government!'

His hand froze on the telephone. One ambulance
would scarcely be adequate: there were sixteen in the
delegation. The vision of sixteen ambulances, each bearing its Soviet diplomat, screaming and clanging out of
the Quai d'Orsay, was quickly replaced with a mental
tableau of sixteen distinguished corpses in sixteen
hearses surging endlessly down the Champs Elysées in
what would certainly be the most well-attended funeral
in history. Every Communist in Europe would march in
that procession; there would be a general strike, and
then—

In the dining-hall another Comrade Commissar could
be heard proposing another toast. 'I give you,' he said,
'the French Revolution.'

'That,' thought the Minister, 'is precisely what we're
going to get.' With sixteen honoured guests of the
Republic struck down at an official dinner in cold
blood, revolution was only the beginning – this was
war!

Dessert was just about to be served when a trustworthy
doctor, under the strictest oath of secrecy, was smuggled
into the Ministry and put to work with Henri in the
kitchen. There are, it seems, only two effective antidotes
for truffle poisoning, and it was felt that neither of them

was sufficiently tasteless to risk introducing in the 'Bombe Surprise'. Obviously the antidotes would have to be surreptitiously administered and if world peace was to be preserved it could only be with the coffee.

'Turkish coffee,' the First Under Secretary urged, 'Café Diable – laced with heavy spirits. Henri must arrange it.'

The chef, mindful of his own responsibilities as a good Communist, laboured mightily.

'Try some tabasco,' suggested the Minister, 'or a bit of curry powder.'

'Your Excellency,' said Henri spitting out a spoonful of the brew, 'at one period of the Occupation I was implicated in a pâté of very young kittens. One has one's resources, but they are now exhausted: the effluvia of the clinic persists. Send for the stomach pumps and the priests – I know my limitations!' And here the good man burst into tears of despair.

At this black moment there entered the Third Under-Secretary. He knew nothing of the present diplomatic contretemps, for his rank was not such as to admit him to the banquet. 'I have been speaking to Madame,' he said, 'on the phone. She was most upset over the news about Fifi—'

The Minister cut him off with an impatient gesture. 'We are *all* upset,' he said. 'Indeed, we've felt the loss most keenly.'

'Madame asks me to request that you fire the assistant gardener.'

'This is hardly the moment for domestic trivialities. My God, man, we're on the brink of—'

'But the gardener left the gate open, and you know how Fifi always *would* run after cars—'

The Minister seized the Third Under-Secretary by the

lapel of his coat, a lapel which will shortly be brightened with the rosette of the Legion of Honour.

'You mean—' asked the Minister.

'Yes, the poor old thing tried it just once too often. A big delivery truck. Death was instantaneous. It was very sad.'

THE WASTREL

Peter Sellers

Peter Sellers was another great show business talent who wrote the occasional humorous short story, now lost in the newspapers and magazines of his time. One tale he delighted in repeating was how he got his first acting job – by phoning a producer and recommending himself for a part using the voices of two well-known actors! His story 'The Wastrel', which appeared originally in the London Evening News *in 1958, is a bit of a spoof, too, on the old-established stiff-upper-lip Englishman – in this instance, an old military buffer with a ne'er-do-well son. It is a comic gem, full of the kind of absurdity and word-play which were Sellers' hallmarks as an actor.*

Richard Henry Sellers, alias Peter Sellers (1925–80), was born in Southsea and got his first taste of the world of entertainment when his parents featured him in their comedy act. At 13 he won a talent contest telling jokes, and during his war service in the RAF he often appeared as a camp entertainer. It was on BBC Radio that he first came to national prominence in The Goon Show *co-starring with Spike Milligan, Michael Bentine and Harry Secombe. Here he began to develop the diverse personalities and voices which really flourished once he entered the world of films in the early 1950s. Brilliant performances in such comedies as* The Lady

Killers *(1955),* I'm All Right Jack *(1959) and* The Pink
Panther *(1963) in which he turned the accident-prone Inspector* Jacques Clouseau *into a contemporary icon, made him
an international star. Sellers later worked in Hollywood,
starring memorably in* Doctor Strangelove *(1963), and
was rarely out of the newspapers, thanks to his various
romantic entanglements and the long-running series of hugely
successful Pink Panther movies which continued after his
death. He can almost be seen and heard performing 'The
Wastrel' as he teases us towards the final twist of his hilarious
parody.*

On a hot and rainy July afternoon in the year 1901
General Sir Charles Hanley-Adamant sat brooding, the
long thin legs of a hunting man stretched out before him,
in the long, oak-panelled dining-rooms of Coplands, the
country home of the Hanley-Adamants for nigh on four
centuries.

In every angular line of him there was something
significant of one of England's country gentlemen, the
pride of many closely knit generations. But at this particular moment his physiognomy was clouded.

With a heavy sigh he ran his hands through his rapidly
thinning hair and, as he did so, rose jerkily from his
armchair until he was very nearly erect. After a moment
or two he lurched, his beautifully shod splay feet making
no perceptible sound on the thick pile of carpets, to the
window and gazed lackadaisically out. He seemed to be
on the point of coming to a momentous decision.

Outside the rain beat a ceaseless tattoo on the bent
back of old Chambers, the head gardener who, with the
deceptive ease born of long practice, was busily engaged
in spraying both the roses and himself with a secret

preparation that had been handed down to him from time immemorial.

Suddenly a kind of muffled sob burst involuntarily from the General's lips and his wife, Lady Cicely who, until this moment and for the past three hours had been industriously, but to little practical purpose, plying her needle, looked up in concern from the music-stool on which she was sitting.

'Did you say something, Charles?' she queried, not without some solicitude.

'No, no, it was nothing – nothing at all, I assure you. I beg of you to dismiss the matter from your mind entirely. It is of no consequence whatsoever.'

With the awkward grace which invariably accompanied nearly all her movements, Lady Cicely Hanley-Adamant set down her embroidery and glided swiftly to her husband's side with a rustle of silk, chiffon and bombasine.

'Something is wrong, Charles,' she urged, grasping her spouse by the upper part of one of his skinny arms. 'I can sense it. Tell me if you will. Have I not always been the one to share your confidences, thereby, to however small a degree, lightening them?'

'It is your son,' he finally managed to ejaculate thickly.

'Lance?' faltered Lady Cicely.

'Who else?' returned the General mechanically.

'I merely wondered, that is all,' vouchsafed his better half somewhat timidly. 'Why, has he done something to distress you, Charles?'

The General made an impatient gesture which sent a small cutglass bowl of antirrhinums whizzing through the French windows.

'It is no use,' he groaned aloud. 'I can stand it no

longer. I will not have a wastrel and a milksop for a son. As the last of a great and proud line he has certain responsibilities – but what has he done since being sent down from Cambridge? Nothing! Nothing but skulk in his room scribbling poetry and slouch about the place like a pickpocket!'

Instantly Lady Cicely sprang to the defence of her only child. 'But surely, Charles,' she temporised desperately, in a wheedling tone, 'you are aware as well as anyone that Lance is – well – sensitive and not quite as other boys.'

A close observer would have seen a vein beginning to throb in the venerable warrior's left temple.

'My mind is quite made up,' was the curt rejoinder. 'As you know his uncle has recently been good enough to offer him gainful employment in the City, and I have decided that either he takes advantage of this opportunity or I renounce him entirely. This is your son's final chance!'

Lady Cicely gave a pathetic little cry and swayed slightly before slithering carefully to the floor in a swoon. Tried beyond endurance the General yanked savagely at the bell-sash and tottered from the room.

After tea that day, in the selfsame room, still half-stunned by the information which had only seconds before been imparted to him, Lance Hanley-Adamant, a comely, well-set youth with a loosely knit face which did little or nothing to belie the thirty-nine summers that rode so easily on his sloping shoulders, stood aghast in a loosely cut pepper-and-salt knickerbocker suit before the stern-visaged author of his being.

'I say, really, look here, dash it all, Pater, it's a bit bally thick on a fellow and all that sort of rot, I mean to say . . .' he blurted lamely.

'Silence, sir!' exploded the General. 'How dare you adopt that tone with me! You have heard the terms of my ultimatum. Either you will do what I have said, or I shall have nothing more to do with you and this house will be barred to you forever. There is no more to be said.'

For a second or two the young fellow stood like one transfixed. His pointed chin worked nervously and there was a look in his eyes that was not easy to understand.

'You really mean that, Pater?' he breathed.

'I am not in the habit, as far as I am aware, of saying what I don't mean,' was the sardonic reply.

There was a short, but pregnant, silence broken only by the sound of a muffled explosion from the wine cellar. Lance Hanley-Adamant seemed to be trying to realise the full significance of his father's words. He was evidently fighting an inward battle too.

Suddenly he reeled and turned the colour of white-wash.

'But what about Ethel?' he cried hoarsely. Pursing his lips, General Sir Charles Hanley-Adamant, his face assuming an even graver mien, leaned back in his chair and, having made one or two abortive attempts at placing the tips of his fingers judiciously together, decided in favour of abandoning the project.

'Ah,' he observed with as much crispness as he could muster to cover his momentary confusion. 'I am glad that you have brought up the matter of your fiancée.'

There followed another short, albeit pregnant, silence, this time broken only by the sound of someone falling downstairs.

'You are no doubt doubtless aware,' continued the older man, 'that I was more than gratified when you first began to pay attention to Ethel Edgbaston. It was what both her father and I had long hoped for. But George Edgbaston naturally has to think for his daughter. I received a letter from him by this morning's post.'

A new light shone in the young fellow's eyes.

'What did he say?' he enquired hoarsely, eagerly, anxiously.

For a full minute, perhaps less, father and son eyed each other askance.

'He says,' returned the General icily, 'that he will have no idle, indolent, listless, useless, moon-struck, dawdling, loitering, footling, dabbling, fribbling, fiddle-faddling ninny as a husband for his daughter. Furthermore, he declares that, until you turn over a new leaf, his doors will also be closed against you.'

'He says that?'

'Yes.'

'But Ethel will stand by me. I know!' babbled the distracted youth. 'I must hasten to her at once!'

A curious smile played about the grim features of his sire.

'It is a trifle late for that,' asseverated that worthy drily. 'Ethel Edgbaston has already been dispatched to stay with relatives in the country for an indefinite period.'

Again Lance reeled, turning even whiter than before. Then, by a supreme effort of will, he regained some of his composure.

'I still cannot do what you ask.' The words appeared to be jerked out of him.

'You are aware of the alternative?' persisted the other.

'Yes, goodbye, Pater,' was the only reply.

With bowed head and leaden gait, Lance Hanley-Adamant somehow stumbled blindly through the door.

On the dramatic scene which took place at Coplands

that night between the parents of Lance Hanley-Adamant there is no need to dwell at length. In fact, there is no need to dwell upon it at all.

Months dragged wearily by and nothing was heard of the prodigal.

Of course, during the whole of this unhappy time, there raged far away in South Africa, the South African War.

Then, suddenly, it was rumoured in Society circles that someone resembling Lance had been seen drilling in a private's uniform, with almost uncanny lack of precision, at Wellington Barracks.

And Lady Cicely, far too excited to keep the news to herself, rashly divulged it to her husband.

'I thought I had made it perfectly clear,' declared Sir Charles, 'that I did not wish to hear his name mentioned again.'

'Yes, yes, I know, Charles,' pleaded the mother, 'but I can't help it. Besides, if it is true, it is a noble thing he has done. He has offered his life for what he believes to be right.'

'As to that,' returned the father harshly, 'many of the greatest scapegoats in the country have gone into the army. Young fools, knowing nothing of what war means and posing as heroes. And consider it! A son of mine a private! A friend of every groom, bootblack, potboy, crossing-sweeper and shop-walker in his regiment. But it's just like him.'

As a matter of fact it turned out that it actually wasn't Lance Hanley-Adamant who had been seen drilling in a private's uniform at Wellington Barracks.

We shall, therefore, never know the identity of the unfortunate warrior who *was* seen drilling etc., etc., and even supposing that we did, it is extremely doubtful whether any of us would be a penny the wiser.

I suppose you will be wanting to know what happened to our hero in the end. But that is another story entirely, and, much as I should like to, I really don't feel quite strong enough to go into it just at the moment.

℩

♌

A
3

MALICE IN BLUNDERLAND

Cases of Crime

mac

STIRRING THE POT

Tom Sharpe

Tom Sharpe is surely the most popular comic novelist of his time. No one writes better farces, crammed with bizarre characters ranging from the Blimpish right to the Loony left. Nor can many others match his ability to make crime amusing and murder funny. With incidents such as the discovery by Walden Yapp in Ancestral Vices (1980) of the body of a dead dwarf in the boot of his car, he demonstrates that the crime mystery need not always be deadly serious – if you'll excuse the pun. It is a viewpoint with which I heartily concur, and the evidence of the stories in this final part of the book amply bears it out. Sharpe, however, has always insisted that there is nothing too far-fetched in his stories. He quotes the occasion, during his days as a photographer in South Africa, when he was sent to cover a witchcraft killing and found two men, totally unmoved by the grisly discovery of a skinned torso without a head, arms or legs, who were calmly going about their business of stuffing an otter. And, he relates, still grinning at the memory, how when one of the men decided at lunchtime that the stuffed otter was not good enough, he took it home for his wife to cook!

Tom Sharpe (1928–) has been described as 'Wodehouse on acid', a comparison he enjoys with the writer he most admires. Born in South Africa, he was educated at Lancing College and Cambridge University, served in the Royal Marines, and then *returned to his native country where he was variously a social worker, teacher and a press photographer in Pietermaritzburg. Finally, in 1961, one indiscretion too many caused him to be deported. He had already begun writing, but it was not until he was settled in Bridport in 1971 that he discovered his talent as a farceur and produced* Riotous Assembly *in just three weeks. It has been followed by eleven more of the funniest novels being written today. 'Stirring the Pot', one of Tom Sharpe's few short stories, was written for* The Daily Telegraph *in 1994, and apart from the usual selection of grotesques, features what is arguably the strangest and most potentially menacing newspaper advertisement ever to appear in a tale of blundering in maliceland.*

It was an unusual advertisement. DEAF MUTE REQUIRED FOR CHAIN-SAW WORK. ESN TEENAGER PREFERRED.

'I'm buggered if I'm putting that in,' muttered Mr Potter, the advertising manager of the *Lexham Gazette*, when he saw it. 'Major Grail again, I suppose?'

Miss Bleyne nodded. 'Comes of him being a recluse. He's out of touch with the present.'

'Out of something. Next time he comes in, tell him to wait for me.'

'I'll try, Mr Potter, but he's ever so difficult. He says he's like Time.'

'Time? What on earth does he mean by that?'

'I think he means he waits for no man.'

Mr Potter looked at her suspiciously. There were moments, more frequently of late, when he had the impression Miss Bleyne was taking the mickey. He went upstairs to consult the editor.

'Unholy Grail's at it again,' he said, thrusting the offending copy on the desk.

Mr Wellstead ignored it. 'What the hell does banausic mean?' he asked.

'Banausic? That's not in the advert.'

'It's in this letter from Miss Roach about the horrors of hunting,' he said and looked at the advert.

'Fairly offensive,' he said. 'Still, it could give us a good headline. MAJOR RISKS LIFE OF TEENAGE HALFWIT ought to raise circulation nicely.'

Mr Potter shuddered.

'In the hands of a teenage moron it could do other things. We could be seen as accessories before an exceedingly nasty fact.'

Mr Wellstead considered this slight problem.

'All right, check it with Ponson first for liability,' he said. If he gives it the say-so, we'll print.'

Mr Potter went out and, ignoring the solicitor's office, headed for the bar of the Ram. Mr Ponson was in his usual place with a brandy and water, marking the racing page of the *Telegraph*. Potter sat down beside him.

'And what can I do for the *Lexham Gazette* this bright and cheerful morning?' Mr Ponson asked.

'Wellstead wants your opinion about Major Grail's latest.'

'Seems a bit odd to me,' said Mr Ponson, when he'd read the advert. 'The Mad Major must intend cutting down Warden's Wood.'

'Using a simple-minded deaf mute with a chain-saw?' said Potter.

'Got to find someone to do it.'

'I daresay, but why the deaf mute?'

Mr Ponson applied himself to the problem.

'See what you mean,' he said finally. 'The poor devil

couldn't exactly scream for help if he did himself a mischief, could he?'

'Don't,' said Potter, visualising a scene of speechless carnage.

'Only trying to weigh up the pros and cons,' said Mr Ponson, and signalled for another brandy.

'Can't you just come down on the side of the cons?'

'It's rather an interesting point of law all the same. Wellstead's worried about liability, is he?'

'Circulation,' said Potter. 'Thinks we're competing with the bloody *Sun*. Anything to push up sales. If it weren't for Lady Bartrey, we'd have full-frontals on page three. Her and the vicar.'

'Full-frontals of La Bartrey and the vicar? What a horrible thought. Now that would lead to an action under the obscenity laws. I'd advise Wellstead to forget it.'

'Yes,' said Potter, thanking God the editor hadn't yet thought of it and wondering at the same time if Mr Ponson added brandy to his early-morning tea. 'Can I tell him to forget the chain-saw massacre too?'

'The what?' said Mr Ponson, still occupied with the dreadful vision of Lady Bartrey full-frontal.

'The Major's advert,' said Potter, stifling a 'For God's sake'.

'Oh that. I must say I can't see anything legally wrong with it. Quite harmless. Stands to reason no one's going to reply. Can't if they're educationally subnormal. Won't be able to read it in the first place and couldn't write a letter even if they did.'

Mr Potter went back to his office despondently. 'The old soak says we can go ahead,' he told Miss Bleyne. 'All the same I think we'll shove it under Agricultural Implements to be on the safe side. No one looking for a job is going to see it there.'

'If you say so, Mr Potter.'

That was Tuesday. On Thursday he came in from lunch to hear Mr Wellstead shouting into the phone on the floor above.

'Mr Wellstead's ever so angry,' said Miss Bleyne.

'I can hear that,' said Potter, as the editor told someone he wasn't going to be called an insensitive swine.

'I can't think what it's about,' said Miss Bleyne. Potter could.

Two minutes later Mr Wellstead burst through the door.

'I suppose you enjoyed listening to that?' he shouted. 'I suppose you think it's funny to hear me called a . . .' He checked himself and glanced at Miss Bleyne. 'All right Potter, I'll discuss this in my office.'

Potter followed him miserably upstairs.

'Now then, you blithering idiot, do you know what you've just done?'

Potter swallowed drily. 'Not precisely.'

'Then shall I tell you?' said Mr Wellstead.

'Am I to take it Major Grail is somewhat put out?' said Potter hoping to delay the explosion. The editor advanced on him.

'Major Grail? The hell with Major Grail. That was the RSPCA. They've had a flood of complaints about that insane advert. My phone hasn't stopped ringing.'

'The RSPCA? Surely you mean the NSPCC?' Potter began but the editor silenced him.

'No I don't. If you put teenage morons with chain-saws in Pets & Livestock you get the . . .'

'Pets & Livestock?'

'Dogs, Cats, Rabbits and assorted Pets,' Mr Wellstead yelled. 'So why in God's name . . .'

'But I thought . . .'

But Mr Wellstead was past listening. 'Thought? Thought?' he bawled. 'You didn't think. You aren't capable of thought. You wouldn't know a thought if it was stuffed under your snout on a bleeding plate.'

Potter thought about handing in his resignation. Mr Wellstead forestalled him.

'Let me tell you this, Potter. If you want to keep your job, you won't even try to think. You'll do exactly what barking lunatics like Major bloody Grail and I . . . You'll do what I tell you to. Is that clear?'

'Yes,' said Potter and looked hopefully at the door. But Mr Wellstead hadn't finished. 'Some damned official from the Education Department calls me up and dresses me down like I was some sadistic monster,' he continued before correcting himself. 'As though I was. She's even got me talking like an ignoramus. Said we had set a terrible example of uncaringness for the educationally challenged.' He paused and looked at Potter almost pathetically. 'Why the Pets & Livestock section, of all places?'

'Hang on a moment,' said Potter and went downstairs.

Miss Bleyne fiddled with her nail file. As usual she had nothing to do. 'I just thought it would look more cuddly like, in with bunnies and hamsters instead of with turnip cutters and the muck spreader old Mr Foulless has been trying to sell.'

Potter went back upstairs and explained this to the editor.

'She may be right at that,' Mr Wellstead admitted. 'I can't begin to imagine what that Education cow would have said if we'd put a mentally challenged dummy down as an Agricultural Implement.'

That was Thursday. On Monday the editor was even more distraught.

'You look awful,' Potter said intentionally when he met Mr Wellstead in the car park.

'You'd feel awful if you'd spent the early hours being shouted at by a madman in New York.'

'God,' said Potter, regretting his unkindness.

'Exactly. God,' said Wellstead. 'The Almighty's taking a personal interest. And we all know what that means, don't we, Potter?'

Potter nodded dumbly. Mr Wellstead went on.

'Wanted to know what the hell I'd done to provoke all these complaints to head office. Nearly a thousand faxes, letters galore, phone calls. You name it. The works.'

'A thousand faxes? I don't believe it. Not a thou . . .'

'Of course it's not true,' said Mr Wellstead. 'But when did truth matter to God?'

'You'd think he'd be pleased with an outcry. Always gone for it before in his national dailies.'

'The proprietor's forte is not consistency. Nor is taste. Remember his Christmas Message last year; "Dig the Dirt on the Virgin Birth"?'

'Christ,' said Potter. 'No wonder they call him the Digger.'

'Pay dirt pays,' said Mr Wellstead. 'Now get out. I want to think.'

Downstairs Potter picked up *The Times*. There were days even now when he dreamt of getting a job on a respectable paper. Anything to get out of Lexham. Idly he turned to job vacancies and instead found the Obituary page. Opposite him Miss Bleyne went on pretending to type. It was then that he saw the small notice. He read it through several times.

'Miss Bleyne . . .' he began and stopped. There was no point in asking her directly.

'Yes, Mr Potter?'

'Do you ever get bored, Miss Bleyne? I mean frantically, almost terminally bored?' he said. She looked at him curiously and said nothing. 'I only ask because Major Grail's just died in Switzerland after a long illness bravely borne.'

THE SUICIDE OF KIAROS

L. Frank Baum

*This story offers a striking contrast to Tom Sharpe's bizarre
tale. It is a deadly serious, locked room mystery, written by the
man for ever associated with a trio of the most fabulous comic
characters in literature: the Wizard of Oz, the Tin Woodman
and the Cowardly Lion. L. Frank Baum's* The Wonderful
Wizard of Oz *(1900) – which, incidentally, provided the
inspiration for the title of my first comic fantasy collection,*
The Wizards of Odd *(1996) – is one of the best known
fantasy novels of all time. With its various sequels, it made
the author famous and his world 'somewhere over the rainbow' immortal. Baum also wrote a number of fantasies under
pen-names such as Floyd Akers, Schuyler Staunton and Edith
Van Dyne, which remain to be unearthed, but 'The Suicide of
Kiaros', which appeared in a long-forgotten magazine,* The
White Elephant, *in September 1897, is unlike anything else
from his pen with its portrait of a cold and calculating bank
cashier. It does, however, contain a strong vein of irony, which
enabled me to include it in this collection, returning it to print
for the first time in more than half a century.*

*Lyman Frank Baum (1856–1919) was born in New York
and struggled to make a living as a journalist until 1899,
when he wrote a book entitled* Father Goose *which became a
bestseller, apparently selling as many as a thousand copies a*

day in the first three months after publication. The following year The Wonderful Wizard of Oz *established his reputation beyond doubt, being acclaimed by one of the leading American critics, Edward Wagenknecht, us 'the first distinctive attempt to construct a fairyland out of American materials.' A stage musical in 1901, with David Montgomery and Fred Stone, followed by the film version in 1939 starring Judy Garland, Ray Bolger, Bert Lahr, Jack Haley and Frank Morgan as the Wizard, confirmed the story as a modern fantasy classic. Baum's story, Ozma of Oz (1907), is also something of a landmark in the genre because it introduces the intelligent clockwork man, Tik-Tok, one of the first robots in fiction. In 'The Suicide of Kiaros', there may be nothing new about what is in the mind of cold-hearted Felix Marston, but the story itself is undoubtedly unique in the career of one of the masters of fantasy fiction.*

Mr Felix Marston, cashier for the great mercantile firm of Van Alsteyne & Traynor, sat in his little private office with a balance sheet before him and a frown upon his handsome face. At times he nervously ran his slim fingers through the mass of dark hair that clustered over his forehead, and the growing expression of annoyance upon his features fully revealed his disquietude.

The world knew and admired Mr Marston, and a casual onlooker would certainly have decided that something had gone wrong with the firm's financial transactions; but Mr Marston knew himself better than the world did, and grimly realised that although something had gone very wrong indeed, it affected himself in an unpleasantly personal way.

The world's knowledge of the popular young cashier included the following items: He had entered the firm's employ years before in an inferior position, and by energy, intelligence and business ability had worked his way up until he reached the post he now occupied, and became his employers' most trusted servant. His manner was grave, earnest and dignified; his judgement, in business matters, clear and discerning. He had no intimate friends, but was courteous and affable to all he met, and his private life, so far as it was known, was beyond reproach. Mr Van Alstcyne, the head of the firm, conceived a warm liking for Mr Marston, and finally invited him to dine at his house. It was there the young man first met Gertrude Van Alsteyne, his employers' only child, a beautiful girl and an acknowledged leader in society. Attracted by the man's handsome face and gentlemanly bearing the heiress encouraged him to re-peat his visit, and Marston followed up his advantage so skillfully that within a year she had consented to become his wife. Mr Van Alsteyne did not object to the match. His admiration for the young man deepened, and he vowed that upon the wedding day he would transfer one-half his interest in the firm to his son-in-law.

Therefore the world, knowing all this, looked upon Mr Marston as one of fortune's favourites, and predicted a great future for him. But Mr Marston, as I said, knew himself more intimately than did the world, and now, as he sat looking upon that fatal trial balance, he muttered in an undertone:

'Oh, you fool – you fool!'

Clear-headed, intelligent man of the world though he was, one vice had mastered him. A few of the most secret, but most dangerous gambling dens knew his face well. His ambition was unbounded, and before he had even dreamed of being able to win Miss Van Alsteyne as his bride, he had figured out several ingenious methods of winning a fortune at the green table. Two years ago he had found it necessary to 'borrow' a sum of money from the firm to enable him to carry out these clever methods. Having, through some unforeseen calamity, lost the money, another sum had to be abstracted to allow him to win back enough to even the accounts. Other men have attempted this before; their experiences are usually the same. By a neat juggling of figures, the books of the firm had so far been made to conceal the thefts, but now it seemed as if fortune, in pushing him forward, was about to hurl him down a precipice.

His marriage to Gertrude Van Alsteyne was to take place in two weeks, and as Mr Van Alsteyne insisted upon keeping his promise to give Marston an interest in the business, the change in the firm would necessitate a thorough overhauling of the accounts, which meant discovery and ruin to the man who was about to grasp a fortune and a high social position – all that his highest ambition had ever dreamed of attaining.

It is no wonder that Mr Marston, brought face to face with his critical position, denounced himself for his past folly, and realised his helplessness to avoid the catastrophe that was about to crush him.

A voice outside interrupted his musings.

'It is Mr Marston I wish to see.'

The cashier thrust the sheet of figures into a drawer of the desk, hastily composed his features, and opened the glass door beside him.

'Show Mr Kiaros this way,' he called, after a glance at his visitor. He had frequently met the person who now entered his office, but he could not resist a curious glance as the man sat down on a chair and spread his hands over his knees. He was short and thick-set in form and both oddly and carelessly dressed, but his head and face were most venerable in appearance. Flowing locks of pure white graced a forehead whose height and symmetry denoted unusual intelligence, and a full beard of the same purity reached almost to his waist. The eyes were large and dark, but not piercing in character, rather conveying in their frank glance kindness and benevolence. A round cap of some dark material was worn upon his head, and this he deferentially removed as he seated himself and said:

'For me a package of value was consigned to you, I believe?'

Marston nodded gravely. 'Mr. Williamson left it with me.'

'I will take it,' announced the Greek, calmly. 'Twelve thousand dollars it contains.'

Marston started. 'I knew it was money,' he said, 'but was not aware of the amount. This is it, I think.'

He took from the huge safe a packet, corded and sealed and handed it to his visitor. Kiaros took a penknife from his pocket, cut the cords and removed the wrapper, after which he proceeded to count the contents.

Marston listlessly watched him. Twelve thousand dollars. That would be more than enough to save him from ruin, if only it belonged to him instead of this Greek money-lender.

'The amount, it is right,' declared the old man, rewrapping the parcel of notes. 'You have my thanks, sir. Good afternoon,' and he rose to go.

'Pardon me, sir,' said Marston, with a sudden thought. 'It is after banking hours. Will it be safe to carry this money with you until morning?'

'Perfectly,' replied Kiaros. 'I am never molested, for I am old, and few know my business. My safe at home large sums often contains. The money I like to have near me, to accommodate my clients.'

He buttoned his coat tightly over the packet, and then in turn paused to look at the cashier.

'Lately you have not come to me for favours,' he said.

'No,' answered Marston, arousing from a slight reverie. 'I have not needed to. Still, I may be obliged to visit you again soon.'

'Your servant I am pleased to be,' said Kiaros with a smile, and turning abruptly he left the office.

Marston glanced at his watch. He was engaged to dine with his betrothed that evening, and it was nearly time to return to his lodgings to dress. He attended to one or two matters in his usual methodical way, and then left the office for the night, relinquishing any further duties to his assistant. As he passed through the various business offices on his way out, he was greeted respectfully by his fellow-employees, who already regarded him a member of the firm.

Almost for the first time during their courtship, Miss Van Alsteyne was tender and demonstrative that evening, and seemed loath to allow him to leave the house when he pleaded a business engagement and arose to go. She was a stately beauty, and little given to emotional ways, therefore her new mood affected him greatly, and as he walked away he realised, with a sigh, how much it would cost him to lose so dainty and charming a bride.

At the first corner he paused and examined his watch by the light of the street lamp. It was 9 o'clock. Hailing the first passing cab, he directed the man to drive him to the lower end of the city, and leaning back upon the cushions, he became occupied in earnest thought.

The jolting of the cab over a rough pavement finally aroused him, and looking out he signalled the driver to stop.

'Shall I wait, sir?' asked the man, as Marston alighted and paid his fare.

'No.'

The cab rattled away, and the cashier retraced his way a few blocks and then walked down a side street that seemed nearly deserted, so far as he could see in the dim light. Keeping track of the house numbers, which were infrequent and often nearly obliterated, he finally paused before a tall, brick building, the lower floors of which seemed occupied as a warehouse.

'Two eighty-six,' he murmured. 'If I remember right there should be a stairway at the left – ah, here it is.'

There was no light at the entrance, but having visited the place before, under similar circumstances, Marston did not hesitate, but began mounting the stairs, guiding himself in the darkness by keeping one hand upon the narrow rail. One flight – two – three – four—

'His room should be straight before me,' he thought, pausing to regain his breath. 'Yes, I think there is a light shining under the door.'

He advanced softly, knocked, and then listened. There was a faint sound from within, and then a slide in the upper panel of the door was pushed aside, permitting a strong ray of lamp-light to strike Marston full in the face.

'Oho!' said a calm voice, 'Mr Marston has honoured me. To enter I entreat you.'

The door was thrown open and Kiaros stood before him, with a smile upon his face, gracefully motioning him to advance. Marston returned the old man's courteous bow, and entering the room, took a seat near the table, at the same time glancing at his surroundings.

The room was plainly but substantially furnished. A small safe stood in a corner at his right, and near it was the long table, used by Kiaros as a desk. It was littered with papers and writing material, and behind it was a high-backed, padded easy-chair, evidently the favourite seat of the Greek, for after closing the door he walked round the table and sat in the big chair, facing his visitor.

The other end of the room boasted a fireplace, with an old-fashioned mantel bearing an array of curiosities. Above it was a large clock, and at one side stood a small bookcase containing a number of volumes printed in the Greek language. A small alcove, containing a couch, occupied the remaining side of the small apartment, and it was evident these cramped quarters constituted Kiaros's combined office and living-rooms.

'So soon as this I did not expect you,' said the old man, in his grave voice.

'I am in need of money,' replied Marston, abruptly, 'and my interview with you this afternoon reminded me that you have sometimes granted me an occasional loan. Therefore I have come to negotiate with you.'

Kiaros nodded, and studied with his dark eyes the composed features of the cashier.

'A satisfactory debtor you have ever proved,' said he, 'and to pay me with promptness never failed. How much do you require?'

'Twelve thousand dollars.'

In spite of his self-control, Kiaros started as the young man coolly stated this sum.

'Impossible!' he ejaculated.

'Why is it impossible?' demanded Marston. 'I know you have the money.'

'True; I deny it not,' returned Kiaros. 'Also to lend money is my business. But see – I will be frank with you, Mr Marston – I cannot take the risk. You are cashier for hire; you have no property; security for so large a sum you cannot give. Twelve thousand dollars! It is impossible!'

'You loaned Williamson twelve thousand,' persisted Marston.

'Mr Williamson secured me.'

Marston rose from his chair and began slowly pacing up and down before the table, his hands clasped tightly behind him and an impatient frown contracting his features. The Greek watched him calmly.

'Perhaps you have not heard, Mr Kiaros,' he said at length, 'that within two weeks I am to be married to Mr Van Alsteyne's only daughter.'

'I had not heard.'

'And at the same time I am to receive a large interest in the business as a wedding gift from my father-in-law.'

'To my congratulations you are surely entitled.'

'Therefore my need is only temporary. I shall be able to return the money within thirty days, and I am willing to pay you well for the accommodation.'

'So great a chance I cannot undertake,' returned Kiaros, with a slight shrug. 'You are not yet married, a partner in the firm not yet. To die, to quarrel with the lady, to lose Mr Van Alsteyne's confidence, would leave me to collect a sum wholly unable. I might a small amount risk – the large amount is impossible.'

Marston suddenly became calm, and resumed his chair with a quiet air, to Kiaros's evident satisfaction.

'You have gambled?' asked the Greek, after a pause.

'Not lately. I shall never gamble again. I owe no gambling debts – this money is required for another purpose.'

'Can you not do with less?' asked Kiaros. 'An advance I will make of one thousand dollars; not more. That sum is also a risk, but you are a man of discretion; in your ability I have confidence.'

Marston did not reply at once. He leaned back in his chair, and seemed to be considering the money-lender's offer. In reality there passed before his mind the fate that confronted him, the scene in which he posed as a convicted felon; he saw the collapse of his great ambitions, the ruin of those schemes he had almost brought to fruition. Already he felt the reproaches of the man he had robbed, the scorn of the proud woman who had been ready to give him her hand, the cold sneers of those who gloated over his downfall. And then he bethought himself, and thought of other things.

Kiaros rested his elbow upon the table and toyed with a curious-looking paper-cutter. It was made of pure silver, in the shape of a dagger; the blade was exquisitely chased and bore a Greek motto. After a time Kiaros looked and saw his guest regarding the papercutter.

'It is a relic most curious,' said he, 'from the ruins of Missolonghi rescued, and by a friend sent to me. All that is Greek I love. Soon to my country I shall return, and that is why I cannot risk the money I have in a lifetime earned.'

Still Marston did not reply, but sat looking thoughtfully at the table. Kiaros was not impatient. He continued to play with the silver dagger, and poised it upon his finger while he awaited the young man's decision.

'I think I shall be able to get along with the thousand dollars,' said Marston at last, his tone showing no trace of the disappointment Kiaros had expected. 'Can you let me have it now?'

'Yes, as you know, the money is in my safe. I will make out the note.'

He quietly laid down the paper-cutter and drew a notebook from a drawer of the table. Dipping a pen into the inkwell, he rapidly filled out the note and pushed it across the table to Marston.

'Will you sign?' he asked, with his customary smile.

Marston picked up the pen, dashed off his name, and tossed the paper toward Kiaros. The Greek inspected it carefully, and rising from his chair, walked to the safe and threw open the heavy door. He placed the note in one drawer, and from another removed an oblong tin box which he brought to the table. Reseating himself, he opened this box and drew out a large packet of bank-notes.

Marston watched him listlessly as he carefully counted out $1,000.

'The amount is, I believe, correct,' said Kiaros, after a second count. 'If you will kindly verify it I shall be pleased.'

Marston half arose and reached out his hand. But he did not take the money. Instead, his fingers closed over the handle of the silver dagger, and with a swift, well-directed blow he plunged it to the hilt in the breast of the Greek. The old man lay back in his chair with a low moan, his form quivered once or twice, and then became still, while a silence that suddenly seemed oppressive pervaded the little room.

*　　*　　*

Felix Marston sat down in his chair and stared at the form of Kiaros. The usually benevolent features of the Greek were horribly convulsed, and the dark eyes had caught and held a sudden look of terror. His right hand, resting upon the table, still grasped the bundle of banknotes. The handle of the silver dagger glistened in the lamplight just above the heart, and a dark-coloured fluid was slowly oozing outward and discolouring the old man's clothing and the point of his snowy beard.

Marston drew out his handkerchief and wiped the moisture from his forehead. Then he arose, and going to his victim, carefully opened the dead hand and removed the money. In the tin box was the remainder of the $12,000 the Greek had that day received. Marston wrapped it all in a paper and placed it in his breast pocket. Then he went to the safe, replaced the box in its drawer, and found the note he had just signed. This he folded and placed carefully in his pocket-book. Returning to the table, he stood looking down upon the dead man.

'He was a very good fellow, old Kiaros,' he murmured. 'I am sorry I had to kill him. But this is no time for regrets; I must try to cover all traces of my crime. The reason most murderers are discovered is because they become terrified, are anxious to get away; and so leave clues behind them. I have plenty of time. Probably no one knows of my visit here tonight, and as the old man lives alone, no one is likely to come here before morning.'

He looked at his watch. It was a few minutes after 10 o'clock.

'This ought to be a case of suicide,' he continued, 'and I shall try to make it look that way.'

The expression of Kiaros's face first attracted his attention. That look of terror was incompatible with suicide.

He drew a chair beside the old man and began to pass his hands over the dead face to smooth out the contracted lines. The body was still warm, and with a little perseverance Marston succeeded in relaxing the drawn muscles until the face gradually resumed its calm and benevolent look.

The eyes, however, were more difficult to deal with, and it was only after repeated efforts that Marston was able to draw the lids over them and hide their startled and horrified gaze. When this was accomplished, Kiaros looked as peaceful as if asleep, and the cashier was satisfied with his progress. He now lifted the Greek's right hand and attempted to clasp the fingers over the handle of the dagger, but they fell away limply.

'Rigor mortis has not yet set in,' reflected Marston, 'and I must fasten the hand in position until it does. Had the man himself dealt the blow, the tension of the nerves of the arm would probably have forced the fingers to retain their grip upon the weapon.' He took his handkerchief and bound the fingers over the hilt of the dagger, at the same time altering the position of the head and body to better suit the assumption of suicide.

'I shall have to wait some time for the body to cool,' he told himself, and then he considered what might be done in the meantime.

A box of cigars stood upon the mantel. Marston selected one and lit it. Then he returned to the table, turned up the lamp a trifle, and began searching in the drawers for specimens of the Greek's handwriting. Having secured several of these he sat down and studied them for a few minutes, smoking collectedly the while, and taking care to drop the ashes in a little tray that Kiaros had used for that purpose. Finally, he drew a sheet of paper

towards him, and carefully imitating the Greek's sprawling chirography, wrote as follows:

My money I have lost. To live longer I cannot. To
die I am therefore resolved.

KIAROS

'I think that will pass inspection,' he muttered, looking at
the paper approvingly, and comparing it again with the
dead man's writing. He placed the paper upon the table
before the body of the Greek, and then rearranged the
papers as he had found them.

Slowly the hours passed. Marston rose from his chair at
intervals and examined the body. At 1 o'clock rigor
mortis began to set in, and a half-hour later Marston
removed the handkerchief and was pleased to find that
the hand retained its grasp upon the dagger. The position
of the dead body was now very natural indeed, and the
cashier congratulated himself upon his success.

There was but one task remaining for him to accom-
plish. The door must be found locked upon the inside.
Marston searched until he found a piece of twine, one
end of which he pinned lightly to the top of the table,
a little to the left of the inkwell. The other end of the
twine he carried to the door, and passed it through the
slide in the panel. Withdrawing the key from the lock
of the door, he now approached the table for the last
time, taking a final look at the body, and laying the
end of his cigar upon the tray. The theory of suicide
had been excellently carried out; if only the key could
be arranged for, he would be satisfied. He blew out the
light.

It was very dark, but he had carefully considered the

distance beforehand, and in a moment he had reached the hallway and softly closed and locked the door behind him. Then he withdrew the key, found the end of the twine which projected through the open slide in the panel, and running this through the ring of the key, he passed the key inside the panel and allowed it to slide down the cord until a sharp click told him it rested on the table within. A sudden jerk of the twine now unfastened the end which had been lightly pinned to the table, and he drew it out and carefully placed it in his pocket. Before closing the slide of the panel, Marston lighted a match, peered through the slide and satisfied himself the key was lying in the position he had wished. He breathed more freely then and closed the slide.

A few minutes later he had reached the street, and after a glance up and down stepped boldly from the doorway and walked away.

To his surprise, he now felt himself trembling with nervousness, and despite his endeavours to control himself, it required all of his four-mile walk home to enable him to regain his normal composure.

He let himself in with his latchkey, and made his way noiselessly to his room. As he was a gentleman of regular habits, the landlady never bothered to keep awake for his return.

Mr Marston appeared at the office the next morning in an unusually good humour, and at once busied himself with the regular routine of his bank duties.

As soon as he was able, he retired to his private office and began to revise the books and make out a new trial balance. The exact amount he had stolen from the firm was put into the safe, the false figures were replaced with correct ones, and by noon the new balance sheet proved that Mr Marston's accounts were in perfect order.

Just before he started for luncheon a clerk brought him the afternoon paper.

'What do you think, Mr Marston?' he said. 'Old Kiaros has committed suicide.'

'Indeed! Do you mean the Kiaros who was here yesterday?' inquired Marston, as he put on his coat.

'The very same. It seems the old man lost his money in some unfortunate speculation, and so took his own life. The police found him in his room this morning, stabbed to the heart. Here is the paper, sir, if you wish to see it.'

'Thank you,' returned the cashier, in his usual quiet way. 'I will buy one when I go out,' and without further comment he went to luncheon.

He purchased a paper, and while eating read carefully the account of Kiaros's suicide. The report was reassuring; no one seemed to dream the Greek was a victim of foul play.

The verdict of the coroner's jury completed his satisfaction. They found that Kiaros had committed suicide in a fit of despondency. The Greek was buried and forgotten, and soon the papers teemed with sensational accounts of the brilliant wedding of that estimable gentleman, Mr Felix Marston, to the popular society belle, Miss Gertrude Van Alsteyne. The happy pair made a bridal trip to Europe, and upon their return Mr Marston was installed as an active partner in the great firm for Van Alsteyne, Traynor & Marston.

This was twenty years ago. Mr Marston today has an enviable record of an honourable and highly respected man of business, although some consider him a trifle too calculating.

His wife, although she early discovered the fact that he had married her to further his ambition, has found him reserved and undemonstrative, but always courteous and indulgent to both herself and the children.

He holds his head high and looks every man squarely in the eye, and he is very generally envied, since everything seems to prosper in his capable hands.

Kiaros and his suicide are long since forgotten by the police and the public. Perhaps Marston recalls the Greek at times.

He told me this story when he lay upon what he supposed was his death-bed . . .

℥

THE RAPE OF THE SHERLOCK

A.A. Milne

Sherlock Holmes has probably been parodied, satirised and made the subject of comic misadventures more than any other character in crime fiction. Within a few years of his first appearance in 'A Study in Scarlet' in Beeton's Christmas Annual *for 1887, his cases were being revamped in humorous style with titles like* Shylock Homes: His Posthumous Memoirs *by John Kendrick Bangs in America, and 'The Adventures of Herlock Sholmes' by the British writer Peter Todd. So prolific have these satires become that an American Sherlockian some years ago published a booklet listing all those titles he had been able to locate. One he missed, however, was 'The Rape of the Sherlock' by A.A. Milne, the creator of Winnie-the-Pooh. Milne actually hinted about the story's existence in his autobiography,* It's Too Late Now *written in 1939, when he said, 'Meanwhile, my first free-lance contribution had been accepted. Sherlock Holmes had just "returned" in the* Strand Magazine *after his duel with Moriarty. I wrote a burlesque of this which I sent to* Punch. *They refused it and so I sent it to* Vanity Fair *who paid me fifteen shillings for my "first story".' The date was 15 October, 1903, and although Milne had no way of knowing it, in the future for him lay the creation of a character now every bit as well known as the sleuth of Baker Street.*

Alan Alexander Milne (1882–1956) was born in London and, after attending Cambridge University, began a career in journalism which led to his becoming assistant editor of Punch. *It was the stories and verses written for and featuring his son, Christopher Robin, especially* Winnie-the-Pooh *(1926) and* The House at Pooh Corner *(1928), that eventually made him famous, rather than the plays and essays which he considered far superior. Milne was also something of a fan of crime fiction, and in 1922 published* The Red House Mystery *which has been described as one of the most important books of the Twenties. It introduced a jolly 'what fun!' approach to crime in the person of a zany amateur detective, Anthony Gillingham, nicknamed 'Madman', and Alexander Woollcott even went so far as to describe the book as 'one of the best mysteries of all time'. No doubt encouraged by this, Milne wrote three more novels in the same vein:* The Fourth Wall *(1928),* Four Days' Wonder *(1933), a humorous satire on crime, and* A Table Near the Band *(1950). 'The Rape of the Sherlock', undoubtedly one of the earliest pastiches of the Great Detective, carried a sub-heading as amusing as the story itself: 'Being the Only True Version of Holmes's Adventures'.*

It was in the summer of last June that I returned unexpectedly to our old rooms in Baker Street. I had that afternoon had the usual experience of calling on a patient, and in my nervousness and excitement had lost my clinical thermometer down his throat. To recover my nerve I had strolled over to the old place, and was sitting in my arm-chair thinking of my ancient wound, when all at once the door opened, and Holmes glided wistfully under the table. I sprang to my feet, fell over the Persian slipper containing the tobacco, and fainted. Holmes got into his dressing-gown and brought me to.

'Holmes,' I cried, 'I thought you were dead.'

A spasm of pain shot across his mobile brow.

'Couldn't you trust me better than that?' he asked, sadly. 'I will explain. Can you spare me a moment?'

'Certainly,' I answered. 'I have an obliging friend who would take my practice for that time.'

He looked keenly at me for answer. 'My dear, dear Watson,' he said, 'you have lost your clinical thermometer.'

'My dear Holmes—' I began, in astonishment.

He pointed to a fairly obvious bulge in his throat.

'I was your patient,' he said.

'Is it going still?' I asked, anxiously.

'Going fast,' he said, in a voice choked with emotion.

A twinge of agony dashed across his mobile brow. (Holmes's mobility is a byword in military Clubs.) In a little while the bulge was gone.

'But why, my dear Holmes—'

He held up his hand to stop me, and drew out an old cheque-book.

'What would you draw from that?' he asked.

'The balance,' I suggested, hopefully.

'What conclusion I meant?' he snapped.

I examined the cheque-book carefully. It was one on Lloyd's Bank, half-empty, and very, very old. I tried to think what Holmes would have deduced, but with no success. At last, determined to have a dash for my money, I said:

'The owner is a Welshman.'

Holmes smiled, picked up the book, and made the following rapid diagnosis of the case:

'He is a tall man, right-handed, and a good boxer; a genius on the violin, with an unrivalled knowledge of criminal London, extraordinary powers of perception, a perfectly enormous brain; and, finally, he has been hiding for some considerable time.'

'Where?' I asked, too interested to wonder how he had deduced so much from so little.'

'In Portland.'

He sat down, snuffed the ash of my cigar, and remarked:

'Ah! Flor–de–Dindigul–I–see,–do–you–follow–me–Watson?' Then, as he pulled down his 'Encyclopaedia Britannica' from its crate, he added:

'It is my own cheque-book.'

'But Moriarty?' I gasped.

'There is no such man,' he said. 'It is merely the name of a soup.'

THE WHITE RABBIT CAPER

James Thurber

In this wonderfully off-beat story, James Thurber switches roles with A.A. Milne to present a mystery in which animals are the main characters. Fred Fox is no Winnie-the-Pooh searching for a jar of honey, but a smart private detective who goes looking for a missing white rabbit who may have been killed for her lucky foot. Like Milne, Thurber is perhaps, a surprising writer to be found in the crime section of this book, but in fact he wrote a number of stories on just such themes, including 'Mr Prebble Gets Rid of his Wife' (1935) – or rather he tries to by luring her down into their cellar – 'The Catbird Seat' (1951), concerning Mr Martin's plan to 'rub out' the awful Mrs Ulgine Barrows, and 'The Night the Ghost Got In' (1953), which is rather more about the intervention of the police than the supernatural. None, however, is quite as unusual as 'The White Rabbit Caper' which Thurber wrote for The New Yorker *in 1949, calling it an example of 'what the boys who turn out the mystery programmes on the air might write.'*

James Grover Thurber (1894–1961) was another of the great humorists of the century. His work was especially enlivened by his little sketches, which have been described as being 'like what everyone thinks he can do himself' although they actually possess a unique technique. Thurber once referred to himself as having been born on a night of 'wild portent and high wind' in Columbus, Ohio. He made his reputation on the staff of The New Yorker *where he wrote the influential 'Talk of the Town' column, and this was later assured by the publication of* The Seal in the Bedroom *(1932),* My Life and Hard Times *(1933),* Fables for our Times *(1941) and other equally successful anthologies. Thurber once light-heartedly suggested that 'The White Rabbit Caper' was 'a story for children' – but you are advised not to be fooled: there is comedy here, certainly, and surprises.*

Fred Fox was pouring himself a slug of rye when the door of his office opened and in hopped old Mrs Rabbit. She was a white rabbit with pink eyes, and she wore a shawl on her head, and gold-rimmed spectacles.

'I want you to find Daphne,' she said tearfully, and she handed Fred Fox a snapshot of a white rabbit with pink eyes that looked to him like a picture of every other white rabbit with pink eyes.

'When did she hop the hutch?' asked Fred Fox.

'Yesterday,' said old Mrs Rabbit. 'She is only eighteen months old, and I am afraid that some superstitious creature has killed her for one of her feet.'

Fred Fox turned the snapshot over and put it in his pocket. 'Has this bunny got a throb?' he asked.

'Yes,' said old Mrs Rabbit. 'Franz Frog, repulsive owner of the notorious Lily Pad Night Club.'

Fred Fox leaped to his feet. 'Come on, Grandma,' he said, 'and don't step on your ears. We got to move fast.'

On the way to the Lily Pad Night Club, old Mrs Rabbit scampered so fast that Fred Fox had all he could do to keep up with her. 'Daphne is my great-great-great-great-great-granddaughter, if my memory serves,' said old Mrs Rabbit. 'I have 39,000 descendants.'

'This isn't going to be easy,' said Fred Fox. 'Maybe you should have gone to a magician with a hat.'

'But she is the only one named Daphne,' said old Mrs Rabbit, 'and she lived alone with me on my great carrot farm.'

They came to a broad brook. 'Skip it!' said Fred Fox.

'Keep a civil tongue in your head, young man,' snapped old Mrs Rabbit.

Just as they got to the Lily Pad, a dandelion clock struck 12 noon. Fred Fox pushed the button on the great green door, on which was painted a white water-lily. The door opened an eighth of an inch, and Ben Rat peered out, 'Beat it,' he said, but Fred Fox shoved the door open, and old Mrs Rabbit followed him into a cool green hallway, softly but restlessly lighted by thousands of fireflies imprisoned in the hollow crystal pendants of an enormous chandelier. At the right there was a flight of green-carpeted stairs, and at the bottom of the steps the door to the cloakroom. Straight ahead, at the end of the long hallway, was the cool green door to Franz Frog's office.

'Beat it,' said Ben Rat again.

'Talk nice,' said Fred Fox, 'or I'll seal your house up with tin. Where's the Croaker?'

'Once a gumpaw, always a gumpaw,' grumbled Ben Rat. 'He's in his office.'

'With Daphne?'

'Who's Daphne?' asked Ben Rat.

'My great-great-great-great-great-granddaughter,' said old Mrs Rabbit.

'Nobody's that great,' snarled Ben Rat.

Fred Fox opened the cool green door and went into Franz Frog's office, followed by old Mrs Rabbit and Ben Rat. The owner of the Lily Pad sat behind his desk, wearing a green suit, green shirt, green tie, green socks, and green shoes. He had an emerald tiepin and seven emerald rings. 'Whong you wong, Fonnxx?' he rumbled in a cold, green, cavernous voice. His eyes bulged and his throat began to swell ominously.

'He's going to croak,' explained Ben Rat.

'Nuts,' said Fred Fox. 'He'll outlive all of us.'

'Glunk,' croaked Franz Frog.

Ben Rat glared at Fred Fox. 'You oughta go on the stage,' he snarled.

'Where's Daphne?' demanded Fred Fox.

'Hoong Dangneng?' asked Franz Frog.

'Your bunny friend,' said Fred Fox.

'Nawng,' said Franz Frog.

Fred Fox picked up a cello in a corner and put in down. It was too light to contain a rabbit. The front-door bell rang. 'I'll get it,' said Fred Fox. It was Oliver (Hoot) Owl, a notorious fly-by-night. 'What're you doing up at this hour, Hoot?' asked Fred Fox.

'I'm trying to blind myself, so I'll confess,' said Hoot Owl testily.

'Confess to what?' snapped Fred Fox.

'What can't you solve?' asked Hoot Owl.

'The disappearance of Daphne,' said Fred Fox.

'Who's Daphne?' asked Hoot Owl.

Franz Frog hopped out of his office into the hall. Ben Rat and old Mrs Rabbit followed him.

Down the steps from the second floor came Sherman Stork, carrying a white muffler or something and grinning foolishly.

'Well, bless my soul!' said Fred Fox. 'If it isn't old mid-husband himself! What did you do with Daphne?'

'Who's Daphne?' asked Sherman Stork.

'Fox thinks somebody killed Daphne Rabbit,' said Ben Rat.

'Fonnxx cung brong,' rumbled Franz Frog.

'I *could* be wrong,' said Franz Frog, 'but I'm not.' He pulled open the cloakroom door at the bottom of the steps, and the dead body of a female white rabbit toppled furrily onto the cool green carpet. Her head had been bashed in by a heavy blunt instrument.

'Daphne!' screamed old Mrs Rabbit, bursting into tears.

'I can't see a thing,' said Hoot Owl.

'It's a dead white rabbit,' said Ben Rat. 'Anybody can see that. You're dumb.'

'I'm wise!' said Hoot Owl indignantly. 'I know everything.'

'Jeeng Crine,' moaned Franz Frog. He stared up at the chandelier, his eyes bulging and his mammoth mouth gaping open. All the fireflies were frightened and went out.

The cool green hallway became pitch dark. There was a shriek in the black, and a feathery 'plump'. The fireflies lighted up to see what had happened. Hoot Owl lay dead on the cool green carpet, his head bashed in by a heavy blunt instrument. Ben Rat, Franz Frog, Sherman Stork, old Mrs Rabbit and Fred Fox stared at Hoot Owl. Over the cool green carpet crawled a warm red stain, whose source was the body of Hoot Owl. He lay like a feather duster.

'Murder!' squealed old Mrs Rabbit.

'Nobody leaves this hallway!' snapped Fred Fox. 'There's a killer loose in this club!'

'I am not used to death,' said Sherman Stork.

'Roong!' groaned Franz Frog.

'He says he's ruined,' said Ben Rat, but Fred Fox wasn't

listening. He was looking for a heavy blunt instrument. There wasn't any.

'Search them!' cried old Mrs Rabbit. 'Somebody has a sap or a sock full of sand, or something!'

'Yeh,' said Fred Fox. 'Ben Rat is a sap – maybe someone swung him by his tail.'

'You oughta go on the stage,' snarled Ben Rat.

Fred Fox searched the suspects, but he found no concealed weapon. 'You could have strangled them with that muffler,' Fred Fox told Sherman Stork.

'But they were not strangled,' said Sherman Stork.

Fred Fox turned to Ben Rat. 'You could have bitten them to death with your ugly teeth,' he said.

'But they weren't bitten to death,' said Ben Rat.

Fred Fox stared at Franz Frog. 'You could have scared them to death with your ugly face,' he said.

'Bung wung screng ta deng,' said Franz Frog.

'You're right,' admitted Fred Fox. 'They weren't. Where's old Mrs Rabbit?' he asked suddenly.

'I'm hiding in here,' called old Mrs Rabbit from the cloakroom. 'I'm frightened.'

Fred Fox got her out of the cool green sanctuary and went in himself. It was dark. He groped around on the cool green carpet. He didn't know what he was looking for, but he found it, a small object lying in a far corner. He put it into his pocket and came out of the cloakroom.

'What'd you find, shamus?' asked Ben Rat apprehensively.

'Exhibit A,' said Fred Fox casually.

'Sahng plang keeng,' moaned Franz Frog.

'He says somebody's playing for keeps,' said Ben Rat.

'He can say that again,' said Fred Fox as the front door

was flung open and Inspector Mastiff trotted in, followed by Sergeant Dachshund.

'Well, well, look who's muzzling in,' said Fred Fox.

'What have we got here?' barked Inspector Mastiff.

'I hate a private nose,' said Sergeant Dachshund.

Fred Fox grinned at him. 'What happened to your legs from the knees down, sport?' he asked.

'Drop dead,' snarled Sergeant Dachshund.

'Quiet, both of you!' snapped Inspector Mastiff. 'I know Ollie Owl, but who's the $20 Easter present from Schraftt's?' He turned on Fred Fox. 'If this bunny's head comes off and she's filled with candy, I'll have your badge, Fox,' he growled.

'She's real, Inspector,' said Fred Fox. 'Real dead, too. How did you pick up the scent?'

Inspector Mastiff howled. 'The Sergeant thought he smelled a rat at the Lily Club,' he said. 'Wrong again, as usual. Who's this dead rabbit?'

'She's my great-great-great-great-great-granddaughter,' sobbed old Mrs Rabbit.

Fred Fox lighted a cigarette. 'Oh, no, she isn't, sweetheart,' he said coolly. 'You are *her* great-great-great-great-great-granddaughter.' Pink lightning flared in the live white rabbit's eyes. 'You killed the old lady, so you could take over her carrot farm,' continued Fred Fox, 'and then you killed Hoot Owl.'

'I'll kill you, too, shamus!' shrieked Daphne Rabbit.

'Put the cuffs on her, Sergeant,' barked Inspector Mastiff. Sergeant Dachshund put a pair of handcuffs on the front legs of the dead rabbit. 'Not *her*, you dumb kraut!' yelped Inspector Mastiff. It was too late. Daphne Rabbit had jumped through a windowpane and run away, with the Sergeant in hot pursuit . . .

'All white rabbits look alike to me,' growled Inspector Mastiff. 'How could you tell them apart – from their ears?'

'No,' said Fred Fox. 'From their years. The white rabbit that called on me darn near beat me to the Lily Pad, and no old woman can do that.'

'Don't brag,' said Inspector Mastiff. 'Spryness isn't enough. What else?'

'She understood expressions an old rabbit doesn't know,' said Fred Fox, 'like "hop the hutch" and "throb" and "skip it" and "sap".'

'You can't hang a rabbit for her vocabulary,' said Inspector Mastiff. 'Come again.'

Fred Fox pulled the snapshot out of his pocket. 'The white rabbit who called on me told me Daphne was eighteen months old,' he said, 'but read what it says on the back of this picture.'

Inspector Mastiff took the snapshot, turned it over, and read, ' "Daphne on her second birthday".'

'Yes,' said Fred Fox. 'Daphne knocked six months off her age. You see, Inspector, she couldn't read the writing on the snapshot, because those weren't her spectacles she was wearing.'

'Now wait a minute,' growled Inspector Mastiff. 'Why did she kill Hoot Owl?'

'Elementary, my dear Mastiff,' said Fred Fox. 'Hoot Owl lived in an oak tree, and she was afraid he saw her burrowing into the club last night, dragging Grandma. She heard Hoot Owl say, "I'm wise. I know everything", and so she killed him.'

'What with?' demanded the Inspector.

'Her right hind foot,' said Fred Fox. 'I was looking for a concealed weapon, and all the time she was carrying her heavy blunt instrument openly.'

'Well, what do you know!' exclaimed Inspector Mastiff. 'Do you think Hoot Owl really saw her?'

'Could be,' said Fred Fox. 'I happened to think he was bragging about his wisdom in general and not about a particular piece of information, but your guess is as good as mine.'

'What did you pick up in the cloakroom?' squeaked Ben Rat.

'The final strand in the rope that will hang Daphne,' said Fred Fox. 'I knew she didn't go in there to hide. She went in there to look for something she lost last night. If she'd been frightened, she would have hidden when the flies went out, but she went in there after the flies lighted up again.'

'That adds up,' said Inspector Mastiff grudgingly. 'What was it she was looking for?'

'Well,' said Fred Fox, 'she heard something drop in the dark when she dragged Grandma in there last night and she thought it was a button, or a buckle, or a bead, or a bangle, or a brooch that would incriminate her. That's why she rang me in on the case. She couldn't come here alone.'

'Well, what was it, Fox?' snapped Inspector Mastiff.

'A carrot,' said Fred Fox, and he took it out of his pocket, 'probably fell out of old Mrs Rabbit's reticule, if you like irony.'

'One more question,' said Inspector Mastiff. 'Why plant the body in the Lily Pad?'

'Easy,' said Fred Fox. 'She wanted to throw suspicion on the Croaker, a well-known lady-killer.'

'Nawng,' rumbled Franz Frog.

'Well, there it is, Inspector,' said Fred Fox, 'all wrapped up for you and tied with ribbons.'

Ben Rat disappeared into a wall. Franz Frog hopped back to his office.

'Mercy!' cried Sherman Stork. 'I'm late for an appointment!' He flew to the front door and opened it.

There stood Daphne Rabbit, holding the unconscious form of Sergeant Dachshund. 'I give up,' she said. 'I surrender.'

'Is he dead?' asked Inspector Mastiff hopefully.

'No,' said Daphne Rabbit. 'He fainted.'

'I never have any luck,' growled Inspector Mastiff.

Fred Fox leaned over and pointed to Daphne's right hind foot. 'Owl feathers,' he said. 'She's all yours, Inspector.'

'Thanks, Fox,' said Inspector Mastiff. 'I'll throw something your way someday.'

'Make it a nice, plump Plymouth Rock pullet,' said Fred Fox, and he sauntered out of the Lily Pad . . .

Back in his office, Fred Fox dictated his report on the White Rabbit Caper to his secretary, Lura Fox. 'Period. End of report,' he said finally, toying with the emerald stickpin he had taken from Franz Frog's green necktie when the fireflies went out.

'Is she pretty?' asked Lura Fox.

'Daphne? Quite a dish,' said Fred Fox, 'but I like my rabbits stewed, and I'm afraid little Daphne is going to fry.'

'But she's so young, Fred!' cried Lura Fox. 'Only eighteen months!'

'You weren't listening,' said Fred Fox.

'How did you know she wasn't interested in Franz Frog?' asked Lura Fox.

'Simple,' said Fred Fox. 'Wrong species.'

'What became of the candy, Fred?' asked Lura Fox.

Fred Fox stared at her. 'What candy?' he asked blankly.

Lura Fox suddenly burst into tears. 'She was so soft, and warm, and cuddly, Fred,' she wailed.

Fred Fox filled a glass with rye, drank it slowly, set down the glass, and sighed grimly. 'Sour racket,' he said.

WOT THE EYE DON'T SEE

Stan McMurtry

Another artist and writer, Stan McMurtry, better known to British readers as 'Mac' of the Daily Mail, has one of the most distinctive styles in modern cartooning and, like James Thurber, is an accomplished writer growing in skill with each new story. Aside from his daily cartoons, Mac has written a number of mystery stories which reveal a more serious side to his nature, and he is also working on his first novel, From Eternity to Here. 'Wot The Eye Don't See' makes its debut in print in this book and combines humour and murder in the best tradition of the comic crime story.

Stan McMurtry (1936–) was born in Birmingham and was keen on art from his childhood. After several years working in an art studio and producing animated cartoon commercials for television, he joined the Daily Mail and his work has since become a distinctive and much admired feature in the newspaper. His cartoons use ribald exaggeration to poke fun at pretensions in all manner of people, from leading politicians to everyday figures – milkmen, dustmen (sorry, refuse disposal operatives) and the clergy. He has twice been named Social and Political Cartoonist of the Year, and in 1988 he received the Cartoon Club of Great Britain's top award, 'Cartoonist of the Year'. Mac has also been honoured as one of Britain's Men of the Year for his 'inimitable comments on British social life'.

This said, he enjoys nothing more than sharing a pint in his local pub with friends and retreating to his word processor after his daily cartoon is finished. To those writers who aspire to be cartoonists, Mac is a man to be envied with a foot in both camps – as 'Wot the Eye Don't See' reveals.

It was a mistake taking on a public house, let me be the first to admit it. I tried, I really did, but whatever the ingredients that make up a successful licensee I seem to have been woefully short of them – or to be more truthful, not just short of but completely devoid of. Every man to his own trade, I suppose, and there are many who can do the publican's job admirably, but I'm not one of them.

I am, however, or have been, a jolly good accountant. For most of my life working as a senior in the firm of Goldenby, Smirton and Chobley in the bustling town of Kingsbarton here in Somerset. However, when Mummy died and left me a bit of money I decided, being of an adventurous spirit, to go forth into the outside world away from that of taxes and investments and try something perhaps a little less dull. So when I was pondering what to do with my inheritance, it struck me that the last time I had been in a hostelry, about six years before, it had all seemed terribly jolly. The landlord had been a rosy-faced fellow with a smile and a kind word for everyone, while his customers were prone to clutching one another, laughing uproariously and occasionally bursting into song, very often from a horizontal position. A far cry from Goldenby, Smirton and Chobley. This, I decided, was the life for me.

Imagine my surprise and delight therefore when I discovered in the columns of the *Somerset Bugle*, whilst midway through my morning muesli with dried banana chips, an advertisement proclaiming the sale of the Rat and Ferret public house on Tindersley moor, the very same hostelry in which I had enjoyed a hearty pint so many years before. Providence, it seemed, was looking my way. Within one calendar month I was owner and 'mine host' at this house of revelry and looking forward to a life of fun and gaiety.

On my first night the bar was soon packed, mostly by ruddy-faced farming folk eager to evaluate the new landlord. Huge men with broad backs and massive, calloused hands thrust battered pewter tankards at me for refilling, with such swift regularity that often I was forced to enquire, 'I say, old chap, do you really think you should? This is your third pint, you know.'

Halfway through the evening I called for quiet, then shouted to the assembled throng: 'Hello, everybody. It's awfully nice to see you all here tonight. I do hope we're all going to become jolly good chums. I'd like to add to the general merriment of the evening by telling you a rather naughty joke my father used to tell at his club, involving a donkey, a tulip and a nun.' I proceeded to tell my father's joke, but I suppose as this was our first meeting they were all a little shy, for the laughter was a little subdued. 'Anyway,' I finished off, 'my name is Rupert Ponsonby-Smythe, but all my chums call me Smithy.'

'Well, we'll call you Poncey,' a rough voice cried.

It is every landlord's aim to put his own personal stamp onto his business, and I tried during the next few weeks to make the Rat and Ferret unique among the pubs in the neighbourhood by injecting into it the ingredients of those proven 'good times' which I had experienced during my life. From now on almost every night was to be a 'party night', an opportunity for me to recall some of the wonderful parties I had attended. Mondays, for instance, were to become 'pass the matchbox from nose to nose racing night', a favourite game of my old school chum, Binky Heathrington. Tuesday was 'pass the parcel night', with me adding to the excitement by turning the volume up and down on one of my Mantovani tapes. Wednesday was 'cold spoons down the trousers racing' and so on. The fun could have been enormous. Alas, this modern world has become too preoccupied with electronic and digital games or with merely standing around with a glass in its hand, talking. So, little by little, the attendances at my party nights began to drop and as the weeks progressed, try as I might, greeting every customer with a joke or a merry squirt of water from my fake chrysanthemum button-hole, the place gradually emptied of customers.

The final nail in the coffin of my dream was when, in my desperation to lure the crowds back, I hired two professional entertainers whom I billed as starring in 'a night of wonder at the Rat and Ferret'. To my dismay, part of their act was fire-eating and they set fire to the saloon bar and most of the roof. Within the space of three months I was almost destitute. My insurance policy did not cover damage caused by fire-eaters, my customers had all but deserted me, the breweries would not provide barrels of beer that had not previously been paid for and the pub itself, because of the unrepaired fire damage, was unsaleable.

I was reduced to sitting under the flapping blue plastic tarpaulin that served as a roof, night after boring night, contemplating my fate with the only regular who had not so far deserted me: Jack Jarvis, a man in his mid-seventies with acute halitosis and very little in the way of stimulating conversation. He was, moreover, a person who had to be watched constantly, having a tendency to reach across the bar and help himself to cigarettes, crisps or the occasional bottle of beer. Forgetting to pay for drinks was another of his bad habits. His favourite saying was, 'Wot the eye don't see, the 'eart don't grieve about.'

Jack was my nearest neighbour, living only a short walk from the pub. Until ten years ago he had worked on a farm as a labourer and cowhand. I felt fairly certain that, since downing his shovel and cattleprod, he had not once bathed or changed his clothes. Why he chose to frequent the Rat and Ferret when everyone else had deserted I had no idea, except perhaps his laziness and the proximity of the pub. Whatever, on the stroke of eight o'clock every evening he would appear, bringing with him all the various odours of the farmyard and last night's meal. His usual nightly consumption was five pints of bitter and six packets of cheese and onion crisps.

It was at about this time that fate took a hand.

One Sunday evening Jack arrived a little earlier than usual, and I could tell straight away that there was something different about his appearance. Incredible as it may seem, he had had a wash. True, the dirt that had been in the centre of his face was now at the sides in a thick tide-mark, but no matter, the face had actually been touched by water.

It seemed that the reason for this new-found cleanliness was to celebrate a modest win on that week's National Lottery. Tomorrow he was going to buy a suit. I congratulated him and revealed that I too had been lucky that week and won myself ten pounds, but when I asked the sum of his win all he would divulge was ' 'Tis enough to keep the wolf from the door.' I remember thinking how well I knew that wolf: he had been hammering at my door for months.

However, the following day was Hallowe'en and I had decided to make one last effort to turn my fortunes around and entice the customers back. I had placed posters on every conceivable blank space in the nearby village and on every tree on the road leading to the Rat and Ferret, advertising a grand fancy dress party at the pub with prizes for the best and most frightening costumes. Fun and games, I assured the readers of my posters, were to go on late into the night, starting at 7.30 p.m.

Monday came and at 6.30 so did Jack. At first I thought he was in fancy dress, the effect was so startling, but then I realised that he was wearing his new suit. It was a lovat green, about three sizes too big, complete with waistcoat and sharp creases. Under it was a white shirt with grubby fingermarks on the collar, around which was wound an extremely loud tie with a huge knot. 'Paid for the suit, pinched the waistcoat,' he said proudly. 'They didn't notice.' He tapped his nose. 'Wot the eye don't see, the 'eart don't grieve about.' Peering over the bar I could see that the trousers were tucked into his old, muddy wellington boots.

'Jack,' I said, 'you look wonderful, but you're a bit early for the party.'

'I'm not comin' to any o' your bleedin' parties,' he growled, frowning at the decorations I'd slaved over for hours. Skeletons and witches were pasted to the walls and some papier mâché skulls dangled from the ceiling. In one corner a massive pumpkin leered evilly, spilling candlelight through it's eye sockets and teeth. 'Me son's comin' down.'

'Oh,' I said, 'about your lottery win?'

'Mind yer business!' Jack mumbled. 'And get me a pint.'

Five minutes later a man entered the bar. He was a younger version of Jack – bigger and fatter, but with the same stooped figure as the old man and the same hooked nose and mean, thin-lipped mouth. He was, however, dressed in a sleek charcoal-grey suit and everything about him reeked of money and affluence. I put on my best welcoming smile and gave him my official publican's greeting: 'Eveninsquire, coldout, wattleyooave?' He ignored me and walked unsmiling to where Jack was sitting. 'Hello, father,' he said.

'Vernon!' Jack cried, genuinely pleased. 'Nice to see you, son.'

The newcomer grunted and deftly avoided his father's attempted embrace, shaking his hand instead as one would shake water off a dead fish. Jack stood back and stared appraisingly at his son. 'You're looking so . . . so . . . well heeled,' he said.

Vernon inspected his hand for signs of contagion. 'Hard work, father, hard work. It brings its rewards.' He turned to me: 'What are you hanging about for?'

'I'm the publican,' I said as breezily as I could. 'Have you heard the one about the . . .?'

'Poncey!' Jack warned.

'What would you like to drink?' I asked.

Vernon turned to his father, ignoring me completely. 'Is there somewhere we can talk in private?' he asked.

Jack turned to me. 'Can't you shove off somewhere?'

'No, I can't,' I said indignantly. 'I've got a crowd of people coming in soon.'

'Hah!' Jack snorted.

Vernon looked at his watch. 'Come along, father. You've got some good news for me, I believe. Now where can we talk?'

Jack glared at me, then quaffed down the remains of his pint. 'Come on, then,' he snarled. 'We'll go back to my place.' They walked towards the door, man and son, both graduates of the Attila the Hun school of manners. Jack turned just before leaving and said with a grin, ' 'Ave a nice 'Allowe'en party.' He slammed the door. He'd forgotten to pay for his pint.

Seven o'clock. Just time to get ready for the fray. Upstairs, under the flapping tarpaulin in my bedroom, I painted my face with actors' greasepaint a citrous shade of green, blackened the area around my eyes and with a headband that could be hidden under my hair, clipped on an astonishingly realistic pair of horns. Next I covered my normal clothing with a long black nightshirt complete with sewn-on tail, then stood back to view the finished effect in the mirror. In all modesty, I must say that the reflected image was devastatingly sinister. It was Satan, the ultimate in evil, staring back at me. I was beginning to enjoy myself. I could hardly wait for the crowds to arrive. Picking up my wooden trident I went back downstairs in a state of high excitement.

Alas. Ten o'clock came and I was still alone in the bar. All my efforts had been in vain. My hours of work on the posters and decorations had been a complete waste of time.

It is not a pleasant feeling to be so deeply unpopular; in all my life I have never felt so utterly dejected and desolate. At 10.15, in a rage of self-pity, I tore down the decorations and cast them into the fire, then sat staring at the smouldering pile and contemplated a bleak, impoverished and lonely future.

My eye fell upon the bottle of champagne which would have been the first prize in the fancy dress competition. I thought of Jack Jarvis and his modest lottery win. I pictured him in his ramshackle cottage playing host to his dislikeable son with possibly not a drink in the house, and it was then, fed up as I was, that I decided to present the bottle to him with my congratulations. Besides, I was badly in need of some company, such as it was.

It only took three minutes to reach Jack's cottage. It was a pitch-dark night but I was guided by the solitary light in the grubby window. I was about to knock when I heard Vernon's angry voice scream: 'You can't give it all to charity, what about your family?'

'Family? What family?' Jack's gruff voice replied. 'You keep them all well clear o' me in that posh house o' yours. I wish I 'adn't told you now. Wot the eye don't see the 'eart don't grieve about.'

'You owe it to your family, not bloody charity!'

'I ain't givin' it all to charity. I've told you, I'm settin' the kids up with a 'andsome trust and you and Ethel get twenty thousand apiece.'

'Twenty thousand? You old fool. I can earn that in a month!' Vernon's voice was getting higher and higher in pitch. I felt guilty of eavesdropping but too fascinated to move.

'Don't call me a fool. I'm your father, remember.'

'Father?' Vernon was screaming now. 'You're not a father. You're a dirty old tramp. I don't want Jeremy and Harriet knowing their grandfather never washes and lives in a pig-sty. You smell. D'you know that?'

Jack started shouting now. 'You don't want to know your dirty old father but you want to know about his money, you greedy young . . .'

'Seventeen million pounds and you intend to give it all away? You're not only filthy, you're mad!'

I pressed my ear to the door, my eyes popping with astonishment. Seventeen million? Did I hear correctly?

Jack bellowed: 'If your mother 'ad 'ad one o' they Di and Alice machines, she'd 'ave been alive today. I'm goin' to buy a few o' them for the 'ospitals and I'm goin' to help a few other o' God's forgotten ones, the poor and the 'omeless.'

'What's happened to you? You've never given anything away in your life.'

'I've never been able to until now. You've got enough, Vernon. You're rich. You don't need any more.'

'It's my inheritance!' Vernon screamed, almost bursting my eardrums through the door.

'Inheritance? Inheritance? You don't deserve nothing. You're a lousy son to 'ave. I want to see my grandchildren. I want to come up and spend a week or two with 'em up at your posh house.'

'Never!'

'Right!' Jack bellowed. 'You're disinherited!'

There was a crashing of furniture. 'You stupid old bastard!' Vernon roared. 'Give me that.' Then came a sickening crunching sound like a coconut being hit by a hammer, then silence.

I stood shivering on the doorstep, wondering what to do. Really, this was no way for a father and son to behave. They should calm down, let the atmosphere lighten a little. I wondered whether they would like to hear a joke. Perhaps I should invite them back to the pub for a drink? I was about to knock when the door swung open and Vernon stood on the threshold clutching his father's lottery ticket in one hand and a bloodied candlestick in the other. I waved my trident at him.

'Come with me!' I cried. I was about to add, 'and have a drink at the pub,' but Vernon was backing away making little choking sounds. His face had gone an unusual shade of red and his eyes seemed about to pop from his head.

'I have come for you,' I said.

Vernon sat down, then with a long gurgling noise he fell onto his back and was quite still, staring at the ceiling. 'I say, old chap,' I remember saying, 'I didn't mean to startle you. Are you all right?' But when I approached him it became very clear that Vernon was definitely not all right. In fact Vernon was quite dead and the reason was soon apparent. As I stooped over him in that squalid cottage with its smell of rotten cabbage and dampness, I caught a glimpse of myself in a fly-blown mirror on the wall and nearly jumped out of my skin. I'd quite forgotten that I was still wearing my Hallowe'en costume. The awful realisation dawned upon me that because of my forgetfulness I had frightened poor Vernon to such a degree that he had suffered a fatal heart attack.

I'm never terribly good with sick people. Visiting hospital has always made me feel queasy, so the sight of a dead person was something I felt I was just not up to coping with. Consequently, when I looked across the room and saw Jack sitting up in an armchair with a huge cleft in his skull, one eye down where his nose should be and a mess of butcher's offal seeping from the gaping wound down onto his new suit, I make no exaggeration when I say I felt distinctly off-colour. I decided there and then that a nice cup of tea and an early night back at the Rat and Ferret were what I needed, so saying a polite goodnight to father and son I closed the door and went home.

All this happened several months ago. The murder caused quite a sensation in the papers and the village became alive with journalists, cameramen and TV crews for some time. In fact, business at the Rat and Ferret picked up considerably for that brief period.

The inquest reached the sad conclusion that Jack, in his desperation to see his son, had telephoned to say that he had won money on the lottery and Vernon had killed him in a rage when he had found that the winnings amounted only to ten pounds. The ticket had been found in Vernon's hand. The coroner said he was convinced that the subsequent trauma of killing his father had caused him to have an immediate and massive heart attack.

Meanwhile the lottery organisers agreed to my claim for the jackpot prize of seventeen million, four hundred thousand and sixty-three pounds, to be paid to me anonymously. I've has such fun spending it. I'm sure Jack would have approved. Quite a portion of it has been spent on kidney dialysis machines and a considerable sum on helping the poor and homeless. Vernon's wife, although comfortably off, was sent a small donation to express my sorrow over her losing two of her loved ones. I believe she also claimed the ten pounds.

I had the Rat and Ferret completely restored and

refurbished and realised quite a profit when it was sold. I can't say I'm sorry not to be living in a pub any longer. As I've already mentioned, I don't think I was cut out for the publican's life and I do so like living on my yacht. I wanted to call her: *Wot the eye don't see . . .* , but that's too long a name. I settled instead for *Jackpot*. Rather fitting, I thought.

The captain tells me that by tomorrow we should be moored just outside Barbados. I intend to give the crew a day off, then throw a gigantic party with lots of fun and party games. I know people will turn up. They do at every port of call. I'm so popular now, I've no idea why.

♌

THE CONDEMNED

Woody Allen

The comedy thriller has become of increasing interest to Woody Allen, the brilliant actor, director, screenwriter and playwright whose understated wit has proved to be a major element in the development of American humour since the mid-Sixties. Two of his recent movies, Manhatten Murder Mystery *(1993), featuring a very average couple who suspect they may be living next door to a murderer, and* Bullets Over Broadway *(1994), a madcap Thirties tale about a bunch of gangsters involved in show business, are merely extensions of the short stories he has been writing on similar themes for the past twenty years. Tales like 'A Look at Organised Crime' (1973) a hilarious spoof on the Mafia, 'Mr Big' (1981), a parody about a Los Angeles private eye written in the style of Raymond Chandler, and 'The Condemned', published in the* New Yorker *in 1976, are just three typical examples of his outstanding contribution to the crime-with-a-laugh genre.*

Woody Allen, alias Allen Stewart Konigsberg (1935–) was born in Brooklyn, New York, and began his writing career while still an adolescent by creating jokes for newspaper columnists and television stars. In 1961 he rather reluctantly began performing his own brand of self-effacing parody in Greenwich Village cafés, and after graduating to appearances on TV shows, got his big break into films as both a screen-

writer and performer in What's New Pussycat? *made in 1965. The following year he created a masterpiece of absurd humour by cleverly dubbing a Japanese film thriller in English and calling it* What's Up, Tiger Lily? *His comic wit was also evident in a Broadway play,* Play it Again, Sam *(1969), which was filmed in 1972. His later movies have all contained a unique mixture of parody, spoof and cynical humour that has made him a cult figure all over the world. No one mixes gloom and soul-searching with the absurd and the fantastic better than Woody Allen, as he shows once again in 'The Condemned'.*

Brisseau was asleep in the moonlight. Lying on his back in bed, with his fat stomach jutting into the air and his mouth forming an inane smile, he appeared to be some kind of inanimate object, like a large football or two tickets to the opera. A moment later, when he rolled over and the moonlight seemed to strike him from a different angle, he looked exactly like a twenty-seven-piece starter set of silverware, complete with salad bowl and soup tureen.

He's dreaming, Cloquet thought, as he stood over him, revolver in hand. *He's* dreaming, and I exist in reality. Cloquet hated reality but realised it was still the only place to get a good steak. He had never taken a human life before. True, he had once shot a mad dog, but only after it had been certified as mad by a team of psychiatrists. (The dog was diagnosed as manic-depressive after it had tried to bite off Cloquet's nose and then could not stop laughing.)

In his dream, Brisseau was on a sunlit beach and running joyously towards his mother's outstretched arms, but just as he began to embrace the weeping

grey-haired woman, she turned into two scoops of va-
nilla ice cream. Brisseau moaned and Cloquet lowered
the revolver. He had entered through the window and
stood poised over Brisseau for more than two hours,
unable to pull the trigger. Once, he had even cocked
the hammer and placed the muzzle of the gun right in
Brisseau's left ear. Then there was a sound at the door,
and Cloquet leaped behind the bureau, the pistol sticking
out of Brisseau's ear.

Madame Brisseau, who was wearing a flowered bathrobe, entered the room, turned on a small lamp, and
noticed the weapon protruding straight up out of the side
of her husband's head. Almost maternally, she sighed
and removed it, placing it beside the pillow. She tucked
in a loose corner of the quilt, snapped off the lamp and
left.

Cloquet, who had fainted, awoke an hour later. For one
panicky moment, he imagined he was a child again, back
on the Riviera, but after fifteen minutes went by and he
saw no tourists it came to him that he was still behind
Brisseau's chest of drawers. He returned to the bed, seized
the pistol, and again pointed it at Brisseau's head, but he
was still unable to squeeze off the shot that would end
the life of the infamous Fascist informer.

Gaston Brisseau came from a wealthy, right-wing
family, and decided early in life to become a professional
informer. As a young man, he took speech lessons so that
he could inform more clearly. Once, he had confessed to
Cloquet, 'God I enjoy tattling on people.'

'But why?' Cloquet said.

'I don't know. Getting them in Dutch, squealing.'

Brisseau ratted on his friends for the pure sake of it,
Cloquet thought. Unredeemable evil! Cloquet had once

known an Algerian who loved smacking people on the back of the head and then smiling and denying it. It seemed the world was divided into good and bad people. The good ones slept better, Cloquet thought, while the bad ones seemed to enjoy the waking hours much more.

Cloquet and Brisseau had met years before, under dramatic circumstances. Brisseau had gotten drunk at the Deux Magots one night and staggered towards the river. Thinking he was already home in his apartment, he removed his clothes, but instead of getting into bed he got into the Seine. When he tried to pull the blankets over himself and got a handful of water, he began screaming. Cloquet, who at that moment happened to be chasing his toupee across the Pont-Neuf, heard a cry from the icy water. The night was windy and dark, and Cloquet had a split second to decide if he would risk his life to save a stranger. Unwilling to make such a momentous decision on an empty stomach, he went to a restaurant and dined. Then, stricken with remorse, he purchased some fishing tackle and returned to fish Brisseau out of the river. At first he tried to dry fly, but Brisseau was too clever to bite, and in the end Cloquet was forced to coax Brisseau to shore with an offer of free dance lessons and then land him with a net. While Brisseau was being measured and weighed, the two became friends.

Now Cloquet stepped closer to Brisseau's sleeping hulk and again cocked the pistol. A feeling of nausea swept over him as he contemplated the implications of his action. This was an existential nausea, caused by his intense awareness of the contingency of life, and could not be relieved with an ordinary Alka-Seltzer. What was required was an Existential Alka-Seltzer – a product sold in many Left Bank drugstores. It was an enormous pill, the size of an automobile hubcap, that, dissolved in water, took away the queasy feeling induced by too much awareness of life. Cloquet had also found it helpful after eating Mexican food.

If I choose to kill Brisseau, Cloquet thought now, I am defining myself as a murderer. I will become Cloquet who kills, rather than simply what I am: Cloquet who teaches Psychology of Fowl at the Sorbonne. By choosing my action, I choose it for all mankind. But what if everyone in the world behaved like me and came here and shot Brisseau through the ear? What a mess! Not to mention the commotion from the doorbell ringing all night. And of course we'd need valet parking. Ah, God, how the mind boggles when it turns to moral or ethical considerations! Better not to think too much. Rely more on the body – the body is more dependable. It shows up for meetings, it looks good in a sports jacket, and where it really comes in handy is when you want to get a rub-down.

Cloquet felt a sudden need to reaffirm his own exist-ence, and looked into the mirror over Brisseau's bureau. (He could never pass a mirror without sneaking a peek, and once at a health club he had stared at his reflection in a swimming pool for so long that the management was forced to drain it.) It was no use. He couldn't shoot a man. He dropped the pistol and fled.

Out on the street, he decided to go to La Coupole for a brandy. He liked La Coupole because it was always bright and crowded, and he could usually get a table – quite a difference from his own apartment, where it was dark and gloomy and where his mother, who lived there, too, always refused to seat him. But tonight La Coupole was filled. Who are all these faces? Cloquet wondered. They seem to blur into an abstraction: 'The People.' But there are no people, he thought – only individuals. Cloquet felt this was a brilliant perception, one that he could use impressively at some chic dinner party. Because of observations such as this, he had not been invited to a social gathering of any sort since 1931.

He decided to go to Juliet's house.

'Did you kill him?' she asked as he entered the flat.

'Yes,' Cloquet said.

'Are you sure he is dead?'

'He seemed dead. I did my imitation of Maurice Chevalier, and it usually gets a big hand. This time, nothing.'

'Good. Then he'll never betray the Party again.'

Juliet was a Marxist, Cloquet reminded himself. And the most interesting type of Marxist – the kind with long, tanned legs. She was one of the few women he knew who could hold two disparate concepts in her mind at once, such as Hegel's dialectic and why if you stick your tongue in a man's ear while he is making a speech he will start to sound like Jerry Lewis. She stood before him now in a tight skirt and blouse, and he wanted to possess her – to own her the way he owned any other object, such as his radio or the rubber pig mask he had worn to harass the Nazis during the Occupation.

Suddenly he and Juliet were making love – or was it merely sex? He knew there was a difference between sex and love, but felt that either act was wonderful unless one of the partners happened to be wearing a lobster bib. Women, he reflected, were a soft, enveloping presence. Existence was a soft, enveloping presence, too. Sometimes it enveloped you totally. Then you could never get out again except for something really important, like your mother's birthday or jury duty. Cloquet often thought there was a great difference between Being and Being-in-the-World, and figured that no matter which group he belonged to the other was definitely having more fun.

He slept well after the lovemaking, as usual, but the next morning, to his great surprise, he was arrested for the murder of Gaston Brisseau.

At police headquarters, Cloquet protested his innocence, but he was informed that his fingerprints had been found all over Brisseau's room and on the recovered pistol. When he broke into Brisseau's house, Cloquet had also made the mistake of signing the guestbook. It was hopeless. The case was open-and-shut.

The trial, which took place over the following weeks, was like a circus, although there was some difficulty getting the elephants into the courtroom. At last, the jury found Cloquet guilty, and he was sentenced to the guillotine. An appeal for clemency was turned down on a technicality when it was learned that Cloquet's lawyer had filed it while wearing a cardboard moustache.

Six weeks later, on the eve of his execution, Cloquet sat alone in his cell, still unable to believe the events of the past months – particularly the part about the elephants in the courtroom. By this time the next day, he would be dead. Cloquet had always thought of death as something that happened to other people. 'I notice it happens to fat people a lot,' he told his lawyer. To Cloquet himself, death seemed to be only another abstraction. Men die, he thought, but does Cloquet die? This question puzzled him, but a few simple line drawings on a pad done by one of the guards set the whole thing clear. There was no evading it. Soon he would no longer exist.

I will be gone, he thought wistfully, but Madame Plotnick, whose face looks like something on the menu in a seafood restaurant, will still be around. Cloquet began to panic. He wanted to run and hide, or, even better, to become something solid and durable – a heavy chair, for instance. A chair has no problems, he thought. It's there; nobody bothers it. It doesn't have to pay rent or get involved politically. A chair can never stub its toe or misplace its earmuffs. It doesn't have to smile or get a haircut, and you never have to worry that if you take it to a party it will suddenly start coughing or make a scene. People just sit in a chair, and then when those people die other people sit in it. Cloquet's logic comforted him, and when the jailers came at dawn to shave his neck, he pretended to be a chair. When they asked him what he wanted for his last meal, he said, 'You're asking furniture what it wants to eat? Why not just upholster me?' When they stared at him, he weakened and said, 'Just some Russian dressing.'

Cloquet had always been an atheist, but when the priest, Father Bernard arrived, he asked if there was still time for him to convert.

Father Bernard shook his head. 'This time of year, I think most of your major faiths are filled,' he said. 'Probably the best I could do on such a short notice is maybe make a call and get you into something Hindu. I'll need a passport-sized photograph, though.'

No use, Cloquet reflected. I will have to meet my fate alone. There is no God. There is no purpose to life. Nothing lasts. Even the works of the great Shakespeare will disappear when the universe burns out – not such a terrible thought, of course, when it comes to a play like *Titus Andronicus*, but what about the others? No wonder some people commit suicide! Why not end this absurdity? Why go through with this hollow charade called life? Why, except that somewhere within us a voice says, 'Live.' Always, from some inner region, we hear the command, 'Keep living!' Cloquet recognised the voice; it was his insurance salesman. Naturally, he thought – Fishbein doesn't want to pay off.

Cloquet longed to be free – to be out of jail, skipping through an open meadow. (Cloquet always skipped when he was happy. Indeed, the habit had kept him out of the Army.) The thought of freedom made him feel simultaneously exhilarated and terrified. If I were truly free, he thought, I could exercise my possibilities to the fullest. Perhaps I could become a ventriloquist, as I have always wanted. Or show up at the Louvre in bikini underwear, with a fake nose and glasses.

He grew dizzy as he contemplated his choices and was about to faint, when the jailer opened his cell door and told him that the real murderer of Brisseau had just confessed. Cloquet was free to go. Cloquet sank to his knees and kissed the floor of his cell. He sang the 'Marseillaise'. He wept! He danced! Three days later, he was back in jail for showing up at the Louvre in bikini underwear, with a fake nose and glasses.

THE MULLIGAN STEW

Donald E. Westlake

*Stories of secret agents and undercover operators in the James
Bond mould have become very popular as a result of the huge
success of the 007 books and films. Such men are also ripe for
parody, of course – witness the famous Sixties Harvard
Lampoon series of J*mes B*nd novelettes, with titles like
Lightningrod, Doctor Popocatapetl and Scuba Do – Or
Die, and short stories such as 'The Mulligan Stew' which
Donald E. Westlake was invited to write especially for the
January 1979 issue of Ellery Queen's Mystery Magazine.
Few contemporary authors are better equipped for the task
than the versatile Westlake who, since the Sixties, has written
just about every kind of mystery, from straight suspense stories
to private eye cases, police procedurals, caper novels, light
comedy and pure farce. He is an acknowledged master of all of
them.*

*Donald Edwin Edmund Westlake (1933–) was born in
Brooklyn, but grew up in Albany, New York. After serving
in the US Air Force he was briefly an actor and literary agent
before publishing his first 'hardboiled' mysteries in the early
Sixties – one of which,* Killing Time *(1961), about a corrupt
upstate New York town, was compared to the Dashiell Ham-
mett classic,* Red Harvest *(1929). Westlake's skill at writing
humour became evident with* The Fugitive Pigeon *(1965),*

the first of a series about inept criminals and unlucky victims. The Spy in the Ointment (1966) was all about a pacifist who becomes entangled with bomb-throwing extremists and proved influential on the developing genre of comic spy capers. Westlake's reputation was confirmed in 1968 when his novel God Save the Mark, *about the exploits of the fall-guy of the title, earned him an Edgar for best novel from the Mystery Writers of America.*

He has subsequently written straight thrillers about a professional thief named Parker, using the pseudonym Richard Stark, and as Tucker Coe produced an equally successful series featuring Mitch Tobin, a guilt-ridden former policeman. Several of these books have been filmed starring Lee Marvin, George C. Scott and Robert Redford. Also very popular are Westlake's ongoing stories about Dortmunder and his comic associates who are always planning crimes that never come off: The Hot Rock (1970), Jimmy the Kid (1974) and Castle in the Air (1980).

'The Mulligan Stew' is a parody about a secret agent and the even more secret science of cloning – but always remember that however outrageous such a story may be, 'imitation is the sincerest form of flattery . . .'

Preston Mulligan sat in the dark with the shades drawn and the TV turned to the wall. Nevertheless, he sensed that he was being watched. 'I'll call the exterminator again in the morning,' he mused, eyes glinting.

The phone rang.

A strong man of early middle age, Preston Mulligan kept himself in shape with daily workouts of handball, tennis, jogging, mah-jong, and backgammon.

The phone warbled.

Today a respected Washington attorney with one of

the large firms down on Pennsylvania Avenue (he could never remember which one, but it didn't seem to matter – he'd enter an office at random, make a few phone calls, reject a supply contract for muddy wording, and on Fridays his paycheque would appear in the mailbox), years ago Preston had worked briefly for BNX, the undercover arm of TPP, the covert organisation within the CIA.

The phone whistled.

His jungle experiences during that time had left him with a slight limp but strong memories of brave men defying the elements and one another.

The phone shouted, 'Hey, you!'

'Quiet,' Preston said, eyes flaring. 'I'm mentally surveying my history till date.'

'It's a phone call,' the phone said. 'Important. For you.'

'Oh, very well,' Preston said, eyes weary. But when he picked up the receiver, the hiss of gas told him, too late, it had been a trap. In .67 of a second, he had been rendered unconscious.

*

Within the deep mahogany walls of the Mahogany Club, an apparently lavish exclusive club for rich and powerful men, was concealed the headquarters of the CFTC, a lavish exclusive club for rich and powerful men.

'Gentlemen,' Thrum said, 'be seated.'

Crash crash crash thud thud crash thud crash crash crash crash thud thud crash thud crash crash thud thud thud crash crash crash crash crash.

'You understand,' the President said, 'the reasons for absolute secrecy.'

'Absolutely, Mr President,' Preston Mulligan said, eyes

narrowing. 'But can you tell me nothing at *all* about my mission?'

'Only this,' the President said. 'The fate of the entire human race hangs in the balance.'

'Mulligan is getting too close,' Thrum said. 'I know it goes against our principles, gentlemen, but I'm afraid Mulligan must be – eliminated.'

'Preston! That car!'

'I see it,' Preston said, eyes grim. 'Hang onto your hat, Lewis, this is going to be a wild ride.'

'Oh, yes, sir, the General's out. I packed him a nice lunch, and he went off for a hike along those cliffs. Sir? Sir?'

'Hurry, Lewis! Pray God we're not too late!'

'Neck broken,' the doctor said. 'Obviously an accident.'

'But we'll need to know a bit more,' the police officer said, 'before we can let you gentlemen go.'

'But there's no time!' Preston hissed, eyes clenched.

'Sergeant,' Lewis said, handing the policeman a small, white card, 'national security is at stake here. Phone that number, and you'll understand.'

'Oh, I will, will I?' Sceptically the policeman retired to the other office. Soon he returned, significantly reaching for his handcuffs. 'That phone number,' he said significantly, 'has been disconnected.'

'Lewis! Look out!'

'That was meant for me, Sergeant,' Preston said, eyes hard.

'I have only your word for that,' the policeman said.

'Sorry, I have to do this, Sergeant,' Preston said, eyes moist, as he struck the policeman down with the scythe. Leaping through the window, kicking the twin orphans out of the MG, he made good his escape.

'It all began,' Preston said, eyes farfetched, 'when an old friend from my Burma days called with an incredible story. A super-secret organization, the Committee For The Crisis, was on the move; no one knew whose side they were on, or what they planned to do.'

'Go on,' Laura Cartwright said, voice husky. An astonishing ash blonde, Laura had been a Washington fixture for years. Apparently merely a legwoman for a TV network news department, Laura in fact held in her hands threads leading to a thousand hidden Washington secrets. She might have sold that knowledge for millions, but she wasn't interested in money; her concern was for something finer – power.

Preston had known Laura for years. After their torrid love affair several years ago in Karachi – while changing planes – they had remained good friends. Now it was to her snug apartment in the Watergate, furnished exclusively in Oriental rugs, that he had naturally turned for sanctuary.

'Since,' Preston continued, eyes sharply focused, 'I perfectly matched the complex membership profile of the Committee For The Crisis, I was the logical one to infiltrate the organisation and find out what was going on. The President himself spoke to me—'

'The President *himself*?' Laura asked, voice quivering.

'Later, it turned out the President too might be implicated. A ring I'd noticed on his finger was the symbol by which members of the Committee recognised one another.'

'The President *himself*?' Laura asked, voice rising and falling.

'It was possible, of course, that he too had infiltrated the organisation, for reasons of his own. But what if the Committee were actually involved in *good*? Dam-building along the lower Gobi, for instance, or food-parcel distribution in Guatemala. In my determination to learn the truth I apparently attracted attention. There have been several attempts on my life.'

'Preston!' Laura said, voice rich with emotion. 'Were you hurt?'

'I've been incredibly lucky,' Preston acknowledged, eyes twinkling. But then his eyes hardened. 'And I've also learned the truth. The Committee For The Crisis is involved in one of the most massive conspiracies the world has ever not known!'

'Preston!'

'It's true, Laura. You understand the principle of clon-ing—'

'Yes.'

'– parthenogenetically creating a new human being—'

'Yes, I know that, Preston.'

'– from just one cell of an existing human being—'

'I've read the literature on the subject, Preston.'

'– so that the new being is identical with the original—'

'I *know*.'

'– except, of course, without the original's memory. With, in fact, a blank mind, ready to be filled with whatever its creator chooses. Well, Laura, that's what's happening here. It's incredible, but true. Within a huge underground laboratory-dormitory beneath Kennedy Center – and I find it significant that every single worker on the construction of Kennedy Center has either died an unnatural death or not – the clones are being prepared to *take over the world*!'

'Preston,' Laura said, her voice weak with terror, 'you can't mean—'

'I do. The world's most powerful human beings, all are being systematically replaced. Senators, Generals, vast industrialists, flinty bankers, Dick Clark, world-renowned sports figures—' Preston leaned closer, eyes half shut. 'The President himself.'

'The President *himself*?' Laura asked, voice snapping in two.

'Not only that, the original clones have turned on their masters, destroyed them, made clones of *them*, and now the Committee For The Crisis itself is completely manned by clones! Clones cloning clones, and ever more clones cloning ever more clones. I have myself just escaped from a circus clown clone and *two* Rosemary Clooney clones! Humanity must clean out this clan of clones before we decline, or it'll be too late!'

'I'm sorry, Preston,' Laura said, her voice vibrant, 'but it *is* too late.'

Preston stared at the tiny gun in Laura's tiny fist, his eyes huge with understanding. 'Laura – you mean— ?'

THE DULWICH ASSASSINS

David L. Stone

This final story is in the same tradition as the very first, by Terry Pratchett, and the author himself is something of a discovery. David L. Stone made his debut in print at the age of 18, much as the world-famous creator of the Discworld novels did in 1961, aged 15. Like Pratchett, Stone has devised his own comic world in a series of stories about the assorted members of the curious Assassins Guild. 'The Dulwich Assassins' is the first of these, in which a young student at the Crumb Lane School for Professional Killing is required to test his expertise in mortal combat with the head of poison-related studies, the formidable Rumlink Banks. The story first appeared in Xenos magazine in April 1997 and is now published for the first time in book form.

David L. Stone (1978–) was born in Ramsgate, Kent, and at school was often accused of not taking his writing seriously enough: 'Whenever I was asked for an essay, whether it was an appreciation of Romeo and Juliet *or a critical study of* Macbeth, *the Dulwich tendencies always crept in,' he says. However, at the age of 12 he won three literary awards – for an essay, a poem and a short story – at the Dover Festival of Literature. After leaving school, he worked in a local estate agency while continuing to develop his decidedly off-beat fantasy kingdom. His biggest influences, he says, have been Terry Pratchett and Mervyn Peake, and he explains his idea: 'I've always been fascinated with the darker professions of the typical fantasy kingdom where kings, queens, warriors and wizards are invariably discussed in depth, while their "employees" like the assassins and thieves are largely ignored. I want to settle the score a little.' Following the publication of 'The Dulwich Assassins', Stone has written three further episodes, 'The Legrash Larcenies', 'Fine Wine', 'Indiscretion' and a novel, After the Organist, all of which promise to make his underworld of inept assassins and unionised criminality a success with lovers of comic fantasy. Read and enjoy discovering how this lugubrious saga began.*

Victor swung his left leg over the cemetery wall and dropped into the darkness beyond. So far so good, he reasoned, although fully aware that the worst was yet to come. Silence had settled on Dulwich Church like flies on excrement and thick swirling mists meandered between the gravestones.

A gorse bush provided ample cover as the young assassin fought with the clasp on his backpack. After a few mild curses he produced the grappling hook and, stowing the pack away for collection later, crept quietly towards the menacing shadows of the church. This, according to his friend Mifkindle, was the most important part of the test. Mifkindle was a fellow assassin at the school in Crumb Lane and shared most of Victor's classes. Mifkindle had amazing good luck: he'd drawn the relatively lenient Professor Crutchluddle for his exam. Crutchluddle was partially blind and had one leg, not an ideal candidate for 'Dead Man's Boots', as he would be the first to admit. Mifkindle had disposed of the elderly master with apparent ease, finishing his S12 assignment in a little under twenty minutes.

Victor, on the other hand, had drawn poison master Rumlink Banks. He knew students who would slice off their own heads rather than sign up for an S12 against Rumlink. The man had a reputation for being slippery as an eel and twice as fast. He had poisoned just about every prominent assassin in the school history and was feared by students and teachers alike. Victor had nearly lapsed into a fit of self-mutilation when he saw the examiner's name printed on the small slip of paper beneath his own signature. He remembered thinking how typical it was that he should draw the most vicious rat in the pack. He had about as much chance of winning the Vanishing Village Olympics as of topping Rumlink this evening, especially on the man's favourite hunting ground. He'd been tracking the wily veteran for the past four hours, in some of the most appalling weather conditions ever experienced this side of the Gleaming Mountains. A sensible student would have given up by now, headed back to the school house and prayed fervently that he'd draw a more reasonable opponent next year. Well, not Victor. Quit? He didn't know the meaning of the word. This was only one of a large number of words he didn't know the meaning of.

Out of the corner of his eye, Victor glimpsed a slight movement beyond the large stone cross that commemorated the legendary battle of Q'harm Forest. He crouched close to the ground, employing a low-level crawl to advance his movement. The area previously of interest was now silent. Instead of the normal silence created by an absence of sound, this silence was the silky smooth quiet created by someone attempting to make no noise.

Victor's gloved hand slipped to his belt and returned with an Orpal throwing knife, which he placed neatly between clenched teeth.

Suddenly, and with almost shadow-like dexterity, a cloaked silhouette moved between monuments. Victor dived behind the north face of the memorial and gasped for breath as a poison-tipped dagger thudded into a tree stump, mere inches from his left leg. The young student allowed himself a brief exhalation of breath, confident in the knowledge that he had successfully earned a point in the 'not-getting-killed' column. A habit he was pretty determined not to break.

After a few seconds of frantic fumbling in the recess of his right sock, Victor produced a small mirror securely attached to a thin stick which he unfolded before sliding the instrument along the ground beside him. When it appeared to be in the correct position, he employed a quick wrist movement to adjust the device at a right-angle to the path. Unfortunately, the only object of interest in the resulting view was a similar device protruding from a marble statue, twelve feet away.

Victor quickly retrieved the mirror and moved surreptitiously around the perimeter of the monument, his gaze not leaving the opposite stone for a second. Subconsciously he was aware that he had the mental advantage of the situation, Rumlink having disclosed his presence. The sneaky old rat must have been fairly confident of his knife achieving the desired target. Victor sighed; perhaps there was hope for him yet.

Making sure that every step was accurately revised, the student advanced along the grass verge, cold steel remaining tightly clenched between his teeth. He nearly swallowed the blade when Rumlink leaped from his hiding-place like a prancing deer and crossed the verge at a dead run. Victor had to admit that the teacher moved extremely stealthily for a man his age. He took a few seconds to wonder exactly what age this was, before sprinting off in pursuit. Even though Victor was some twenty seconds behind him, Rumlink's preferred destination was clear. He was heading for the church itself. Once inside, the maze of chapels and bell towers would render tracking the man virtually impossible. Dulwich was a large church, large in the true sense of the word; the vestry was so well hidden that people got lost looking for it. Victor had no choice, he would have to dispose of the adept Mr Banks before he reached the building.

He grabbed the knife from his mouth and accelerated his speed, clearing small bushes and low headstones in a complex series of leaps and bounds that would have injured a shorter man for life. He saw Rumlink struggling (apparently without success) at the large double doors, set firmly into the wall of the church. Slowing slightly as he neared his target, Victor took aim and fired his blade which imbedded itself into the back of the portal, about three inches from his teacher's ear.

Finally forcing the reluctant entrance, Rumlink took advantage of the careless shot and disappeared into the silky darkness behind the door. Amidst sudden disappointment and confusion, Victor lost his footing and crashed to the ground, quickly curling into a foetal position to protect his head from any stray daggers. None came.

Allowing a few minutes to pass before attempting any sort of pursuit, Victor collected his thoughts and reached into his chest pocket for the Arlington Brassey blowpipe he always kept there. Keeping one eye firmly focused on the church entrance, he located his neck pouch and pulled a small, yellow-feathered, acid-tipped dart from within. He loaded up the pipe, flipped the safety cap over to cover the exposed hole and stepped cautiously forward.

The church door creaked open ominously on rusty hinges. So much for the element of surprise, Victor thought bitterly as he peered around the wooden portal. The entrance hall was deserted, with only a single candle to cast its meagre light, illuminating the immediate area only. Rumlink must already be in the main section, waiting patiently for his prey.

Victor plucked the flickering candle from its resting-place, quickly stepping aside as a large black cat scurried out from under a desk to his left. Steeling his nerves, the student assassin applied gentle pressure to the inner door, forcing it ajar just enough to get a clear view of the east wing. The pews were empty but candlelight was plenty here, the elegant holders stretching the length of the aisles, almost three stands to a row. At least it wouldn't be a case of 'Blind Man's Buff'. Victor had known many a pupil whose test had ended in that scenario; usually by judging the angle from which they had been stabbed. Life was not kind to the trainee assassins; brief, but not kind.

Increasing pressure on the creaking oak enabled a more focused view of the centre aisles, and Victor flipped open the tube cap as he caught sight of Rumlink crouching down beside the altar. With a turn of speed that surprised himself as much as his tutor, the apprentice dived from the entrance portal and landed neatly behind the rear pew of the centre row. He heard Rumlink curse briefly as a lone dagger thudded into the stuffed model of an eagle suspended above the door, behind him. Badly judged, Victor mused. Perhaps the old snake was panicking.

He crawled, on his belly, to the edge of the pew and grabbed a prayer cushion, thrusting it out experimentally. A blue-tipped dart wedged into it. Ah, he was already resorting to Gantolin.

As head of poison-related studies at the Crumb Lane School for Professional Killing, Rumlink Banks had known many poisons considered foreign to other professors. Usually he introduced all his new finds to the staff; on occasions, quite personally. This procedure did not apply to the use of Gantolin, Bank's own brainchild.

Gantolin consisted of the blood of the Gallows frog and the urine of the Prolonged bird, one of the saddest creatures in existence. These were distilled using methods and procedure used only by the master himself until the resulting substance formed itself into a light blue powder, perfect for dart-tips. The effect of having this poison injected into the system would arrive in the form of immediate paralysis, during which time you would generally be dispatched by knife or, if you were lucky, suffocation.

Victor quickly reached out and plucked the dart from the prayer cushion, hoping to employ it later, to his own benefit. Then, placing both hands firmly on the edge of the pew, he peered carefully over at the altar. Rumlink was reloading his blowpipe. Needing no further encouragement, the young assassin put the black tube to his lips and blew, sending a red blur across the church at his superior. There was a brief (but satisfying) yell and then, silence. Victor waited. Nothing.

Slowly, employing as much caution as excitement would allow, he ventured a quick glance back towards the altar. A single boot was visible from behind the steps. Victor wondered if there was a foot in it. Only one way to find out.

Slipping into the shadows of the seat wing, he proceeded towards the appendage, another dagger drawn and poised to strike. He was almost upon his destination when memory invaded his subconscious and metaphorically tapped him on the shoulder. The 'empty-boot', of course! The oldest trick in the book and Victor had nearly swallowed the bait. You approached the (supposedly) inanimate corpse and found just an empty boot, which you were bound to make a grab for out of curiosity alone. That harmless-looking piece of leather footwear was (unbeknownst to the approaching enemy) filled with Opiolk Six, a poison so deadly that even inhaling its alluring aroma could paralyse the average man. Victor hesitated. While he never liked to think of himself as average, he had a sense of strange foreboding and firmly decided against advancement in his current line of inquiry. He had to find another route of approach, but how?

The young assassin quickly shook himself from his reverie when he noticed that he was absentmindedly drumming his fingers on the rough wooden armrest of one of the pews in the left row. He had to pull himself together, there was always a chance that his mentor had survived and was watching him carefully from somewhere near the pulpit, waiting to take him. Height, that was what he required; a position of technical brilliance where he could view the entire chamber while remaining concealed himself. Slowly, carefully, his wandering eyes scaled the walls of the church interior, finally coming to rest on the creaking beams that supported the gallery.

Victor cursed himself when he realised a serious mistake. In the confusion of pursuing his erstwhile teacher, he had mislaid his grappling irons! There was no practical alternative, he would have to tackle the wall himself. Damn this assignment, it was tantamount to physical labour! After failing to spot a single feature of the wall that might double as a foothold, Victor settled on taking a leap from one of the pews in the left row nearest the door. Thirty seconds later our young assassin hung from the jutting nose of a particularly menacing gargoyle that occupied the gallery above. Offering silent praises to Sirlgynflinnexume the Weary (an extremely difficult deity to pray to), Victor swung back and forth for a few moments before building up the momentum to vault over the parapet and into the shadows beyond. Catching breath and regaining balance, he raced along the gallery towards his predefined vantage point, pausing briefly to check for any movement from the silent expanse of darkness below.

Victor reached the corner of the parapet, leaned out over a statue of Ohnmix the Everlasting in her incarnation as a buffalo and craned his neck for a better view of the altar. The shoe remained inanimate but no foot protruded; Banks was still alive. A shiver of uncertainty ran along the length of his spine and Victor quietly retracted into the bowels of the gallery floor. Now everything seemed alive. Tapestries with travelling eyes explored his every movement, gargoyles blinked as he passed and attempted to grab him with awkward, incapable limbs. Victor admonished his wild imagination and prepared a mental summary of the many possible locations of concealment that the building offered to a fully trained and equally adept master of deception.

Probably twice the number of hiding-places available to the average apprentice, he surmised grudgingly.

Victor examined a few of the stacks, eventually pausing by an old piano to blow the thick overcoat of dust from a big blue hardback that perched jauntily on the lid. He squinted in the half dark, just recognising the title. It was *Lady Shankley's Friend* by Maurice Kozlowski. Some of the ornate gold lettering had worn away over the years, altering the title of the book to *Lady Shankley's Fiend*. Victor suppressed a juvenile giggle as he successfully attempted to recall the nature of the story.

There was no obvious exit from the chamber apart from the portal through which he had entered, but this didn't fool the young assassin. Churches were notorious for all manner of trapdoors, priest-holes, sliding panels and rotating walls; besides which, there was a distinct chill on his back. He turned round to face a sturdy-looking bookcase with a difference that set it firmly apart from the other items of furniture strewn around the room; there were no books piled on top of it.

Victor crossed the decorative flagstones and scrutinised the old wooden construction. It stood approximately two inches away from the wall and was obviously concealing the source of the breeze that currently occupied the vestibule. Throwing all his weight against the oak monstrosity, Victor pushed the bookcase away from the wall, noticing two important and valuable points in the process. First, the fact that the case was as light as a feather because of all the books inside were simply painted deceptions and consequently, all were glued in place. Second, there were handles adorning the inward-facing side of the case giving Victor the distinct impression that it had been left ajar on purpose.

Remembering his lessons in tactical illusion, Victor returned to the corridor outside and began to search for further access to the roof. When the fourteenth wall-panel offered no secret mechanisms or sliding tendencies, Victor decided to ascend to the bell tower from outside the building. A decision he was fairly certain that Mr Banks would not be expecting.

Seventy feet above the gravel drive of Dulwich Church, Victor clung to the concrete neck of a grimacing gargoyle and wished, quite fervently, that he was dead. Being the last son in a long line of vertigo sufferers did not equip the assassin well for the task assigned to him by his own quick-thinking stupidity. Employing a smile of grim determination, the apprentice swung round with his legs, twisted his upper body and landed atop the statue, straddling the stone beast like a jockey. Then, gripping the creature's ears for leverage, he took the whole of his body weight onto his forearms and hoisted his lithe frame to a standing position atop the head, quickly snatching the guttering to regain his balance. Cautiously, he peered over the roof of the church. Banks was squatting just above the trapdoor which led down into the vestibule, obviously expecting him to emerge at any moment. Perhaps the master was not as cunning as his reputation promised. Victor reached down, his tongue between his teeth as an aid to silence, and produced a short, stout dagger from his belt pouch. He clenched his fist tightly around the handle and jammed it hard into the brick wall, beneath the guttering.

Using the imbedded dagger as a foothold, Victor balanced on his left leg and swung his right onto the roof, gripping a handy metal rail which was wedged just above the slate for a purpose Victor couldn't imagine under the circumstances. He pulled a long, needle-thin stiletto from his foot-strap and proceeded. The teacher appeared to remain blissfully unaware of his student's stealthy approach until the young assassin was almost upon him. Then, with surprising agility for a man of his girth, Banks dived aside as Victor lunged with his blade. With a deft sweeping motion the master swept the young assassin's legs from beneath him, sending Victor crashing to the slate. The apprentice let out a yelp of pain but managed to roll swiftly aside as Banks brandished a gleaming dagger and steadied himself for the duel. He noticed that his opponent was limping and offered Victor a malicious grin, displaying two rows of dingy, yellow-stained teeth. When his junior produced no weapon, Banks perceived this a fatal miscalculation of need and darted forward. He was inches away from Victor when he lost his footing on the slates and staggered.

The trainee assassin spotted his momentary advantage and went in for the kill. Disregarding the now acute vertigo, Victor cleared a miniature steeple and careered into his mentor. The two figures crashed to the slate and somersaulted over one another, each in a desperate attempt to gain possession of the single dagger which Victor brandished over Rumlink Banks, teeth clenched in grim determination. The slanted roof gave way to a short space of levelled tiles over the vestry where the two men slowed to a halt and Rumlink finally managed to remove his aggressor by kicking hard against the student with both feet. Victor regained his footing quickly and moved the blade in a severe arc, describing Robis' Fourth Syllabus in the cold evening air. The teacher leaped to his feet and produced a similar stiletto from a breast pocket.

They circled wearily, meeting in quick succession to the accompaniment of screaming metal. Neither teacher nor student uttered a curse at the other. Each man had the same purpose, no words would alter the situation.

Rumlink Banks' life had been fraught with incalculable risks. It was all part of being an efficient assassin. Professional killers often suffered numerous depressions and bouts of deep foreboding – death always did that to you. The most common characteristic of all true assassins was described by Reno Altiman, world-class killer, as the ultimate risk. The moment where normal men end and assassins begin. That fateful leap from a tower, the last grasping attempt to dispose of your opponent before he disposed of you. Every member of the school was given a lecture to this effect before signing up. It was designed to be the final deterrent for all but the most serious applicants. Rumlink was well aware of the ultimate risk. He took it.

Victor had never possessed the gift of anticipation. Mother Nature had simply never endowed him with the insight this skill required. Luckily for him, stealthy reactions more than made up for the disability. Rumlink, blade poised, darted forward like a rogue streak of lightning. When the master was mere inches from his prey, Victor swung round to avoid the blow with terminal velocity, sending the senior man headlong into the darkness beyond, waving his arms in a flail for mercy. Acting on instinct rather than aptitude, the apprentice quickly cast his last opal-studded dagger into the air after him. For a few seconds, seconds that he would never forget in his lifetime, Victor waited. He swallowed, breathing in frequent, desperate gasps. Slowly, he approached the edge of the guttering and peered over.

Rumlink Banks lay motionless on the church steps, the jagged knife protruding from his back. Victor winced, barely containing the overwhelming feeling of victory that was brewing up in his stomach. There was no doubt about it, the man had breathed his last.

Victor turned away from the scene and produced the pink slip of paper from beneath his belt. There was the space for Mr Banks' signature. A pass at Crumb High was achieved by the absence of a master's signature, its presence usually indicating that the student had suffered a failure of no reprisal. Victor walked back along the roof and took one last look down at the corpse. He found himself wondering who would have the inevitable job of tidying things away. He didn't have to think very hard before a suspect came to mind. Candle-holders smashed beyond repair; pews damaged and chipped. On the whole, he reflected, it could have been a lot worse.

ACKNOWLEDGEMENTS

The editor and publishers are grateful to the following authors, publishers and agents for permission to include copyright stories in this book: Colin Smythe Ltd. for 'Hollywood Chickens' © 1990 by Terry Pratchett; A.P. Watt Ltd. for 'The Angry Street' by G.K. Chesterton; David Higham Associates Ltd. for 'The Party at Lady Cusp-Canine's' by Mervyn Peake; Ellie Bloch for 'The Little Man Who Wasn't There' by Robert Bloch; Abner Stein Literary Agency for 'The Year the Glop-Monster Won the Golden Lion at Cannes' by Ray Bradbury; A.M. Heath Ltd. for 'Lila the Werewolf' by Peter Beagle; Scott Meredith Literary Agency for 'The War With the Fnools' by Philip K. Dick and 'Dream Damsel' by Evan Hunter; Spike Milligan Productions Ltd. for 'The Creation According to Spike Milligan' by Spike Milligan; Samuel French Ltd. for 'Ethelred the Unready' by Ben Travers; Virginia Kidd for 'How I Lost the Second World War' by Gene Wolfe; Davis Publications Inc. for 'Fifi and the Chilean Truffle' by Orson Welles, 'The Suicide of Kiaros' by L. Frank Baum and 'The Mulligan Stew' by Donald E. Westlake; Standard Features Ltd. for 'The Wastrel' by Peter Sellers; Sheil Land Associates Ltd. for 'Stirring the Pot' © 1994 by Tom Sharpe; Curtis Brown Ltd. for 'The Rape of the Sherlock' by A.A. Milne and 'The White Rabbit Caper' by James Thurber; Stan McMurtry for his story 'Wot the Eye Don't See'; Virgin Publishing Ltd. for 'The Condemned' by Woody Allen; and David L. Stone for his story 'The Dulwich Assassins'. The illustrations in this collection are reprinted by permission of Borden

Publishing Company, Laurence Pollinger Ltd. and Stan McMurtry. While every care has been taken to clear permissions for the use of the stories in the book, in the case of any accidental infringement copyright holders are asked to write to the editor care of the publishers.